Black Roses

by

Deanna Dellia

A Dark Romance

Printed in the United States of America
First Printing, 2024

ISBN: 979-8-218-55512-2

Publisher: CoolBird Publishing House
            2036 Cherokee Rd PMB 38
            Alexander City, AL 35010

Cover Design: Dark Romance Press
              www.DeannaDellia.com

This is a work of fiction. Unless otherwise indicated, all the names, characters, businesses,
places, events, and incidents in this book are either the product of the author's imagination
or used in a fictitious manner. Any resemblance to actual persons, living or dead,
or actual events is purely coincidental.

COOLBIRD
PUBLISHING
HOUSE.

Author's Note

This story takes you on a journey in which the characters face heavy mental health issues. Like many dark romance novels, this book highlights the morally gray shades that live within us all. That being said, it is not my intention to blur the lines of consent or abuse. My hope is that you, the reader, will be able to see the line with clarity. My goal is to take you inside the mind of someone who is being abused to help you understand how and why they make certain decisions and engage in risky behaviors.

My perspective on these mental health topics come from my experience of being a trauma survivor as well as my work as a clinical psychotherapist who specializes in trauma therapy. If you personally relate to the struggles that any of these characters face, I hope this book makes you feel less alone. If you have seen the rain too, I hope you find the healing in feeling. And, above all, I hope this story reminds you that you matter, you always have.

Also, don't worry... There's a lot of fun, a lot of scandal, a lot of love, and a lot of spice. Happy reading, my dark-minded friends.

TRIGGER WARNINGS:

- Domestic violence
- Substance abuse
- Suicide
- Sexual assault
- Emotional abuse
- Coercion
- Depression
- Stalking
- Sexual content
- Manslaughter
- Panic disorder

To those of you that were taught to believe
that you don't matter, they were wrong.
You matter. You always have.

Chapter 1

Present Day

My glass is half empty in more ways than one. The quiet pounds on my eardrums like an off-rhythm middle school choir. I twist off the cap of my asylum and watch as my familiar old friend streams slowly into the crystal glass. I take a long, leisurely swig, and suddenly, the sun comes out. It's not that I want to be drinking this incredibly stiff martini at 9am, but everything comes with a price to pay, and maybe this is mine. I need something to chase my racing thoughts before they catch me first. I rub my hazel eyes which are burning from being open all night. I reach my hand up to the top of my floor-to-ceiling window and notice how heavy my arms feel today, they always do, but today, they're particularly heavy. Today, it's particularly hard to be alive.

I power through, pulling back the cream-colored drapes to let the actual sun spit morning in my face. The brightness of the sky makes me wince, the softness of the clouds taunting me with false hope. The magnolia trees are lit up by the sun in a way that makes them glow. It's beautiful, yet somehow it makes me feel… I don't know, embarrassed. I'm embarrassed by how uncomfortable the outside world makes me feel. *You're pathetic, Delilah.* I gaze out to the backyard through the gazebo and over the saltwater pool. The warm Georgia winds ripple the water like an angry ocean. I peer beyond, and immediately notice that our hedges need to be higher. Unfortunately, I catch a glimpse of our neighbor, Beth, a

7

53-year-old woman who claims to be 45 with the biggest prosthetic boobs I've ever seen. She's talking to a younger man with deep brown eyes that sparkle in the sun he's squinting in protest. I assume he is her gardener with the way he's submerged in the dirt. She's pointing to the leaves and licking her lips between each sentence, I can't tell if she's commanding him to do something or if she's trying to seduce him, you never know with Beth. The man gets up off his knees and grabs a leaf blower. Beth's eyes trail up and down his tanned chiseled body. I let myself bask in staring at her stare at him. She strokes his sweaty olive skin while tracing her fingers around each one of his muscles. Her delicate hands caress him like it's not the first time. My mouth waters. Pleasure shoots through me at the thought of trading places with Beth. Although, I highly doubt being a middle-aged divorcée washing down the lonely nights with Klonopin cocktails is much fun. I picture her eating at an empty dinner table, sleeping in an empty bed, questioning why her husband left her to start a new family with a 20-something-year-old. Perhaps that's why she's desperate for a man half her age to give her validation that the party isn't over yet, that she's not entirely alone. For the first time, I feel a slight kinship with Beth. Loneliness is a song I never forget the melody to. My eyes study her mannerisms, the way she leans all her weight to one side of her body, the way she purses her big lips. I'm enjoying observing all her idiosyncrasies, when suddenly, she cocks her head and glances in my direction. God, I think she caught my idiotic stare. She doesn't wave, though; she's probably learned not to by now. Beth swivels her breasts in the direction of her mid-century modern home and strides towards her back door. She will most likely spend the day glued to her phone screen, endlessly swiping on dating apps and stalking her ex-husband and his new family on Facebook.

Like I said, everything comes with a price to pay. I can't help but wonder what other prices she's paying. Me, I'm left looking for answers at the bottom of the bottle. Maybe in another life, Beth and I could be friends, but in this life, I just can't deal with hearing about her overgrown peonies one more damn time. I'm truly not nice enough to endure that. Besides, every time she says the word "overgrown" my eyes can't help but linger down to her chest.

My eyelashes flutter back to the attractive man weeding away his youth in Beth's garden. You'd think that someone so brutally obsessed with gardening would do her own yard work instead of paying someone else to do it, although I'm sure the leaves aren't the only thing getting blown around there. I take a nice, long sip and stare down at the crystal glass. My lips pout into a smirk as my guilty bloodshot eyes shimmy back up toward Beth's little friend. Although, this time, her little friend is staring right back at me. His dark brown eyes are fixed below mine; I follow them down to my collarbones. It's then that I realize I'm wearing nothing but a thin, silk-white slip dress that is translucent in the sun's fiery glare. My pale nipples are ferociously hard and ferociously exposed. I bring my arm to my chest to cover up. Shock fills my face, burning my cheeks. But the man across the way doesn't share my disturbance. Instead, I notice a smile stretching on his full, dark lips. His smile grows with confidence like he knows exactly who I am, and his head cocks to the side with intrigue like he wants to know more. I lower my arm, allowing him to examine my body. Goosebumps rise on my pastel skin. My eyes hit the floor with a bashful grin, then I hear the slam of a door. Shit, it must be Beth. I yank the curtain closed and shake the temptation off me. *Look at you, you're disgusting, Delilah.* Stomping over towards the marble counter behind me, I pour myself another, desperately trying to convince myself that what happened didn't just happen, and that the lace thong I'm wearing is completely dry. It's fine, it was merely two people making eye contact. People do that, right? Beth didn't see anything. I wonder what her opinion of me is, it's likely not much higher than mine of her. I imagine she thinks I'm rude considering I avoid her like a plague. It's not personal though, I avoid every plastered-on smile in this neighborhood which is why I've acquired the reputation of being the resident bitch of Peach Street. It's not that I don't want to have small talk and make friends, but what these picket fenced-in zombies don't understand is that it's a privilege to be friendly, to speak up, to take up space. They were probably raised to believe that other people are safe. I don't have the luxury of believing that people are safe, I know that they're not.

I feel the vodka slide down my throat and circulate into my empty stomach, burning each one of my organs and wrapping my brain in a blanket warm enough to melt the anxiety away. I should probably wince at the sensation, but I know that there are things far more painful than setting your internal organs on fire... like forgiving someone who will never be sorry.

Martini in hand, I cruise around the kitchen island and onward until I find myself in the dining room. I gently sit my glass down and brush my French tips over the chestnut mahogany table to straighten one of the China plates. I designed this room myself. I went with a warm, Hygge look with all brown furniture and golden chandeliers. I was inspired by a hotel lobby I once saw in Norway. I look around, taking some pride in my work until a rush of shame swirls up from beneath my toes and through my body until it submerges my head. Because the truth is, decorating this dining room has been my greatest accomplishment in the last 15 years. And that makes me feel… I don't know, useless. I pick up my glass and carry on. I barely notice where I'm walking until I somehow find myself in front of our black baby grand piano. The keys taunt me as they get bigger and bigger. The deeper my stare grows, they begin to move as if they're playing themselves. I try to ignore the Debussy composition that lives in my mind like a tumor that won't stop growing. I feel my finger tap on the stem of my martini and immediately slam the crystal glass down on the cast-iron frame of the piano. A bit of liquid splashes up and leaps over the rim. I glue my hands to my hips to keep my fingers from playing along. I sigh and stare at the keys. They look more inviting today than they have all week. I try to think of a song to play, one I haven't butchered on stage in front of an audience. What else could I play? Maybe something more modern. What was that song I heard on the radio on the way to the liquor store yesterday? A soft melody and a silky voice begin to play in the speakers of my mind. I don't recognize it at first.

"Da da da da da, watching the tides roll away…"

And then, I can't help but think of him, all of the long nights, all of the secrets shared, all of the black roses. He was… sunset. Rivers of original thought streamed through his brain. A thousand suns radiated in his voice. The entire solar system was painted on his broad back. If only the world existed under his feet, instead of on top of his shoulders, maybe he would have had a chance. Transported in time, I smell the comforting scent of cigarette smoke wafting through the crisp air. I feel the warmth of his breath on my lips at the piano. I hear the pattering of the rain hitting the dock while his big arms wrap me in safety, my broken heart beating just for him. I see the silver cross dangling between his pecks, flirting

11

salaciously with the silver in his gray eyes. Out on the river, the sun retires on the horizon, making the teal ripples in the water glow orange, my favorite. I can still hear his low, raspy voice. I can still taste his warm breath, his heart-shaped lips. I can still see his toned chest and broad shoulders glistening in the water under the moonlight. I can still feel his stubble on my cheek, my legs wrapped around his thick waist. I can still feel my lips stretch when his mouth flares into a half smile on the left side of his face. He once told me I was his version of heaven, but honestly, he was lucky if I could make it through the night. He broke me. He broke me like a promise.
No.

I shake my head to snap out of my daze, a daze that's been following me like a demon after my soul for as long as I can remember. I lift my glass off the piano and use the corner of my white slip to wipe off the small ring it left. I turn away from the black baby grand that has become my greatest enemy and turn towards the vodka that has become my closest friend, my only friend. I hear the familiar click of my jaw as I empty the glass down my throat before heading back to the kitchen. I'm so tired of myself. I know that my husband is too, that's why he's been traveling so much for work even though he's a financial analyst who works from home. He doesn't love me anymore, and I don't blame him. I wouldn't love me either. I'm going to make this marriage work though. I was lucky enough to find someone who could provide for me and put up with me for this long. I know how good I have it, and I'm not going to fuck this one up. I've done enough of that for one lifetime. I'll just have to do better; I know that I can do better. I straighten my pearls, letting my hands rest on top of my necklace for a minute. I swear, I can almost hear the off-white family heirloom whispering to me in a waspy voice, telling me to stop feeling sorry for myself. Who am I *not* to listen? After all, if I were to be kidnapped right now, these perals would rank higher in ransom money than my ass would.

I head back towards the counter, ttwist the cap off the Belvedere and take in the beautiful cadence of the vodka hitting the bottom of the glass, it's like velvet on my ears. I swish around the two olives and take a bite of one, probably the only thing I'll eat today. Maybe to the feeble mind, I seem like I have some sort of drinking problem. But I think those people don't understand what it's like to want to forget all the things you never deserved to know. My mind was broken long before I took my first sip, this is the only thing that can at least bandage it for a little while.

I pick up my glass, spinning around, and I catch a glimpse of the paper invitation on my refrigerator. My 15-year high school reunion. Here, I thought those only existed in lame 80s movies. I cannot fathom that it has been 15 whole years. I scan the invitation until I'm lost in a pair of striking eyes. Those eyes are still like nothing I've ever seen. It's truly a great photo of him. He looks handsome. The promising young boy taken too soon. I guess they plan to dedicate part of the reunion to have a memorial for him. I look down at my white slip and make a mental reminder to buy a new dress for the occasion, something elegant and regal. I know I shouldn't bother trying to impress these people, my stomach curls at the thought of having idle conversation with them, pretending like that fateful night never happened. Pretending like I didn't do what I did. Pretending like the shards of my shattered heart don't still cut me every day. But that's the Georgian way for you – plaster on a fake smile, put on your Sunday best, and you've conquered the world. Bailey never did that, perhaps that's why things went down the way they did. I squeeze my eyelids shut and open them, hoping the image in front of me will disappear, hoping the past 15 years will disappear. I can't stop staring at the boy in this grainy photo. It pains me to look into his eyes, yet I can't bring myself to look away, just like back then.

Then all of the sudden, I open my eyes. I'm on the floor, my back is against the wall. There's so much screaming but all I can feel is the throbbing, searing pain in my jaw. I look beneath me and I see a pool of scarlet lurching towards my Manolos, and immediately I know that he's dead. How did this happen?

No.

I shake my head, pick up my glass, and take a sip that drains the whole martini. See? There it is, all those things I never deserved to know, forgotten. I guess it doesn't totally wipe away the memories, but it softens their sharp edges at least. I wipe the lipstick mark off the rim of the glass then shut my eyes. I try to think positively. That's what Sandra, my old life coach, used to say. She said to think positively, and you will manifest your brightest inner goddess. I search my brain for happy memories, and not to my shock, I come up with nothing. Maybe Sandra is a toxically positive middle-aged white woman with no degree who is full of shit, or maybe she has a point. Maybe there are some happy memories that I choose to ignore. Maybe we're designed to only remember the bad, or maybe that's just me. Maybe I'm just miserable. Maybe I choose to be miserable because it's all I know. Maybe I'm too miserable to love. Maybe if things were different, the nightmare would have ended when I woke up. *Why are you like this, Delilah?*

Sandra was no help with my insomnia. She told me that to find my peace, I have to look within myself. But okay Sandra, I'm looking. Where the fuck is it? She doesn't understand. She doesn't get what it's like to be scared to shut your eyes because the darkness squeezes your brain so hard that it explodes. Or, how you want to claw out your eyes to erase everything you've ever seen. How you want to break your ear drums to drown out all the screams you've ever heard and rip out your tongue to forget all the blood you've ever tasted. That's what happens when I close my eyes, I'd love to know what positive affirmations Sandra has to fix that. I learned my lesson about life coaches the hard way which is why I chose to bite the bullet and go legit with a real therapist, regardless of how much my husband detests paying her $300 per session for me to just 'sit there and complain'.

My racing thoughts are suddenly interrupted by the screech of a doorbell followed by three painful knocks. Why do both? I'm pulled out of my daze, or 'Lila Land' as my mother loved to call it, and I'm brought back to the hole I dug for myself. At least this hole is a 3.2-million-dollar hole. I peek over from the kitchen table into the foyer and see a 40-something-year-old blonde woman wearing Lulu Lemon. She's accompanied by a 7-year-old girl in a dress and bow that makes her look like an American Girl Doll. Fuck. It's Mrs. Chamberlain and her daughter, Ashley. I must have forgotten that we had booked a piano lesson for today.

"Yoooo-hoooo," Mrs. Chamberlain exclaims.

I don't think I've ever found someone more annoying than her in this moment.

"Uh, be right there! I'm just… straightening up a bit."

"No rush, don't worry about us." Mrs. Chamberlain says.

I throw my glass in the sink and stash the bottle in the overly stocked liquor cabinet. I run to the laundry room and grab a pair of pants and t-shirt from the dryer that have been there for days. Running to the guest bathroom, I squirt toothpaste onto a small travel sized toothbrush, and I can't help but wonder what the hell I'm even doing here. I'm not supposed to be living in this picket fenced purgatory, exhausting myself to get through one hour of Chopsticks with one of the twins from The Shining. I always promised myself that I wouldn't be one of these women, locked in a shiny hell of my own making, just like my mother. My life wasn't supposed to end up like this. But I reached for the stars and all they did was burn me. Now I have a spoiled, tone-deaf kid and her controlling pickleball-playing mother at my door. It's not as if I don't like kids, I do, I used to love them. That love is what made me decide to be a teacher in the first place. Kids have such an innocence about them, it's infectious. I used to feel a world of hope every time I was around them. Now, when I look at them, all I see is what I've lost. I allow my hand to float down to my stomach. I touch my fingers to the jagged scar. My hand flies up at the sound of another knock. I suck in a deep breath and spit into the sink. No time for any of that. I peek my head out of the bathroom door. Through the window, I see Ashley holding her mom's hand and swaying to music that isn't playing. I don't think I've ever had the kind of innocence that Ashley has, not even as a young kid. The ribbons were ripped out of my hair and the crayons were stolen from my hand. No nightlight could brighten the darkness that was coming for me. My black roses were set on fire, and I was drawn to it like a moth. And now here I am, left in the ashes praying for a day when insults don't scream, and compliments don't whisper. But that day will never come because you're invisible when you're sad. Nobody sees me. Nobody has ever really seen me... well, except for *him*.

"Delilah, you there? I do have a pickleball scrimmage in a bit, so..."

16

Pickleball, nailed it.

"Coming!"

Snapping back to reality, I ransack the guest bathroom looking for mouthwash. Mrs. Chamberlain doesn't strike me as the sharpest tool in the shed, but I swear that the look she gave me last week when she picked her daughter up… She was on to me. I need to be more careful. I finally spot a travel-sized bottle of Scope in the bottom drawer of the vanity. My jaw clicks as I open my mouth, reminding me of exactly who I am. I gargle what's left of my sanity and spit it down the drain. I turn off the bathroom light and hurry towards the foyer when my phone buzzes. I'm surprised to be getting texts at all, my husband has barely bothered to check in since he's been away. I'm sure whatever concubine he's with this time is occupying him just fine. I pull my phone out of my pocket, type in my passcode and see a text from an unfamiliar number.

Unknown number: Delilah, I'm out. I'm telling them everything. See you at the reunion.

And suddenly, the sun disappears.

Chapter 2
2009 - Richmond Hill, Georgia

I watch the wind blow through the Spanish moss, focusing on the beauty of the greenery around me, trying to drown out the cadence of insults flying between my parents. Blocking out the noise is a skill I mastered long ago. My brother, Liam, seems to have the same idea as his eyes basically shoot Cupid's arrows through the voluptuous redhead posing for pictures on the staircase. I follow Liam's gaze and admire the pre-war steps that are accompanied by tall colonial columns. We've been coming to the Richmond Hill Country Club for so long, I often forget how beautiful the architecture is. I'm sure I would find this whole town beautiful if I didn't live here, but all I know is that it feels like suburban purgatory right now. It's a place where narrow minds can come together and bury their hot heads deep in the sand. I can't think of a single thought more exciting than getting the hell out of here and never looking back.

Continuing to ignore the future murder-suicide that is my parents, I close my eyes and take in the jazz melody coming from the lobby's ceiling speakers. It's the kind of music my dad would refer to as elevator music, the kind of music he has banned me from playing on our black baby grand piano at home. I'm afraid my repertoire is confined to the works of Bach, Debussy, Beethoven, and a plethora of other dead dudes. It's not that I don't love playing classical piano, I do. And Dad is right, if I'm going to play for the New York City Philharmonic one day, I need to stay focused. Still, I can't help but sway my body to the pure soul I hear coming out of those speakers. There's just something about jazz. Something about playing it feels so, I don't know… free, I guess. It's a feeling I don't get often. Most days, I'm a prisoner held captive in a dungeon of my insecurities. My fingers play chords along to the free-flowing melody, when suddenly, I'm interrupted by a shrill, familiar sound.

"Delilah, earth to Delilah, anybody home?" My mom shrieks in her long, southern drawl. Her ice blue eyes lock with mine, once again reminding me that I have the worst genes in the family when it comes to looks. My brother has those same baby blues that glow flecks of green when he looks into the light, while mine are a strange cross of dark green and dirt brown. Mom says they look like muddy water, sweet lady she is.

"Are you ready to leave Lilah Land and join the rest of society? The waiter said our table is ready," she screeches before flipping her long dark curls away from me as she heads up the stairs. I get smacked in the face with a strong whiff of her new Dooney & Bourke perfume. She tries a new scent every week, an attempt to win my father's attention back from his two young female secretaries. Although, I'm sure it would take a lot more than designer perfume to lure the great William Monroe in like a siren seducing a sailor at sea. He hasn't shown interest in my Mom in years. Dad is all about value and what a person can add to a situation. He says the key to success is to make sure you hold the highest value in any room you walk into. For him, that looks like being the smartest, wealthiest, and most powerful. If they're playing checkers, you best be playing chess. For Mom, her value once existed in her gorgeous face and her southern charm. She rode that train all the way to becoming Miss Georgia which she used as leverage to bag one of the most successful men in big oil. Dad was immediately charmed by her beauty and poise. Lady Katherine, they used to call her. But eventually, the train skated off the tracks. The older she got, the things that put a bedazzled crown on her head began to dwindle. As Dad became more successful, Mom became more complacent. She became lazier, angrier, more reactive, and sometimes insufferable. My parents changed a lot over the past 20 years. Dad's value went up and Mom's went down, and they both resent each other for it. I guess that's what my brother and I can blame for the daily screaming, the nightly drunken dish breaking, and the bruises around Mom's neck which are tactfully hidden under her Burberry scarf even though it's 80 degrees outside. My mom is still a beautiful woman, with her long dark hair and her high cheekbones. The Botox has preserved her at a solid 40-years-old, but my dad doesn't see the beautiful Southern Belle when he looks at her. These days, all my Mom is to him is a washed-up beauty queen with a vodka-soaked heart and bourbon stained soul.

"D, let's go, I'm hungry," Liam pleads.

"This girl is just slower than a Sunday afternoon," Mom remarks as she turns towards me. "Why must you always do this, Delilah?" She scoffs as she struts away. My cheeks glow red as I hang my head down.

Liam turns around and pats me on the shoulder. "Ignore her, she's mad at Dad for God knows what. Come on, I see some underaged drinking in our future."

I laugh and follow him up the pre-war steps and into the lobby, hoping and praying that none of my family members will bring up the events from today.

Mom orders a Belvedere martini the minute we are seated at our regular table. Dad orders a bottle of wine from the southern regions of Italy, and I already know this will be continued by a 20-minute-long breakdown on the history of the grape and region it comes from. I swear, he makes up half the things that he says, but he is so damn convincing that you end up taking his word for it. He could have been a lawyer, but the money to be made in oil was always going to rank higher than any passion of his. Wealth, that's the real siren in William Monroe's life. And she's always singing.

Dad's monologue comes to a halt when the waiter brings over the decanter of dark red bliss. Dad puts his hand up and stops the waiter from filling our glasses, insisting that the wine needs to breathe. I roll my eyes, as does Liam. If we're forced to listen to his sommelier-wannabe ramblings, we should at least be able to enjoy the cause. Dad turns his head to Liam and begins his usual line of questioning about school and how he is doing in his finance classes. My brother, the golden child, answers with the perfect amount of 'yes sirs' and fake enthusiasm. Liam wanted to study psychology, he's always been great at listening to people and reading them. But that dream was crushed into a million pieces when my Dad got hold of the essay that Liam wrote for his college application. Two paragraphs in, my dad smashed the papers in Liam's handsome face, bloodying his lip. Dad genuinely thought Liam wrote the essay just to mess with him, like he was playing a sick joke on him. *'Shrinks are just that, weak hacks with shrunken brains. You want to help people, be a man and get a real job.'* William doesn't believe in therapy, or depression, or feelings at all, which is why I have always made sure to button up mine. My mom doesn't like to talk about feelings either. Though, she never seems to have a problem expressing her rage, nor does Dad. They constantly get on Liam for being too sensitive, and me for being too quiet. But every time I open my mouth, everything that I say is wrong, even when I'm right. So, I've opted to only speak when necessary to save myself from embarrassment. But Liam, my sweet brother, is an incredible speaker. He would have made an amazing therapist, but that's not the Monroe way. And, at the end of the day, he will do anything to make my dad proud. If only he knew that nothing he ever accomplishes in this life will be good enough for William Monroe.

Once Dad gives us the nod, I pick up my crystal glass and take a sip of my wine. I close my eyes and savor the bold taste making its way down my throat. I reach in front of me to grab another cheese straw from the center of the table. Lady Katherine catches my grab and subtly moves the bowl away from me, inching it with her pinky. Mom treats the slowing of a metabolism like it's like a monster under her bed at night waiting for her to fall asleep. I give Mom the side eye and see her face light up as she spots two men in $1000 suits, holding glasses of $100 dollar scotch approaching our table.

"Well look what the cat dragged in. Katherine, looking as exquisite as ever," the taller gentleman says in a flirty voice.

"Kids, you remember John and Oliver, they own the winery downtown."

The winery is an understatement, John and Oliver Preston come from some of the oldest money in town, they pretty much own the whole county. Mom nudges me with her elbow, and I know she's signaling me to say something polite and endearing that won't embarrass her, but my mouth won't move. Instead, a rapid ray of heat travels up my body from my abdomen to the top of my head.

"How are you doing, boys? It's great to see you. I'm home for the week on fall break, so we thought we'd come to our good old trusty stomping ground." Liam jumps in, no doubt trying to take the pressure off me. I flash him a look of gratitude and chug my wine. I reach for the decanter and pour myself another glass of probably the only thing I will enjoy about tonight.

"Yes, Liam is a finance major at Duke, he's at the top of his class just like I was at his age," Dad exclaims, showing off. It's as if Liam is nothing but a mere extension of him instead of a living, breathing humn being.

"Well, that's very impressive Liam, good for you."

"What are yinz doing here on this fine evening?" Dad asks, and my mouth nearly drops at his Pittsburgh accent peeking through. His face remains unpinned and unphased like a professional poker player, but I notice his chest becoming flushed with scarlet patches, like mine does when I'm nervous. Mom lets out a little nervous laugh, immediately noticing the slip up. Dad tries with all his might to hide his Pittsburg accent. The last thing he wants to do is remind guys like this that he didn't come from old southern money like everyone else in this town. Dad grew up in a foster home but worked his ass off to get a scholarship to Duke. He bussed tables at night to support himself. The fact that Liam doesn't have to work as hard is something Dad hangs over him like the moss from the trees outside. And, although Liam has expressed his deepest appreciation many times, something tells me that's a debt that will never be paid in William's calculating mind. Dad never did stop hustling, his quest to get in on big oil is what brought him to Georgia and falling for the beauty queen, Lady Katherine, is what made him stay. Her being what tied him to this magnolia tree is something he will never stop punishing her for. He hates it here. You would think that growing up with nothing and building an empire all by yourself would be celebrated, but not here in Richmond Hill. Here, the only money that is respected is accompanied by generations upon generations of lineage.

"Honey," my mom chimes in with disingenuous affection in her voice. "We should let these gentlemen get back to their dinner, I'm sure they're just as starving as we are." I roll my eyes, knowing that the only thing Mom will be eating tonight is seven stiff martinis and under-handed insults from her devoted husband.

"You got that right. Well, it was great to see you lovely people. Enjoy your evening, and Liam, keep up the good work."

Liam gives them a respectful nod as they head back to the bar.

"Fucking pricks," Dad whispers under his breath.

His jealousy is wildly transparent. Dad treats life as a competition, and in his mind, he is always losing, weighed down by that Pennsylvania sized chip on his shoulder.

After the waiter comes back to take our order, my phone buzzes. I flip open my light pink razor phone and see that I have a text. Damn, it's just Mia.

"Delilah." I jerk my head up at my Dad's voice.

"How is Philly doing? Is he ready for the state playoffs? I'll tell ya, what that kid can do on the field is incredible," Dad says before taking another sip. His comment, disguised as a compliment, is really a dig directed at Liam. He's pointing out that Liam wasn't half the football player that Philly is. His heart just didn't seem to be in it, but he continued to play because that's what Dad wanted. Now, here my Dad is years later, still finding subtle ways to criticize him for not being the next Ben Roethlisberger. Liam seems to take notice of the dig as he shakes his head and looks away, peering through the large window to his right. I can only imagine what's going through his head. Maybe he's thinking of traveling to whatever planet my mom landed her ship on three martinis ago.

"Um, I don't know, I think he's ready," I respond, sheepishly while searching my brain for ways to change the subject.

"His dad was busting my balls last week at the bar about all the new young players they have, but those pricks weren't the ones who won the Super Bowl last year, we did." My Dad trails off into sport mode as if he's the 1968 mint condition Camaro that sits in our garage. He's going on about the rivalry between the Philadelphia Eagles and the Pittsburgh Steelers, something mine and Philly's Dad immediately bonded over a few years ago, the two of them being the only ones in this town from Pennsylvania. Philly's Dad is the chief of police in Richmond Hill and he's running for Mayor this year, but that doesn't stop him from being the life-of-the-party guy's guy that everyone adores. Sheriff St. James understands my Dad in a way that most people don't, especially his pride and love for his home-town's football team. The St. James' have so much Philadelphia pride that they went as far as to name their only son Philly. I always loved that name. *Philly*. Every time I hear it my heart skips like a rock over a pond. But, to my dismay, he hasn't texted me all day, and I know that if I text him first, he's going to see it as desperate, get turned off, and ignore me the rest of the week. I don't know why things need to be so complicated all the time. I love him more than anything in this world, and I know that he loves me, he's just scared.

Liam joins in on the Steelers versus Eagles conversation, attempting to relate to Dad in some way. Dad continues his rant, he'll never pass up an opportunity to hear his own voice. As for me, the Eagles are the last thing I want to talk about. I tuck my dark hair behind my ear and touch the back of my head, wincing as pain surges through the raw area. I still have the remnants of a pounding headache from Sunday. *Ugh, Sunday. Fucking Sunday.*

Chapter 3

25

2009 - Richmond Hill, Georgia

On Sunday, the Eagles were playing the Ravens, and we all gathered in Mia's basement to watch it on her new flatscreen TV. The boys sat on the leather couch drinking Natty Ices while Mia and I sat on the floor and shared a water bottle filled with cheap vodka. I'm not even sure what brand of vodka it was, probably whatever Mia's sister could snag us with her fake ID. Philly was excited that night, and he was more affectionate than usual. At one point, he even sat on the floor and put his arm around me. His black eyes peered into mine, slicing my corneas with lust. His fair complexion was lit up by the basement lights, illuminating his sharp angles and jawline. He bit his bottom lip, and suddenly everything in me wished he was biting mine. My head leaned into his chest as I savored his scent, a combination of Axe body spray and Abercrombie cologne. He even called me his girl; he had never done that before. He's never wanted to put a label on our relationship which has been going on since kindergarten. I still remember the we met. It was my first day of kindergarten and I was so nervous, I cried the entire car ride on the way to the school. Mom practically dragged me through those double doors by my little moppy head of hair. Philly and I were put in the same class, and we met that first day during recess. I was sitting in the corner trying not to make eye contact with anyone when I noticed a monarch butterfly. I could tell what kind of butterfly it was by its orange color and black spots. I had this big book of all the butterfly species. I wanted to bring it to school that day but when Mom went through my backpack, she took the book out and slammed it on the kitchen counter. She said I needed to grow up and make some friends and that no kid wants to play with the weird bug girl. I'm sure she was right, but shit, I just liked butterflies. I thought they were magical. I don't find much magical anymore, but back then, I was full of false hope. I stared at that butterfly slowly flapping its wings as it drank the nectar from a purple coneflower for at least five minutes. I was infatuated. When the butterfly finished its business and started flying away, I began to chase it. Philly noticed me before I noticed him. He ran up behind me, startling me, and asked what I was doing. I struggled on stutters, trying to explain to him that it was a monarch butterfly and that they were an endangered species. Just when I thought he was going to walk away and label me as the weird bug girl, his eyes lit up and he started chasing the butterfly with me. We ran and laughed, forgetting the rest of the kids, forgetting the rest of the world. I remember the way the sun reflected off his captivating black eyes like a full moon off the night sea. I still see that boy when I look at him. Even on Sunday, when the Eagles lost the game on a technicality. Philly and the other boys screamed at the TV, throwing beer all over Mia's mom's fancy Persian carpet. When Mia yelled at them for acting like animals, the other boys apologized and knelt to help her scrub the stains off the ground. I did the same until I noticed Philly stomping away to the bathroom. I know how much it hurts him when his team doesn't win. Football is way more than just a game to him, it's his future and his greatest passion.

I got up off my knees a few minutes later to try and catch Philly in the hallway to console him. We were having such a good night and he was so happy just half an hour ago. I didn't want the loss to ruin it. I rounded the corner of the hall and was immediately met by Philly's dark eyes as the bathroom door swung open. I grabbed his broad shoulders.

"You okay, baby?"

In one motion, he swatted my hands away, pushing me off him and into the wall. My head hit the linoleum so hard, I was completely stunned.

"Get off me, slut. I'm not your baby."

"But, I—I—"

"What? Are you gonna cry now, Delilah?"

Philly stormed off in a huff. My hand flew up to the back of my head to check if it was bleeding, and I was surprised to find out that it wasn't. I quickly scanned the perimeter to make sure no one witnessed what just happened. The last thing I needed was more embarrassment. Baby? Baby? Why the fuck would I have used that word? I've never called him that, I have no idea where that came from. Of course, he's not a baby, he's almost eighteen, a full-grown adult. Perhaps I drank too much, I tend to do that. Whenever I drink, there's this part of me that wants to throw my whole life in the fire, and every single time, I burn along with it.

I walked into the bathroom and let out a few deep sobs. I stared at my reflection for a moment, trying to toughen my facial expression. I took my fingers to my eyes, wiped the smudges under my eyeliner and headed back out, hoping that I could apologize to Philly and forget it ever happened. When I finally made my way back to the basement, no one was to be found besides Mia, still scrubbing the stale beer off the carpet. I sighed and bent down to help her. That was when she told me that the boys left to try and sneak into Mulligan's, a local bar on the river whose bouncer will sometimes look the other way for the right price. I decided to stay at Mia's that night, wanting to avoid the night show of my parents' drunken arguing. I had already caught the matinee show earlier that afternoon. I didn't tell Mia what happened. I said I had a headache and blamed it on the cheap vodka. She plied me with Advil, but I'm sure she saw through me. She always knows when something is wrong, I never have to tell her, which is convenient because I never would. After I lied that I was fine for the sixth time, she stopped pushing. I told her that I wasn't tired even though I was completely exhausted. I wanted to make sure I stayed awake in case I had a concussion. I remembered learning that protocol in middle school when Liam hit his head in practice. Mia nodded her head and perched up on the couch. She put a warm blanket over both of us then turned-on reruns of The Hills she had saved on DVR. I pretended to watch Kristen and Audrina squabble in silence until the sun came up while quietly trying to untangle my twisted mind.

Why must things be so complicated with Philly? I know he can be a dick, but no one understands him like I do. When I look at him, I still see the boy that chased butterflies with me. I see the boy who was scared to go to the pool party because he was self-conscious about his stomach. I see the boy who smiles with his mouth shut because he doesn't like the white mark on his tooth. Deep down, Philly St. James has a sensitive soul. He once cried in my arms for three straight hours in eighth grade after his dog died. Philly took care of her throughout her entire cancer journey. I guess some things never change. The pure love that he felt for that animal was beautiful. I've always thought that Philly loves *too* hard, and he's afraid of it, he's afraid of me. He didn't speak to me for an entire month after the time he cried in my arms, and I wondered if I was maybe too comforting that it scared him. Maybe I said too much, maybe I didn't say enough. I guess I'll never know what I did wrong.

I'm snapped back to reality by Liam's voice.

"You okay, D? You hit your head or something?"

It's then that I notice that my hand is still rubbing the back of my head. I quickly remove it, burying it under my pale legs.

"Yeah, I'm fine."

That should honestly be my catchphrase by now, the most common lie in the world must be that we say we're fine when we're not. But let's be real, when someone asks how you are, do they ever really want to hear the truth?

"Oh, that girl is in Lilah land, don't pay her any mind."

Mom's accent gets thicker the more the vodka drenches her mind, and it causes my Dad to grow a familiar, disgusted look on his face. His attention is averted when the waiter brings over his filet mignon that is so rare, it may just be able to get up and walk right out of here. He puts my salmon down in front of me. I ordered fish instead of the truffle mac and cheese, wanting to avoid unsolicited criticism from Mom. Once the waiter has set down Katherine's arugula salad and Liam's roasted chicken, Mom bows her head and begins saying grace. After a minute and a half of her drunk attempt at ministry, Dad pipes in.

"Alright, Katherine! Get on with it and let us fucking eat."

Mom quickly finishes by thanking Jesus for the bountiful meal we are about to eat, and we break hands. Dad murmurs something under his breath about how Jesus isn't paying for our meal, he is, but Mom ignores him and takes a sip of her freshly shaken martini. Dad has never been quite on board with the Christian thing. My mom got extremely involved with the church a few years ago after Dad told her she needed to find a hobby. I assume he was hoping she would pick up cooking, gardening, or Pilates, but instead, she found God.

"So," Mom chirps up again, "I wanted to talk to y'all about something I heard in my church group today."

"Was it the story of Samson and *Delilah*," Liam teases as he tickles my arm.

I chuckle, but Mom is, of course, unamused.

"Young man, I swear, your corn bread ain't done in the middle. The bible is off limits for your silly comedy routine."

"Yes, ma'am," Liam returns sarcastically and winks in my direction.

Mom's serious demeanor continues. "It's about that girl from your school who..." Mom lowers her voice to a whisper. "The girl who…" She struggles to find the words as her face turns pale, she looks like she's going to vomit.

"Killed herself, Mom, the girl who killed herself," I blurt out.

Shock fills my mom's face which would show if her face was still capable of movement. She looks at me in horror. My Dad glares at me as Liam keeps his gaze down towards his chicken. I don't know why I blurted it out like that, but like I said, every time I speak, I say something wrong even when I'm right.

Chapter 4
Present day

The Georgia wind blows the door closed behind me after I practically clear each stair, lunging up the wrap around porch. I push the door behind me once more to make sure it's locked. I kick off my black Louboutins and savor the feeling of the cold floor underneath my throbbing feet. Whoever said 'the higher the heels, the closer to God' must have been an atheist. I turn away from the door but am then pulled back at the sound of a creek on the porch. What was that? Is someone out there? Is it *him*? It can't be. My hand flutters faster than my heart as I carefully creep towards the window. I peak my head around the corner, barely letting my face touch the glass. I swivel to get a better view, but all I'm met with are the same old rocking chairs and the same old colonial columns that have always been here. I sigh at myself and close the black shutters. I move towards the kitchen, abandoning my Draper James purse on the floor as I practically rip off my black cocktail dress. I toss it on the counter and yank a chilled martini glass out of the freezer, wrapping the French tips on my other hand around the tall bottle of Belvedere. I set the glass and bottle down on the kitchen island and admire the two entities that have been waiting patiently for me to get home all night, like loyal puppies. I pour a Delilah-sized glass of vodka and set the bottle back on the freezer shelf. I grab the handle to shut the door but I'm stung with the stare of a face I can't forget no matter how hard I try. They say when someone dies, you have to make an intentional effort to remember them, to keep their memory alive, or else you forget. But I've never forgotten. Those eyes, the way they used to look at me. That voice, and what it used to say to me. I haven't forgotten. Not for a day, not for an hour, not for a minute, not for a mother fucking second. As much as I want to swim to the other side of the world and drop the memory of him off the edge of it, I will always be haunted by the cadence of his sadness and the echo of his soul. The words he said, and the words I was too afraid to say. It's my fault, I did this, it's all my fault. I've heard that grief is just love with nowhere to go anymore. Perhaps that's why I try to stuff it in this Belvedere like a message in a bottle, but I can't seem to drift it out to sea. My glassy eyes stay locked with the boy in the photo, no key to salvation in sight.

Then all of the sudden, I open my eyes. I'm on the floor, my back is against the wall. There's so much screaming but all I can feel is the throbbing, searing pain in my jaw. I look beneath me and I see a pool of scarlet lurching towards my Manolos. And immediately I know that he's dead. How did this happen?

No.

Jesus fucking Christ. I slam the freezer door like it's my enemy… Oh wait, that's me. *Why must you always do this, Delilah?*

I turn my body away from the door and shove myself into the counter, nearly knocking the wind out of my stomach. I'm sinking, I'm sinking into the abyss again. I lift my martini to my glossed lips and drain it into nothingness. There, now I'm anchored to shore, at least for a little while.

The peach fuzz on my arms stands straight up as a chill breezes by my body. It's then that I notice I'm no longer wearing my cocktail dress, only black-lace lingerie from Victoria's Secret, a cheeky thong and a push-up bra that does me wonderful favors. It felt like the perfect little secret to hide under the perfect little black dress I wore for the charity auction in Savannah tonight. What we were raising money for… I couldn't say, nor could the rest of the women on the country club committee. But it didn't matter. Charlotte Vanderheiden, chair of the committee and resident stuck up snob of this town gave me the simple task of choosing the music, something I'm actually good at. I went with piano and soft guitar acoustic versions of popular songs one may hear on the radio. Always a crowd pleaser. Even Charlotte thanked me for a job well done after a night of idle conversation and dodging questions about why my husband didn't accompany me. Pitying looks from women, lingering looks from their husbands. It made me feel… I don't know, like the loneliest woman in the world. The looks they gave me, like I was sub-human because I was there solo. The way that everyone phrased the question as 'where's your better half?'... I know it's just an expression, but it reminded me that I am, indeed, the lesser half.

After pouring myself another martini, one with room temperature vodka from the liquor cabinet in an effort to avoid the photo on the fridge, I grab my phone from my purse and take a seat in the living room. Still in my bra and panties, I lay myself out long on the white velvet couch. I take a deep breath before checking my text messages to see if there is anything new from the unknown number. What did he mean he's telling them everything? Was that a threat? I can't risk finding out. I drag my fingers across the screen and hit the block button. I sit up, grab the remote and turn on the plasma screen. I click the channel button a few times until I come up on my childhood favorite, Fried Green Tomatoes. It looks like it just started, hell yeah. I grab my garnish-less martini and lean back on a furry white pillow. I take a sip and swish the vodka around my mouth, waiting for the sun to come out. I lick the rim of the chilled glass, hoping the bite of the alcohol will puncture my tongue the way it's punctured my heart. I set the crystal glass down on the coffee table, not that it's ever used for coffee. I open my phone back up and flicker my eyes over the text I sent to my husband while at the gala tonight. It's a mirror picture of my tight dress and a text that says, 'wish you were here tonight.' The word underneath the text is the one that pierces me like a jellyfish sting. *Read.* He opened the text right after I sent it and never responded. I continued to make the rounds of small talk and fake air kisses at the party as I silently reiterated to myself that he's just busy with work. But six hours have gone by now. If he had a compliment about the picture, he would have said it. If he had any interest in my body, he would have shown it. My hazel eyes continue to linger over the photo. I should have edited it or used one of those filters I see the other women use on Instagram. I usually mock those women, attempting to pass a shape shifting filter as their own face, looking cartoonish instead. But, hey, it's not like I'm freaking winning over here. Maybe they're onto something. I pull up Instagram on my phone and scroll past the pictures of tonight's event and young mothers using their babies as props, then open the camera. I click on a filter I saw a young 4th-wife-of-a-wealthy-man-cliche use at the country club. I tuck my balayage golden hair behind my ears and stare into the camera. The filter makes my skin look like I've never carried a burden in my life. I try out different angles until an idea floats into my buzzed brain. I reach behind me and snap the hooks of my bra undone. I let the lace fall to the floor as I scan my reflection on my phone. I grab one of my breasts, cupping it and pulling it up until it reaches my neckline. I keep my French tips over my pale pink nipple and purse my shimmery lips. I snap the same photo a few times until I land on one I don't hate. I upload it as a text to my husband and click send. There, that ought to get his attention. I keep my phone in one hand as I pick up my martini with the other. I bask in the daydream of him in a lonely hotel room, staring at that photo of me, getting hard as wood. I imagine him calling me to whisper mellifluous nothings in his ear while he rubs himself up and down to completion. I imagine him cumming to the sound of my voice while he screams my name. A smile presses on my glossed lips as I take another sip of my martini. Almost all of my teeth are showing as I put down my drink and look down at my phone. *Read.* Read! He read it four minutes ago. Four fucking minutes ago. I throw my phone across the room, knocking over one of our wedding photos. Luckily, it hits the soft carpet and doesn't shatter. I yank my head backward and let out a gentle scream. He's with *her*. I know it. I know it like I know every note and chord in Claire de Lune. He doesn't want me. He wants *her*. Maybe he always has.

I pick up my martini and gobble it gone. I'm trying. I'm trying to make this marriage work, to spice things up. But instead, I'm over here sending him nudes like a desperate teenager and he could care less if I'm dead or alive. It makes me feel... I don't know, humiliated. I don't matter to him; I don't matter to... anyone, not anymore. I destroyed that more catastrophically than I'm currently destroying my liver.

I stare at my black bra on the white couch. I think it's warranted to go topless after a long night of feeling like a caged animal in a cocktail dress. I leave the bra where it is. I pick up the remote and surf the more adult sections of television. I click through a few different PlayBoy channels. They have some girl on girl, not my thing. Some missionary, boring. Some porn star game show, what in the world? Finally, after the seventh flip, I see something that catches my eye. The camera is panning across a dungeon lit in red lighting, scandalous for TV porn. A woman walks into the center of the frame wearing nothing but a black lacy thong that resembles mine. Behind her, there are a variety of whips, chains, ropes, and sex swings. Ah, this could be interesting. A large man walks into the frame, he's wearing some sort of masquerade mask that covers the space around his eyes and cheeks, but his body looks like it was built by the gods. He comes up behind the woman and grabs her neck. I watch the attractive woman melt into his body as I slip off my panties. I quickly saunter over to the cabinet underneath the TV stand to grab my vibrator. It's brand new and has one part that goes inside me and another part that stimulates elsewhere else. I leave it under the TV for this exact reason. I sneak back over to the white couch, tiptoeing as if this isn't my home, as if there's someone else here, which there never is. I focus back on the screen. The large man reaches around the woman from behind and puts his fingers in her mouth. She sucks on them dutifully with her big, red lips. His other huge hand glides up and down her neck, taunting her. He then grabs her shoulders and spins her around with force, her large breasts swinging with the grace that only breasts under 30-years-old can have. She begins to say something, but he stops her by putting his finger to her red lips. She hushes at his command, as he slowly removes his finger from her mouth and points in towards her underwear. She nods at him submissively and slowly takes off her thong, throwing it on the floor of the red dungeon. He studies her toned, curvy body up and down. He inches towards her and whips out a feather toy from behind him. Has he had that whole time? He brings the feathers up towards her neck and slowly moves them down, tickling her chest. He continues to drag the feathers down her breasts, her stomach, and her hips until it's lingering between her legs just above her skin, teasing her with pleasure. The woman throws her head back and lets out a yearning moan of desire. She's aching for more; *I* am aching for more. But the masked man yanks the feathers away from her inner thighs and walks off the screen, leaving the woman alone. Her skin is illuminated red underneath the dungeon lights. All she's wearing are her high heels. After a few beats of her standing there alone, I'm about to flip to a different channel. Then, the large, masked man appears back on the screen. He comes up behind her and grabs her neck, choking her. His hand squeezes her neck while the other travels all around her smooth body. He pushes her from behind down on to her knees and the woman smiles as she looks back at him. The woman positions herself on her hands and knees and begins to beg the man for more.

"Please," I hear from the surround sound speakers. The man leans down behind her round butt. There we go, now we're cooking with gas. I get my toy ready and try to position myself in doggy style on the couch. My arms sink in between the couch cushions and the pillows behind me fall over. I roll my eyes and push the coffee table slightly away, making room on the carpet. I lower myself off the couch and get down on my hands and knees. Once I sturdy myself, I slip my hand between my legs to find I'm wetter than the Savannah River. I replace my hand with the toy and press the button. Elation floods through my body, the current flowing rapidly and wildly. I almost have to stop myself to savor the moment. I look back at the screen and see the man thrusting in and out of the woman.

"Fuck me harder!" She yells.

The masked man slaps her round bottom. I pretend my hand is his and slap my own butt, and it hurts so good. I whip my head back towards the screen, my honey hair falling over my shoulder. The masked man in the frame pulls out another BDSM toy, and he wraps it around her neck. She gives him a kinky smirk as she gets up from her hands and leans backward onto his chest. He pulls tightly on the chain around her as he thrusts inside of her. She moans in ecstasy; her facial expression is euphoric. I'll have whatever she's having. I look around me, wondering if I have anything like that to choke myself with... in a fun way, of course. I come up short as I search around the minimalistic white furniture the living room is decorated with. I touch my hand to my neck to find the family heirloom I had almost forgotten about. I brush my fingers over the large off-white pearls. Fuck it. I lean up off my hands and unclasp the necklace. I bring it back to my neck and tie it in a knot. I get back down into doggy style and place my toy in its rightful spot. My legs quiver, throbbing for more.

I watch the big, masked man pull the black choker around her neck tightly as he pounds her from behind. I pull the pearls tighter around my neck and moan even louder than the woman in the dungeon. I keep choking myself, pulling the pearls tighter and tighter. I pant and swoon until I can barely breath. A sweet darkness comes over me like it's a curtain and I'm a bare window. The masked man moves his hips rhythmically in a circular motion, and I do the same with the toy inside me. My gasps and moans blare louder as euphoria entraps me, starting from my toes and rolling up me like a beautiful marble on a hard floor. This is paradise, this is heaven. My body pulsates, and just as the orgasm is about to overtake me, I feel a cold air on my neck and hear the pearls explode from the chain and smash onto the ground. I leave them, ambivalently, as I look back at the screen. The man let's go of the chain, puts his big hands on her curvy hips and pushes off of her. He leans his body back from the woman, exposing his big manhood that glistens red under the light. The woman turns around to meet his gaze. He smirks at her as she slowly opens her legs in front of him and lies back. I turn myself around and do the same on my rug, adjusting the position of my vibrator. The large, masked man slowly lowers his body on top of hers. Fear flushes through my blood. Discomfort tickles my bones. I close my eyes, trying to stay in the moment, desperate to finish what I started. I move the toy rapidly side to side, in and out until I'm practically stabbing myself with it. I squeeze my eyes tighter and tighter, focusing on nothing but the sensation and the moans of the people on the screen I've begun to grow fond of. My hand keeps moving, my body stays still, but my mind wanders to a place far away.

The sky above me is dark, the pavement beneath me is cold. Get off the ground. Get off the ground. Get off the fucking ground, Delilah.

My eyes fling open. A roar of frustration rages out of me as I throw the sex toy out of my hand. I shoot up off the ground and bring my hands to my face, heaving in and out. When I lower my hands, I see the sex dungeon on the screen in front of me. Suddenly, the two people that I found compelling and attractive, the people I was ravenous for just minutes ago, are now revolting to me. Nausea swarms in my stomach. What are you watching? A sex dungeon? BDSM? Who are you? *You're a slut, Delilah.* I slam my finger on the power button of the remote until the TV fades to black. I scoop my lingerie off the couch and floor and re-assemble it back on to my body. I return the coffee table to its normal position and pick up my martini glass. I tilt it back towards me, but sadly, it's empty, like my life. My gaze travels to the ground to find priceless pearls scattered. Shit, how am I going to explain that one? I go to take the glass towards the kitchen until I spot my vibrator on the white carpet. I pick it up and walk it back towards the cabinet under the TV stand. I wouldn't want my husband finding this if he ever decides I'm worth coming home to. I tuck the toy towards the back of the cabinet when my hand grazes something, a silver frame. I pull it out to see the picture I had hid from myself years ago. I never thought my husband and I would be the type of people to frame something like this, but we were so excited at the time, we couldn't help it. We wanted to do all of the things, all of the celebrations. I run my left hand over the photo gently. My oval wedding ring reflects sparkling spots on the white wall. I stare at the photo as pressure builds in my throat. Tears sting my bloodshot eyes as I'm forced to relive everything I've lost. I try to take a deep breath, but it's caught in my throat. *What, are you gonna cry now, Delilah*? My arms move faster than my body as they lift the photo over my head and launch it straight into the ground, glass shattering all over the floor. I look around beneath me. The shattered glass of broken dreams and the scattered pearls of a shambled marriage all rest across the floor. I bury my pale face in my hands. I wish there was a remote for my mind like there is for the TV. I wish there was a power button that could turn *me* off and fade my life to black.

Chapter 5
2009 - Richmond Hill, Georgia

The looks of shock begin to fade as Mom relays the news we have all heard already. It was about 8am this morning when the whispers began, and the phones started buzzing at school. I treaded lightly down the hallway to my locker. I ran late this morning after dozing off at Mia's around 6am. I had to scramble to run home and change before catching the bus to school. I didn't think my Eagles jersey that I cut into a crop top and low-rise jeans would be a suitable outfit for fifth period pre-calc.

I twisted in my locker combination and threw my books onto the bottom shelf. I loitered in front of my locker for a bit, trying to make out the conversation the sophomore girls were having next to me. *Great. They must be whispering about me*, I thought to myself. I should have figured, most rumors that fly around that school tend to be about me or my friends. Mia gets it the worst. There was that one rumor about her getting Eiffel towered by community college guys. We did go to a college party and Mia did go home with a guy, but I'm pretty sure it was just the one. Mia pays no mind to it though. If people are whispering, she'll put on her stage makeup and give them a real show to watch. Me on the other hand, I burn under the spotlight. That's why I haven't participated in a piano recital in years. At my last recital, I had such bad stage fright that I had a full throttle panic attack backstage. Once I got to the piano, my hands locked up and my vision blurred. I bombed so badly that my Dad threatened to stop paying for my lessons. 'If you are not going to be the best, you are not going to be doing it at all.' I can't ever let that happen again which was why this morning I desperately needed to find Mia to get to the bottom of whatever was going around. I wanted to get it over with then spend the rest of my free period in the music room practicing.

I raced down the narrow hallway towards the cafeteria hoping that our friend group would be there as usual. My chicken legs covered by Sophie shorts, I hauled ass as fast as possible. When I finally hit the end of the white, barren hallway, I entered the cafeteria. Black and white paint covered the walls to represent our school colors, and 'Go Jaguars!' posters were carpet bombed along the far wall. I scanned the room for my friends, not wanting to walk in all the way in case they weren't there. I didn't want to risk looking like loner girl again, that phase of my life ended when I met Mia in 6th grade. She had been walking by the practice room as I was playing some freestyle. I was shocked when she came in and leaned her elbows on the other side of the piano. My wrists were shaking as I continued tapping the keys in front of the most popular girl in school. After a minute or two of her studying me, I got tired of her cat and mouse game. I looked up at her to take whatever verbal beating awaited me. But instead, she flashed me a smile then asked if I knew any Nelly Furtado. We both laughed, and I couldn't believe that Mia White was giving me the time of day. She stayed and listened to me play for over an hour. After school let out, she said that my music touched her soul. She believed in me. We were inseparable ever since. I found out later that it was Philly that told her she should befriend me because he thought I was cute. This was a shocking revelation to me because Philly had not acknowledged my presence for two whole years prior to that, not to mention I had frizzy hair and hadn't discovered mascara yet. But Mia took me under her wing and fixed all of that. She taught me how to straighten my hair, how to do my eyeliner, and what clothes to wear. She introduced thongs to me. She even taught me how to use a tampon. Lord knows my mother wasn't going to do it. Mia taught me everything. She is the best friend I've ever had.

I had scanned every inch of the cafeteria and was about to give up until I spotted a pastel Lily Pulitzer dress in my peripheral. Mia was sitting on top of a lunch table with our friends, Chloe, and Mary Lu, who were sitting in the black seats below her. Both carbon copy minions were wearing different variations of Mia's outfit, although they could never pull it off quite as well. I walked up to the table, approaching the three of them with a light-hearted smile, but Mia's face was sullen and pointed towards the floor. *Oh no, is she mad at me? What did I do? Was I weirder than I thought last night?*

I stumbled on my words. "Hey, uh, what's uh, what's going on?"

Mary Lu gasped, "You mean you haven't heard?" She and Chloe exchanged looks like they had just heard the juiciest piece of gossip Richmond Hill High ever had. Getting increasingly nervous, I could feel my heart speeding up, matching the rhythm of the pounding in my head from the night before. Just as I was ready to make a break for it, Mia looked up at me with a frown as she whispered, "you know Bailey Garcia?"

"Yeah, she's that girl with the black hair, Sam's twin. He's that dude in our gym class who smokes cigs under the bleachers while coach Carter hits on us."

"Yeah." Mia nodded.

"What's up with Bailey?"

"She... she took her own life last night. Like committed suicide, she's dead." Mia hung her head back down with a heavy breath. I brought my hands to my mouth trying to cover the gaping hole it had become. I was in complete shock as I joined Mia in staring at the tile. I had no idea what to say or what to do. I racked my brain. I couldn't believe that she was gone, she was just there. I saw her in chemistry on Friday and she was helping a kid at the eye wash station after he splashed something toxic in his face. Bailey seemed kind, she didn't seem suicidal to me. Then again, I know all too well how easy it is to hide who you really are. We all have a mask we wear.

I began to recall all the interactions I had with Bailey over the past few years. She was on the quieter side, like me. If I weren't sworn into a friend group that would completely ostracize me for branching out, I bet Bailey and I could have been friends, but now I'd never know. And that made me feel... I don't know, guilty. Guilty and vapid. Maybe my Dad had been right all along about my head being stuck up my own ass.

"H-how?" I asked hesitantly, unsure of why I wanted to know. Maybe it was a morbid curiosity.

"She hung herself," Mary Lu exclaimed, like she was proud to have the inside scoop on this tragedy.

"Apparently it was with a scarf... from Walmart," Chloe added, not even trying to mask her distaste.

"Chloe!" Mia snapped, "who the hell cares where the scarf was from?"

"I would. If I'm gonna choose to go out, I'm going out in style. Give a girl a little Hermès at the least." Chloe teased as she flipped her blonde hair. Just like Chloe, callous to the core.

"You don't own anything Hermès," Mia coldly reminded Chloe. That one cut deep as Chloe perched her head down, deflated. Chloe's Dad filed for bankruptcy and is facing some fraud charges. It has been quite a scandal in our small town. Mia continued to reflect on what we had just heard. "I feel bad, you know. Yesterday, while we were at my house drinking our faces off and yelling at the TV, Bailey was, you know."

"Wait, y'all drank at your house last night? Why wasn't I invited?" Mary Lu interrupted.

Mia ignored her and continued, "it's just crazy."

"What's crazy?"

Suddenly, I was stunned as if someone flashed a bright light directly into my eyes. There I was, sucked into those same black eyes that won me over while chasing a monarch butterfly all those years ago. They still sparkle, even under the fluorescent lighting of our school. They give me chills that excite me as much as they scare me.

I locked eyes with him for a little too long until I was yanked back down to earth by a familiar voice that has never failed to make me cringe. Like clockwork, in walked Link, Philly's loyal sidekick. The Robin to his Batman, a dynamic they both seem to know and accept. Link looked at me up and down with a smug little smirk, no doubt thinking of some snide remark to make. I'm no stranger to it. Link picked on me in middle school before I was socially adopted by Mia. He made

45

it his mission to torment me daily about my flat chest. It became such a problem that I started wearing my mom's C-cup bras. They were padded with enough push up material that it almost looked like I had full breasts when I wore them. Link, however, was not convinced that someone could grow boobs overnight. To his credit, I suppose he was right. He came up to me that day in the lunchroom and put his fist into my bra which, of course, completely inverted, showing the audience he had acquired that there was nothing in there to fill the bra out. He convinced a bunch of other kids to punch me in the boob when they passed me in the hallway. I went home with bruises all over my chest every day for months. I try not to take it personally when I think about that phase of life. Link also called Chloe a slut because she was the first girl to develop boobs in middle school. None of us girls can win at this school. Big boobs, small boobs, we are all targets. The minds are even narrower than the hallways and the hearts are even blacker than the walls. It's not like Link is nicer to me now that we're in the same friend group. If anything, he's meaner. But, I'll admit, he's sometimes funny... somtimes.

"Sup Stevie Wonder," Link gestured to me while simulating an air piano with his eyes closed.

Okay, maybe he's not funny.

"Always so clever," I joked, sarcastically.

"Sup hoes," he politely addressed the rest of the group.

"Fuck you, Link," Mia hissed.

"You already did, bitch."

"What's crazy?" Philly repeated himself. His thick eyebrows pulled together, annoyance etched across his features. I looked at Philly, hoping to wrap the conversation up so I could whisk him away and apologize about the night before, for the stupid name I called him.

"We just filled Delilah in on the Bailey thing," Mary Lu enlightened him.

"Oh yeah," Philly stated, "that girl was crazy, bat shit."

"Can you two just pretend to have an ounce of compassion in your tiny grinch hearts for one second? She is dead for fuck's sake," Mia cried before burying her face in her hands.

"Well, we're not wrong. It's not like any of you are going to miss her vibrant energy. She was a weirdo, so quiet and lurking in the corners, watching people," Philly said.

I tried to remind myself that he wasn't talking about me, though he very well could have been. I'm not exactly bubbly and outgoing, which has historically been Philly's type.

"Tell me I'm wrong," Philly challenged, and the girls all shrugged in agreement, even Mia couldn't disagree.

"You're not wrong," Link chimed in. "She dressed like Hot Topic fucked her, ate her, then threw up on her. All those skulls and goth shit. She did have a nice ass though, I gotta say..."

"She did, yeah." Philly nodded his head in agreement as I shoved down the wave of jealousy that surged through me.

This poor girl is dead, how could I possibly be jealous of a dead girl? I'm always jealous though. I feel... I don't know, like I'm always competing with whoever Philly is telling me is hot that day. Usually the girls are bubbly, have blonde hair, big boobs and blue eyes. And I'm yet again reminded that I'm not actually Philly's type, I'm just what he got. I took a deep breath and decided to compartmentalize the feeling like any polite southern girl would as I picked up my Vera Bradly bag off the floor. The one-shoulder design kills my arm, but two strap backpacks are social suicide. *Suicide.* That word snapped me back to the present as I threw my bag over my shoulder and lifted my head. That's when I saw him. Of all the people I could make eye contact with, I locked eyes with him. *Why the hell is he here?* I thought to myself. I kept my eyes interlocked with Sam's for a moment, feeling like it would be rude if I looked away. I imagined his grief was excruciating. What I didn't anticipate was the way my eyes were drawn to him like magnets. And the way he peered back at me, it was as if we were compelled by greater forces. It was then that I noticed how tall he was, towering over the rest of the kids who glared at him with fear and pity. I noticed the scruff along his jaw line that matched the jet black hair that framed his face. I noticed his biceps busted through the thin fabric of his black T-shirt. Sam squinted his eyes at me, and the corner of his mouth rose, forcing a soft smile to the left side of his face. It was effortlessly charming, alluring even. I smiled shyly as a strange tingling sensation stirred inside of me. Then, the whispers grew louder, and Sam's half smile faded to a half frown. He broke eye contact with me and glanced over his shoulder. I followed his line of sight to see a large group of students behind him, staring. The seconds felt like they were passing in slow motion. My gaze snapped back to Sam who dropped his head down. I wondered if he hates eyes on him as much as I do. Although, I don't believe I've ever had every single student in the cafeteria staring at me all at once. That seemed like a special kind of hell. Once Sam swam through the cafeteria of piranhas, our table reconvened.

"Fucking freak. Those beady eyes and black hair." Link barked.

"You're one to talk, Bieber cut." Mia hissed.

"Why would he be here today? His sister just died. He should have stayed home. That's so weird," Mary Lu stated.

"Maybe he needed to pick up his schoolwork." Mia sighed. "Oh, he looked so sad. Can you imagine?"

"No, he didn't," Link disagreed, "did you see that smug smirk? He was practically smiling. Kid is a freak like his sister, the fucking skeleton twins. I bet he's the one that gave her the damn scarf to hang herself."

Just then, in perfect unison, every single one of us shot our heads in Link's direction, silently conveying that he had gone too far this time.

"Damn dude, you're dark," Philly chuckled.

"Whatever, who cares?"

Mia rolled her eyes as I shook my head, both of us knowing that getting in a debate with that half-pint wouldn't be worth it. Link will never change. I adjusted the strap of my bag as one of the girls from the Christian Youth Group Club came over and handed Mia a flyer for a prayer vigil they were holding for Bailey later that night. I was waiting for the right time to speak so I wouldn't interrupt. Finally, after what felt like five minutes, I interjected.

"I gotta go!"

It came out louder than I intended it to. I looked around at everyone's surprised faces, but I didn't have time to linger on the embarrassment. I turned on my heels towards the exit.

"Wait, D, there's more that I need to tell you," Mia pleaded.

"Later!" I shouted over my shoulder as I began to head for the door.

"I'm heading that way too," Philly called out, "later losers."

I was completely caught off guard by him wanting to walk with me. I knew that some guys walked their girlfriends to class, but Philly and I weren't like that. There were some days he pretended I didn't even exist. Sometimes I feel… I don't know, like maybe he's embarrassed of me. I don't get it. I try so hard. He tells me I'm too quiet, then tells me to shut up when I talk. He tells me I wear too much makeup, but then tells me I don't look good without it. It's never enough.

I heard the faint sound of a kick drum, and it was then that I noticed we were approaching the music room and neither one of us had said a word the whole walk. We strolled up to the door, and I finally had to break the silence.

"Hey, um, I just wanted to say uh, I'm sorry about last night."

"What? The Eagles losing? It's all good, we'll get 'em next week." He shrugged, casual as ever.

"No, I'm talking about when–"

He cut me off. "It's all good, I said. Don't worry."

I was a little shocked. *Is he trying to pretend nothing happened between us last night? Does he not even remember? Or maybe he truly doesn't think it was a big deal. Maybe it wasn't.*

"Anyway, gotta get to Chem. Those beakers aren't gonna fill themselves," he joked.

"Y'all are working with beakers?" I asked, following his lead on changing the subject.

"I don't fucking know, have fun with your little band geeks. I'll text you later, *baby*." Philly bit his bottom lip as he traced mine with his black eyes. Then without another word, he turned and walked away. I should have kissed him. I should have grabbed his chiseled face and smashed it into mine so hard that we absorbed each other, then we'd be together forever. That word, he said it. *Maybe he does feel the same way about me after all,* I thought. *Maybe I was right all along. He was just scared; he needed time. He loves me, I know he does.*

My attention is yanked back to our dinner table by my mom's acrylic French tips tapping on the services. I snap out of it enough to see Liam pondering. He seems deep in thought while Dad is deep in his mashed potatoes. He must have finished his wine while I was zoned out because he's switched to Macallan, neat. This means Liam or I will have to drive his Bentley home. He is the worst backseat driver, especially when he's been drowning his frustrations in the bottle all night.

"What do you think, Lilah?" Mom asks, more chipper than usual for this hour.

"I don't know," I respond. I truly don't, considering I have no idea what we're discussing, but I'm sure that answer won't please her.

"It's a terrible idea, Katherine, a stupid one," Dad answers for me.

I'm still lost in this conversation. How long was my mind racing this time? Perhaps Mom has a point about Lilah Land.

"Maybe there's somewhere else that they can go," Liam says as more of a question than a statement.

"Sorry," I finally say after not being able to pick up on context clues, "who are we talking about?"

"The Garcia's, that poor family who lost their daughter. Girl, did you just fall off a turnip truck? Are you listening at all?"

"What about the Garcia's?"

"Sofia Garcia is a member of our church, she's a sweet little Mexican woman."

"Um, I think the Garcia's are Brazilian."

"Yes, that's what I said. Anyway, she told our pastor that their house is being foreclosed on. And with all the funeral costs, their family is in the weeds. They need a place to stay for a while, and as a good Christian family, I feel it is our duty to help the down trotted." She folds her hands and draws her attention to Dad. "William, we have a whole guest house, and we don't use it. It practically sits there like a dead fish in the bayou. They can stay there."

"And I'd have to turn on the gas, and air, and Wi-Fi and everything else in there. Who do you think pays for that, Katherine, you?" He scoffs, like the decision has already been made.

"I mean, Mom is right. We've never used that guest house, and what they're going through, I can only imagine. I mean, for that girl to get to that point... I feel awful for her," Liam says with empathy in his aqua eyes.

"Yes," Mom corrects, "we do feel awful, for her family. For someone to have the heart to do that to their family, it is unimaginable. Her choice was selfish, and now her poor mother has to live with the consequences of her actions. I mean just the scandal of it all. Bless that poor woman's heart." Mom throws her dark hair back and wipes a crocodile tear from her eye.

"I'm sure she had a reason to do what she did, she must have been in a lot of pain," Liam argues.

Mom glares at him in disdain. "There is never a reason that is good enough to do... something like that. It is a sin under God and a sin to her poor family. We all have pain."

"I know that, Mom. I'm not saying I think she should have ended it, but I'm sure it wasn't what she wanted for herself either. Maybe something bad happened to her. I don't think anyone *wants* to die, but you know, sometimes life just gets too hard to live and sometimes it just hurts too bad to be you."

I stare at Liam for a second, trying to read his mind. What he's saying, how would he know all of that? Maybe he's felt that way before. I never would have thought, he's always been so happy-go-lucky. He's the golden child. Perhaps I don't know him as well as I think I do.

Mom takes another sip of her martini and swirls it around. "I have nothing to say to that, Liam," she admits in a high-pitched voice. "That girl had a loving family. Please, tell me what could have possibly happened that was so terrible that she would put them through this shame?"

"I heard she was raped," I blurt out without thinking, yet again. What the hell is wrong with me tonight? My head does a pan of the mahogany table, and each member of my family is looking at me with wide eyes, even my dad has put his fork down.

"Delilah Grace, how could you... how could you use a word like that?" Mom pleads with her hand over her heart.

I feel like a child that got in trouble for breaking a vase after running in the house.

"Wait, D, what do you mean? How do you know that?" Liam asks.

"Mia told me."

"Ugh, right, Mia. Crude, just like her mother. Last time I saw her in town, her hem was so short, she could catch old *and* new-monia in that dress," Mom spits, but I pay no mind to her. Mom judges Mia's Mom for divorcing her husband after she caught him cheating. But I think she's a total badass. She has her own career, her own money, and most importantly, she has some freaking self-respect.

"What did Mia tell you?" Liam asks again.

"It's not just Mia, everyone was talking about it at school. Apparently, the story is that she was raped... I mean..." I change my wording to not rile obliterated Katherine up any more than she already is. "Apparently, she was assaulted at a party on Friday night by some guy, no one knows who the guy is. But, when she went to the cops to report it, they didn't believe her. Mia thinks that's why Bailey…. you know, did what she did."

"Wow, I had no idea. That's horrible," Liam says.

"Oh, give me a break," Dad murmurs, causing our heads to swing in his direction.

"It sounds to me like this little girl cried wolf then didn't want to deal with the consequences, so she took the easy way out."

My brow furrows.

"I'm not sure that I would call death by hanging the easy way out," Liam interjects.

"I don't believe it for a goddamn second," he reiterates.

Mom scoffs at the 'G' word, and I get a strong whiff of Belvedere from her breath.

"How often do people lie about being raped? Who would lie about that?" I ask.

Mom scoffs again as she folds her hands and looks to the ceiling. I forgot the 'R' word was off the table tonight as well.

"I'm with D, I doubt it's common for people to lie about…" he catches himself, "that."

"I bet she did the deed with some boy then got pissed at the knucklehead, so she made up a bullshit assault allegation to ruin his life. Happens all the time."

"So, you're saying you think she made the whole thing up?" Liam asks.

"Yes. Or…" Dad holds up his finger like he's a judge holding a wooden gavel. "Yinz know, boys will be boys. I bet the girl went to a party wearing next to nothing looking for attention, and when she got it, she took it the wrong way. I saw it in undergrad all the time. Happened to a frat brother of mine. If you ask me, it's her fault for leading the guy on."

I don't know why, but I start to feel tears welling up in my eyes.

"I don't think there's any right way to take rape," Liam challenges.

"What don't you get? There was no rape," Dad raises his voice. "It's a made-up fucking word that women use to ruin mens' lives and put them in prison. How would you like it if you were flirting with a girl at one of those sorority parties yinz are always at, and the next day you wake up to the police busting down your door because you didn't call her the next day, or did God knows what to piss her off? But all she has to do is say 'oh he raped me' and now you're facing 15 years. You could kiss your whole career goodbye. Really, son, use your fucking head. How would you like it, huh?"

Liam sits, stunned for a minute. I can feel the eyes of the other restaurant patrons on us. I'd love to crawl in a hole. I'd even go back to Lilah Land at this point, as dreadful of a place it can be.

I see Liam out of the corner of my eye calculating his next move, playing the game of chess just like our father taught us. He finishes off his wine and looks completely emotionless as he responds in a robotic voice. "Of course, sir. You're right, girls lead guys on all the time. Perhaps she gave him the wrong idea."

Dad gives Liam a look of pride, knowing he has won the match. I can't read Liam's expression. I wonder if he's as disappointed with himself as I am.

"I have to use the bathroom," I share before darting away. I can feel it. The heat traveling through my whole body, the pins and needles in my hands, my shoulders shaking uncontrollably, my heart absolutely racing. Keep breathing, keep breathing, you can breathe, just keep breathing.

Seven minutes was all it took this time. These episodes are a cycle I know all too well, like a pop song on the radio that I can't get out of my head. I open the gray door of the bathroom stall and make my way over to the full-size mirror in the parlor. I set my Louis down on the vanity and reach inside to search for my concealer and eyeliner. Once I've fixed myself up, I stare at the girl looking back at me for a moment. I've always heard people say that as they get older, they no longer recognize themselves in the mirror. But now, being face to face with this hazel eyed girl, I recognize her entirely. I know exactly who this girl staring back at me is, and that's the problem.

I pull the hem of my skirt down before exiting the bathroom to avoid the looks of contempt from Lady Katherine. I take a deep breath before I swing the door open, and to my surprise, my freshly painted face smacks right into Liam's chest.

"Hey, was just looking for you. You got any of those Addy's left that I gave you? I could really use them. Got a beast of a paper to write tonight."

"Yeah, you can take the rest since I'm done with SAT's for the year. They're in my room though, so we'll have to wait until we get home."

"Fuck," he yells.

My eyes widen. "What?"

"Nothing."

"I think you can wait a half hour between now and home. What's your deal?"

"Whatever, it's fine. How'd you do by the way? On the SAT's."

"I don't know yet, we haven't gotten our scores. Probably didn't do as good as you though."

"Didn't do as *well* as me," he teases.

56

"Oh, shut the fuck up you pompous Ivy League ass," I say rolling my eyes, not reflecting the same facetious tone as Liam.

He seems a little taken back and gives me a sympathetic look. "I'm sorry, I haven't even asked how you're doing? I'm sure it hasn't been an easy day, losing one of your friends this young, and in that way."

"She wasn't my friend," I snap, avoiding his kind eyes.

"Still, she was your classmate, and she was 17. That's some dark shit."

"Yeah, it is, not that you care."

"What does that mean?"

"Oh, girls always lead guys on, you're right Dad, you're always right, you know everything. Let me bow down to you and kiss your feet," I imitate him in a nasally, taunting tone, knowing full well he sounds nothing like that.

"You think I actually believe that? I don't. I'm not one of those boys' club guys. Last week I went to a rally that was protesting date rape on campus. I think that shit is vial, only the most disgusting of scumbags would do that to someone."

"Then why did you have to agree with Dad? Why do you always have to be the suck-up-golden-boy?"

"Oh, knock that chip off your shoulder, Delilah. It's not about being the golden child. I say what I have to say to keep him happy. He pays the bills, and that's all he is to me. Dad *and* Mom. I don't want to suck up to those motherfuckers, but everything in this world comes with a price to pay, D, and this is mine. Humoring Dad as he recites his epic poem about the difference between Bordeaux and Burgundy, and yes, sometimes also fake agreeing with his outdated views," he argues.

I look down at the ground for a while, still afraid to make eye contact.

"I don't ever want any of their money."

Liam chuckles. "Then you're dumber than you look, D."

"Thanks… Good talk."

I turn to walk away but he grabs my shoulder, spinning me back to meet his eyes.

He lets out a long sigh. "What I'm saying is that unlike most of the world's population, we actually have privilege and opportunity. I mean, look around you."

Liam opens his palm to pan the area of the country club like a Broadway chorus saluting the orchestra. I play along and observe the crystal chandeliers and marble flooring. This *is* a beautiful place, obviously.

"I know, I know, I've heard it all before. I should be grateful for what I have because someone in the world has it worse than me," I roll my eyes. "That's the oldest lesson in the book."

"No, no, fuck that. I'm not saying that you can't feel sorry for yourself."

I raise an eyebrow in confusion of what his overall thesis will be this time.

"Saying that you can't feel sorry for yourself because someone has it worse than you is the same thing as saying that you can't ever be happy for yourself because someone has it better than you. Someone will always have it worse, and someone will always have it better than you, that's irrelevant."

I stand there for a moment staring blankly at him. As usual, I am speechless.

"Never thought about it like that before. What are you saying then?"

"I'm saying you're allowed to have empathy for yourself and your situation. I mean yeah, we got a pretty big house and a nice yard but look at the price that it comes with for us. Living imprisoned side-by-side with Morticia and Gomez Addams," he chuckles, lightening the mood.

"Life would be a hell of a lot easier if I lived with the Addams family, then all I'd have to worry about is a severed hand running around, trying to cop a feel in the middle of the night." I laugh a little, until I remember that I'm mad. "Seriously though, they've gotten worse since you left. You don't even know. Clearly they get worse with age."

"So, they're not like a 1995 vintage Bordeaux? Are you saying that our parents were not stored at the proper temperature and now they're corked?" Liam says, continuing to use his charm to lighten the mood.

"Do you remember the first time you tried to break up one of their fights? Dad had Mom's head against the wall, and you picked him up by the back of his shirt collar and laid him out on the ground. The fear in his eyes when he looked up at you and realized that you might finally be stronger than him, it was bone chilling." An actual shiver travels down my spine.

Liam looks away. "And still, I'm the one who wound up with 12 bone chilling stitches in my head."

"Yeah, from Mom, not even Dad."

"That's when I learned my lesson."

"What lesson?"

"Not everyone wants to be helped," he states with a look that tells me he's lost a great deal of the happy-go-lucky optimism he once had and I once idolized.

"Is that why you chose to study finance instead of psychology?"

"I didn't exactly have a choice, but yeah, that too."

We're silent for what feels like a whole minute. The air in this restaurant feels thicker than Lady Katherine's southern accent. "Anyway," Liam finally says, "we don't deserve to have extraordinarily shitty parents when other kids get to have loving ones. And we also didn't deserve to be born into wealthy suburbia with silver spoons in our mouths while other kids are born in crack dens with heroin needles in theirs. We don't get what we deserve in life, no one does. We just get what we get, and we must make do with it the best we can. What we have, Delilah, what you have right in front of you is opportunity. An opportunity to go to college, have it paid for in full and not have to work a dead-end job just to pay for books. You can go to Carnegie Mellon or Yale to study music, you can go anywhere you want to go."

"And a large inheritance if Mom and Dad drink an entire bottle of bourbon that was accidentally spiked with arsenic," I taunt, half smiling and only half kidding.

Liam laughs. "Nah, Dad will probably leave all his money to this country club or whatever concubine is his flavor of the week just to spite us. The old prick."

"True."

"Anyway, D, you have privilege and opportunity that most people don't have, the least you can do is use it. Take the money and fucking run."

"Is that your plan, take the money and fucking run?'

"Essentially, yeah, once I've accumulated enough. I won't need to interact with anyone I don't genuinely like, that's the beauty of being an adult," He smirks, as if he is 20 years older and wiser than me instead of just 2.

"Including me?"

"I'll always wanna interact with you, D. Besides, you need me. I'm the only one that can get you out of that racing head of yours. Well, except for Philly, of course."

I give a quiet and awkward laugh. We let cool air and the soft jazz hang over us for a minute.

"Kids!" We hear Mom shriek from around the corner, "where in good heavens did y'all run off to? Come say hello to Mr. And Mrs. Caldwell!"

Liam and I both roll our eyes, gearing up to trot like the show ponies Katherine raised us to be.

"Hang in there, D, only a few more years of playing the part, then you're free. Come on," he grabs my clammy hand. "Can't keep Mr. And Mrs. *Cuntwell* waiting."

We both giggle as we make our way out of the hallway. *A few more years, then you're free.* I wonder what that feels like.

Chapter 6
Present day

"I don't really have anything to talk about today," I say blankly as I stare at the different pieces of black and white artwork around the spacious office.

"Well, okay great then, looks like our work here is done! I'll see ya later," Dr. Veizer exclaims as she lifts herself off her leather chair and onto her feet. She is quite spry for a woman who I assume is in her 70's. I throw my head to the side and offer a little chuckle which she returns before lowering herself back down into a cross-legged position. I know what she's thinking, we've done this song and dance before. Every other session I come in having nothing to talk about, and every single time she makes that same joke. We both know we will have to spend the next 50 minutes together no matter what, and we both know that she'll reach into my mind like a treasure chest and take whatever jewels she pleases. It's as if Dr. Veizer treats these therapy sessions like games of chess, and she's goddamn Bobby Fischer. I like her though. I like her low, raspy voice, it's smooth like velvet, smooth like Jazz. Although, I can't imagine she likes me or the sound of my voice. I'm nothing but a pirate on an abandoned ship, singing the same old sea shanty for eternity.

"Well, not much happened this week, so I don't know where to start," I tell her, avoiding her kind eyes that droop a bit at the corners.

"Why don't we start with the number one goal on your treatment plan, to change your relationship with alcohol."

I sigh, "I know, I know, you want me to stop drinking and become one of those bible thumping AA cult members who spend their free time going on hikes or going to museums, or whatever the hell it is sober people do." I let a huff as I press my fingers to my temples to will this headache away.

"I want what you want," Dr. Veizer states matter-of-factly. When I look up at her, she holds eye contact with me for an uncomfortable amount of time. She stays silent, she always stays silent when she wants me to speak more. I think she may be the only person in the world who is comfortable sitting in silence. I don't share that quality with her, for me, silence is violent.

"The thing is, I don't think I really want to stop drinking. I know how it sounds, but it's the only thing that makes me feel good. At least I'm not a pill popper like all the Xannied out Stepford wives in my neighborhood. So, I like a strong martini, so what?"

"Then how come you made it your number one goal on the treatment plan we created together?"

"Because of my husband."

"Right, your husband."

Immediately, I see Dr. Veizer's wheels turning in her brain like a race car, she's revving the engine like she's concocting some sort of master plan to reveal all my secrets.

"You don't mention your husband much, I've noticed. Tell me more."

"There's not much to tell. He's traveling a lot for work, at least that's what he says he's doing. Maybe he's just tired of me and doesn't want to come home until I've gotten my shit together. I can't blame him. I'm tired of me."

"I see, you want him to see an improvement. And so, what does getting your shit together look like?"

I try not to grin as Dr. Veizer asks that, but there's something about a woman her age cursing that gets me every time. Shit, maybe that's ageist. Either way, I hide my grin.

"I don't know…"

"What *do* you know?" Dr. Veizer claps back like she already knew what I was going to say before I said it. *Check mate.* This player is not letting me leave this couch without saying something real.

"I guess not drinking as much."

Dr. Veizer stays silent and stoic, and it's clear she's yet again challenging me to move my chess piece and say more.

"Not drinking as much," I continue, "like just drinking a normal amount, or only drinking when I'm out to dinner or at an event."

"Right, right. You want it to be more sporadic. That makes sense and I think that's a great goal. Let me ask you something, do you believe you have a drinking problem?"

"I don't know, you tell me. You're the expert, aren't you?" A ray of heat spreads from my chest to my face. That was probably the wrong move and a rude thing to say, although she looks the least bit phased.

"I mean, sure, I can tell you about the neurological implications of alcohol, how it gives you temporary surges of dopamine while depleting your brain's capability to naturally create it and all the other good chemicals, but you could also Google that. I'm not your teacher and these sessions aren't about neurology. These sessions are about you, and I'm not the expert on you. Only *you* are the expert on you."

"Well, okay then. I guess I am an expert on me and that's the problem. Living inside my head is a fucking Shakespearean tragedy." *Why are you so dramatic, Delilah?* I shake my head, "Sorry if that sounds dramatic." I quiet my mouth and perch my head down.

Dr. Veizer waves her hand, telling me to go on.

"In terms of neurology, yeah, I have googled that once or twice when I was hungover and anxious, right after I googled if you can die from a hangover. I know that drinking gives you a rush of dopamine- it's dopamine, right?"

She nods.

"Dopamine is that rush you get that feels so good, it's like an escape from all your problems. But then you crash, and the dopamine is gone, and you feel even worse than before. But that's the thing, I don't think I ever had dopamine or serotonin or any of those things to begin with, that's why I had to start drinking. I drink so I can feel okay at least for a few hours of the day, is that so bad? It keeps me going."

"Right, I hear you. It's not a bad thing to want to help yourself feel good. I'm glad you want to feel good. But it's not only a few hours a day that you're drinking, is it?"

"No, that's the issue, I suppose."

"Mhmm," Dr. Veizer mutters, one of her therapist noises. She quickly jots something down in the black notepad that's resting on her thin thigh. She doesn't break eye contact the entire time she's writing; I don't know how she does that.

"So… does drinking everyday make me an alcoholic?"

"It's difficult to define what an alcoholic is, there's not an exact way to measure how many drinks it takes or how often one drinks to label them an alcoholic. I tend to believe in an Abnormal Psychology approach when it comes to addiction. I can ask you some questions that may help you better understand where you're at, but at the end of the day, you are the only one that can decide if you have a problem with alcohol, and you are the only one that can decide what you want to do with it. Do you want to hear some of those questions and ponder on them for a bit?"

I nod my head.

"Has drinking alcohol ever interrupted aspects of your life such as career or interpersonal relationships?"

I nod with shame, thinking of my marriage, my teaching career, and my countless other failures.

"Does the amount that you drink seem out of the social norm compared to what you observe in others, and if so, has anyone ever taken notice?"

I nod again. I'm always a few drinks ahead of everyone else. It's like I'm physically incapable of just sipping a drink; I need to down the whole thing upon arrival, at least that's what my husband says.

"Has drinking alcohol ever caused harm to you mentally or physically?"

I'm forced to think about two weeks ago when I tripped over my own foot while going up the stairs and landed like a tree on the crystal glass that was in my right hand. I had to pull the three-inch shard lodged in my knee out with tweezers. Now, every time I pick up those tweezers to shape my eyebrows, I swear my knee starts to throb, like it remembers. But that was one time, and I didn't even need stitches. I have been hurt way worse than that, and it had nothing to do with my drinking habits. There are things that cut deeper than a shard of crystal glass, like being told that you're nothing enough times that you start to believe it. Still, I let out a sigh and nod.

"Does drinking alcohol ever inhibit your ability to complete daily tasks like chores or personal hygiene?"

I look up and give Dr. Veizer a look then motion down towards the $600 Ralph Lauren dress hugging my hips, not to mention my bi-weekly manicured French tips that accompany my five carat oval wedding ring. I twirl my very high maintenance blonde balayage hair extensions with my finger. Then, I think back to the fact that I have not done laundry in weeks or cooked a meal in months.

I nod to Dr. Veizer and hang my head, wondering how many more damn questions she's going to ask me.

"Last one," she says.

Thank God.

"Would you say that drinking alcohol ever causes you to become distressed?"

"I was born distressed," I joke.

Dr. Veizer looks up from her notepad, and her furrowed brow is wildly unamused. I'm not winning this chess game. If anything, I am the pawn.

"Look, I get it. I check all the boxes, but what am I supposed to do? Sobriety doesn't work for me. You remember last time I tried that, I almost ended up in a noose. And we've tried all of those mindful drinking things, counting my drinks, timing them, putting a physical activity between every sip. None of it worked. Sobriety doesn't work, and moderation doesn't work. Maybe I had the right idea when I was tying that noose."

"Maybe you *were* right."

My head jerks up to Dr. Veizer as my mouth falls wide open. "Damn, well okay then, noose it is."

"No, no," Dr. Veizer lets out a small laugh, "that's not what I meant. I was referring to what you mentioned earlier, about believing that you never had high dopamine levels in the first place."

"What about it?"

"I think maybe you're onto something. Like you pointed out, we've exhausted every CBT intervention in the book, I don't think that's the way we approach this."

"We?" I raise an eyebrow.

"Yes, we. I am right here with you, Delilah. I need you to know that. If you go into the abyss, I'm swimming down with you. If you want to float on the surface, I'll tread that water with you too. My job is to meet you exactly where you are at."

"I thought your job was to pretend to care about me for $300 per week," I snap, instantly regretting it. That was way too honest, I'm never that honest, or ill-mannered. Still, to this day, everything I say is wrong, even when I'm right. I keep my head down, avoiding the horrified look I suspect is on Dr. Veizer's face. I hear her sigh lightly.

"Delilah."

I look up to meet her deep brown eyes.

"What you pay for is my time, but my caring is free."

I keep my focus on her corneas without blinking as my eyes rim with tears. I begin to wipe them before letting the salty liquid fall. I grab a tissue from the glass table in front of me. I usually never do that in this office, it's like admitting defeat in the game.

"Sorry," I mutter between holding in sobs.

"I don't accept your apology," Dr. Veizer states. "Because you don't owe me one. You don't need to be sorry. That's what this is for, if you can't cry in this office, where can you cry?" She aks with a smile, even though her eyes seem to be slightly glassy as well.

"So, anyway, back to what you were saying."

"Right, that inability to create dopamine and serotonin, that sounds to me like depression."

No shit.

"Okay… what fixes it?"

"Well," Dr. Veizer says deep in thought, "nothing fixes depression. There's nothing that is going to fix you. You don't need to be fixed because you are not broken, you work perfectly."

I let out a gasp and laugh at the same time. "Me, Delilah, *me*. I work perfectly?"

Dr. Veizer may be a chess champion on her best days, but I have no idea how she's going to move this piece forward.

"You do," she corrects me with diction in her voice, "you work perfectly, it is your strategies that are not working. Those are what need to be changed, but we can't change your strategies without understanding why and how they became your go-to strategies in the first place. Take drinking, for example, there are many reasons as to why someone drinks to excess. With you, it seems to be a coping skill that you use to regulate an already dysregulated nervous system. That's all it is at its core, a dysregulated nervous system, and a coping skill you're using to survive. But the thing is, nervous systems don't just dysregulate on their own. And most coping skills don't just show up out of nowhere, they're learned." Dr. Veizer stares at me.

"So?"

"What dysregulated your nervous system? And where did you learn drinking as a coping skill?" My stomach turns, and I'm once again lost inside of the war in my mind. *I swear, I can hear that long southern drawl over the stench of Belvedere.*

I look off to my left to glance at the clock. Dr. Veizer follows my gaze, probably wondering how much time we have left as well. 20 minutes, damn. I wonder if I should make up an excuse to leave early. If I do, I may be able to catch a glimpse of Beth's gardener before he packs up for the day. Watching how the sun beams down on his bare chest, lathered with sweat and grit… Watching his swollen muscles and huge hands dig, and beat, and massage the soil… He makes planting tomatoes look more erotic than hardcore porn.

I feel Dr. Veizer's eyes burning a hole through my cheekbone as I peer off out the window. The sun is being pushed out by nimbus clouds. I need to get out of here before my date with Belvedere and pleasuring myself to tomato planting stands me up.

"Delilah?" Dr. Veizer says my name like it's a question.

I turn my eyes back to her. "I don't know," I respond, robotically.

"What *do* you know?"

I smirk. "I hate it when you do that."

"I know."

We both let the heavy, quiet air hang above us for a minute. I can't seem to think of anything else to say, shocker.

"You don't talk about your past much. We've never delved into your childhood at all, really. It's a topic you seem to deflect quite well from."

I steal another glance at the clock as I feel a burning sensation rip fire through my throat. I take a hard swallow and shift the white pillow next to me. I look back out towards dark clouds.

"I'm noticing you're getting uncomfortable because I brought up that topic, am I correct?"

I don't say anything, I just swallow hard again and nod my head.

"I'm sensing that this is not something that you want to talk about right now."

I shake my head and bow it down. What am I, a kindergartner? Why can't I speak? If this isn't broken, I don't know what is.

"Okay, that's okay. I'm never going to force you to talk about anything you don't want to, but I do think that it's important to know who you *were* so that we can better understand who you *are*. I hope that we can work up to that."

I give Dr. Veizer another nod. All I want to do is zip the Range Rover home and pour myself a glass of glory, kick my feet up, and watch my favorite program.

"Can I ask you something?"

"Yeah."

"What is depression? I mean, what does depression look like to you?"

"I guess I don't know what it really is, I just know what it feels like."

"Tell me, what does it feel like?"

"I don't know-" I catch myself, "I mean, um, it feels like…"

Dr. Veizer sits steadfast in her silence, and I imagine she's growing impatient of this stalemate we've reached in the game.

"It feels like the devil's back."

"The devil?"

"Yeah."

"Mhmm. That's interesting. I like that you've externalized depression into more of a character in your story rather than something permanent that you can't control. I'm impressed. After all, we are nothing but the story we tell ourselves about ourselves."

"Uh, thanks?" I'm not sure what she's impressed with, I sound like a fucking lunatic. "Listen, I know what you're probably thinking. I'm just another spoiled housewife that curses her life because she can't recognize how good she has it. I'm sure I sound ridiculous compared to the people who come in here with actual problems, who have actual excuses to be depressed."

Dr. Veizer takes a deep breath. "Oh, Delilah. If there is anything I've learned in my time here on earth, it's that depression doesn't discriminate. Mental health issues don't skip you because your life does or doesn't look good on paper. You don't need an excuse. Sometimes feelings don't have a reason or a rhyme. Sometimes, they just *are*. And, that's okay."

I sink my face into my hands, nearly scratching my pasty cheek with my wedding ring.

"So, depression, this devil, what does this devil do to you? What's his role in your life?"

I think for a moment, wondering if my train of thought has derailed, until my mouth starts moving against my will.

"He sits on my arms and glues me to the floor. He makes it hard to move or want to move. I feel heavy, I guess. I feel like everything is heavy from the minute I wake up in the morning. It starts with my eyelids, then it's my arms, then my legs. It's like gravity is constantly betraying me. It's like the devil is trying to drag me to hell before I'm even dead. That's what depression is, feeling dead before you're actually dead."

"Wow, that's powerful."

"And that's just when I first wake up, before my thoughts start surging and I'm reminded of what I did." Those magnetic eyes from the photo on my refrigerator flash through my memory so bright, they may blind my brain. I blink back a tear. "Reminding me of who I am."

"And who are you?"

"Nobody."

"Really…"

"Yes, nobody, I am really nobody with nothing going on, nothing to do, nothing to call my own."

"I see," Dr. Veizer says in a skeptical tone as she adjusts herself on her leather chair and crosses one ankle over the other. "Let me ask you another question. What do you believe causes depression, that heaviness that you're feeling, that devil that's following you?"

I slowly tilt my head back and gaze up towards the ceiling.

"If I knew what caused it, I would fix it and I wouldn't need to be here in the first place. So, yeah, *I don't know*," I reply, aggressively. Dr. Veizer opens her mouth like she's going to say something then clenches her jaw again. She glances towards the clock and closes her black notepad. I'm sure she's relieved that the session is coming to an end and she can be rid of me.

She releases a long sigh. "Come on, Delilah, you need to try harder than that. We have a few more minutes together, just humor me at least. What is one thing that you can pinpoint as a catalyst for your depression?"

I sit up a bit. I'm shocked that she didn't just say 'welp, that's our time for today' as I've noticed it's about 3 minutes past our usual ending time. She's right, I'm being an asshole. She's working her ass off over here. I owe her to try. I notice the tingling pricking my hands as I search my scattered mind for an answer. God, I need a fucking drink. *Say something, Delilah.*

"Purpose," I finally blurt out.

"Purpose?"

"Yeah, I think that's what I'm missing. It's like I don't have a role in society, I don't have anything to do, no life's calling."

"And is that what purpose is to you, a life's calling?"

"I guess so, like something that you were born to do," I shrug. "Like you, you seem like you were born to be a therapist and help people. I thought I had that kind of purpose once before, something I was put on this earth for, but I was wrong." The black and white keys dance in the most distant part of my reminiscence.

"And is that how you feel it works? We're all born with preconceived purposes right out of the womb, and we need to fulfill that purpose or else we become depressed? Is it that black and white?" Dr. Veizer asks. She seems sassier than usual today, and I kind of like it.

"Well, when you say it like that, it sounds kind of stupid. Of course, not everyone is born with a purpose, only the lucky ones are. And the rest of us, we're just hanging out. We're nothing, nobody."

"I don't think it's stupid, I'm just trying to understand," Dr. Veizer reassures me, "is just hanging out such a terrible thing? Is it not enough to just exist?"

"Not like this."

"I see. Okay, so let's say you're right, and some people are born with a specific purpose or prophecy to fulfill, if you were one of those lucky people to be born with one, how would your life be different?"

I look off towards the window and think for a moment. "I guess I would have something that I truly cared about, something to do with my time. I would probably have a fulfilling career, money of my own, friends of my own, maybe even hobbies of my own. Life would be full. The world would matter to me because I would matter to it."

Dr. Veizer remains silent and nods for a minute as she takes in what I said. *I don't understand what I just said, I can't imagine she will.*

"It sounds like, and correct me if I'm wrong, but it sounds like it's not purpose that you're referring to. It sounds like *meaning*. You know, things that would matter to you, a life that would *mean* something to you."

The room is quiet as the energy falls flat. A tidal wave of feelings crashes right over my head, feelings that I can't place nor sequester. I swivel my head towards the window again and I notice little round, translucent droplets clinging to the glass. It's raining. Of course, it's fucking raining.

I can still see the tiny drops clinging to his thick eyelashes and the scruff on his jawline. I can still see the way the bay water glistened on his broad shoulders, the way the moon illuminated us as we treaded the cold water. The way he looked at my body when I took off my shirt, like it was something to be treasured instead of trashed. I remember the way his wet hair felt running through my fingers, like every strand was sculpted for my dainty hand. I remember the taste of his skin as my lips skimmed his thick neck. I remember the way my head felt pressed on his soaking chest, like it had finally found its home. I remember it all. I remember him.

I bring my hand to my mouth in attempts to wipe off the smile that forms, but it only grows wider.

"What are you smiling at?" Dr. Veizer asks with an amused curiosity as her thin pink lips stretch into a grin that mirrors mine.

"Nothing, you- you just remind me of someone, someone that I used to know."

"And who is that?"

Chapter 7
2009- Richmond Hill, Georgia

"I can't believe he's moving in with you, that's insane!" Chloe exclaims, loud enough for the entire lunchroom to hear. Her cat-like screech seems to bounce off the 'Go Jaguars' banner the art club made this week. I sit and admire the banner for a moment, the details are incredible. It looks like a professional designed this, although I doubt the football team will ever appreciate the artistry that went into it.

"It is weird, D. I mean, clearly there's something wrong with that family if their only daughter took her own life. I see them in church every Sunday, and I have to say that they're totally strange. The way they act, the way they sit there in silence. It's like they have some sort of secret, something they need forgiveness for," Mary Lu chimes in with a hushed voice like she's telling a ghost story at a bonfire.

"And asking for forgiveness is a bad thing, why? Isn't that what church is for?" I ask.

"It just seems like they have a lot of skeletons in their closet, that's all."

"They're the skeleton twins, I'm telling you," Link exclaims, throwing his freckled hand palm up in the middle of the black table. I deny him eye contact by reaching into my bag and grabbing my razor phone. I know that no one is texting me, as pretty much every person I know is currently in this building, but flipping open my phone every few minutes has become a habit of mine.

"Aren't you jealous your girl is gonna be living with Sam Garcia, resident burnout of Richmond Hill?" Link taunts, grabbing Philly's shoulder and shaking it.

Philly slams down his empty Coke can. "Pshhh, no," he snorts, "she's not my girl, he can have her."

The flurry that builds in my chest is indescribable and it feels like my throat is closing. I honestly might vomit. I force flip my phone back open and stare at the screen. My face is so hot, it may as well be melting off. I don't understand. He walked me to class and called me 'baby' the other day, and now I'm nothing to him. I'm worse than nothing, it's like I'm fucking garbage. What did I do wrong? I look down and assess my outfit. I made such an effort today; I picked out a light green tank top with black hearts on it to bring out the small bit of green in my eyes. I'm wearing my only bra that squeezes enough to make me look like I have cleavage, and I'm wearing the black lacy thong Mia picked out under my Hollister jeans, it's my best one. I look down further at my heeled brown boots. *Fuck*. Maybe that was the mistake, heels. My mom picked out these heeled boots, she said they'd make my chicken legs look longer. But, damn, I should have known better. Philly hates it when I look taller than him. He's insecure about his height and his teeth even though both are perfect. The heels being problematic for him didn't occur to me when getting ready this morning. I should have been more sensitive. I can be so selfish sometimes.

"Don't you feel weird about it at all? That the family whose daughter just killed herself will be living in your house?" Mary Lu asks.

I let out a breath I've been holding in for what felt like minutes and grab my soda off the table. I take a quick sip to clear my throat. "Well, it's not like they're actually living with me in my house or like Sam and I will be sharing bunk beds. They'll be staying in the guest house only until they can find a new place. They'll probably be there a few weeks at the most."

I hate having to explain myself to my friends. I feel… I don't know, like I'm constantly having to justify everything, and no answer that I give is ever good enough.

"Yeah, I still think it's really weird," Chloe rolls her eyes to the boys looking for approval. Link nods as Philly smirks. I catch a glimpse of that sparkle as his eyes meet mine. I try to adjust my expression to something more mysterious than heartbreak. Philly severs the eye contact as his stare darts above my head. I turn around and see that he's looking at Mia. She's sandwiched between two guys, the three of them linking arms. I recognize them, they're both on the wrestling team and they're both cute, Mia's kryptonite.

"Why thank you fellas, I think I can take it from here. The escort is much obliged," Mia draws out an exaggerated southern accent.

"See ya later hot stuff," one of the boys exclaims as they unlink arms and walk to the other side of the cafeteria. Mia watches them walk away before pivotting towards our lunch table with a big smile on her face. I smile back, shaking my head in awe of how she always manages to wrap these guys around her finger like that. I swear, one day, that girl will rule the world.

"Fucking bucket," Link murmurs under his breath.

Philly and Chloe chuckle, Mary Lu widens her eyes and jerks her head to Mia.

"Pardon?" Mia asks, squinting her eyes. The way she kinks her neck when she looks at him terrifies me. Mia can be quite frightening when she wants to be, and from the look of her scowl, she wants to be.

"A bucket, that's what Mia is," Link gestures to the rest of the group, "a fucking bucket because you can put anything in her."

Mia has been called a lot of things like 'slut' and 'whore'. I thought she had been called every name in the book, until now. Only Link could take a toy that toddlers play with at the beach and spin it into a way of calling girls promiscuous. If only he would have applied this clever nature to our English project last week, then maybe I wouldn't have ended up doing the whole damn thing on my own.

I turn my head back to scan the faces of the rest of our friends. Philly's holding in laughter with a closed lipped smile. Chloe has a grin on her face as well. My head turns back towards Mia, and to my surprise, she doesn't look angry. Instead, she looks like she's deep in mentation, calculating.

"You can't though," she finally says with a mocking, confused look on her face.

"What?"

"You can't put anything in a bucket, not everything would fit in a bucket. A car can't go in a bucket, a chair can't go in a bucket. You can't fit a human into a bucket."

"You know what I mean," Link sneers.

"Come to think of it…" Mia's voice is high pitched. She puts her hand on my shoulder and leans her weight on me. "The only grown-up human small enough to fit in a bucket is you, Link."

The whole table breaks out into laughter, and I hear a few 'oooos' from the table next door. Link pretends to be unbothered as he rolls his eyes towards the back of his head, but his face is getting redder than mine usually does, and my rosacea is hard to beat.

"Fucking whore," Link murmurs under his breath as he puts his elbow on the table and drops his cheek into his hand.

"Oh, well that's more like it, give him a round of applause for the creativity folks."

I can't contain my laughter as everyone at the table joins in clapping.

"Stick to what you know, Linky boy." Mia takes a seat at the table with a smile full of pride stretched across her face. "Anyway, what did I miss?"

"That freak and his freak family are moving into Delilah's house," Chloe adamantly shares.

"Guest house."

"Ah, nice. Papa Monroe actually okayed it? I'm surprised."

"He didn't exactly have a choice in the matter. My mom is blackmailing him."

"With what?" Mary Lu asks.

"You don't wanna know."

Chloe gives Mary Lu a look.

"Anyway," I continue, "they're moving in next Monday."

"I think it's insane. If your mom wants to prove to this town that she's a decent Christian woman and not a trashy pageant chick has-been, she could donate to the Humane Society. She doesn't need to shack up with the Manson family," Chloe blurts out in her meanest tone of voice. I've heard this tone before, but it's never been directed at one of my family

79

members. I know she's not wrong in what she said about my mom, but hearing someone else say it feels... I don't know, humiliating.

"Manson's?" Mary Lu draws her head back, "I thought their last name was Garcia."

"Manson, like the Manson family. Charles Manson, the cult leader, the serial killer..."

"Use your fucking brain, Mary Lu. Like, read a goddamn book for once in your life," Philly barks.

Mary Lu hangs her head down as she pretends to look for something in her backpack. I know this move well. I can almost taste the tears she's trying to hold back. If it were anyone else at this school that talked to her like that, her clap back would be more pernicious than Chlamydia. But Philly has a unique ability to shake you to your core and sew your lips shut. He is incredibly smart, and he can read people like they're children's books.

"Chloe," Mia calls out, "fix your ponytail before you leave the caf. It's too low, you look like fucking Paul Revere."

"Who?" Chloe asks, picking up a tater tot from her tray.

"Ah, look who's the dumb one now," Mia continues, "just fix it. And, uh, go easy on the tots. Your double chin is bad enough, the last thing we need is for our bases to drop you at halftime tonight. I knew it was a mistake making you a flier."

Damn. I guess Mia can spot an Achilles heel too because Chloe drops the tater tot that was in her hand, walks her tray over to the garbage can and chucks it. She sits back down and stares at the black lunch table in silence. That was freaking harsh, but Mia is the only one who can put Chloe in her place. Lord knows I could never stand up to Chloe, or anyone for that matter.

"Well, I like your hair."

My head swings at the sound of Philly's voice, I catch that glimmer in his black eyes that drives me crazy enough to be institutionalized.

"It's sexy," he says while carcassing Chloe's ponytail. Her stupid fucking colonial-looking ponytail.

"You've always had a thing for blondes," Link chimes in.

Damn, I forgot he was even here.

"It's true. Blondes are way hotter than brunettes. Like they say, blondes have more fun. And they're more fun in the sack. Brunettes are fucking boring," Philly states with his dark eyes locked on mine. He and Link cackle when I notice that Philly is still petting Chloe's stringy platinum hair. I look down at my lap and flip open my phone again. I've never colored my hair, as it's strictly against Lady Katherine's orders for me to end up a 'trashy bottle blonde Barbie'. I imagine she was referring to whatever blonde stole her Miss USA crown. But, Christ, maybe Philly is right. Maybe my shit brown hair *is* boring. Maybe *I'm* boring.

It's about 30 seconds later when I depart from Lilah Land and crash down in to the cafeteria. I notice that it's five minutes past when I'm supposed to be in the practice room. I asked one of the guitar girls to help me with an original song, I can't stand her up. I gather my things off the floor in a hurry.

"Shit, sorry y'all, I gotta go. I told Laura May I'd meet her five minutes ago in the practice room."

"Now there's an example of a blonde who is not hot," Link proclaims, and Philly nods in agreement. Link never misses an opportunity to rag on people, well, rag on girls, at least.

"She doesn't actually play for your team, so I doubt she gives two fucks whether or not you think she's bang worthy," I snap. Mary Lu and Mia laugh.

"Lesbian!" Link holds up his hand for a high five and Philly slaps it.

Really though? I roll my eyes.

"Speaking of teams, you're coming to the game tonight, right D?" Mia asks, standing up to meet me at eye level.

"The game?"

I totally forgot. I look around at the group and notice Mia, Chloe, and Mary Lu are all in their black and white cheer costumes, or *uniforms*, as Mia always corrects me. I glance over at Philly and Link who are also in their football uniforms. It's customary to wear their gear to school on Fridays before the game. I guess I didn't notice today. At this point, these uniforms look like their skin to me. I look down at Philly, trying to gage his expression. I wonder if he wants me at the game or not. He looks away, rejecting my shit brown eyes and my shit brown hair.

"I'll be there, cheering in the stands as usual."

"I wish that you would cheer with us on the track instead of in the stands," Mary Lu says sarcastically, flipping her curls. I know this entire crew looks down on me for not being on the cheer squad, but I'm as athletically coordinated as a catfish. Mia is the team captain, and the squad means a lot to her. I wouldn't want to embarrass her, or me, or Philly.

"Nah, Delilah has more important fish to fry. She's going to be a professional pianist at the New York Philharmonic one day, she doesn't have time for childish things like sports," Mia jokes.

"I'll be there."

"Be there, be square, whatever, it's a dumb football game. Now, go practice, my little protégée, one day we're gonna see your name in lights!" She grabs my elbows and gives them a good squeeze. I look back down at Philly to check if he's listening, but I see that he's playing Brick Breaker on his Blackberry. Mia follows my gaze to Philly then looks back at me with a sympathetic smile.

"They're all addicted, it's an epidemic."

"See ya, tonight."

"See ya, D," she responds solo, as the rest of the group is engulfed in phones and/or iPods. I turn around and head for the exit. I can't believe I agreed to sit in the stands another Friday night. I guess my date with Alanis Morrisette and box hair dye will have to wait.

Chapter 8
2009- Richmond Hill, Georgia

"You look like a fucking penny," Mom says, disgust filling her ice blue eyes. This is one of Lady Katherine's infamous facial expressions, although it's usually reserved for my father. However, today, I'm the lucky winner. Mom stomps around the kitchen island and yanks open the freezer. She rips the bottle of Belvedere off the shelf and slams it on the marble counter. She turns around and opens three different cabinets with no luck. I duck under the island and pull out the silver martini shaker.

"It's right here, Mom," I pick up the shaker. "I can make it," I offer, attempting to make amends.

"Fine. Extra dry, Lilah, and I mean *extra*."

"I know." I stride over to the bar and fish out the vermouth. I bend down to get the blue cheese stuffed olives out of the mini fridge.

"Twist, no olives. I don't want the salt to bloat me."

No olives means no dinner for Lady Katherine, as these olives tend to serve as her nightly meal.

"Did you eat anything today?"

"Ugh, worry about yourself, Lilah. I'm fine. I raised almost $600 for the church today. Pastor Craig was so impressed with my hard work and dedication to Christ."

"I'm sure that's not all he's impressed with," I whisper under my breath, eyeing her full lips that are painted dark red, going with her translucent white blouse that's hugging her big breasts. Mom glares her icy eyes at me. She picks up the bottle of vodka and jams it into my hand. I twist off the cap and pour the rest of the chilled bottle into the shaker. I hope to God that we have another bottle in the garage freezer. The only thing scarier than a hammered Katherine is a sober Katherine. I grab a crisp lemon from the glass bowl in the center of the counter and begin to carefully cut a twist. If I get it wrong, she will make me redo it until we're out of lemons completely, then she'll blame me for it. I take the knife to the skin and gently drag it.

"Honestly, Delilah, I just don't understand why you would do that to yourself. You mutilated your beautiful natural hair, and for what, to look like some white trash bimbo on one of those reality shows y'all watch? You will never be able to get it back, you know. You'll have to keep dying it and dying it until the day you die yourself. You'll be a slave to the bottle."

That's ironic.

My mom is referring to my hair, of course. I bleached it over the weekend, not because Philly likes blondes, I just wanted a change. Well… perhaps it did have a tiny bit to do with Philly. However, the endeavor did not go as planned. I knew that Mom would never pay for me to get my hair dyed at a salon considering how against 'bottle blondes' she is. So instead, Mia helped me do it in her basement. We left the bleach on for as long as possible, the directions said to keep it on longer if you have dark hair. I was going for Britney Spears blonde, but after we washed it out and Mia blew my hair dry, it was Orphan Annie orange. We ran to the nearest pharmacy to look for something to fix it. Finally, after several rounds of toner and a million showers with purple shampoo, I got it to this weird copper color. According to Lady Katherine, I look like a penny, which is funny because it cost a pretty penny just to get it to look like this. I managed to dodge Mom all weekend, which is not very hard to do in this house, but I knew I would have to face her wrath at some point. What I wasn't expecting was what a spectacle I became at Richmond Hill High today. It was as if me changing my hair color was the most interesting thing that's happened all year. Some of the nicer girls in the grade said they liked it, but mostly everybody hated it. It was as if I personally offended them by doing something to my own body. That's Richmond Hill for you, though. Besides, I only cared about one person's opinion.

My heart was pounding like a snare drum as I made my way down the hallway to English class this morning. My plan was to sneak in and sit in the back before anybody noticed me, but I took longer than needed in the bathroom staring at my copper hair under the fluorescent lights. I managed to make it to English class right as the bell was ringing. I was met with 20 eyes on me as I rushed through the doorway.

"Nice of you to join us, Miss Monroe," Mr. Stoff sighed.

"Sick hair!" An unmistakable voice shrieked.

"Link, that's your second warning for the week, and it's only Monday. I suggest you don't keep it up. But your hair does look very nice, Delilah, a great color for fall. Have a seat," Mr. Stoff gestured to the only open seat, right behind Link and Philly, of fucking course. My eyes locked with the twinkle in Philly's as usual. I swear, he is the only person that can look that handsome under that harsh light. My orange locks were accompanied by under eye bags while Philly looked like a fair-skinned God dancing under the sun, his sharp cheekbones highlighted to perfection. Butterflies flurried through my empty stomach as I averted my gaze to the white tiles on the floor and sunk into my seat.

"A great color for fall," Link mocked. "I think Mr. Stoff has a crush on you, D. He's always been a fucking creeper."

"Shut up," I hissed.

Mr. Stoff lit up the projector and put a translucent piece of paper with text of The Crucible on it. Usually, the only classes I enjoy in school are music based, but I was desperate for the distraction. I leaned down to grab my pencil case. As I rolled my head up, I was struck by Philly's gaze. I stared back for a second, trying to read his expression. Part of me didn't want him to know that I tried to go blonde for him, but another part of me wanted him to know how much I was willing to do to make him happy. My love for him is the opposite of my parents'. My love has no limits, no bounds. True love never should, right? Nothing worth having comes easy. I opened my mouth, unsure of what I was going to say until Philly's soft whisper beat me to it.

"You look like shit, Delilah."

Chapter 9
2009- Richmond Hill, Georgia

"Ugh, here, give it to me."

I hand the small knife and the seedless lemon over to Mom and she begins to peel.

"I mean, why Delilah, just why?"

"I don't know."

"There you go again with the 'I don't know'. You never know anything, do you? I called the Lucia Ferrara salon in Savannah. They said you'll need to wait at least a month until they can touch your hair because of all the damage you did to it. So, you'll have to look like a cheap coin for a while."

I shake the contents of the martini hard in the metal shaker, hoping it will be loud enough to drown out Lady Katherine's squawking. I pour the crisp drink into her signature chilled glass and hand it to her. She rubs the lemon peel around the rim and tosses it in the drink. The second she looks back up at me, I shoot my head down.

"Eye contact, Delilah."

I slowly roll my head back up. The ice in her eyes freezes over the muddy water in mine.

"You're just mad that I don't have the same hair as you anymore, and without that, we look nothing alike."

"Darlin', you're as lost as last year's Easter egg. It would take a lot more than hair to look like me. You got your looks from your father, that horrible Irish skin," Mom looks up and makes a shivering motion with her body. "Your hair was your best quality; it was a gift that the Lord and *I* gave you. And what is the thanks I get? You throw it away trying to look like some cheap, blonde hussy at the county fair."

"Jesus, Mom, I said I was sorry!" I throw my hand up, waving an invisible white flag.

"Do not use the Lord's name in vain. You watch your tongue in this house, little girl."

"Yes ma'am, sorry."

Mom sighs, "of course you bleached it at Mia's house, her mama is never home. She follows those young men around town like she's got a bee in her bonnet. That house is an unattended garbage can."

"You're one to talk," I mutter under my breath. I close my eyes out of fear of the scowl I know is on my mom's face. If looks could kill, Katherine would be Ted Bundy.

"I'll have you know that I am out spreading the word of our Lord and savior, Jesus Christ. I am working tirelessly to reform the sinners around here into God fearing folks. I do so much for this town, all while running this house. Look around you, Lilah, who do you think does all of this?"

I follow her hands to scan the marble countertops, the smooth oak wood cabinets, and the crystal chandeliers she's pointing at.

"I'm sure your father would say he's the one that pays for all of this, but he is blinded by sin and ego. That man has always been ungrateful for all I do around here. Anyone can pay with money, but I'm the one who really pays. Your father thinks he's smart with his fancy education but he doesn't know the difference between a white wall and an eggshell one, if it were up to him these walls would be painted bright red like some whore house. He'd be worthless as gum on a boot heel. He would be lost without me, you all would." Mom turns her boney body away from me and puts her hands on the refrigerator. When she whips her torso back around, I can see that her shocking blue eyes are filled with tears. A pang of sorrow rips through my heart.

"You know, your dad was nobody when I met him. I was the one who had it all. I was Miss Georgia. There were plenty of men beatin' down my door to ask your Granddaddy for my hand. He practically had to chase them off with a stick. But I chose William, a nobody from the slums of that wretched state."

"Pennsylvan–"

"When I met him, he didn't even know what a cotillion was. I taught him how to dress, how to speak, which fork to use, everything. I made him who he is. And how does he repay me? He treats me like I'm…" Katherine's voice fades to black as she reaches for her freshly made drink. I imagine what she was going to say is nothing, that my dad treats her like she's nothing. Like she's a burden he couldn't scrape off his shoe, resenting her with each step he takes. I could not imagine living 20 years with someone who saw me that way. I study my mom's face which is turned towards the kitchen window. As beautiful as she is, and as perfect as her white picket fence life may seem, I can't imagine anything more horrible than ending up like her.

I wipe my cold, vodka drenched hands on my jeans. "I know, Mom, I'm sorry. We do appreciate you, Liam and me. And Dad loves you, he just, I don't know, can't show it. But that's how all men are, right?"

"Right," she laughs sarcastically, "they'd be damned without us. They'd only have one oar in the water. They need us more than we need them, you remember that, you hear?" Mom walks over to the sink and leans her weight on it, letting out an enormous sigh.

"Mom, I'm sorry, I didn't mean to upset you."

"You didn't upset me," she snaps back immediately, turning around. "Why are you so dramatic, Delilah?"

"Sorry."

Mom picks up her drink, closes her eyes and takes a sip. When she opens her eyes, the tears are gone, and her full lips stretch into a Cheshire Cat-like grin. She looks like she's possessed.

"This drink is great, Darlin', thank you."

"Um, you're welcome?"

Mom straightens her pearls and pats down her white blouse.

"And don't worry about your hair, Sugar. We'll get it fixed as soon as we can, and you'll be back to looking... well, how you looked before."

"Okay."

She never misses an opportunity to take a dig. Just when you think she's softened, she whips out the shovel, jams it into your insecurities and buries you in them.

"Come on now, we don't want to keep our guests waiting. I slaved over this supper all dang night."

Tonight's dinner was catered by the country club, but okay. I attempt to mirror the southern charm in Lady Katherine's plastered on smile as I follow her out into the dining room.

I don't think I've ever been this close to Sam Garcia in all the 10 plus years that I've known him. It's strange, seeing him sitting in this dining room, in the house I grew up in. It feels so... I don't know, surreal. Before this, he only existed at school in my mind, passing me in the hallway with his head down and hoodie on, or smoking cigarettes under the bleachers during gym class. But now, here he is, sitting across from me eating Chicken Francese off Lady Katherine's newest China set. My eyes stay fixed on the scruff around his jaw. It lines his tanned face with perfect symmetry, as do his dark black eyebrows. They arch up slightly, making it look like he's constantly curious. I study his black hair that shines under the chandelier. I wonder if the gleam is gel or sweat, but either way, it makes the hair fall flawlessly over his forehead, like he's straight out of a James Dean movie or something. I poke at my salad, trying to distract myself before Sam realizes I'm staring. The last thing I want to do is make him uncomfortable. I glance next to me and see Mom chugging her martini with one hand while the other hand is pressed over her heart. What is she doing? Is she praying? Now? I guess stranger things have happened in this house. Mom does love to put on a show when she has an audience. I hope that the Garcia's being around will prompt her to be on her best behavior. I peer passed her towards the head of the table and see my dad washing down his mashed potatoes with a scotch, neat. I'm not sure I've ever seen Dad eat a meal that didn't include mashed potatoes… or scotch. The contrast between William Monroe and the man next to him is astounding. Mr. Garcia makes my dad look like a giant in comparison. I look down at his hands and see that they're riddled with calluses. My eyes travel over to my Dad's hands, one of which is strangling a steak knife. I analyze them, checking them for calluses but they're as smooth as the butter on his potatoes. Mr. Garcia's wife, Sofia Garcia, is also a tiny woman. She's beautiful, just like Bailey was, regardless of what my friends say. My eyes travel down to the wine in front of Mr. and Mrs. Garcia that neither of them have touched. I feel a sting of jealousy, as my mom didn't offer me any tonight to keep up appearances.

Only screeches of forks and knives hitting plates can be heard amid this ear ringing silence. The quiet has my stomach doing backflips. I think I'd rather be locked in a padded cell forced to listen to the entire soundtrack of Cats than listen to the nothingness between the Garcia's and the Monroe's. I risk a glance up from my plate towards Sam who's looking right back at me. I look back down and shovel a fork full of lettuce into my mouth, pretending like I wasn't just studying his face like a flash card. So far, I can see that he has the same jet-black hair and scruff as his dad. He has a heart shaped mouth and full lips like his mom. But his eyes are different from both of his parents. Sam's look lighter, but I can't tell if they're blue or green.

"You have a lovely home, Mrs. Monroe," Sofia Garcia says in a meek voice. I can hear she has a subtle accent.

"Why thank you, Darlin'. I work tirelessly day and night, it's nice to see someone appreciate my hard work."

I don't even need to look at my Dad to know his eyes are rolling. He won't make a scene in front of company, but I'm sure I'll be needing noise canceling headphones to drown out the rip roar of his impending rage later tonight.

"Lisa Warner is the most sought-after interior decorator in Georgia. I'm sure you've heard of her."

Mrs. Garcia smiles politely.

"Well," Mom continues, "she is a very close, personal friend of mine."

"Oh that's… great."

If only Lady Katherine were aware enough or sober enough to realize that Sofia is just trying to be polite, or maybe she's trying to fill this mind-numbing silence before it consumes us all. I highly doubt she gives two shits about who picked out the colors of our banisters.

"Michael, is it?" Dad motions to Mr. Garcia.

"It's Miguel," Mr. Garcia corrects him with a smile.

"Meeg-Well, I see."

Oh God. I look to Sam who is twirling his fork in his spaghetti. I'm sure he's thrilled to have a front row seat to how uncultured my family is.

"Meeg-Well, you a scotch guy? I got a single malt that'll knock your socks off," William sputters with a colossal grin like it's the most exciting thing in the world.

"No, thank you, I- uh-"

Mr. Garcia is cut short by his wife who snaps right to his ear. She's whispering something in Portuguese. She's quiet enough that I wouldn't be able to make out what she's saying even if I could understand the language, yet her low octave still somehow sounds like a yell.

"Um, yes, I mean. I will have some. Thank you."

"That's my guy!" William jumps up and heads to the bar. Miguel doesn't share Dad's enthusiasm. His face reads like someone just asked him for a ride to the airport. Dad returns to the table, slamming down the glass of whiskey in front of Mr. Garcia. He stares at the glass, pensively. His wife says something to him in Portuguese again, and he takes a tiny sip followed by a wince. They both flash Dad variants of disingenuous smiles.

"Oh, I just love Spanish, such a beautiful language."

"Oh, it's actually—"

"Shhh," Mrs. Garcia hisses at her husband, "Miguel, do not interrupt."

Mom doesn't seem to notice. "There's just something so romantic about it. It's a beautiful language. Isn't it just a beautiful language, Darlin'?" I hear Mom ask, and it takes me a minute to register that by Darlin', she means me. Certainly, she's not referring to my dad, his contact is stored in her blackberry as 'Satan'. I suppose I'm up.

I break eye contact with my barren salad and look at the Garcia's. "Oh, yes. Yes, it is. Beautiful, I mean. It's uh- a beautiful language."

I catch a look exchanged by Mr. And Mrs. Garcia. There I go again. Why can't I ever respond in a normal manner? Why is that so fucking hard? Luckily, Lady Katherine doesn't take notice as she continues her drunk ramblings drenched in fake southern charm.

"We just love your culture so much. We have many people from South America in our lives," Mom's eyelashes flutter.

"Really?" Sofia asks with a curious crease between her brows.

"Oh yes, of course. We have Jose who keeps the backyard looking immaculate, and we have Rosia who cooks for us on occasion when I'm too tired from working."

Okay. I don't believe that my mom even knows how to boil water. She has never cooked for us, and most nights she's too drunk to even remember that food exists long enough to call Rosia. Most nights, I'm on my own for dinner. I don't mind cooking; I like to keep my hands busy when they're not pressing on the keys. Although, scrounging for ingredients can pose as a challenge and outings to the grocery store are a rare occurrence. I wish I could drive there myself, but I failed the written part of the driving test. I choked, as per usual. I have to wait a few months until I can try again. The look on Philly's chiseled face when he found out I failed. *"Why are you so fucking stupid, Delilah?"* I thought I might die of a bruised ego and a broken heart.

I shake my head and look back at Mom who is, evidently, still talking.

"And of course, we have Juana and Val. They are the most important people to me; I would die without them."

"Oh! And who are they?" Sofia perks up.

"They're our maids," Mom says with a smile.

I see Sofia's shoulders roll down and her expression go flat. She's disappointed. She probably didn't expect that when my mom mentioned all the people from South America in her life that she was referring solely to people who work for her, not actual friends. My God. Katherine can be severely dense sometimes. The crazy thing is, I know she believes that she's being sweet as tea by relating to Sofia right now. But the truth is, they have nothing in common. As elegant as Mom tries to appear, she's just a country girl who has never left the state of Georgia. Looking at the Garcia's at this comically large dining table, eating off our China; it's obvious that they feel out of place in this house. But it never occurred to me that they likely feel out of place in this whole town. We have very little diversity here. I don't think we have many other Brazilian residents, if any at all. That must be so strange for them, to have no one around them that can speak their first language. I've always thought of myself as a black sheep in this town, running from the Shepherd but getting lost in the herd. I've felt out of place here for as long as I can remember, and I was born here. I can only imagine how the Garcia's must feel.

I sink back into my mind, wandering around Lilah Land in efforts to drown out the tipsy ramblings. I hear 'The Lord' in my peripheral and immediately know it's a conversation I want no part of. Although, most conversations are ones that I want no part of, it's not like I add much as a conversationalist anyway. Damn, I really wish I could reach across the table and pour Mrs. Garcia's full glass of wine down my esophagus. My pupils linger, landing back on Sam who hasn't looked up from his plate once this entire dinner. I wonder how he feels about being here, living at a random classmate's home. I wonder how he feels about people knowing that their family is struggling financially. I wonder how he feels about his twin sister dying. I wonder how he feels about *everything*. I also wonder how he feels about me. Usually, what people think of me is based on what they think of my friends considering I have the smallest personality of the group. I wonder if he thinks I'm a slut because people call Mia a slut, even though she's not. I wonder if he thinks I'm a bully because people think Philly is a bully, even though he's not. I wonder if he thinks I'm dumb because people think Chloe is dumb, even though… no, they're right about that, she is pretty dumb. Wow, high school sucks. I can't wait to get out of here and make a name for myself as a pianist. I can see it so clearly, me on stage, so confident that I had scored into the New York City Philharmonic. I see myself sitting behind those keys. I don't look nervous or awkward, I look poised and regal, elegant, and… I don't know, beautiful? I look out into the crowd and see the faces of all the people I used to know watching me with big, admiring eyes, thinking to themselves how wrong they were about me. When I picture my future, that's all I want, really, to prove everyone in my life wrong. "Claire de Lune" plays melodically in my head as I'm transported to a place far more euphoric than this one. The keys flow in a legato bliss. The spotlight beams on my piano, not even half as bright as the light radiating from my aura.

I don't notice that my fingers are playing along to a Debussy melody until my mom subtly slaps a hand on top of mine, gesturing for me to get out of Lilah Land and come back down to hell.

"Ugh. Why can't you just be normal, Delilah?" Mom hisses under her breath. I slide my hands into my lap. I am a freak. I feel a lump in my throat. I look around the table, terrified that everyone saw, but the men at the table are engulfed in their dinners while Sofia has her eyes politely entangled with my mother's. I look around at each full plate on the dining table, comparing them to my tiny side salad. Mom put the order in for everyone. I'm not surprised that she went with plain salads sans the dressing for both of us. It's probably for the best, Mom thinks that I'm getting a 'belly.' The way she says 'belly' makes it sound like the ugliest word in the world.

All the sudden, I hear a faint sound. Is that Mom? Is she crying right now? I look over and see tears leaking past her long eyelashes. She puts a hand to her chest.

"It just breaks my heart, Sofia, it really does. The choice that your beautiful, beautiful little girl made. I can't imagine what you are going through." Mom puts a hand on my shoulder. "If my daughter did that to us, it's… it's just too horrible to think of. We need our children with us, they're our angels from God."

Half the time, Mom doesn't even know her own name, let alone mine, but I digress.

"I'm so sorry, Sofia. I am so very sorry for what you are going through," Mom wipes her tears and dabs her face with her cloth napkin.

"Thank you, Mrs. Monroe."

"Oh please, Sugar, call me Katherine."

"Thank you, Katherine. We appreciate your condolences, and we are very grateful that you are allowing us to stay here, very grateful. Right, Samson?" Mrs. Garcia nudges Sam with her elbow.

"Yes, of course. We are incredibly grateful. This place is amazing. Thank you."

I avoid eye contact as Sam's heart shape mouth curls up into a polite smile. His voice sounds sincere, and it's lower and raspier than I thought it was. He sounds like an actual man. I'm surprised he had an answer ready, and he was so confident about it. I didn't think he was paying attention. I assumed he was also lost in a dark cave somewhere deep inside of his mind, maybe that's just me.

"You are a very kind woman," Sofia states.

"Oh, shucks. I do what I can. So then, as we have the opportunity, let us do good to everyone. Proverbs 31:8."

I hate it when she speaks in scripture to show off. I will say though, Mom has memorized a lot of those quotes, or whatever they are. You'd think the memory part of her brain would have been condemned due to the daily monsoons of Belvedere.

"I..." Mom continues, "did she even leave a note?"

Sofia bows her head. "No, she did not, I wish she had."

Now, why on planet fucking earth would she ask that? If Bailey did leave a suicide note, why would her parents wish to share that with Katherine Monroe?

"Sofia," Mr. Garcia firmly speaks to his wife, "I don't... I don't think this is appropriate table conversation."

"Of course," Mom exhales, "where are my manners, I'm like a piglet in a barn."

I can't help but chuckle a little. Lady Katherine has many Katherineisms like this, hazards of being raised in the country. I glance back at Sam and notice that he's smiling a bit too. His eyes dart my way and I look back down at my hands.

"Excuse my wife," Dad says.

"Oh, no, it is no problem," Sofia assures him.

"I get it," Dad says to Miguel. "You give these kids the world, and they throw it away. Kids have no gratitude these days."

"Dad," I exclaim. He doesn't hear me, as usual. He is not about to go there, is he? I look down at his empty scotch glass. He is, he is about to go there.

"My son, Liam, he is a bright, good-looking kid. He has everything going for him because I gave it to him, and what does he want to do with it, he wants to throw it away. A therapist," he laughs, "that boy tells me he wants to be a therapist. What a quack. Don't worry, he's a finance major at Duke now."

I'm sure he was so worried.

"All he needed was a good ass whoopin." Dad puts his large hand on Miguel's thin shoulder. "I understand what you are going through, my good man. Yinz are good parents, and your daughter should have appreciated that more."

Oh. My. God.

Mr. Garcia keeps his eyes fixed on his plate.

"The Lord forgives all, and he will forgive your darlin' daughter," Mom spats.

"Thank you, Mrs. Monroe," Sofia says.

"Oh, I told you, Sugar, call me Katherine."

"Right, yes, Katherine." Mrs. Garcia looks left to right at her husband and her son, neither look back at her. She wipes her mouth with her napkin and folds it onto her place setting. "Well, we should be going now, we have to unpack. Thank you very much for dinner, this has been a lovely evening."

Mom stands up to walk the Garcia's out. She pulls Sofia in for a hug, wrapping her boney arms around her. I hear her whisper that she will be praying for her family. Right, because that is what will heal their grief, inebriated prayers at 2am washed down by Xanax and a 12th martini. Thank God for you, Mom. Thank *God*.

Chapter 10
2009- Richmond Hill, Georgia

"Hey."

"Hey." Sam looks back, startled as the smoke from his cigarette dances with the warm Georgia winds. The water below us shakes the dock under our feet ever so slightly. I look out onto the river, the breeze causing it to rage like my parents after their 10th drink of the night. The smell of sea water violates my nose as I sink down onto the worn wood, dangling my white Converse sneakers over the edge.

"Sorry, I thought this would be a good place for a smoke, it looked... private. I can go."

"You can stay," I say, flickering my eyes to the spot next to me on the dock. I look back up at him. Damn, he's tall. Sam looks back past the pool towards the house then back at me. *Shit.* This is awkward, he probably wants to be alone. Of course, he wants to be alone, his twin sister just died, and here I am encroaching on his bereavement time. I'm just about to hoist myself up when he lowers down next to me, exhaling a bit of a groan. My shoulders soften. "Those things will kill you, ya know," I joke in my nerdiest sounding voice.

Sam smirks, but only with one corner of his heart-shaped mouth. I stare at that corner a little too long. I've never noticed it before, just like I've never noticed his wool gray eyes before, the eyes I kept trying to guess the color of during dinner. They're not quite as captivating or mind blowing as Philly's black eyes or Lady Katherine's ice blue eyes, but there's something about them. They're deep, and they seem... warm. Not striking, yet far from ordinary. A wave of heat pummels through my body. I take a big gulp and focus on the river flowing beneath my feet.

"You ever try one?" he asks, holding out the cigarette to me.

"No."

"Good, don't. These things will kill you, ya know."

I laugh, surprised he's still able to make jokes after what he's been through.

"I tried a Black and Mild before, does that count?"

Sam chuckles, "you would."

"What's that supposed to mean?"

"Nothin'," he says, owning the half smirk on big lips. He slides over the top one with his tongue, and I nearly lose my breath.

"What are you doing down here anyway?"

"This is my night cap spot," I say, spinning the glass of scotch that I stole from Dad's open bottle. I snuck it from the bar after he went into his study. Not that my dad is one to judge anyone for drinking, it's just, it's a really nice bottle of Macallan. It's more sacred to William than my mom and I will ever be.

"Anyway, I love it down here. This dock is probably the only thing on this property that has never been touched or renovated."

"I bet."

"I come out here pretty much every night because…" I stop myself. "Um… because I just love hanging here by the river, it feels like I'm in an Otis Redding song."

"Otis Redding, really…" He says it as more of a sarcastic statement than a question. His scruffy, tanned face has quickly gone from titillating to aggravating.

"Um, yeah. Is it so shocking I listen to Otis Redding? He *is* from Georgia." I put my glass down on the wood and cross my arms.

"I just… nothin."

"What?"

"I just thought you were more of a top-forty girl. Thought you'd be into, I don't know, who's that new chick on the radio? Key-shah?"

"You mean Kesha?" I laugh.

"Yeah, that's the one."

"Well, I'm not." I take a small sip of scotch. "Well, maybe, sometimes, only when we're pregaming," I say, nudging him a little with my shoulder which I'm now regretting. The Macallan has possessed me.

"Pregaming?"

"Yeah, you know, like taking shots at someone's house before going to the party."

"I don't really go to parties," he takes a drag, "not my scene. Not like I'm invited anyway, I'm not exactly the prom king."

"You're not going to prom then, I take it?"

Sam laughs sardonically. "Maybe I will. Guess it's the only party I'll get an invite to."

Wow, I am a dickhead.

"The parties around here aren't that great anyway; you're not missing much." I try to save the conversation. I don't know why, but every fiber of my being doesn't want this tall stranger to get up and leave.

"Then why do you go to them?"

"I..." I choke on my words, "I don't know, I guess it's just... what my friends do so it's what I do."

"Right." Sam rolls his eyes then looks out onto the ripples in the water. "I'm sure your little gang would send out a search party for you if you ever missed one of those things."

"My gang?"

"Yeah, your jock boyfriend."

"Jock, what is this? The fucking Breakfast Club?"

Sam laughs a little. "I love that movie."

"You would."

"Touché. You know what I mean though. Y'all are like that group at school that everybody knows. The infamous *Mia* and her loyal minions, Chloe and, uh, what's her face, Mary Jane?"

"Mary Lu," I correct, smiling slightly, "but I'm not one of the minions, Mia is my best friend."

"Really?"

"Um, yeah. What?" I dart my eyes at his face as I attempt to read his thoughts, those of which are becoming blurrier to me by the minute. I think my brain needs glasses.

"It's just, you seem…. nice. And, Mia, she's so…"

"So what?"

"Nothin'."

"No, go on, Mia's so what?"

"Nothin'," he sharpens his inflection.

I'm wondering if I should get up and leave now. I have an iPod Touch full of Otis Redding waiting for me in my room. A musician who, to Sam's shock, I genuinely do listen to. It's clear that Sam and I have zero in common. I bet he thinks I'm some dumb party girl or mean girl or whatever the hell girl he wants to see me as. I sigh and look away towards the little sand patch just below the dock, the one Liam and I used to hide out on when we were young, when our parents were doing their usual fight song and dance. Just the thought of that makes me want to stay as far away from inside of my house as possible. It's safer out here swimming in the tides of Sam's judgment.

"Look, I know what you must think of us, what you must think of me. But no one is going to talk shit about my best friend. You don't know her; you just know her reputation. You're judging a book by its cover." I sigh, disappointed that the warmth in Sam's eyes and the lust in his smirk may have been a mirage.

Sam lets out a puff of smoke then dabs his cigarette out on the splintered wood. "That's fair."

"Mia's just, she's honestly the best person I've ever met, truly."

"Really? I guess you're right then. I don't know her, tell me more."

"Well, for starters, she's the only person on this planet who actually sees me when I'm there and hears me when I speak."

"What are you talking about? Everyone knows you. You're like one of those girls that everybody knows."

"Maybe, but there's a difference between being known and actually being seen and heard."

Sam thinks for a moment, and I wonder if I've said too much. "That makes sense."

"It does?"

"Yeah, it does. I'm sorry, I didn't mean to be a dick. You're right, I don't really know you or Mia. I know *of* y'all, but it's not the same."

I jerk my head back at him, meeting his kind stare. I've never heard someone admit that they were wrong before, let alone so quickly. What is his angle? I study his expression for signs of ingenuity. Now I feel… I don't know, bad, guilty.

"You weren't being a dick."

"No, I was. It's okay to say it."

He flexes his broad shoulders back, exposing the pecks that peek through his white shirt. It's tight on him, and it gives me a full view of chest. I don't think I've ever seen someone this comfortable in their skin. He stretches his arms back behind him, almost touching the tip of my finger with his, like he's not afraid to… like he's not afraid to take up space. I keep my hand where it is, hoping he'll graze it again.

"Anyway, Mia encourages me musically. She's been my number one supporter from the day I met her. She believes in me; I think she's the only person that ever has."

"You're a musician?" Sam asks, his forehead wrinkling.

"Yeah," I say, looking down to avoid his silver eyes. "I play piano, mostly classical."

"Oh, wow. I never knew that. That's pretty cool. Guess you were right about the book and cover thing."

"Thanks." I pat my cheeks in anticipation of rosacea. I take another swig of scotch and notice Sam's gray eyes locked on my glass. "You wanna sip?"

"Nah," he says, pulling out a pack of cigarettes from his pocket. "I like to stick to one vice at a time."

He takes out his lighter and lights the cigarette. I'm relieved when he does it because it means that he's not rushing back inside, away from the crazy bitch who's house he's forced to stay at. I set my glass down and look back out at the blue river. The sunset is casting orange tones over the teal waves, my favorite. I shift my hips on the dock. I know I should go back inside soon, practice a little, do homework, call Philly. Even my scotched-up brain can see that I should call it a night. But the sensation in my chest and the goosebumps on my arms give me a different command. I can't stay here long, but maybe, I can stay here for just a little while. Just a little while longer.

"I'm sorry, by the way, for… for what happened, at dinner. Sorry about my mom, and about my dad. Sorry about… all of it."

Sam wraps his full lips around his cigarette. He takes a drag and blows it out slowly while squeezing his eyelids shut. "It's fine. He wasn't wrong, you know, your dad. What Bailey did was... I don't even want to say it. She broke my mom's heart."

I can sense the anger in his words, and I get an intense feeling rushing towards my forehead.

"I'm sure…" I stutter, "I'm sure she didn't mean to hurt anyone."

"But she did," Sam pounds his large fist down on the dock.

"She was depressed though, right? Like, she was sick."

"Yeah, I'm not saying she wasn't. For a long time, she would say things like her life was meaningless and nothing matters. But like, okay, if your life is meaningless, don't end it. Go make it mean something, volunteer in a third world country, give yourself something important to do, that'll give you some fucking meaning," he shouts, his volume rising with every word. He takes another drag. "Sorry."

"It's okay."

I'm surprised he's sharing this with me. And I'm surprised how easy it is to talk to him. I don't feel that surge of panic I usually do when conversing. I haven't slipped into Lilah Land at all since we've been talking either. It's like someone else has taken over my body and mind on this dock, perhaps it's Old Man Macallan sitting heavy in my glass. I look over at Sam who's staring at his dangling Doc Martins. I consider putting my hand on his thick arm or shoulder or something for comfort, but it feels... I don't know, strange. We've known *of* each other since first grade, but like he said, we don't actually *know* each other.

"It's just... I don't know," I hesitate.

"What?"

"It's just, I don't think it's that simple. I don't think it's that black and white."

"What's not black and white?"

"Life."

"I think it is. I think the entire point of life is simple, it comes down to meaning, like what means the most to you. Take you and your music. I'm sure that gives you meaning."

"Yeah," I say, pondering, thinking of four-year-old me smiling from ear to ear while pounding on the keys until every member of my family wanted to send me away to a farm like a pet they no longer cared for. I think about how exciting and full everything felt back then anytime I played our baby grand. I feel a small grin creep onto my lips. "I guess it does."

"See, Bailey never found her meaning because she never even tried to look for it. It was like she wanted to be sad. I know how that sounds, but that really is what it felt like."

"Okay, so then what is your meaning? What do you live for?"

"Fuck if I know, dude," Sam laughs while flicking his cigarette, "but I plan on sticking around to find out unlike Bailey who bowed out of the race not even a mile from the starting line."

My eyebrow raises in confusion, Sam picks up on it right away.

"My mom doesn't like for me to say that Bailey killed herself, so…"

"Yeah, neither does mine. Guess we have more in common than we thought."

Sam laughs, "doubt it, I mean, look at this place."

He turns his head back towards the house and pans over it from side to side. Looking back towards the river, he takes out the box of cigarettes from his jean pocket. I wonder how many of these he goes through in a day. I lift my eyes up, and that half smirk on his lips is still invading my space.

"What?"

"Nothin' just seems you have it made here. You have everything you could ever want. I'm just jealous, that's all. All I have is no home and a twin sister six feet under. I mean damn, I'd trade lives with you in a heartbeat."

"You don't want to be me, trust me," I whisper with my head down towards the water.

"Oh, no? Why is that?"

"Nothing."

"Eh, you just don't know how good you got it because you don't know anything else."

A sick feeling comes over me as heat sprinkles through my legs and up through my stomach, they meet in the middle, both dancing together in my chest. Sam doesn't know how I have it. Sam's parents seem sweet and pure. He has no idea what it's like to live with William and Katherine. I'm sure he also doesn't know what it's like to love someone head over heels for 12 fucking years. And he definitely doesn't know the indescribable pain of realizing that that person may never love you back. There are more ways than one to suffer, he'll never understand mine and I'll never understand his.

I stare down at a loose string on my jeans and anxiously pull at it. I'm hoping the cool breeze will wash off the redness on my cheeks.

"Sorry," Sam finally breaks the silence, "I didn't mean to be rude, it's been a rough couple of days."

"Yeah, that's understandable. Anyway, you're probably right. My dad works his ass off to give us the life that he does, I need to remember that and be grateful."

"Nah, I'm sorry, I'm sure you got your own shit, everybody does. I didn't mean to like compare tragedies or anything. It's not about you, it's about Bailey. I'm just so...so..." his words are caught in his throat.

"Angry?'

"Yeah," he says, relieved, "I'm so goddamn—" Sam bows his head, "sorry, I didn't mean to say that. I never say that."

"Oh please, I've heard it all."

It's then that I notice the silver cross dangling between his pecks. I stare at the shiny necklace. The silver glimmers on it match the ones in his eyes. I travel my gaze up his chest, stopping on the hair that peeks through his collar and leads to his neck. I re-focus my eyes on his, shoving down the realization that Sam Garcia is hot. He is really fucking hot. Sam blows out smoke and sucks in air. "I'm so goddamn mad at her. Is that fucked up?"

"No, I don't think so," I shrug, captivated by the vein popping out of his skin between his black hair and one of his gray eyes. "It's just that, my parents immigrated here from the Favela when they found out that my mom was pregnant with twins."

"Favela?"

"It means the slums, the ghetto. My parents are from Providencia, it's in the center of Rio de Janeiro. It's a dangerous area, at least it was at the time. There was a lot going on in the country before my parents fled, a lot of corruption and gang violence and just awful shit. My parents wanted to give their kids a better life than they had. So, they left everything and everyone they knew behind and risked their lives to come here. Then they worked tirelessly to become citizens. It's not easy here, let me tell you. They did that all for us. That's never been lost on me, but it was completely lost on Bailey. Towards the end, she refused to come to church with us or eat dinner with us. She rejected all my mom's attempts to spend time with her. She hid and sulked in her room all day and all night. Anytime she did come out, it was an explosion of angry outbursts. She even punched my dad in the face one time. And then finally, the cherry on top of it all, she repays my parents for giving up both of their lives for her by taking her own."

"Bowing out of the race before the finish line?"

"Yeah," Sam chuckles a little and drops his shoulders.

"I know it sucks, Sam, more than sucks, it's the worst thing in the world, losing her, especially in that way. But I'm sure she had her reasons."

His eyes dart towards me, and I feel myself jump back a little.

"What reason could possibly cause you to kill yourself?"

I look away from him and out towards the water. I'm entirely unsure if I should bring this up. Would he even know what I'm talking about? Did it actualy happen? I should just keep my mouth shut, I'm good at that. However, the scotch I inhaled seems to have other plans.

"I heard she... she..." I trip over my words like two left feet, "I heard she was raped."

Sam lights the cigarette sitting in the corner of his heart-mouth. "Yeah."

"It's true?" I ask in utter shock, "I thought maybe it was a rumor, I just heard people talking about it in school."

"That's how I found out as well, probably the same time as you. I can't believe she didn't tell me. I could have-"

"What? What could you have done?"

"I don't know, help her somehow, be there for her, but she never gave me the fucking chance," he lets out a big sigh. "I should have known something was wrong. I had felt physically sick all weekend before it happened, like I was feeling her pain."

"You don't mean like..."

"Yeah, twin telepathy, it's a real thing."

"Wow," I say nodding my head. "Do you know who it was? You know, the guy who..."

"The vile monster that raped her? No, I don't know. But I found one of Bailey's diaries under her old bed. It's mostly gibberish, but I'm hoping there are some clues in there. Mark my words, when I find out who the dirtbag is, he's fucking dead." Sam practically spits out a puff of smoke. It's quiet between us for a moment, and I take in the sounds of cicadas singing in the trees behind us.

"Do you think that's why she did it? Because she was, you know, raped?"

"I guess so, I don't know. Do you think being assaulted would make someone want to die?"

"Yeah, I do," I respond way too quickly and immediately regret it when I see the look on his face.

"You do? Have you been—"

I jump in with urgency. "It sounds though, from what you said, she wasn't happy for a while. Maybe it was a bunch of little things that added up, then what happened to her, whatever that guy did to her was the last straw," I say quickly. I feel relieved when I see the expression on Sam's face transform slightly.

"Maybe, but I'm not sure that there should be straws when it comes to life. Killing yourself should never be an option, no matter what. It's just so fucked up."

Sam leans back onto his elbows and forearms, and I join him. Suddenly, we are much closer than before, our faces inches apart. My skin burns like I've been stung by a hundred jellyfish. His breath on my face feels like the only cure.

"I can't imagine what she was thinking in that moment, you know, right before she did it."

"Maybe she was thinking that life was too painful to live, and it just hurt too bad to be her."

Sam gives me an entertained look. "It sounds like you know from experience."

Fuck. I spring up off my elbows and take a sip that infests every part of my body. I'm pretty sure I swallowed a bug, but I don't care. The only notable thing crawling in my throat right now is embarrassment. Why did I say that? Why do I speak at all, ever?

"No, it's, it's something my brother said once."

"Ah, got it," Sam lifts off the dock to meet my eyes again.

"It's, ugh, it's fucking eating me alive. Like really, what could she possibly have been thinking when she went into her closet to get that scarf? Didn't she know how badly this would devastate my parents?"

"Probably not."

"What do you mean?"

"She probably *didn't* know how badly it would devastate your parents. She probably believed that no one would miss her, that the world would be a better place without her." I inhale deeply and stare out towards the bay. I pick up the scotch glass and hold the last sip in my mouth for a few seconds. Then I swallow it, along with the memories of all the times, I too, have eyed the scarves in my closet, wondering if I was never meant to be here in the first place. I see that same concerned look roll over Sam's face again and know I need to retreat.

"I mean, at least, that's what I've read. I uh, did a project on the topic for school once."

"Really? That's a strange topic for school, what class?"

"I don't remember."

"Oh. Well, yeah, I guess what you read makes sense. She couldn't have been thinking logically or she never would have done this to us, to my parents, to me. It's unnatural. As animals, we're born to survive, to literally do whatever it takes to fight for our lives, no different from wild animals in the jungle. We're like tigers that will fight and kill anything in their path to survive. They fight to survive at any cost, and we're supposed to do that too. But, Bailey, dude, she didn't fight at all."

"Maybe she did."

The arch in Sam's eyebrow raises.

"Maybe she was fighting for a long time, and you couldn't see it. I get what you're saying, it's unnatural, but that's probably a testament to how much pain she was in. I've watched Planet Earth with my brother before. Even animals give up the fight with their predator at some point. There's only so much energy that one has to fight. Maybe Bailey ran out of energy."

Sam stares at me, flickering his eyes from my left cornea to my right. He breathes in deeply through his nose.

"Ya know, you're a smart person, Delilah. You're cool. I'm sorry if I was being, whatever I was being earlier. You were right, I judged a book by its cover because the cover was just so…" he pauses.

"What?"

"Beautiful."

Sam's gray eyes stay locked with mine, and it feels like our minds are slow dancing to Otis Redding in the moonlight. I feel a dry wind brush over my eyes, but I don't want to blink, not yet. Not when the painting in front of me is this seductive. Sam inches his hand slowly and cautiously, like he doesn't want me to notice. I feel the touch of his warm finger brush against mine. The ripples in the bay feel as though they're suddenly flooding me, leaking from my pours with lust. I slowly shift my hand until it is under his. He puts subtle pressure over the top of it, and I savor the warmth. It resembles the warmth in his eyes. I stare down at our laced fingers, unable to breathe or think. And, I don't try to think, all I do is feel. I feel the sensation of desire run through me, tickling every nerve I have, sending pleasure to their endings. I pick my head up, and I can taste his breath on my lips. It's sweet, despite the cigarette smoke. I grab his arm and stroke it with my free hand, feeling each of his black arm hairs on my fingertips. I slowly tighten my grip, my nails gently digging into his perfect dark skin. Sam lets out a quiet moan, like he's as desperate as I am to be closer. I slide my hand up to the back of his neck, trailing by each muscle along the way. I grab the back of his black hair. He slowly glides his arm towards the small of my back. I lean in and he begins to lean too, until…

Right then, our dance is interrupted by the slam of a screen door, it sounds like it came from the main house. *Shit.* I don't want either of my parents to see me out here with him. I jump back, untangling myself from Sam's warmth, from the fever dream I would have elected to stay in forever. I'm nearly choking on air as I pick up my glass to take a sip, forgetting that I already drained its contents into my bloodstream. I place it back down.

"I, uh, I better go before the sun goes down." I can barely catch my breath, let alone form words. I lift my bottom off the worn wood and struggle up to my feet. Sam jerks up fast. "Oh, don't forget this," he says while picking my glass up off the ground. His finger brushes mine when he gently places it in my hand. His lips grow into a half smile, leaning to the left of his face. His deep eyes travel over my body. I cross my legs and arms, not wanting these old jeans to be his vision of me.

"That glass probably costs more than most of the things I own."

I give him a shy smile and look down. "I'll see you in school then?"

"Ah, my favorite place. Can't wait," he says sarcastically.

I turn towards the house and start walking through the mossy trees when I hear Sam call out. I pirouette around.

"Hey, Delilah! I love your hair by the way, it looks…
beautiful."

Sittin' on the dock of the bay,
Watching the tides roll away,
Just sittin' on the dock of the bay,
Wasting time...

Chapter 11
Present Day

The cool air brushes my legs, freezing the droplets that cover
them. I put one foot under my bottom and spring myself off
the ledge of the pool and onto my feet, the limestone ground
underneath me burns my heels. I grab my towel from the
lounge chair and wrap it around my black Victoria's Secret
plunging-neck one piece. I look down at the deep V-line and
instinctually cover my breasts with my towel. I'm approaching
35 and I'm worried my boobs are starting to show it. I wished
on all my lucky stars for years that my breasts would reflect
how old I felt, but now that they do, I'd give anything to have
my flat chest back. I wonder if my husband would be willing
to dish out the doe for a boob job. It's not like I haven't
noticed him gawking at the plastic trophy wives at our country
club charity galas. I look down at my exposed breasts again,
they're bolstered pretty well by this tight spandex. I run my
French tips between my cleavage. Perhaps I'll wait on surgery,
I've heard that augmentation is quite painful. Although, there
are things that are far more painful than surgery… like
realizing the people meant to protect you are the people you
need to be protected from.
I grab my phone out of my oversized Louis Vuitton bag and
type a reminder into my notes app to research the best plastic

surgeons in the area. It can't hurt to look. I check my texts to see if the unknown number has texted again, but there's nothing. It's not him... it can't be. He wouldn't dare. Would he? I put my phone down and walk around to the other side of the pool, trying to keep my body moving. I take a deep breath in for four seconds, hold it for four seconds, let out a breath for four seconds, hold it again for four seconds, then let the rest out. I repeat this a few times. Dr. Veizer calls this rectangle breathing or something like that, it's supposed to soothe me. 'Like a mother's hand petting her child's head while she hums', she says. If only she knew. It does sound nice though, someone cradling me, making me feel safe again. I haven't felt that since...

No.

I'm broken out of my daze by a slight rustle behind me. It's *him*. I whip around with my hands in front of me, my frail arms ready to attack. I steady my feet and release a sigh. It's just a squirrel, he's climbing the magnolia tree in front of me with an intense urgency. My heart flutters faster than a butterfly can flap its wings. I put my hand to the left of my chest and rub gently. *I am safe, I am safe, I am safe.* It's an affirmation Dr. Veizer suggested I repeat to myself when I'm anxious, but I'm always anxious. Fight, flight, freeze, or fawn mode is what anxiety is, apparently. It's when your mind perceives a threat where there is no real danger. I don't think there's any real danger here, but I've been wrong before. I look around my 3-acre yard, scanning each bush, each tree, making sure there's no one hiding behind one of them, watching me. My God, there I go, making things up again. My paranoia has made me delusional. *Why can't you just be normal, Delilah?* I don't know who is more squirrely today, me or the actual squirrel I just saw in my magnolia.

I return to breathing in and out through my nose. It's odd that focusing on my breathing makes me feel like I can't breathe at all, hence why that meditation app my former life coach made me download did jack shit for me. I continue to walk laps on the flat stones that surround the pool, still trying extra hard to make sure I'm breathing. I know that I am, but it feels like I'm not. I ball my hands into fists, feeling my French tips dig into my palms, then I let them go. I do it again, and again, and again. Dr. Veizer calls this progressive muscle relaxation.. But my hands are completely numb at this point, and I'm afraid that they'll stop working all together. My legs are tingly too, but I keep walking, my pace picking up until I make my way over to the jacuzzi. I unwrap the white towel hugging my waist and throw it on the ground. The wind blows over my bare thighs. I push my honey hair behind my shoulders then lower myself into the hot, bubbling tub. I feel the sting of the water scorch my pale skin for a second before I spring up. I walk out of the jacuzzi and onto the limestone towards the pool. I stare at the ripples in the salt water. The sun is casting orange tones over the teal, tiny waves, making them glow, my favorite. The faint smell of cigarette smoke breezes through the air above me.

No.

I catapult myself off the stone, leaping into the water with the grace of a baby giraffe. It's not until I'm completely submerged at the bottom of the pool that I even realize I jumped in. The cold saltwater stings my skin and burns my eyes. I try to take a calming breath in through my nose, but my lungs fill with water. I toss my body around, fighting the primal urge to swim up to the surface. The water shoots rockets through me as I force myself to stay limp at the bottom of the pool. The feeling in my nose is a pain like no other. Although, there are things far more painful than asphyxiation... like being rejected by the people who are supposed to love you the most. Eventually, my body betrays me. A foot presses on the pool floor and launches me up to the surface. I doggy paddle to the ledge, splashing my heavy arms on the thick ripples. I cough from a place that feels like my heart and see the saltwater splatter onto the stone. I heave in with a roar. Once I catch my breath, I lay my head on the edge of the pool and let my body float on the fake ocean water. I bring my palm up to my chest and whisper the affirmation again, out loud this time. "I am safe, I am safe, I am safe." I keep repeating the mantra, knowing in my heart of hearts that it's entirely untrue. I am not safe; I never have been. Dr. Veizer is wrong about me perceiving a threat that isn't there. The truth is that there is a threat to my life present, and it's me. I'm a danger to myself and anyone who is unlucky enough to come into my path. Everything I touch burns to the ground.

Not wanting to kid myself any longer, I stop repeating the affirmation and float lifelessly in the water for a minute. I don't want to drown in depression again, but no one ever taught me how to swim.

Once I'm out of the water and back in my towel, I continue walking in circles around the pool. Oddly enough, my hands and legs don't feel tingly anymore. Something about going from hot water to cold water, to warm air, I'm starting to feel... I don't know, calmer. I guess some of those self-soothing tricks Dr. Veizer taught me worked for once. Apparently, I just had to do them 50 million fucking times. I'm walking my seventh lap around the pool when I notice that a strand of my hair is dripping onto my shoulder. I put my fingers to my face and see that my eyeshadow smeared onto my fingertips. Ugh. I know I should probably be more concerned about the fact that I just blacked out and came to under water, and also kind of, sort of tried to drown myself, but all I can think about is that I got my hair wet and will now have to wash it, blow dry it, straighten it, curl it, then style it with my extensions before today's escapades.

I'm finishing my last lap when I come face to face with a big rose bush under the gazebo at the end of the pool. I stop in my tracks, my feet basically stapled to the grass. Every fiber of my being wants to walk away, but I don't. My stare grows deeper and deeper like a scalpel digging into my skin. The red roses on the bush slowly turn darker, shade by shade, until finally they're... black.

No.

My chest protrudes as my lungs catch my breath without my permission. I inhale grandly. I avert my eyes from the rose bush and speed walk back over towards the lounge chair. I reach into the leather bag sitting on it and pull out my phone. I hover my thumb over the home button but it's not reading it. *Stupid fucking phone.* This is my thumbprint, I swear. I flip my hand over and see that my skin has pruned into wet wrinkles. I wipe my right hand on my white towel then abandon the towel onto the ground. I type in my password three times until the screen unlocks. Even though I still have no notifications, I open the messages app anyway. Still nothing from the unknown number. Goddamnit. Why now? What does he want from me? I feel my hands start to tingle again.

"Buongiorno."

"Ah!" I yelp as my phone hits the hard limestone with a thud. I look up to see a dark-haired, olive-skinned stranger a few feet away from me. I squint my eyes; my eyelashes are still damp with salt water. It takes me a minute to place where I've seen this man before. The sun kisses the sweat on his pecks, on his nipples, and suddenly, I realize how I know him. This is the guy that works for my annoying neighbor, Beth, the one who's obsessed with peonies. My eyes tilt up and down over the man in front of me, wandering down his torso. Damn, he's even sexier up close. His chiseled six pack abs glimmer as if they were painted onto his stomach. His arms, swollen with muscles, look as if they want to wrap around my waist, lift me off my feet, and spin me like a merry-go-round. His shoulders look broad enough to carry the weight of my problems and all the baggage I've ever acquired on them. And his lips, oh my God, his lips. They look like they want to slide all the way from my neck down to my thighs. I feel a slight tingle, but it's not in my hands or legs this time. I lean in closer to take in the masterpiece in front of me, his eyes twinkle like stars in the summer sky. But not just any summer sky. His eyes look like what you see when you look up at the Alabama sky after a long day of washing all your problems away in the clear ocean water, losing yourself in the soft sand. I'm almost salivating while my mind dances with the thought.

Wait. Why the hell is this stranger on my property?

Once I fly out of Lilah Land and the Alabama sky, I take a step back and bend down to pick up my phone. "Um, hi, can I help you?"

"I, no. I— I help you," he says, his accent thick and poetic. Judging by the way he greeted me and the olive tint in his smooth skin; I'm assuming he's Italian. We went to the Amalfi coast for our honeymoon. I learned a little bit of Italian before we left so that I could get us around and order at restaurants without sounding like a southern hick. I know the greetings and how to say more wine, 'piu vino' but that's about it. What does he mean he'll help me? With what? I mean, I guess I could imagine a few things…

"Your hedges," he says, his voice firm, "I cut for you." He points over to the hedges beyond the gazebo, the hedges that are already low enough to have a full view into the fascinating world of Beth. I don't know what to say, and my cheeks are burning with flush and desire.

"Um, okay," I stutter, "Th— thank you."

Looking at this striking man in front of me, I realize that he's not as young as I thought he was. He looks about my age. Still, he's far too young for Beth. The only thing not prehistoric about Beth is her post-divorce boob job. *Boob job, wait, oh God.* I look down to see the black spandex squeezing my breasts, my entire chest exposed. It didn't even occur to me how I must look right now, black makeup smeared all over my face, half of my areola out in plain sight. I lean down and rip the towel off the ground, holding it to my chest. I take a palm to my cheek and wipe off the tar-like consistency that's caked onto it. I run a hand through my hair. My face is on fire, and I'm sure it's a nice shade of maroon by now.

"Uh, sorry," I grimace, utterly mortified. I look down at the ground, making sure my feet are still planted on it. I don't look up as I see the man's thick legs stepping closer to me until the tips of our toes kiss. I gradually roll my neck up, inch by inch. When my face finally meets his, his smoldering stare kidnaps me. His hair falls just to his shoulders, kissing his broad traps, tickling his clavicles. He squints his dark bedroom eyes at me, then he lifts his hand slowly. I watch as his hand makes its way up to mine, which is still clutching the towel. He gently wraps his fingers around the white towel and gingerly pulls it away. My dainty hand goes limp with zero protest. Once he removes the towel from my chest, he lets it fall onto the stone. I stand in front of him, still as a rock. I look down at the ground, letting him inspect each corner of my body, as I have done to his. I feel his eyes burning into my flesh, temptation streams through my blood. My eyes travel up his muscular thighs, fixing on the bulge bursting out of his gray work shorts. Excitement ignites between my thighs, screaming for more. Sweat drips down my bare chest as my lips part.

"Bellissima," he sings, his voice wispy.

My head jerks up. "Um, what?"

"Beautiful."

Chapter 12
Present Day

The searing water hits my red-tinted skin with a vengeance. I adjust my stance, shifting directly under the shower head as the pressure pushes on my scalp. I run my fingers through my golden hair, trying to wash all the salt water out. I wipe my hands over my eyes and gaze out the clear shower door, finding the His & Hers sinks that mock me with the illusion of a happy marriage. God, I need a drink. I haven't had a drink all morning, and I've detested every healthy second of it. The only reason I haven't drank yet is because I must brave the gang of polished Stepford wives at the country club today. I'm on the charity and event planning committee. My husband thought it would be a good project for me ever since I got fired and became a directionless loser. I have to say, it does force me out of the house once a week, a house that has slowly become my 3.2 million-dollar prison cell. They should honestly pad the walls in here. Thinking about spending the day with that motley crew of old-money hags and new-money trophy wives, I feel… I don't know, like my blood is going to boil over and spurt out of each one of my pores. Maybe I should have a drink, just one… or two. No, I can't, I have to drive there. Last week, I took an Uber, not wanting my vodka drenched hands on the wheel, running over every suburban zombie in this town. I thought I was being responsible, a good Samaritan. But, then Charlotte Vanderheiden, the president of the committee, saw me getting out of the back seat of an unfamiliar SUV. Ugh, Charlotte, she's everything Katherine hoped I would be. She's Christian, wealthy, pompous, popular, and completely devoid of a soul. When Charlotte saw me getting out of an Uber that day, she asked where my Range Rover was with suspicion. I told her it was in the shop, but she followed up by asking why I didn't take my husband's car. I panicked and told her that he had it with him overseas. Yeah, overseas, I really said that. Overseas, as if he drove his new Tesla through the Atlantic Ocean all the way to London. At least, I think he's in London, I honestly wouldn't know. After my colossal fuck-up of a lie, I overheard Charlotte gossiping to one of the other women on the committee. Their pearls sparkled in the hot southern sun as they traded conspiracy theories as to where my car really was. They eventually landed on bankruptcy, speculating that our cars were taken by the bank as assets. Damn, all I had wanted was a little liquid courage, how else was I supposed to sit at that same freshly clothed table with those same feckless shrews? It's decided, I'll stay sober until I get there then pace my martinis at the club. Although maybe I should have a little something while I get ready to calm my nerves. Surely, I don't want the ladies at the club to see me clenching my fists and repeating affirmations to myself to avoid a panic attack the whole day. So, maybe I will have just one, one shot to take the edge off.

No, I shouldn't. If I drink now then order drinks at the club, I'll be too buzzed to drive. I'd have to leave my car at the country club which may lead to more conspiracy theories. But what if I just had a glass of wine while I do my make up? Wine is barely even alcohol, that's what Mom always said. Do we have any white wine in the cellar? No. I can do this, I can stay sober for two more hours, it's only two more hours, then there's a light at the end of the tunnel, a pot of gold at the end of the rainbow. I'll bring a flask in my Gucci and take a shot before I walk in; the bar sometimes takes forever with our drinks.

I grab the purple shampoo off the shower shelf and squirt a comical amount onto my scalp. After getting this balayage and going a few shades lighter to a honey blonde color, purple shampoo is a must to keep the brass away. The hell if I'm going to look like a copper headed penny ever again. I guess not everybody hated it, at least *he* didn't.

I massage the shampoo into my hair with brute force, willing my brain to catch the train out of Lilah Land and travel to any other destination. I close my eyes and begin to recap the morning. That was strange today, the thing with Beth's gardener. His brown eyes all but licked every inch of my skin. He called me beautiful. *Beautiful.* Perhaps I'm reading into it, maybe he really did approach me to talk about trimming the hedges. He just wanted a job, I'm sure that's it. I guess we never negotiated payment. It's odd he didn't mention it. He didn't mention much at all, he just said he wanted to help me. But, with what? Probably just the hedges, but still, my mind wanders to an Italian island. My hand travels down between my thighs, the wetness between them is no match for the shower head above me. I begin to gently rub with three fingers, slowly, in wide circles. In my mind, I'm standing on an Italian beach.

I'm staring at the sunset on the horizon, my eyes burning from the beauty of the cotton candy sky. Suddenly, I feel two large hands on my hips. I savor the warmth of his palms until he yanks me into him, my butt gracing his manhood. He moves my hips back and forth, grinding on his thick bulge. He breathes deeply into my ear, tickling my neck, arousing me down below. I lift my hand up backward and rub it gently over his chiseled chest. I take my hand behind me and trace his entire body down, feeling each one of his washboard abs. I can almost taste the chills I'm sending up his spine. My touch falls below his abdomen and onto the bulge in his pants. I rub up and down until he grabs my hand with his, lacing our fingers together. He takes his other hand and cups my breast, massaging my nipple. He begins tracing little circles around my pink areola. I feel a spike of heat surge through me as he kisses my neck, tickling my sensitive skin with his stubble.

"Bellissima, Delilah," he whispers in my ear.

I swoon at the cadence of his masculine voice. I want to whisper his name back between quiet moans, but I don't know it. He trails his fingers lightly over the peach fuzz on my arm until he settles his hand on my other breast, massaging both with synchronicity. I close my eyes as his perfect, olive-skinned hand slides down my stomach. Rubbing all around my abdomen and my thighs, he teases me with bliss. I am starving for him, my lips are hungry. I feel my mouth start to salivate as my lips part slowly. He strokes up my thigh, grabs it, and nudges it out further in the sand, opening my legs. His fingers trace over me gently. I feel wetter than the ocean in front of us, and he savors each drop. He presses his fingers harder, the pressure shoots all the way up me as he moves his hand side to side. I feel a wave of ecstasy crash over my body. I open my eyes, wanting to look back into his until I'm captured by the view in front of me. The sunset is beaming over the ocean, making the teal ripples glow orange... my favorite.

And, suddenly, I see his face. I see *him*.

No.

I'm snapped back to reality by my windpipe gasping for air. I pull my hand out from between my thighs and yank the faucet all the way to the cold side. The temperature changes in an instant, the heavy stream like ice cold bullets piercing my skin. I force myself to stay under the shower head for as long as I can take it, then turn the water off. I sink down into a sitting position, hugging my knees to my chest. My hair feels like icicles on my shoulders. My body shaking profusely, I bring my head down onto my knees. I can't stay here long, but maybe, I can stay here for just a little while. Just a little while longer. I lay down on the wet shower floor and begin to hum a song; a song I was almost sure I had forgotten.

It's about 2:15pm when I finally smooth down my hair extensions, straighten my pearls, and slip on my Prada patent leather slingbacks. I take one last trip into my walk-in closet and look into the full-length mirror. I pull the neck of my dress up then pull the hem of the skirt down, not wanting to expose my chest or cellulite. I turn half-way to see my side profile. I rub a hand down my stomach, aching with disgust at how it protrudes slightly. I should have listened to my mom about all those cheese straws. I feel a rumble come from my stomach; it hits my hand like a boxer hitting a punching bag. *You look like shit, Delilah.* I brush my fingers over the scar on my abdomen. Pushing in the layer of fat on my stomach, I suck in as hard as

I can. I walk over to the dresser and take the Spanx out of the bottom drawer. I put my feet in the two holes then pull with all my might. They're barely over my hips when I realize that you can see the black Spanx under the white dress I'm wearing. I drop my hands, letting the Spanx squeeze my hips like a plastic bottle of ranch dressing. My God, these things are tighter than the prenuptial agreement my husband made me sign. I don't have any other Spanx, and I don't want to change my dress. I meticulously chose this white dress to create the illusion of a good, put-together, wholesome, innocent woman. Too bad I'm the furthest from all those things, but as Mom always said, it's important to dress for the role you want, not the one you have. I wanted to be a professional classical pianist on a big New York City stage. I didn't know how to dress for that though, maybe that's why things worked out the way they did. It's difficult to imagine that my dreams were once so big, and now, my only dream is to make it to 3pm without having a drink.

I slowly roll the tight Spanx down my hips and walk them over to the hamper. I take my light pink lipstick from my vanity and paint my lips with one last coat then walk back towards the full-length mirror. *The shoes*! Yes, it's the shoes, that's the problem. I slip off my Prada's and place them gently back into their place on the shoe shelf. I stare at the wall in front of me, the shelf taking up its entirety. I scan it from left to right like I'm reading a Sylvia Plath novel. That's a lot of freaking shoes, it's excessive. Nobody needs this many shoes. I should donate the ones that I don't wear to Goodwill. Who knows, maybe donating something to charity will make me feel good. I've heard that dedicating your life to a cause gives you meaning, or something like that. I walk over to the far-right side of the shoe wall and pick a pair of black Dior, low chunky heels. These are better, more modest, perfect for the crowd of heckling hens I'm about to break bread with, not that I've eaten a carb in over a decade. I slip into the new shoes and head back over to the full-length mirror. I brush my hair gently with my fingers, spreading it around my shoulders. I stare blankly at the woman in front of me, recognizing her wholly. But, today, when I look at her, I don't recognize her as Delilah. I recognize her, well, but as someone else. My stare grows deeper as I study her with intensity. She looks like… Katherine. I shake my head and turn away from the mirror. Walking back over to the vanity, I grab my phone off the charger. I unlock it with my thumb and see that I still have no new messages, and also, *fuck*. It's 2:30pm. I was supposed to be at the country club at this exact time. Fuck, fuck, fuck, fuck, fuck. *You are so fucking stupid, Delilah.* I grab my keys, throw them into my black Gucci with my phone and my flask, and high tail it out of the house.

Chapter 13
Present Day

I ignore the clicking sound my jaw makes as the warm Belvedere travels down my throat and splashes into my empty stomach. I can practically hear the vodka sloshing around inside me as I step out of my white Range Rover and hand my keys to the valet.

"Thank you," I shout over my shoulder.

"You are very welcome, ma'am."

I'm halfway to the colonial stairway when I hear the young man yell to me.

"Miss, if you need to leave your car here overnight, we can accommodate that for you. Anything you need."

A ball of embarrassment shoots from my knees up to my stomach where it explodes into a searing pain. I grab the pained area and turn halfway around. "Thank you," I utter, shakily. I'd love to be able to say, 'Thank you, though it will not be necessary' but who are we fucking kidding? It wouldn't be the first time I've stumbled out of this place, the maître d' having to call my husband to come pick me up. I need to be careful today, I know that, but I still need something to take the edge off. Something to still my shaky hands. Something to tape over the cracks in my brain. I have no idea how this afternoon is going to go or which one of my demons will decide to possess my body, vodka being the only priest able to exorcize it. A chill shivers over my head and swims through my blood all the way down to my feet. I can feel sweat welling up in my lace push-up bra. I pat my cheeks with my hand as I make my way up the stairs. My face is likely cherry red, my cheeks filled with rotten, sour juice. I breathe in through my nose and out through my mouth in a sequence. I take my phone out of my black Gucci to see if there are any messages. Still nothing. What do I do, block him? I suppose I could go to the police, but that would require being honest, and Lord knows that is out of the question. I sold my soul to the devil long ago, and if there's anything I've learned since then, it's that a soul is non-refundable. I reach into my purse to feel around for the flask when suddenly the large door in front of me swings open.

"Good afternoon, Ma'am. Welcome to the Richmond Hill Country Club."

I walk into the lobby and let out the breath I've been holding in for what feels like an eternity. I inhale the familiar scent of freshly groomed linen tablecloths and old mahogany wood. I look around at the old building I know far too well. Welp, this is going to suck.

I walk past the large French doors of the fireplace room which are ajar enough for me to see a group of men in crisp, tailored suits. Most of the men are holding glasses that have some variation of whiskey in them. Standing in a tight circle, one of the tailored suits looks up from his scotch and offers me a quick smile. I throw my head down towards the ground and saunter away from the French doors and woodsy aroma. When I finally walk into the main room, I'm shocked to see our usual meeting table empty. I look around the well-lit room. Did I get the date wrong? Am I wasted again? Wait, no, I only had one shot from the flask when I got here. Did they change the meeting place without telling me? Is this their way of kicking me off the planning committee? Panic blooms in my throat.

"Hey, Sugar," I hear a male voice whisper from behind me, "we're over here." He guides me with one hand on the small of my back while the other gestures to a table right by the clear picture windows leading to the patio and the golf course. I follow Sebastian over to the table of Chanel infused gaggling geese.

"Delilah, how nice of you to join us," the mother goose honks. Charlotte Vanderheiden gives me a smirk as she subtly chastises me. Her bright red hair is lit from the window behind her, wrapping around the back of her head like a halo. I glance slightly above her head to see gorgeous hills of greenery behind her that match her eyes. This would be a fantastic photo-op for Charlotte's Coalition of Savannah Republican Women Facebook page but fuck if I'm going to tell her.

"Um, sorry," I flounder, "I, uh, couldn't find y'all."

"Yes, well we saw you come in."

"The valet was slow as sin today, it took eons for one of the boys to approach my vehicle," one of the women chimes in, flicking her wrist downward. It seems rather odd to refer to a new Rolls-Royce Phantom as just a vehicle, but okay. The woman's eyes stay locked on mine. I believe her name is Dixie, or maybe it's Daisy. This isn't the first time Charlotte has embarrassed me in front of the group on one of her power trips. She needs to be in control, I wonder if that's why she only drinks sweet tea while the rest of us have real drinks. *Drinks*. God, I need a drink. I scan the white, round table, seduced by what everyone is drinking. I don't even have to look at Charlotte's place setting to know that she ordered her usual iced sweet tea. I glance next to her, to see Dixie or Daisy nursing a white wine. Judging by its color, it's a glass of dry Sauvignon Blanc. My eyes linger to the right of Charlotte to see Anastasia sipping on a fruity drink with a cherry in it that's probably 2% alcohol. It's only fitting considering she barely looks old enough to drink. Of course, she is sitting next to Charlotte, and she is doting on every word with wide Bambi eyes. Anastasia has been desperately seeking Charlotte's approval since the day she married the twice-divorced Arthur Turner, a wealthy real estate investor who does business dealings with Charlotte's husband. I'm sure Anastasia believes she's playing the long game, that the more she kisses Charlotte's ass, the more she'll build rapport. But, somehow, I don't see Charlotte putting an end to calling her a Russian-mail-ordered-bride behind her back. I look past Anastasia's boring fruity drink and have come face to face with a glass of dark red wine, I'm guessing Cabernet. The cabernet's host, Blanche Burton, is staring at the stem of her crystal glass, her eyes dull, her gray hair lifeless. From what I hear, she's changed quite a bit since she was widowed. Allegedly, she used to be spirited and vivacious. I once heard her described as the 'life of the party'. Looking at her now, it's hard to imagine her being the life of anything, and that makes me feel... I don't know, horribly sad. I trail past the other two glasses of white wine until my eyes lock on a martini. *Thank God.* It's clear, no signs of olive juice. There may be some vermouth in it, but if so, it's very little. The frost inside of it tells me that it's clearly been shaken, not stirred. My shoulders drop in relief when I see that the hand that picks up the martini glass belongs to Sebastian. I don't know him well, but his energy has always felt... I don't know, inviting. At least, it's more inviting than the rest of the judgmental pearl-clutchers at this table. Sebastian pulls out the empty seat next to him and I sink down to it in appreciation. I place my purse on the arm of my chair and flatten out the wrinkles in my dress. I peer back towards the window to see Charlotte still glaring at me, shooting daggers from her lime green eyes and breathing fire from her freshly blown out red hair.

"How darling of a day we're having," Sebastian turns to me, his voice colorful, "I just love that we're overlooking the golf course. This table is never open, but today, when I walked in, it was empty and I said, Lord, it's a sign. So, I went and snagged it faster than a one-legged man in a butt-kicking competition. I even told Anthony, that's the maître d', you know. I said, Anthony, if you want to move my big behind off this here seat, you're gonna need a forklift." Sebastian snorts as he grabs my shoulder and cackles at his own joke. The other women around the table giggle in unison. I look back at Sebastian and give him my most convincing smile and polite chuckle. I'm not sure if anything that Sebastian says is particularly funny, but the women find him amusing. Sebastian is the only man on the committee, and I'm pretty sure he's the only man who has made the cut in the history of the committee, not that many of the men in this town are vying to spend hours of their week arguing over raffle prizes

132

and gift baskets. But Sebastian is a different breed of southern gentleman. He's gay, for starters, one of the few openly gay men in this town, though I'm sure there are many men here that are hiding in their walk-in closets. Sebastian moved here from Louisiana a few years ago. One of the first things he told me about himself was that he's gayer than a Fifth Avenue Barney's display, and I kind of loved that. It's hard to find people who are willing to be themselves around here. Charlotte, however, seems to be less than a fan of Sebastian. I imagine she was a bully in high school, like one of those old-school bullies who would shove kids into lockers and put gum in girls' hair. If that was ever her, she hasn't changed much, she's just gotten smarter and sneakier. That's the thing about monsters, the real ones will never come out in the light of day, they'll hide in your shadow until you become too small to have one anymore.

I silently let out a sigh as I see Charlotte whip out multiple binders and folders that she's organized for a live fundraising auction. She hands a folder to Blanche, who I believe is our secretary, but she leaves the folder in front of her, untouched while she continues to stare at the stem of her wine glass. Charlotte hands another folder to Anastasia who… I'm not actually sure what her job on the committee is, but I'd say that her youth, long platinum hair, and pretty, Botox-less face bring up the group average. Anastasia scoops up the folder and flings it open with excitement. She studies the numbers on the piece of paper and nods, pretending to know what she's looking at. Dixie or Daisy takes a sip of her Sauvignon Blanc and looks at Charlotte with an expectant smile, but Charlotte doesn't hand her anything. Instead, she slams open her three-ring binder that has way too many tabs in it and asserts, "Okay, ladies, it is time to get down to business."

Wow, I didn't realize we were in the fucking CIA. I roll my eyes practically out of my skull, and they land, once again, on Sebastian's drink. He must catch my stare because he puts his hand on top of mine.

"Girl, let's get you a drink," his voice lulls into a whisper, "because there ain't a single bitch in this world that can tolerate this old hag sober."

I cover my grin with my hand. I chose the right seat today.

"Would you like something to drink, ma'am?" A voice asks from behind me.

"Get her a Belvedere martini, very dry, very cold. Shaken, not stirred, obviously, and uh, throw some stuffed olives in there, will ya, Sugar? God knows this skinny little thing ain't gonna touch those things," Sebastian says, pointing to the bowl of cheese straws in the center of the table. The way that Sebastian speaks, with just the right amount of sassiness and confidence, like he himself invented every word that's ever been spoken. I stare at him in awe. He kind of reminds me of—

"Um, excuse me y'all, if we can get back to the matter at hand," Charlotte squawks from her thin-lipped beak.

Ah, yes, the matter at hand. I forgot that the annual winter fundraiser for the country club, where one membership fee is already the price of a college tuition, is a life and death level matter. I didn't realize that we are filling all the mysterious holes within the Big Bang theory. Come to think of it, I doubt Charlotte even knows what that is, she seems like the epitome of a Creationist. My foot bounces on the ground anxiously as I keep my hands pinned to my side, willing myself to not play along to the smooth jazz melody softly caroling through the speakers. I let out a huge breath and keep my eyes glued on the table, ignoring the music and focusing on the voice speaking. Charlotte Vanderheiden's shrill mouth makes me want to stab a cocktail kingdom channel knife into my eardrum.

"Here you are ma'am." A waiter who looks young enough to be Blanche's grandson sets down a perfectly cold and crisp martini in front of me, olives stuffed to the brim with jalapeños. I couldn't possibly be more excited. The combination of Charlotte's evil spirit, Blanche's grief, and my sad girl routine has cast a gray cloud over this table that is darker than a David Foster Wallace novel. I pick up my drink from the top of the stem, squeezing it like a lemon so my shaky hands don't spill any of the precious liquid inside. I bring the glass to my lips. I open my mouth, and the clicking sound my jaw makes causes heads at the table to turn towards me. I pretend not to notice as I take the longest, most satisfying sip I have had in a long time. I keep the glass to my face as I look out onto the hills. A buzzing sound from my bag vibrates the table, and I nearly leap out of my chair.

"No phones at the table, Delilah."

Shit. It's him.

Chapter 14
Present Day

Slipping a $20 out of my Coach wallet, I slide it across the wood table.

"May I do my usual? In a tall glass, please."

"Right away ma'am."

The adolescent waiter does a quick take of the area around him before nonchalantly pocketing the twenty-dollar bill. This is why I love the bar in the east wing of the country club. I often sneak over here during our committee lunches on the pretense that I'm using the ladies' room to freshen up. It's more casual at this bar, less pretentious. It's only here that I can order 'my usual in a tall glass" and they know exactly what I mean: double Belvedere and club soda with ice, no lemon or lime, in a glass that's meant for water. The cocktail glasses at the country club are short, but the water glasses are tall which allows me to disguise my last drink or two of the afternoon as virgin, the only thing I've ever been able to disguise as such. Most of the women on the charity committee tend to get buzzed and loose lipped halfway into their second drink. Anastasia gets dull-eyed and giggly after three sips of her first cocktail, for Christ's sake. I do not share that quality. It takes a hell of a lot more than two, three, four or even five drinks to make me feel normal. *Why are you like this, Delilah?*

"Here you are ma'am."

"Thank you so much," I say, sliding another $20 directly into the young waiter's hand. A smile pulls at the corners of his mouth. He looks so youthful, so innocent, so unknowing of how unkind the world can be. I hope he never finds out. I give him a warm smile in return and head out towards the patio overlooking the golf course, desperate for a minute to myself.. I cannot hear Charlotte's shrill roar right now nor can I handle the chattering fake laughs, the flat southern smiles, or the sounds of forks and knives scraping on glass plates. I turn the handle of the door and gasp the clean air of freedom. Immediately, the social bricks that were weighing on my shoulders fall to the ground, breaking on the hard rock patio. I can breathe again. Sensory sensitivity is what Dr. Veizer calls this. I think she said it's when your senses become overstimulated so much that your body can't process it and you feel like you're going to crumble or explode. She says it's a normal thing for someone with social anxiety. She said that fresh air and quiet can help. I take a sip of my fake water from the straw floating inside of it and allow the salvation to trickle down my throat, delivering my mind from Charlotte's evil. From the outside, I'm sure I look the same as the rest of the cackling hens on the club planning committe. Eh, who am I kidding? I am the same. I'm nothing but a washed-up, old housewife with nothing better to do than sip drinks and pretend to eat in the middle of the day with a table of women cut from the exact same cloth as I. Each set of their eyes may as well be mirrors reflecting my past, present, and future. It's imbecilic of me to think that I am any different from them. Although, I'm not sure that any of the women on the committee are carrying the secrets that I am. I doubt any of them go to therapy. I doubt any of them have restricted numbers threatening them over text message. I doubt any of these women jump every time they hear a small noise. And I definitely doubt that any of these women have ever loved someone as hard as I have.

Suddenly, a voice breaks into my thoughts.

"Well fancy meetin' you here!"

I hear Sebastian's long drawl to my left. He's seated at the very edge of the patio, his Armani loafers dangling above the turf. He has a cigar firmly planted between his fingers. I rock back on my heels and observe the area around me. Other than the polo-wearing golfers in the distance, there's no one in sight.

"Don't worry, the brigade is busy going over numbers. Our dictator is laying into the Russian one about some miscalculated costs of chairs or this, that, and the other. I feel bad for the young girl, I think that poor thing is dyslexic or somethin'. I don't know why on God's good earth she insisted on being the committee's treasurer, she's useless as gum on a boot heel."

I put my fist to my lips, trying to hide my chuckle. I have noticed that Anastasia seems to invert numbers when she's copying them down, but I never wanted to say anything. Again, we are not cracking cold case murders or operating on brains, we are raising money for a country club that already profits more than most businesses in the South. I'm sure the world would go on without us.

"Bless her heart though, she's a sweet little thing. Her elevator don't go all the way up, is all." Sebastian stares me up and down, "you get yourself another drink?"

"No, well... yes, but it's— it's just water." My eyes are cartoonish with fear.

"I see. Well, don't just stand there, pop a squat, Sugar."

I look back through the big, picture windows. I can see the stern force of Charlotte's teaching finger and the frustrated crease in between Anastasia's eyebrows. The other women at the table continue to sip their wine in total ennui. I sigh and walk over to Sebastian, delicately lowering myself to the ground.

"I didn't know you smoked cigars."

"Why would you think that? Church going gay boys can't smoke a manly cee-gar?"

"No— I— I just meant, um..."

"Relax, Sugar. I'm just messin' around with ya. Besides, I don't know why cee-gars are a masculine straight guy thing," he holds up his cigar, "having your mouth wrapped around something that's shaped like this? Why, there ain't nothin' gayer than smoking a cee-gar."

Laughter fills my gut as my back hunches. I set my drink to my right and shift on the patio ground with more comfort. I point to Sebastian's cigar. "If that's the size of what you normally wrap your lips around, then I think you need to expand your dating pool."

"Damn girl," he says playfully. "You'd be surprised. I dove and dove into that dating pool for way too long. And let me tell ya, some of these boys done have some messed up junk."

We both giggle as a cool fall breeze flows through the space between us. There's something about Sebastian that feels so... I don't know, comforting. He's not like anyone else on the committee.

"Anyway, I thank God every day for my husband. He rescued me from that dirty cesspool. Plus, he's hung like an Ox."

I smile, catching my reflection in his round eyes. "How long have y'all been married?"

"Why, it's been almost two years now. Two magical years," he cheers with bliss. His eyes might as well be shaped like hearts.

"That's wonderful," I say through my teeth, attempting to hide my envy. Two magical years. I remember that phase, it *was* magical, until a hawk ripped my heart out and flew away with it. I can feel it getting further and further every day.

"Yeah, I'm a lucky boy."

"Do you have any kids?"

"Ugh, hell to the no. Disgusting," Sebastian sticks his tongue out. "Babies are for bored people… and poor people."

I laugh, "I'm sure a lot of the well-off women in this town would beg to differ."

"Don't I know it, Honey. I'm forced to live it in every restaurant I walk into, every store. Babies wailing everywhere. It's an epidemic. I look at so many folks in this town and I think, well, that person should not be breedin'. It should be mandatory that certain people get fixed like dogs."

"Certain people like…"

"Like our tyrant, Charlotte Vanderheiden? Yes, that's the one. She has her nose so high in the air, she could drown a rainstorm. But have you met her three sons? Demons straight from hell, each one worse than the last." Sebastian's hand flies around the crisp air.

"Well, luckily for us, Mama Menopause will be coming for her soon if it hasn't already."

"You said it, girl. I'm sure her husband is tired of sleeping with her anyhow. That old hag's got cobwebs in her snatch."

My jaw practically drops onto the golf course below us, and Sebastian puts both of his hands on his cheeks.

"Oh, I am so bad. Excuse my naughty tongue. My mama taught me better than to speak such profanities in front of ladies."

"Oh, don't worry. I'm no lady."

"Good, don't ever become one." Sebastian takes a big puff of his cigar. "Anyway, how about you, Sugar? You and your husband got any demons of your own?"

"Uh, what?"

"Kids, Honey. Are you somebody's mama?"

Nausea swirls in my stomach and floods my diaphragm. Salt begins to sting my eyes as liquid leaks out of the corners. I focus on the hill in front of me as I swallow the vomit that has intruded into my throat. I can feel Sebastian's glare on the side of my red cheek.

"You okay, Sugar?"

I choke down my entire being. "Yeah." I wipe my bottom eyelashes. "Just... allergies."

"Tis the season. That's the only bad part about fall here."

I pick up my glass and suck the straw as hard as I can. "Anyway, I—uh, I don't. Kids, I mean. I'm— I'm not a mother."

"Good, don't ever become one," he repeats himself then continues on, "yeah, no rug rats for me, no Ma'am. I do adore being married though. I haven't even thought about being unfaithful since the day we said I do, not once, and that's a first for me."

"Yeah?"

"Oh yes, Honey. Like I said, my husband is hung like an ox and he's richer than God. I'd be a dang fool to give up a man like that, the life he gives me. I know when I got it good, and Sugar, I got it good. When I met Jeremy, he was already a millionaire. I was frying bacon at a Waffle House. Can you believe that?" Sebastian wipes his forehead with the back of his hand.

"Sounds like he worked hard."

"Oh please. The only thing that worked hard for Jeremy's money was his mama's hooha spitting him out 40 years ago. He was born into it like most of the spoiled brats in this town. Some of us aren't so lucky, some of us have to work for opulence like this."

"Is that what you did?" I ask. Maybe I shouldn't have, I don't want to pry, but he's suddenly revealed himself as the most interesting person I've met in a long time.

"Hell yeah, I did. But not by flipping the best burgers or folding the neatest omelets. With no money for a fancy degree, I had to *really* work for it." Sebastian takes a long drag of his cigar and stares down at his loafers. The usual color in his face seems drained by melancholy. I know I should probably politely change the subject and head back inside to the rest of the women, but my curiosity is yanking on me harder than my extensions are yanking on my hair.

"So then, how did you do it?"

He sighs, keeping his head down. "Oh, it's not the prettiest of stories. There was lots of champagne, nice designer gifts, parties on yachts."

"Doesn't sound so bad."

"But there was also lots of men, lots of bad men. Lots of drugs, lots of booze. Jeremy, he saved me from all that." Sebastian suddenly perks up and swings his face to meet mine. "Speaking of, can I have a lil swig of that flask? I'll trade you the rest of this cee-gar."

"What? I, I don't kno—"

"The flask, the one you keep in your purse. I saw it sparking like a diamond in the sun peeking out of your Gucci today... and in your Louis last week, and your Chanel the week before."

"Okay, okay," I cut him off. I zip open the gold zipper of my Gucci and pull out the flask. I rush it down to my side and quietly sneak it into Sebastian's hand. "It's a little warm, sorry."

"It don't matter to me none." He twists the silver cap and downs a double shot. When he sighs in relief and the color comes back to his face, I see that he and I are way more alike than I thought.

"So, how did you know it was a flask in my purse? It could have been anything shining in there."

"Oh, Sugar. I got your number. You and I are cut from the same cloth, I knew it the moment I met you. I could see it straight away in your eyes, the way they're afraid to meet anybody else's. I could tell, Lord, this woman has seen the rain."

"The rain?"

"Yeah, the rain, the bad stuff. You've seen it, I can tell. You're not like these judgmental, empty-headed tramps. The most pain these women see comes from a Botox needle."

I keep one hand on my jaw as I take a sip of my drink. I'm hoping that my hand will keep my jaw in place enough to not make a clicking sound. I've gone this long without having to explain it, I'm not about to change that now. I take a sip and hear the click, but Sebastian doesn't seem to notice. I hold the cold glass in my lap, swirling what's left of the ice. "Yeah, they're kind of the fucking worst."

"You said it, Honey. But that's okay. I can deal with anyone for the status that being on this committee gives me. If only my mama could see me today. Women like that would have never given her the time of day, she was their servant, a faceless cog in their machines. I never wanted to be like that. So, if it takes sucking on catty Charlotte's tit like a baby cow and dealing with red wine-teeth miserable Mildred, then that's what it takes."

I can't help but laugh a little. "You mean Blanche?"

"Ugh, does it matter?" Sebastian passes the flask back to me and I quickly stuff it in my purse. "Anyhow, I know the part these here women want me to play. The flamboyant token gay that they can use to make them look chic and woke, as the kids say. I'm good for a laugh or two, and I'm fine with that. I know my role."

"So, that's the price you're paying?"

"Exactly, you get it. Nothing comes free in this world, especially not in this town." Sebastian's expression grows sullen again, and I'm realizing that this may be the first time I'm seeing him, the real him, not the persona he puts on for the ladies-who-lunch. "But, as they say, there are no small parts, just small actors," the vibrance comes back into his voice as he frames his face with his hands. And, just like that, the persona returns.

"So, who is the real you then? The real you when you're not playing a role?"

Sebastian sticks his hand out in response, and I instinctually grab the flask out of my purse and hand it to him. He unscrews the top and swallows the vodka hard. "Oh, Sugar. I'm just a gay kid from the Louisiana bayou who got picked on in school for the way my voice sounded. I lived in a double wide for most of my life with a mama who could barely afford a loaf of bread because all the men in her life were dead beat hillbillies without a pot to piss in. I prayed and prayed and prayed to God for things to be different until I realized that he wasn't gonna answer me until I answered myself. So, I went out and found a different path than my mama's. It wasn't easy. Lord, I have my demons. I have my ups, my downs. I can flood hell with light when I'm happy and drown heaven in darkness when I'm sad. But, like you said, everything comes with a price to pay, at least this one comes with a mansion on the water, a home movie theatre, and full-time access to a spa with a sauna." Sebastian hands the flask back to me and motions for me to take a sip. Looking down at my nearly empty glass, I happily oblige and take a swig.

"Anyhow, look at me, goin' off like a heard of turtles, I must be boring you to tears." Sebastian folds up the sleeves on his Hugo Boss button down. "Well, I am just sweatin' like a pig on the Fourth of Ju-ly."

I let out a small snort and cover my bared teeth. His Louisianan sayings remind me of what I used to call my mom's 'Katherinisms'. Suddenly, a ripple of sorrow rushes through me and a lump accumulates in my throat. I feel like... I don't know, like I miss her, maybe. *Ew.* I take another small sip then put the flask back in my purse and zip it tightly. I'm about to suggest to him that we go back inside to make the last few minutes of the meeting when I see Sebastian dabbing his cigar in the ashtray on his left. The inside of his arm is in full view, and I notice a bunch of red and purple marks tainting his pale skin. They're too big to be cuts, maybe they're burns. My mind shivers a little. My eyes flicker back to his cigar then back to his arm. That's when I notice the red marks on his arm are in the shape of fingerprints. It's a hand mark. Someone must have grabbed him…. hard. Really hard. I remember the tune to that song. Sebastian moves the ashtray behind him and turns back towards me. He must see my eyes lingering on his arm because he follows my line of sight and rips his sleeve down with force. He stares, expressionless, out at the golf course, like he's waiting for me to ask. Should I? It's none of my business.

"Is that the real price you're paying?" I blurt out. There I go, always wrong, even when I'm right.

Sebastian sighs with a familiar heaviness. "I guess it is."

"Is— is it worth it?"

"I don't know, Sugar. It's not that simple."

"It's not?"

"Not as simple as what I saw my mama go through day in and day out. Useless men beating her silly, bloodying her lip every dang night. Always taking from her, never giving a dime in return. Jeremy is nothing like that. He's successful, charming, giving, and thoughtful. He has a temper, sure, but it's not like he beats the shit out of me, pardon my language." Sebastian flicks back his short hair with his hand, and I can tell he's about to put the act back on. "I'm no battered housewife, Honey, that's for sure, just a rich one. I should have my own show."

"But…" I probably should let it go, but for some reason, I can't. "He's hurting you, isn't that simple enough?"

"Oh Sugar, the world is not that black and white."

"It's not?"

"No." Sebastian sighs as his lips grow sympathetically flat. He rubs my shoulder with his hand, like he's just had to tell me bad news that I didn't already know, like that Santa isn't real. I try with all my might to force a frown, but I can't tame the smile that stretches on my lips. Sebastian's face lights up in response.

"What?" He asks, excitedly.

"Nothing, it's just… It's nothin'."

We're saved by the bell with the ding of a phone. I jump and scramble towards my purse. I riffle through it to find my phone and open it as fast as I can. I look at the screen and see I don't have any new text messages, just the unopened one from my liquor delivery service during the meeting.

"Ah, Grindr notification. Ooo hot new single in my area is down to get teabagged," he sings, flicking his hand and waving his phone around.

"Um, I thought you said you were never unfaithful to your husband."

"And I thought you said that was just water in your glass."

I look down at my empty cup and shrug in omission. He's good.

"Word of advice, Sugar, don't trust any hoe in this town, not even me."

"Touché."

"Come on," he says, rising to his feet, "I'll drive you home."

"But I—"

"I'm sure you're fine to drive but you cannot mess with these cops on Main Street, they're looking for any reason to pull you over and breathalyze you. Jeremy has an in with the new sheriff though, so I'm untouchable," he flaunts. "Come on, we'll sneak out around the side of the banquet room then text the table of coquettes that we needed to go walk your dog or something. The valet won't mind keeping your car here over night."

"But I don't have a dog."

"Well, then bitch, get one, I don't know. Let's go. I have to dip my you-know-whats in a hot Australian's chops."

I sigh and laugh at the same time, climbing to a standing position, abandoning my glass on the outdoor table next to me. I follow Sebastian inside and tiptoe with him around the side of the banquet room, winding up in the front lobby. I pull the hem of my skirt down and straighten my pearls. I walk out the big French doors of the country club and head down the colonial stairs.

Chapter 15
2009- Richmond Hill, Georgia

I trudge up the steep colonial stairs and walk through the big French doors of the country club. I close my eyes as the smell of cigar smoke infiltrates my sinuses. I approach the front desk to see a familiar faux smile.

Anthony, the maître d' of the main dining room, nods at me. "Right this way, Miss Monroe." He gestures for me to follow him down the hallway towards the east wing and I oblige.

We pass the fireplace room, my curiosity peaked as usual. Women aren't allowed in there. As my dad says, 'the fireplace room is for the men who make the money, not the women who spend it'. We pass the main bar and the main dining room, the banquet hall, the bathrooms, until we arrive at the east wing bar, just as I had assumed we were headed. I scan the wooden bar top. I lose count of the empty martini glasses on the counter holding nothing but untouched olives. I trace the row of glasses along the bar then tilt my line of vision up to their drainer.

"What are *you* doing here? This is the east wing, no kids allowed," my mom slurs. Anger breaks through her Botox, wrinkling her forehead and the space between her brows.

"Thank you, Anthony," I say with my head down, avoiding eye contact.

He nods and exits out the back door towards the golf course.

"What do you want, Lilah?"

Lady Katherine is still as elegant as ever in her white tweed Chanel skirt-suit. I catch a whiff of what she's drenched in today. The vodka odor is the same as usual, but the perfume is new, maybe Marc Jacobs? I imagine she is, yet again, hoping that the new scent will attract my dad like a moth to a flame. I don't understand why it's always perfume that she uses as a seduction tactic. Perhaps it's because she can't possibly get any more plastic surgery than she already has without looking like Frankenstein's monster, a look quite a few housewives in this town proudly sport. God, please don't ever let me become like any of these women.

My attention draws back to Lady Katherine who looks less lady-like than usual with her elbows resting on the bar top, her frail arms barely holding her up. My eyes dart to the freshly shaken martini that's placed down in front of her by a bartender she's undoubtedly been torturing for the past few hours.

"Paging Delilah? Earth to Delilah?" Mom mocks. "Oh, don't mind her, Darlin'," she says to the bartender, "she's got her own little world up there, under that horrific orphan Annie orange hair."

"Thanks for reminding me," I roll my eyes and take the bar seat next to her. I press her fresh martini to my lips. I nod to the bartender, and he begins to make another.

"I am done with your father, you hear? My goose is cooked."

"I figured something was going on, that's why I came, to pick you up."

"And, how did you know I was here then?" Mom attempts to inspect my face, but her light eyes are too glazed over to focus.

"Anthony called the house," I hesitate, "he— he thought you might need a ride home."

"Ugh, Anthony," she scoffs, "nosy as ever, that one. People 'round here need to start minding their own dang business."

Lady Katherine is Richmond Hill's most esteemed queen of gossip, but okay. Did you hear Jennifer Wilson is having an affair with her husband's business partner? Because I have. Did you hear that Mr. and Mrs. Campbell are swingers? Because I have. Did you hear that Mom's weird friend from church married her cousin? Because I have. Lady Katherine told me right before telling everyone else she's ever known. Mom spouts that gossiping is a sin, but I suppose Jesus has different rules for her.

"So, um, what happened with Dad?" I regret asking before the words slip between my teeth.

The bartender sets a fresh martini down in front of Katherine. The crystal glass looks colder than her heart. She picks it up from the base and takes a big gulp.

"That man, he is rotten to the core. I tell ya, my goose is cooked."

"Yeah, you said that already."

"Do you know where he is right now? Your father, the great William Monroe? He's rolling in the hay with tramps and floozies. He's probably got more than one at a time. That man, born in sin, raised in sin. He's gon' die in sin." Mom laces her fingers together into a prayer position. "But the man who committed adultery is an utter fool, for he destroys himself."

I assume that's a bible quote considering she whipped out her drunken preacher voice. It's a typical occurrence when she's all greased up with vodka. Though, I can't recall the last time she wasn't. I'm fairly confident that she spikes her coffee in the mornings. I could muster up a decent response, but I'm sure anything that comes out of my mouth will be wrong. Still, I feel… I don't know, like I'd say anything just to make her feel better even if it's wrong.

"Mom," I sigh, "Dad's not cheating, or… he's not committing adultery. He wouldn't do that, he loves you." My teeth chatter at her chilling stare. I look away and take a sip of my martini, hoping she didn't catch the lie in my beady eyes. After a few long seconds of silence, I turn back towards her, and to my surprise, she's laughing. It's a diabolical, bone shivering laugh.

"Oh, Darlin', don't you play dumb with me. You don't need to cover up your father's sins. I know he's y'all's favorite."

"That's not true."

"But you don't know that man like I do. 20 years. 20 miserable, worthless, wasted years."

"I'm sure they weren't all bad, we've had some good times, you know, as a family."

Mom picks her heavy head up and gives me an unconvinced look. "Like what?"

Fuck. I dug myself into a hole. I search over each part of my twisted mind for some shred of family bonding or wholesome memories. Mom shakes her head with a sarcastic laugh.

"Oh, oh, that time we went to the county fair and Liam entered the peach pie eating competition then went on that teacup ride with his crush and hurled all over her."

Mom rolls her blue eyes.

"Then you and I went into that haunted house they had that year, and you slapped a zombie in the face for sneaking up on you!"

Mom chuckles and chokes a little on her vodka. She turns to me and has a warm smile on her face, a look I thought I'd never see again. "Well, I have no patience for someone who claims to rise from the dead. Only our Lord and savior can do that."

"Yeah, well, that was a fun day. We all had fun, ya know, as a family."

"You and I had fun," she corrects me, holding up her finger, "your dad spent the whole day hitting on some carnie slut running the ferris wheel."

The bartender stops in his tracks and stares at Lady Katherine like a deer in headlights. I grab his stare with my eyes and give him a little head shake, hoping to clairvoyantly tell him to mind his own business if he wants to keep that attractive baby face intact. He turns away from us and begins to polish glasses that are already sparkling.

"You don't know that he was flirting, and you don't know that he's doing anything now."

"Oh yes ma'am, I do."

"How?"

"Because I called his office today, thinking that maybe, just maybe we could have lunch together for the first time in five years. When I called, that 20-something-year-old hussy assistant of his told me he wasn't in, said he was having lunch with some investors at the country club. I could smell it. Something wasn't right. I could hear that harlot laughing on the other end of the phone. So, I drove down here to give him the benefit of the doubt, like a good wife. And when I got here, sure enough, no William Monroe in sight. Anthony said he hasn't been here all day and he doesn't have any lunch reservations. So, Daddy's girl, where do you reckon he was?"

Anxiety pinches my throat with nails sharper than the knives the bartender is now polishing. I feel... I don't know, so fucking sad for her. She wanted to have lunch with him. I know better than anyone that Katherine is not always easy to be around, but she's trying. There's clearly some part of her that wants to save their marriage. Why can't Dad see she's making an effort? I shouldn't be surprised. For as much of a genius as William Monroe is, he's an absolute idiot. He only sees what he wants to see, which apparently is an assistant, not much older than Liam or me, named Tiffany. I want to say something, anything to get that warm smile back on my mom's lips. I didn't know how much I missed it until I saw it again.

"Um, well maybe there's an explanation. Like, maybe he was going to meet investors at the country club but then changed the plan. Maybe they decided to go to a different restaurant or meet at a different office."

Mom's lips form a thin line. "Or maybe he's bumping uglies with that teenage hooker at his office, or at the local college doing the dirty in some filthy dorm room. That's what he wants, that's what all of them want, some perky, bubbly, nubile sex doll less than half their age. They don't want…" Mom turns her head away from me, towards the window. I hear a small whimper that she immediately hushes with the vodka she pours down her throat. I sigh and put my hand on top of her cold fingers, but she pulls her hand away. I watch her squeeze her eyelids shut like reality doesn't exist as long as she doesn't open them. I want to tell her how beautiful she is, as much as she's always been. I want to tell her that she's sharp and witty and formidable. I want to tell her how much I admire her efforts to fight for her marriage, the different perfumes, the weekly hair blowouts, the failed lunch date. I want to tell her that she's worthy of happiness, that she's worthy of love. But we've been down this road before, and there's no highway to reconciliation. We all know my dad cheats on her, religiously, like more religious than the churches in this town. Usually, ignorance is bliss and Mom is able to look the other way. But having blatantly caught him like a spider in its own web, she can't exactly turn a blind eye this time.

I sigh and scoot my empty martini glass towards the edge of the bar. "Come on, let's get out of here. I'll drive us home and make you a real drink."

Mom laughs a little under her breath. "Ugh, please, Darlin'. These over-vermouthed drinks are for toddlers. You should serve this in a sippy cup." Mom empties her glass into her esophagus. She pulls herself off the chair and stands up straight. She grabs her lambskin quilted black Chanel purse and looks at me with defeat in her light blue eyes.

"Maybe we can watch a movie or something. We haven't done that in forever. We can watch something nice. Nothing with zombies you have to slap, I promise."

She smiles again, and the tears in her eyes drip onto my soul, drowning my cracked heart.

"Maybe we can watch Fried Green Tomatoes, it was your favorite as a girl."

"Yeah, Mom, that sounds nice."

I grab her by the hand and lead her down the hallway towards the lobby.

Chapter 16
2009- Richmond Hill, Georgia

I blast Kelly Clarkson as loud as my speakers can handle. My jean skirt squeezes my narrow hips with a vicious vendetta. I stride over to my keyboard and play along with the melody. I pound on the keys like each one of them is my enemy. Drowning out the sounds of my parents' screams became a skill I had no choice but to master over time. But tonight... tonight is different. I knew that there would be some sort of reckoning, some hell that Dad would have to pay for being caught in a lie when he came home, if he came home. But Mom seemed to be in such a state of exhaustion that she was acting... nice. And, it felt... I don't know, nice. It was like the fight in her was gone, like that dark passenger that normally overtakes her drunken body had been evicted. I was even able to get her to eat some popcorn, only two handfuls, but still. When she passed out at the part where Ruth dies in Fried Green Tomatoes, I was sure that tonight would be a relaxing, quiet Friday. I was just putting the Wizard of Oz disk in the DVD player when Mom's head shot up at the sound of the garage door closing. Then, I knew the storm was here to wash over the calm, and I would get swept up in the cyclone just like Dorothy.

I turn my keyboard off and tiptoe over to my full length mirror. I sink down onto the carpet and smudge my eyeliner with the little sponge on the other side of the pencil. My heart jumps at the sound of a crash. Fuck. What was that? Mom probably just threw a plate. Dad is seasoned enough to dodge incoming kitchenware with precision by now. My room is right above the kitchen, so I'm used to being privy to the nightly riffraff. Once upon a time, it made me sad when they fought, and scared, but there's only so many times that you can feel sad and scared until it becomes normal, another day at the office. I hear another crash over my Dad's beastly roar. Damn. I thought that having the Garcia's in our guest house would cause my parents to be on their best behavior. But that was before Mom spoke to Dad's young assistant today. I wonder if he has the energy to deny the cheating at this point, but I hope he at least has the decency to. I flip open my phone and see that it's already 8:30pm. I've got to get going. I wasn't planning on going to Mia's party tonight. I had texted her that I was taking care of Katherine as usual. Mia understood, being that she's witnessed just how passionate my mom is about the stiffness of her cocktails. Alas, my quiet evening got interrupted by the black parade, the one that marches through this house any night in which both of my parents are drunk… which is every night ever. My phone buzzes.

Philly: Be there in 5, don't make me wait
Delilah: K! <3

The heart was probably too much, but I can't help it. I'm elated, practically floating, even with the horror movie occurring below me. I flip my phone shut and put it in my Juicy Couture purse. I close it with the J zipper and hang it on my arm.

A minute or so after Dad had walked through the door tonight, Mom lunged towards him. I retreated to my room and grabbed my phone from its charger. I couldn't believe my eyes when I saw the text from Philly telling me he wanted me to come to Mia's. It was such a sweet gesture, and it couldn't have come at a better time. It was like he knew I was having a bad night and wanted to save me from this hell I call home. Philly is good like that, he's so intuitive. He even offered to give me a ride. I think tonight is the night, the night where we finally do it, like for real this time. We tried it once before, a few months ago. At first, I was scared, but Philly worked really hard to convince me. It hurt like hell, and I wanted to stop the whole time, but I was set to power through it because I knew he wanted it. He's had sex a bunch of times before, at least he says he has. Come to think of it, he didn't know how to put on a condom. It's not like we have sex-ed classes in our conservative, southern high school. He had to read the directions on the back of the pack while I lay there naked, trying to cover my chest so that he wouldn't see how flat it was without a push-up bra. When we finally started, a rocket of nerves launched through me. But I savored the closeness of our faces, the entanglement of our legs, the warmth of his chest on mine. I looked up into his black, sparkling eyes, distracting myself from the pain that was beginning to feel kind of okay. A smile crept onto my lips at the fantasy of staring into those eyes for the rest of my life. I grabbed the back of his sweaty neck to bring his face to mine for a kiss, but he pulled away instantly. He lifted his body off of mine, looked down and yelled that I was bleeding. He screamed at me for not telling him that I was on my period, but I wasn't. I had two whole weeks until my next period. I didn't understand why there was blood. I get why he was mad and repulsed, that's disgusting. I never would have done it if I knew I would bleed. But then, when I told Mia about it, she said that it happens on the first time. She swore to me that it wouldn't happen again, it's just a first time thing. God, I hope she's right. Having that happen again would be humiliating. I need tonight to go perfectly, the car ride, the party, the sex… Well, maybe sex. If it goes well enough, I think Philly will finally put a label on us. He's been extra sweet lately, and I think it's time. Philly is the one, I know it in my heart of hearts. This is the man I am going to marry.

I douse myself in my Pink Sugar perfume. After a last look in the mirror, I turn off Kelly Clarkson, walk out my bedroom door and head down the spiral staircase. I try my best to tip toe straight to the front door, avoiding the kitchen. I'm three feet from the door when I hear my dad's booming voice to the left of me. I guess they graduated from fighting in the kitchen, and they are now fist-to-cuffs in Dad's study. My hand is on the knob of the front door when I hear my mom let out a loud, high pitched, earth-shattering cry. *Shit*. I can't leave her like this. Maybe I can help diffuse the situation. I turn to my left and walk into the study. I see my dad sitting at his desk, holding a glass of scotch with one hand and spinning his gold globe with the other. My eyes travel over to my mom who is on her knees in front of the bookcase, she's hunched over and hyperventilating. Her long, dark hair is plastered around her face. She can't catch her breath. Did he punch her in the stomach?

"Mom, are you okay?"

"Oh, shut up, she's fine. Once a pageant queen," he mocks, "now just a fucking drama queen." Dad rolls his eyes and takes a sip of his scotch.

"You are evil! He is evil! Do you see this?" Mom grips the side of her stomach and continues to yell. "This is who he is!

An evil, disgusting man who hits his own wife. He's a liar and a cheater!"

"Anyone would cheat on you!" Dad yells back, his Pittsburg accent peeking through. He rises off his chair and circles around his desk towards the bookcase. "You're a washed up, worthless bitch who spends all my money and has never worked a day in her life. You have no respect. I'm your fucking meal ticket. You're a freeloader, a waste of space." William towers over my mom with his glass in the air. "Here, Katherine. Why don't you have another drink? Drink yourself to death for all I care, the world will be a better place without you."

He flips his wrist and dumps his whole glass of scotch on top of her head then throws it at the wall, shattering it along with my mom's dignity. She screams a guttural scream that makes each one of my organs vibrate. She grabs her hair with her hands and sobs on her knees.

"Jesus fucking Christ, Dad, what's wrong with you?" The words come out before I can stop them.

"What's wrong with me?" His volume turns up. "What's wrong with me! I'm the one who puts a roof over your head and food in your mouth. I'm the one that buys you all your stupid designer clothes and pays for those ear bleeding piano lessons of yours. What's wrong with me?" Veins pop out of his neck, accompanying the beat red fire that has flamed up to his face. I turn in the doorway and shake my head.

"Fuck off," I mumble under my breath.

"What did you say to me?" Dad lunges towards me and I quickly slam the office door. I sprint towards the foyer and run out the front door. When I see Philly's Beemer, I take a deep breath and try to walk as casually as possible, praying to God that my dad doesn't chase me into the front yard and drag me back inside by the hair. It's happened before. I yank open the passenger side door and climb in.

"Sup? You look hot," Philly says with more ease and charm than Gene Kelly. A breath of fresh air flows over me, or maybe that's just the blaring air conditioning. All I know is that all of the sudden, the sun comes out. I stare at Philly's sparkling black eyes and smooth skin the entire car ride, pinching myself to not say 'I love you' with each mile. He is so damn gorgeous, and smart, and sweet, and absolutely nothing like either of my parents. William Monroe has always been a morally corrupt human, but the way that he degraded my mother tonight, he's gone too far this time. I will never be treated like that by a man. Never.

Chapter 17
2009- Richmond Hill, Georgia

Mia's basement looks the same as it always does, nice long couches, expensive carpets that have subtle bleach stains on the spots we've spilled drinks on. Link passes me a bottle of Captain Morgan. I don't know what kind of liquor this is, whiskey maybe? It doesn't matter. I take a swig from the bottle and pass it back, forgoing the diet coke in front of me.

"No chaser? Damn, impressive," Link says.

Yeah, I know it is, Link. I've been drinking since I was nine-years-old. Liam and I stole a bottle of William's scotch after he passed out on a lounge chair outside by the pool. Liam took a tiny sip and made a face. 'Gross,' he said, 'I'm never touching that stuff again.' I grabbed the bottle from him, determined to take a bigger sip than he did. The second the dark liquid stung my taste buds, I knew liquor and I would have a life-long love affair. I didn't hate the bitter taste or the way that it burned my organs on the way down to my stomach. I didn't hate it at all.

I snatch the open bottle out of Link's hand and take a double shot from it.

"Damn, Philly. Your girl can drink."

"She sure can," Philly agrees, putting his arm around my shoulder. Oh. My. God. He just called me his girl. Or, well, I guess it was Link who said it, but Philly didn't protest at all. I'm his girl. Does that mean I'm his girlfriend? Is that the same thing? I should ask Mia; she knows these things. Where is Mia? I scan the basement. I think she might be in her bedroom with one of those wrestling dudes she had on either arm the other day. Good for her, she always knows what she wants. Me, I'm not so sure. I sincerely thought that tonight was going to be the night we'd do the deed, or whatever, but now I feel... I don't know, scared. What if I bleed again? What if I don't know how to do it right? What if he doesn't like the way my body looks?

My plane to Lilah land is emergency landed when Chloe and Mary Lu stumble onto the couch. Mary Lu sits next to Link and grabs the bottle of Captain from him. Chloe rounds the corner of the coffee table in front of us and pops a squat right in front of Philly, her short black skirt leaving nothing to the imagination. I catch a peek of her bright red lace thong as she parts her toned legs before crossing one thigh over the other.

"Hey y'all," she squeals, over the sounds of Rihanna playing through the speakers. Her platinum blonde ponytail bobs back and forth as she sways with inebriation. I brush my brassy, copper hair back, hiding it behind my shoulders. I glance back to Chloe who's staring at Philly in awe, no doubt transfixed by that same glimmer in his black eyes that blinds me with love every time I look his way. But Chloe will never truly know

Philly like I do, nobody will. There is so much about him that only I know, things he's only shared with me. And I feel like... I don't know, like maybe that gives us a bond more special than anyone else in the world.

"So, how's Sam?" Mary Lu asks.

"Who?"

"Sam, Sam Garcia, you know the guy that's living in your house."

"Oh, right, Sam. And it's the guest house."

I look to my right then my left to see everyone's eyes on me. "He's, um, good, I guess? All things considered. The Garcia's are really nice. I think you'd like them."

"Oh, well that's good then."

"Nah," Link chimes in. "Dude is a fucking freak show, I don't care what you say, D. I bet he's the one who killed his sister and covered it up to make it look like a suicide. There can only be one skeleton twin in these here parts," Link draws his words out in an exaggerated southern accent.

"He's not a freak," I snap.

Eyes widen on the couch around me. I sink into myself. I tighten the reigns of my mind as it attempts trot back to the sunset on the dock last week and Sam's silver eyes that chilled and warmed me at the same time. His confident half smile, his heart-shaped lips. The way his pecks showed through his white shirt, and the way I wanted to rip it off. The tickle of his hand grazing mine, the taste of his sweet breath on my glossed lips.

I shake my head. Focus, focus. What happened with Sam was nothing, it meant nothing. It was a nice conversation fueled by my scotch buzz and his smoker's high. I am so close to living happily ever after with Philly. This is what I've always wanted, I'm not going to let one heated interaction with a stranger on a dock soil it. Nothing will stand in the way of my forever, not even Sam Garcia, as tall as his stance may be.

I lock eyes with Link and realize I should probably follow up. "I mean, his sister died, you know? Like, just let up a little."

"Yeah," Mary Lu sways into Link, pushing his shoulder.

"Whatever," he spits.

I glance over at Philly, wondering if he picked up on any strange undertones in my response or if he realizes how much of an ass Link is. But when I meet his side profile, I realize that he's staring straight into Chloe's eyes, her light and wicked eyes. What is she trying to do to me? I thought we were friends. Well, friends may be a loose term. She thinks I'm a nerd for being in the music program at school and I think she's an air-headed warm body with pompoms. But we're at least in the same friend group. She has to know how much I'm into Philly and how long our saga has been.

I rest my hand on Philly's thigh and pretend to laugh at whatever idiotic thing Link just said that has Mary Lu practically falling over. I glance back at Philly to see if he notices the placement of my hand, but he doesn't. That's it, it's time. It's now or never. I have to. I pick the bottle up off the coffee table and swallow three colossal gulps.

Let's. Fucking. Do. This.

I put my lips to Philly's ear, lowering my voice to sound as sensual as possible. "Let's go somewhere private. I want you."

Philly perks up, breaking eye contact with bottle blonde Barbie. A grin appears on his face, revealing the W-shaped white mark of his left front tooth. He hates it, but I think it's the sexiest thing on this earth. He springs up from the couch.

"Fuck yeah," He exclaims.

I haven't seen a smile this wide on his chiseled face in a long time, not with all his family has gone through this past year.

He looks so happy. All I want in this life is to make him happy, that is all I want, and I will do anything to make that happen, anything.

Mia's sister's room is pitch dark, just as I hoped it would be. I had pulled Philly's hand away when he tried to flick on the light switch. It's better in the dark. This way, he won't have to see my frail body and flat chest. I'm lying on my back on the firm mattress while Philly opens the condom. He must have practiced after that first time because he puts it on with ease. Wait, does that mean he practiced with someone else? Has he been with anybody else since that one time? Ugh, shut up, Delilah, just enjoy this. You want this… right? I lay my head back and wait. He comes up to my face. He's holding his dick in his hand. It's thicker than I remember.

"Well, are you just gonna lay there like a dead fish or are you gonna do something?"

Shit. I don't know what to do. Does he want me to put my mouth on it? I don't know how. I don't want to, but does *he* want me to? I stick my hand out and grab it, unsure of what I'm doing.

"That feels so good," he moans.

Okay, that's good. I think this is going okay. He climbs on top of me, and I brace myself for the pain but excite myself for the deep connection we're about to make. He jabs at me a few times, and it doesn't go in. I don't know what I'm doing wrong. Maybe this was a mistake. I can't back out now, can I? It's too late to change my mind… right?

"Um, Philly, I think I–"

"Shhhhh."

He uses his hand to guide it and it pushes inside. He thrusts back and forth, and it hurts, but not in a horrifically bad way.

It actually feels kind of good, kind of, I think. God, I hope I'm not bleeding again.

He looks into my eyes. "Do you like that?"

"Um… yeah. Thank you."

Jesus fucking Christ, are you serious? Did I really just say that? I am the absolute worst, most unsexy being to walk this earth. I hear Philly moan quietly. Am I supposed to be doing that? Am I supposed to be making noise? How the fuck should I know? My mom taught me porn was the devil's worst weapon against us. I've been too afraid of getting caught to try to look for it on the family computer. All I know is what Mia has told me, and we never covered sound effects.

Philly thrusts towards me for a few more seconds. He's grunting with his motions, then he groans loudly and pulsates at the same time. Is he okay? He pushes himself off of me and onto his knees. I lift my head to make sure I didn't bleed all over the place again. No blood, thank God. I see him rolling off the condom.

"That was amazing," he says, out of breath.

Hallelujah. I didn't ruin everything again. I think this is it, I think he's going to ask me to officially be his girlfriend after this. I mean, he has to now… right? I sit up and cover my tiny breasts with my arm. His hand caresses my face and I lean into his palm, wishing I could stay there forever. His hand travels down my neck towards my chest. I shiver at the light touch on my milky skin. I get butterflies as he feels around my chest, exploring it. I hope he's not horribly disappointed. I arch my back, allowing his fingers to travel freely. I look into his eyes and smile, pink staining my cheeks. But Philly doesn't return my smile, instead, he quickly moves his hand from my chest to my shoulder and pushes me back down onto the pillow.

"Where the fuck do you think you're going?" He barks.

Um… what? Aren't we done?

"But, but, we already…"

"You're not going anywhere, slut."

I jerk my torso up, but he pushes me back down on my back, this time with two hands and brute force.

"I don't—"

"Look at you, with that piss yellow hair, you know what else is piss yellow?" He holds his dick out and hovers over me.

"I don't understa—"

It's then that I feel a warm liquid burn my skin. I look up to see Philly over me, swerving back and forth, leaving a trail of urine. Mia told me that guys cum a white, thick liquid when they finish, but this isn't that. The sound, the smell, it's unmistakable. I squeeze my eyes shut and block my face as the stream shoots bullets at my innocence. What is happening? Why is he doing this? I grind my teeth and press my knees to my naked chest. I keep my head down, trying desperately to protect my eyes and mouth. Hot liquid drenches my copper hair, drowning it, drowning me. Finally, I feel air chill over me, the smell of pee wafting around the bed.

"Why did you—"

He surveys over my naked, fetal-positioned body. "Look at you, you're disgusting, Delilah." he scolds before pulling up his jeans and buttoning them up. "Clean yourself up, fucking whore." He rises to his feet and walks out of the dark room.

I look up at the ceiling fan above me illuminated by the full moon bursting through the window. I want to move but I'm paralyzed. Tears stream down my cold face faster than they ever have before. What did I do wrong?

Chapter 18

2009- Richmond Hill, Georgia

The strong winds send warm, salty air through my hair, blowing a copper strand into my eyelashes. Yanking the scrunchie from my wrist, I twist my hair into a messy bun. I stare out onto the dark river. The sun has gone down already, but it's still light enough to see everything. The wind rips through the water with force and little drops fly up, wetting my legs. I wish there was anything in the world that could wash away this feeling, that could wash away me. This feeling, I can't describe it. It's excruciating, like bugs are crawling all over my body. I feel… I don't know, dirty. I feel like I can scrub and scrub until my skin falls off, but no matter what I do, I will never be clean again. I still don't understand what I did wrong. Why would he do that to me? And why did he call me a whore? Was that what he said or was it slut? Was it both? He's the one that's been trying to convince me to have sex for years, and now that we did, he thinks I'm a whore. I wish I could talk to Mia about what happened, but I can't. No one would understand. I haven't been able to look at myself. I've never loved the way that my body looked in the mirror, but now, it's different. Now, every time I see my reflection, I want to punch the mirror and shatter it into a million pieces.

I fight the acid swarming up my throat and throw back a huge sip of red wine. It's an incredibly expensive bottle of Pinot Noir that my dad brought back from a business trip in France. Lady Katherine decided that opening up this sacred bottle and drinking the whole thing without Dad would serve as one of his many punishments for the other night. But, when she opened it and tasted it, she made a disgusted face and slid it across the counter into my hands before making herself 'a real drink'. So, I guess it's all mine, thanks Mom. I haven't seen my dad since Friday, and I haven't slept since then either. I know my mom is having restless nights too. Anytime I'm not playing my keyboard at 3am, I can hear her below me in the kitchen speaking the gospel to herself, like she's leading her own drunk ministry. It's funny how after what happened, after what my dad did, Mom and I are the ones who can't sleep. Yet, I'd put money on it that Dad is at some five-star hotel sleeping like a baby. Why is that? I know that everything comes with a price to pay, but why does this one have to be ours and not his? I didn't light this fire, so why am I the one getting burned?

I swirl the dark liquid and bring the glass up to my face. I breathe in through my nose and mouth at the same time, just like Dad taught me. I'm getting hints of berry, and maybe, chocolate? Whatever, it doesn't fucking matter. Wine is wine. I take my iPod out of my jeans pocket and put the earbuds in. I adjust the wire and select my first playlist on shuffle. I lay my head back on the wooden dock and close my eyes.

A little pain in my heart,
Just won't let me be,
Wake up restless nights,
Lord and I can't even sleep...

My fingers tap on invisible keys, half playing along to the melody and half free styling. I take a deep breath in and start humming to the tune. The song is on its last chorus when I notice a new darkness above me, making it pitch black behind my eyelids. My chest hoists up to a sitting position. I gasp with fear, ripping my headphones off.

"Oh, sorry."

I put a hand on my heart and try to catch my breath.

"I didn't mean to scare you, I just, I was asking what you were listening to."

I catch my breath and look up to see Sam standing at the edge of the dock. He's wearing a white T-shirt and black sweatpants. This T-shirt is too small for him, like the last. I can see his dark nipples and thick chest hair that rises from the collar of the shirt. He brings a hand to the back of his head and ruffles his black shiny hair. I scan his incredibly tall body up and down, it's almost a mere silhouette in the darkness.

"Oh, um, I um..." It appears I've lost my ability to speak and I'm not hopeful that I'm going to find it. Panic stabs at my ribs and I hunch over in humiliation.

"Sorry, I didn't mean to disturb you. Clearly, you're trying to be alone. I'll go."

"No!" I yell, "I— I just— I mean—"

Sam points to the spot next to me and raises a thick, arched eyebrow. I nod, my tongue still caught by the world's most malicious cat. He lowers himself next to me and puts up two fingers, silently asking to share one of my earbuds. I take the bud and hand it to him then put the other one in my ear. He listens and bobs his head along to the music.

"Otis Redding, you weren't kidding about being a fan. And it does kind of go perfectly with this river view," he says, handing me back the ear bud.

"Told ya," I force a little laugh and wrap the wire around my iPod before stuffing it back into my pocket.

"What did your butler or personal bartender make you tonight?" He asks, pointing to my drink.

I playfully roll my eyes. "We don't have one of those. And it's Pinot Noir."

"What? I thought all rich people had butlers named like Chives or Jives or Smives."

"Smives, really?"

"That'd be my butler's name."

"I'm pretty sure you can't just name a butler whatever you want. Like, they come with their own names."

"Well then, I guess I would have to scour the earth until I found someone named Smives, then I'd make them an offer they couldn't refuse."

"Sounds like a solid plan." I take a sip of my wine. "No cigarettes tonight?"

"Ma'am," he scoffs, pulling a pack out of his pocket. "I have an addiction. I always have cigarettes." The corner of his mouth goes up, just like I remember. I giggle as I stare at that corner right above his black scruff. I smile at him, grateful I'm still able to laugh. I shiver as the breeze picks up more power. Sam lights a cigarette, and I watch his eyes as he concentrates. They're darker than usual in this lighting, but the gray in them warms my shoulders better than a letterman jacket could.

"What?" He asks, stuffing the pack back into his pocket.

"Oh, uh, nothing." I jerk my head away from him and stare down at my lap. The beat of my heart sends earthquakes through my bones. I press the glass of wine to my mouth and watch as Sam smokes his cigarette. Ashes fall onto the dock next to his leg, and I notice that he has a book next to him.

"Whatcha reading?"

"Oh, this?" He holds up a little black notebook. "It's not uh— it's not a book exactly. It's Bailey's journal. Think I mentioned it."

"Wow," I say, examining the notebook. "What's in it?"

"Well, I don't really know, that's what I'm trying to figure out. Everything is written in short poems or like riddles, or something. I'm trying to make sense of it all to see if it'll lead me to the fuck head that raped her." Anger fills Sam's silver eyes.

"Oh." I have no idea what to say. "Wow."

"What? You think it's a lost cause?"

"No, that's not— It's just a big thing you're tasking yourself with. Finding a rapist, the guy who made her... you know."

"Well, somebody has to. The police are doing jack shit, and my parents are too worried about getting deported to demand they do their job and investigate."

"I thought your parents were citizens. They can't deport them if they're citizens."

"Yeah, that's what I told them. But they're convinced it can happen. They'll never feel safe here." Sam takes a drag if his cigarette. "Anyway, do you think it's crazy if I launch my own investigation?"

"No, not at all. It's just... it's a lot."

"I know, but she's my sister, Delilah. I— I have to." Sam's eyes get the slightest bit glassy, and I nod, letting him know that I understand. He needs to do this. He needs to exhaust every possibility even if it leads him nowhere. He couldn't save Bailey, but maybe this is the one thing that he *can* do for her, find the monster and seek justice.

"This journal or diary or whatever isn't much, but it's something. Besides, you're only the story you tell yourself about yourself. Maybe in these scribbled pages, I can see what story Bailey was telling herself, and where the story changes, where everything went wrong."

I gulp. I've never thought of life that way, like a story we tell ourselves. I too wonder what genre Bailey's would be, but seeing as how it ended, I don't think it was a happy one. Not that mine is either.

"Will you read me something?"

"Really?"

"Yeah."

"Okay, well," he opens the journal, "like I said, it's mostly scribbling and scattered thoughts. It's hard to make sense of, but there's something here, I know it." Sam flips the pages. "There's this thing that comes up a lot, this same line that's repeated on every page. *All because he bought me black roses.* Black roses, what's a black rose? Do those exist?"

"I don't know, but if they do, they don't grow here in Georgia."

"I don't think they exist," he continues, "I've never heard of a black rose. So, why does she keep saying that? Who bought her black roses?" Curiosity and concern bite Sam like a snake as his forehead wrinkles. He takes a drag of his cigarette and blows the smoke out towards the water. The wind pushes it back and it floods my nose. I try not to cough; I don't want to be rude. Sam notices my lack of breathing and starts waving the smoke away from my face.

"Sorry, I'll put this out."

"No, don't be silly. It doesn't bother me." I hold out my wine glass for a cheers. Sam taps his cigarette to the glass, his finger brushes against mine again, like a paint brush stroking its canvas. My heart hammers in my sternum.

"So, what do you think that means? *All because he bought me black roses,*" Sam asks, looking deep into my muddy water eyes.

"I'm not sure. Maybe Bailey wasn't talking about real black roses, maybe she meant it more metaphorically. Lots of songwriters use metaphors in their lyrics. Like, maybe black roses symbolize something."

"Like what?"

"I don't know. Let me think. I mean, a rose is beautiful, right?"

Sam nods.

"But, when you think of a beautiful rose, you think of it as red or pink or white, not black. Maybe saying that it's black, maybe she's saying that it's not beautiful, like it's evil. You know, like how someone has a black heart or a black soul. Maybe a black rose is something that seems beautiful, but it's actually bad."

Sam's eyes widen as he nods. "Damn. That's insightful as hell. I came to the right place."

A timid laugh escapes my lips. "It's nothing."

"No, Delilah, it's something."

Sam's gray eyes wrap around mine. I blink slowly, unable to look away. His heart shaped lips curve as he inhales sharply. His head jolts back down to the book. "But who is he? She writes that *he* bought her black roses."

I think for a moment. "Maybe she's saying that someone sold her something? Like, sold her on an idea that seemed beautiful but was actually bad, deadly, even."

Sam perks up "Yes. *All because he bought me black roses.* She's talking about him. She's talking about the man who raped her. He sold her on something she didn't know she was buying. Like, he lied to her, or pretended to be someone else, or something."

"It's a theory."

"It's a good one."

I take another sip and lick my lips. "Now, I'm tempted to Google what black roses look like."

"Me too," Sam agrees.

We both laugh a little, until we remember that we're talking about the assault of his dead sister. We both look away from each other.

"Not that I have a computer to do that with," Sam sighs.

"Oh, well, we have one in the den. You can use it any time you want."

"Of course you do."

"What's that supposed to mean?"

"Nothin'." He smirks with his half smile, amusing himself.

I can play this game.

"Or you could always go use one at the school library. Lots of neat stuff in there," I tease.

Sam laughs. "If I walked in there, I'd burst into flames like a witch in a church."

I spit up my wine and catch it in my palm.

"Damn, I'm not that funny."

"Don't flatter yourself," I roll my eyes, wiping my chin. "Can I see that?" I ask, nodding my head towards the black journal.

"Be my guest." Sam hands me the little book and I open the cover.

"Property of Mileena Gale. Who's Mileena Gale?"

Sam laughs. "That was Bailey's alter ego. She always said that she was going to run away from this place and join the circus. Vowed she'd change her name to Mileena Gale. I'm the only one who knows about her alias. She said she didn't want my parents to know where she'd end up, but always wanted me to be able to find her." Sam's half smile begins to fade, probably at the realization that Mileena Gale is gone forever, she died with Bailey.

I nod gently and flip through the pages, looking for something legible. Having Bailey's most personal thoughts in my hands feels... I don't know, strange, like a violation of privacy. I barely knew Bailey, what would she think if she knew I was reading about her deepest darkest secrets?

Sam's low voice breaks into my thoughts. "Anything?"

I flip another page. "Oh, here. She writes: *She knows no one would believe her, so she believes in nothing. All because he bought her black roses.* Wow, that's deep."

"Hmm," Sam ponders. "She knows no one would believe her, so she believes in nothing."

"What do you think she meant?"

"Maybe she was talking about God, our faith. Maybe that's why she stopped coming to church with us on Sundays, she didn't believe anymore." Sam blows cigarette smoke away from me and shields his face. He tilts his head up towards the sky, I do the same. Twinkling stars brighten the darkness above us as the moon shimmers onto the small wave in front of us.

"Do you believe in God, Delilah?"

I nearly choke on the wine in my mouth. How does one respond to that? I relax my shoulders and hold up my glass. "Well, I heard Jesus turned water into wine, so I think we'd get along just fine." I giggle and take another sip, but Sam's expression remains flat. Fuck. Why did I say that? I think I'm drunk. Mom says you can't get drunk off wine because it's not real alcohol. She may have been wrong. I lift my glass to my lips and take another sip because... might as well at this point. I turn away from Sam as shame stings me like a wasp. Then, I hear a quiet laughter escaping from that corner smile, and I turn back towards him. He nudges my knee with his. My head shoots down to his thigh which is touching mine, the fabric on our pants sharing their warmth while our mouths share our demons. I scoot, subtly, towards him. I stare down at his lap, my eyes able to trace the shape of his crotch in his sweatpants.

"You're funny, Delilah Monroe."

"You sound shocked."

"I am."

"Hey. Book and cover, dude."

"I know, I know. You were right, again."

That's strange. People never tell me that I'm right.

"You know, you're rather quick to admit when you're wrong."

"Why wouldn't I be?" Sam stretches a long arm behind me.

"I don't know… It messes with your ego, your pride."

"Nah, ego is the type of shit that ruins you. It doesn't come from confidence; it comes from fear. Fear that you don't matter enough, so you do anything you can to prove yourself to yourself, to have control. That's why people don't apologize or admit when they're wrong, they're scared it makes them small. It's just a mask they're wearing."

"Not you though, you don't wear that mask. At least, it doesn't seem like you do, obviously I don't know you that well."

Sam's lips bend into a side smirk. "You know me better than you think."

"So why don't you then, wear a mask like everyone else?"

"Because I don't need to prove to myself that I matter." Sam lets out a puff of smoke, breathing over the dark river. I ponder on Sam's philosophical words, trying to make sense of them.

"Anyway, what were we talking about?"

"God." Sam adjusts his posture. "Do you believe?"

I swallow a lump in my throat, afraid to open my mouth again. "Um, honestly?"

"Honestly."

"No. I'm sorry, I know that's bad to say. I don't— I don't want to offend you."

Sam waves a hand in the air, "No, no, you don't offend me at all. You can believe or not believe anything that you want. I want to know how you really feel."

Shock consumes my gut. "Really?"

"Yeah, of course, really."

I've never known anyone that wanted to know how I truly feel. Most of the time, I don't even know what I truly feel. I take a long swig of my wine and lay back on the wood. Sam dabs his cigarette out and lays back. I face him with tired eyes and wine-stained lips. Putting two hands under my head, I lay on my side. My face gravitates closer towards his until the tips of our noises are practically touching. Being on this dock with him, breathing in his warmth, it feels righter than anything has in a long time.

"So, what about you? Do you believe in God?" I ask.

"I do."

"You do?"

"Yeah, why?"

"It's just, I don't know."

"I don't seem like the Christian type, do I?"

"Honestly?"

"Honestly."

"No, you don't." My face pinches at my own words. My eyes leer, fixated on the crucifix hanging around Sam's neck. It dangles just between his nipples; his pecks all but squeeze the chain. The silver in the cross dances with the silver in his eyes.

"Your necklace, I've seen it before."

"Bailey had the same one."

That makes sense. I recognize it from Bailey's eulogy photo. Sam tilts his head, stares up at the stars and sighs. "My family is Christian, like everyone else around here. I don't believe in

176

the cultural part of our religion, ya know, the social gatherings, the judgment, the gossip."

"Sound like my mom," I wince.

"Mine too."

"So then, what do you like about it? What's in it for you?"

"Faith, I guess. God. I mean, how can you know anything when you believe in nothing?"

I turn my head up to glistening stars, my thoughts lingering on that concept. I think Sam may be the smartest person I've ever met.

"So, do you believe in heaven then?"

"I do."

"What do you think it's like?"

"Something like this." Sam's gray eyes peer into mine, titillating my fragile soul, stimulating my discarded body. I close my eyes as Sam jerks his head away. "This dock, I mean. Being on the water and stuff, it's nice." Sam stutters on his words. He seems nervous.

I cock my head in his direction. "Can I ask you a question?"

"Shoot."

"Never mind, it's stupid." I turn my head away.

"Stupid is what stupid does," Sam mimics an exaggerated southern accent.

"Okay, Forrest Gump," I laugh.

"For real though, what is it? You can ask me anything."

I look back towards Sam. The crescent moon shines on his face, lighting up his dark features and the black scruff on his chin. "Are you angry with him? God, I mean. For what happened with Bailey?"

Sam sighs and looks up at the moon. "I was, especially when it first happened. There was this moment at her funeral where the pastor was going on and on about Bailey's contagious laugh and infectious smile. He knew nothing about her. It was such a generic speech he probably recites at every funeral. Bailey would have hated it. Then this choir singer started singing this song, and the only lyrics in it were 'the Lord is kind and merciful'. She sang that damn line over and over and over. And I couldn't help but think it was a load of crap. If the Lord was kind or merciful, how could he let this happen to Bailey? How could he have taken a young girl with so much life left to live away from her family? So, yeah, I was angry with God."

"Isn't that, like, a sin though?"

"Nah, it's not a bad thing to be angry with God. It's not a bad thing to feel. God wants to hear all of our feelings so he can help us heal. Have you ever heard the story of Hannah?"

I shake my head.

"It's from the First Book of Samuel. Hannah was the wife of Elkanah, and all she wanted was to be a mother, but she couldn't bear children. So, Elkanah went and had children with another woman and made her his second wife."

"Rat bastard."

Sam chuckles. "It had been thought that expressing anything other than praise towards God was the ultimate sin. But Hannah was so overcome with emotion that she went to the Tabernacle and unleashed all of her emotions, cursing God for not giving her the one thing on earth she needed to be happy."

"Then what?"

"God listened to her grievances and rewarded her for her vulnerability by giving her a son, and Hannah became a prophetess."

"So, what happened with the husband and his mistress?"

"Hmm, good question. I assume they all just lived together and raised Elkanah's children."

"Like a throuple?"

Sam laughs, "I guess so."

"Do you think they had threesomes?

"Well, it would be wrong not to."

We both giggle.

"But the point of the story is that it's good to have feelings and express them even if they're not positive ones. If you don't feel the bad stuff, you'll never heal from the bad stuff. God is here for us no matter what."

"I see," I nod my head. "You know that bible story pretty damn well."

"My mom used to make me learn and recite them. In English *and* Portuguese."

"Damn, that's hardcore. All my mom did was force us to go to Sunday school. But I think she realized after a few years that my brother and I were lost causes. Born sinners."

Sam laughs and sighs. "Yeah, that's my mom for ya, hardcore as they come. She's way more into how everything looks on the outside versus actual faith. She wants all of us to seem perfect and pure. She tries so hard to keep up appearances and make people in this town see her as the perfect Christian woman. Too bad they'll never see past the color of her skin."

"That must suck for her."

"Yeah, and I bet it sucked for Bailey too. All those rigid standards my mom has for herself, she put those onto Bailey. She made her believe that she had to be pure and innocent to be worthy. Always dressing her up like a doll in these white dresses, begging her to wipe off her black makeup. Constantly trying to shape her into someone she wasn't."

Wow. I guess I was wrong at dinner. Maybe Sofia Garcia and Katherine Monroe *do* have something in common.

"Do you—" I hesitate, "do you wish Bailey would have been more innocent?"

Sam's silent for a moment and takes a deep breath. "Honestly?"

"Honestly."

"No. I don't wish she was more innocent. I just wish she didn't fucking kill herself. I get that she felt pressure from my mom to be this perfect Christian daughter. I get that she felt like an outsider in Richmond Hill. And I get that some horrible monster attacked her. I get all that shit is horrific, but I wish that she dealt with it better."

"Easier said than done," I sigh.

"You would know?"

Heat wells in my forehead. "No, I mean, uh, I wouldn't know." I force myself to relax and look back up at the stars. "I don't think there's anything pure or innocent about me." I swallow back the tears that sting my eyes.

"Well, good, innocent is boring. Being innocent just means that you don't know much, you haven't seen much." Sam turns to me and wraps me in a warm blanket with his eyes.

"Well." I cover my yawn with my palm. "I've seen some shit, and I don't know that I'm a better person for it."

Sam's yawn mirrors mine as he looks back up at the black sky. "Well, I happen to like you the way you are. You're pretty damn cool, Delilah Monroe." Sam starts humming Otis Redding and I hum along. My stare at the moon grows deeper, creating a white halo around the curve of it. Sam swivels his head, laying it on the worn wood to face me. He inches his body into mine until we can't get any closer. I blush at the sensation of his body touching mine. Sam lifts his hand and runs his fingers through my hair, tucking a strand behind my cold ear.

"Is this okay?" He whispers.

"Yeah. Yes."

Sam's hand stays in my hair, petting my head lightly. His soft hand then slides down my face, my neck, my shoulder, and onto my arm. He rubs the goosebumps from my shoulders to my wrists, willing them away. My breathing shallows as I wet my lips, licking them slowly. Is this really happening? Sam's soft hand moves up my arm, walking his fingers up my shivering body. He places it on my face and strokes my skin tenderly.

"Look at you, you're perfect, Delilah."

Suddenly, my eyelids shoot open. In front of me, I see Sam's warm gray eyes staring back at me, but the voice I hear in my peripheral is not a low, raspy whisper. *Look at you, you're disgusting, Delilah.*

I hurtle up off the wood, catapulting myself. My breath is caught in my fractured heart. Sam's wrong, I'm not perfect. Not one bit. I'm disgusting, and dirty. I'm a slut, a whore. If only Sam knew the real me, he would be repulsed by me too. I choke back tears.

Sam rolls up and puts a delicate hand on the small of my back. "Hey, you okay?"

"Yeah, yeah, of course. It's just…"

"Just what? Talk to me."

I yank the glass of wine off the dock and chug the rest of the Pinot Noir then hurry to my feet.

"I's just… It's a nice night." I try to change subject, desperately. I try to do anything to not catch the look in his eye, the one that sees me for someone I'm not. Sam may not wear a mask, but I sure as hell do. If I dare to take it off, it's over.

"It is a nice night." Sam smiles.

An idea sparks. "A nice night for a swim." I peer out towards the water, the tiny waves are completely black, the only light shines from the moon and stars above us.

Sam stands slowly. "It's a little cold, don't you think?"

"Come on, Socrates, is that philosophical mind allergic to spontaneity?"

"No, it's just…"

"Just what?"

I feel Sam's eyes widen as they stay fixed on my body. I let him watch me kick off my converse and rip off my socks. I pull the scrunchie out of my hair and shake my head, freeing the copper curls, losing them to the wind. I gather the bottom of my black shirt in my hands and slowly pull it up, lifting it over it over my head. Sam's stare grows, his eyes deliberating over my bare stomach, tracing up to my white bra. Without a rational thought in sight, I pout my lips at him. "Just what? I repeat. "Is swimming not your scene?" I mock him.

Sam's eyes light up in the darkness, his lips press into a seductive smile. "Nothin'." Sam rips off his tight white T-shirt, and I'm stunned by his abs that glisten under the starry sky. He joins me at the edge of the dock. I grab his hand and cradle it in mine, savoring the smooth texture. I bring our interlaced hands down to my hip.

"Ready, Sam?"

"Ready, Delilah."

We both bend our knees and leap into the cold, dark, shimmering bay.

Lover's prayer,
With my head down and my hands up high,
Lover's prayer,
How I hope he will answer my,
Lover's prayer…

Chapter 19
Present Day

He grips my breast while he pushes inside of me, ecstasy not being the only thing to fill me up. A ravenous moan escapes my lips as he breathes hot air on my neck. A river of pleasure flows through me as his tongue runs up and down my shoulder. His big, wet lips travel up to my neck and he bites down gently, it hurts so good. His hands float down to my hips which he grabs with tender intention. He pulls me towards him and pushes deeper into me. I bend over the bed until my back is flat so he can see my butt bounce on him. He pulls out for a moment, scanning and savoring the scene in front of him. Then, he slides back inside me and thrusts in as deep as possible. I whimper as he hits all my spots with beautiful fluidity. He slows his thrusts and moves his hips in a circular motion, his fingers gliding up and down my back.

"Belissima, Delilah."

I was surprised that things with Salvatore escalated so fast. Then again, I suppose I'm not all that shocked. The way he took my towel from me and looked me up and down that day at the pool, I knew exactly what he wanted. I grappled with the fact that he was Beth, my annoying neighbor's gardener, and has probably trimmed *her* hedges a time or two. But I figured it was fine since I didn't plan on actually sleeping with him. I'm not a cheater, at least not anymore. But, what's the harm in some casual flirting and a pretty Italian view? I'm sure fiddling with a sexy Italian stranger wasn't what Dr. Veizer had in mind when she said I needed to create more meaning in my life, but it's a hobby, at the least.

It was last week that I went out to the pool in hopes of seeing him over the hedges. I fished my best push up bikini out of the bottom of my summer drawer. It's a high waisted black Versace bathing suit with white trimming. I hadn't worn it since my honeymoon in Italy. Salvatore's wispy voice and sensual accent made me recall that I had it. Once I stuffed myself into the bikini, I blew out my hair and clipped in my extensions as if I were going to a gala instead of my backyard. I paired the Versace bathing suit with a black Revolve cover up and white oversized Dior sunglasses. I baked in the sun for nearly two hours, pretending to read a copy of Us Weekly. I flipped through the pages with fatigued fingers. Jen and Ben are back together, Kanye is losing his mind, blah blah blah. It was all the same. I threw my head back on the lounge chair, admitting I had wasted my time. I had fasted for two days straight just to fit into that Versace bikini, and the dizzy spells were starting to begin. I thought I might have been hallucinating when I heard a bewitching voice sing.

"Ciao Bella."

I shot up and met the beautiful cadence with a smile. Salvatore formally introduced himself, as did I. He complimented my bathing suit, my hair, and my eyes. The charm in voice and the sun glistening on his chiseled body, I was practically dripping wet by the time I invited him in for some lemonade. I poured him a glass of water and mixed some Crystal Light lemonade powder in it.

"Grazie," he said.

"Prego."

He was impressed that I knew how to respond, and I pretended like I learned Italian in school, as if I didn't spend the entire week on DuoLingo brushing up on the common phrases. Honestly, I needed any distraction to take me away from obsessing over those anonymous texts and the reunion.

Salvatore sipped his lemonade as I gulped down a vodka with fresh squeezed lemon, an adult lemonade. We made small talk in broken English and third grade level Italian until I eventually couldn't take the throbbing in my panties anymore. I was practically salivating over Salvatore. I asked him if he wanted a tour of the house. He put down his lemonade, his face lighting up with lust. We both knew where the tour was going to end.

This is my second time giving Salvatore a 'tour' and it ended in the same place as last time, the master bedroom. This time is even better than the first.

He squeezes my butt with a firm hand, and I throw my head back, flipping my long balayage hair. His fingers trail along the bottom of my back and chills tickle my entire being, making me forget where and who I am. I roll my body up and touch my cheek to his lips. I moan with bliss as he pants in my ear. I look back to see his olive skin glowing under the chandelier above us. Placing my hands back down on the bed, I thrust my butt towards him. He grunts like a wild animal, like he's starving for me. He grazes down my whole body with his hand until it slides in between my thighs. He hovers his hand above me, just barely touching me, teasing me. He finally presses down and rubs in a circular motion until I feel like he is a God, and I am his loyal servant, worshiping at his feet, begging for more. I scream out in pleasure, my toes curling as an orgasm begins to flutter up my whole body. "Salvatore!" I moan loudly and gutturally. My chest heaves as I pulsate between my thighs, shaking with delectation. My breathing slows but my moans continue, as Salvatore slips his hand out from between my thighs. His hand wraps around my neck. I grip his thick arm, it's crusted in dirt, like a real fucking man. I dig my nails into his muscle and kiss it, then I push my head back to graze his cheek. Suddenly, he pulls out of me, grabs both of my shoulders, and spins me around to face him. He gently pushes me back onto the bed and I slowly sink down the silk linens, landing on the floor. Salvatore smiles salaciously and joins me on the floor, lowering himself between my legs. He kisses my breasts, sucking delicately on my pink nipple before peppering kisses down my torso. His lips make their way down to my inner thigh, and I feel the tickle of his stubble as he spreads my legs open. His tongue grazes me, soft and sweet. I try to push down the feeling that overcomes me. Here, on my back, staring up at the ceiling, I feel… I don't know, like I am going to implode. I try to focus on his mouth tickling my clit. My legs quiver as he holds them open with force. After a few more circles with his tongue, Salvatore rises up to his knees and hovers his large body above me. He puts his hands on the carpet and pulls himself up until he's on top of me. His weight presses on me like the tire of a car rolling over a bunny. I look up at his brown eyes, and a monsoon of panic washes through me, flooding my logic. *Get off the fucking ground, Delilah.*

"Stop, stop!" I scream. I push on his chest as hard as I can, and he jumps to his feet. I shoot up and back towards the bed. I crawl backwards on my hands, putting as much distance between us as possible. My chest heaves as all the air in the room disappears. *You're a slut, Delilah.*

"I'm sorry, Bella. Are you—" he looks for the words, trying to translate, "okay?"

My breath is still lost as I choke out, "I'm fine. Just stop."

"I'm sorry, I want to make you feel good. It was not good?"

"It was good, it's fine. It's just— you should go." I press my hand to my chest and try to box breathe.

"I go? Why, Bella? What's happen?"

I turn towards the edge of the bed and lift to my feet. "Just go!"

"But, Bella..."

"Go, just fucking leave! Go fuck Beth instead. I'm sure it makes no difference to you."

"Beth?" He raises his dark, thick eyebrow and stares at me, dumbfounded. "Beth? I work on garden for Miss Beth."

"Really? You're telling me that's all you do for her?"

"Yes. I— I do not understand," he pleads.

"Whatever." I throw his pants at him. "Just go, please."

He puts his pants back on and throws his white T-shirt over his shoulder. It's covered in dirt. He lets out a heavy sigh.

"I make garden for Miss Beth. That is all. I do not want Miss Beth, I want *you*."

I look away from him and towards the doors of the master bedroom, terrified of the kindness in his eyes.

"Ciao, Delilah," he whispers with an intense sadness as he leaves the room through the double doors. When I hear the back door close, I take the white, down-feather pillow from the bed and cover my face with it, hoping that it will suffocate me and put me out of my misery. After a minute or two, I drop the pillow and head towards the closet. I sit at my vanity and stare into my muddy eyes. They look almost green under the vanity lights, but not enough to be pretty. I wipe the smudged mascara off of my face. I check my phone and notice it's almost 2pm. Shit. I throw my phone in a tote and put on the first thing I see. It's a not-so-flattering black maxi dress with white polka dots, but I don't have time to do my usual sad, lonely fashion show in the mirror. I run around the kitchen looking for my keys. Why do I always do this? *You are so stupid, Delilah.* I glance around the table and notice a few sips left of my vodka and lemon drink. Should I... Just one sip so the chills don't take over? No. I shake desperate hunger for respite off of me and keep looking for my keys. Ah, yes, there they are. I bend down in front of the refrigerator and scoop them up. I roll up and do a double take. I'm face to face with a familiar pair of eyes that I could never forget if I wanted to. I stare at his picture, burning holes through the paper. If I stare hard enough, maybe it will bring him back to life.

Then all of the sudden, I open my eyes. I'm on the floor, my back is against the wall. There's so much screaming but all I can feel is the throbbing, searing pain in my jaw. I look beneath me and I see a pool of scarlet lurching towards my Manolos. And immediately I know that he's dead. How did this happen?

No.

I throw my keys in my tote bag and take the vodka drink off of the counter. I chug the whole thing in two sips. Putting on my sunglasses, I head for the door when my phone dings. I sigh and open it up.

Unknown caller: You're going to ignore me, I see. You can't run from me forever, Delilah. The past has a way of haunting us all, even you…

I nearly faint. I am so fucked.

Chapter 20
Present Day

The droplets of rain slide down the window with grace. Some drops move faster than others, meeting fellow drops in the middle then doubling in size. While others travel down the windowpane solo before they evaporate. I've never thought about it until now, but the lifespan of a raindrop is incredibly short. Most fall from the sky with force then meet their demise when they splatter on the ground, while others get lost in the wind. I wonder what that would be like, to be a raindrop. Probably pretty painful, free-falling through the air then splattering on the concrete. Although, there are things far more painful than hitting the pavement, like hating your body forever because of what someone else did to it.

How was he able to text me again? I blocked his number. Does he have multiple phones? Does he have other people working for him? What kind of operation is he running? I should get a new number. I should board up the house or leave town all together. I can't face him, I can't. If I do, I will lose everything.

"Delilah? Are you still with me?" Dr. Veizer straightens her back and stares at me inquisitively.

"Oh, yeah, I—um, sorry." I knew I shouldn't have had that drink.

"Where did you go just now?"

"Nowhere, sorry. Nowhere." I press my hand on my thigh to stop it from shaking.

Dr. Veizer puts her notebook on the side table next to her. She crosses her arms. "I don't believe you. I can tell when your wheels are turning. So, tell me, where did you go?"

Dr. Veizer came to play today. I have a sneaking suspicion that she plans to push me over like a domino.

"I honestly don't remember what I was thinking about, it was probably stupid."

"There are no stupid thoughts in this room."

Okay, now I'm the one that doesn't believe *her*. She's spent the last 30 years or so listening to people for a living. I am sure she's heard some dumb shit in her day.

"I honestly just don't remember." I sigh and glance at the clock.

"Okay, then, fair enough. Let's talk about how you're feeling. What are you feeling in this moment, sitting here talking to me?"

"I don't know."

"What *do* you know?"

Damn, nice draw, she didn't even shuffle me before snagging me from the boneyard.

"Ugh," I huff, "sorry."

I bet she's as sick of me as I am. It's not that I don't want to tell her an answer, I just don't know how. My mind and mouth don't connect, they are mere strangers to each other.

"You don't have to be sorry, Delilah. But I have noticed that every time you say, 'I don't know', it's in response to my asking how you feel about something. That tells me that perhaps you don't know how to identify your feelings. I think I may have something that can help." Dr. Veizer's loafers hit the floor. She smooths out her pencil skirt as she rises from her leather chair. She walks over to the desk behind her, slowly and with a bit of a limp. She rifles through papers on her desk, and I can't help but admire her outfit. She's wearing a long-sleeved white blouse that hangs over a long pencil skirt and black stockings. Her jewelry is understated and elegant. She looks classy and wise.

"Ah, viola!" She exclaims as she returns from her desk with a piece of paper. She hands it to me. I scan the paper. On it are a bunch of printed faces making different facial expressions. They look like bootleg iPhone emojis. Each one is labeled with a word underneath like exhausted, fearful, excited, etc.

"It's a feelings chart. I use it sometimes as a guide to help patients identify their feelings."

I clutch the paper in my hand. "It looks like it was made for elementary school children."

Dr. Veizer laughs. "Well, technically it was. But you'd be surprised how similar adults and children are. At the end of the day, we are all just humans with big feelings, and we will all do anything to avoid feeling pain."

I think back to every kid I've ever taught and how explosive their emotions could be. I guess all of us feel emotions like that, adults have just learned how to hide theirs…. Or drink them away.

I search the chart of faces to find one that matches mine. "I don't—"

"Try, please."

I breathe in and out deeply through my nose. "Embarrassed."

"Embarrassed."

"Yeah."

"Okay, thank you for your honesty."

I swallow hard and arch my back. I cross one leg over the other. I can already feel my hands growing numb, they're in the fun in between phase where it feels like little needles are stabbing into my palms. I place the feelings chart on the cushion next to me and ball my hands up into fists, straightening my fingers a few times.

"I'm glad to see you're using the progressive muscle relaxation we talked about." She studies me, counting my dots.

"Uh huh."

Dr. Veizer picks up her notepad and jots something down in chicken-scratch before clicking her pen.. I can feel her eyes on the side of my face, but I'm still entranced by the raindrops on the window. *Eye contact, Delilah.*

"I noticed that you seemed to get uncomfortable when I asked you to identify your feelings, am I correct?"

I nod.

"You know, Delilah…" She leans in. I'm still avoiding her warm brown eyes, keeping mine glued to the rain. "Identifying feelings is a lesson that's taught to us at a young age. Our parents teach us with their words and their actions. That being said, if you grow up in a house where it's not okay to feel feelings, it's unlikely that you're going to learn how to identify them."

I look up at the ceiling and blink away tears.

"Growing up, was it safe for you to feel your feelings?"

I squeeze my eyelids shut, feeling an eyelash stab at my iris.

I picture that house on the river that I still know all too well. I mentally walk through the front door and into my foyer. The ghost of my mom's heavy perfume haunts the whole house. There, in the foyer, I see myself at seven-years-old being dragged out the front door by my hair because I was nervous for my first day of 2nd grade. I walk further towards the kitchen, and I'm nine-years-old standing in front of the kitchen island, my tears are wiped away with a smack to the face because I was sad that my friend from piano class moved to Tennessee. I keep going. I pass the dining room where Liam had broccoli smashed into his face until he bled because he wouldn't finish his dinner. I keep moving towards the back door, still, even mentally, trying to break myself out of that house. I open the door and walk through the fresh cut grass, passing the pool. I float by the magnolia trees, cicadas singing their familiar song. I find myself barefoot, standing on the old dock gazing out towards the water. The warm breeze blows by me, when suddenly, the smell of cigarette smoke fills my nose. No.

I shake my head and press my thumb and index fingers together at the bridge of my nose, begging the tears not to fall. My head throbs like a kick drum. "I don't want to talk about this," I whisper, my voice shaking.

"That's okay, we don't have to. I know we talked about working up to inner child work, but it seems like today is not the day. I'm sorry if I pushed too hard."

"No, it's not you. It's me, I'm—"

"Not ready?"

I nod.

"Well, are you open to talking about something else?"

"Sure." I take my hand away from my face once I'm sure the tears are dry. I take a deep breath of relief, thrilled to move on from this.

Dr. Veizer flips the pages in her notepad. "Last week we did some meaning exploration, and we identified that perhaps you don't have enough meaning in your life to make it feel like it matters. I was happy that you brought it up because I do believe that meaning is the most important thing that a person can have. Meaning is what makes life worth living. Right now, honestly, do you feel like life is worth living?"

"I don't kn—" I catch myself. "No, I don't."

Dr. Veizer nods her head in silence. I notice her eyes getting slightly glassy. I didn't mean to upset her. I must have said something wrong. Every time I speak, I say something wrong, even when I'm right.

"If I'm being honest," she begins, "that upsets me because I care about you, Delilah. When I look at you, I see someone with so much intelligence and empathy. I see potential for you to be happy, so many reasons for you to live. But, at the end of the day, I can't convince you to stay alive and I can't give you reasons to live, only you can do that."

My hand flies up to my mouth as the tears stream down my face faster than the raindrops stream down the window. I wipe them as quickly as I can and swallow the lump in my throat.

Say something, Delilah.

"I want to have reasons to live, I want to have a million."

Dr. Veizer puts her hands on her knees. "Then let's find them. Let's find a million."

"How?"

"Let's create some meaning."

I want to ask her how in the hell she expects us to do that. I'm nothing but an alcoholic housewife who plays 'Twinkle Twinkle Little Star' with spoiled brats twice a week and fucks her neighbor's gardener. I want to tell her all of that but instead I just mutter, "okay."

"Okay," her thin pink lips stretch into a smile.

I unclench my fists and realize that the pins and needles are gone.

"So, there are multiple aspects of life that one may find their meaning in. I'm thinking that I can give you a list of a few aspects then let you pick which one you want to explore."

"Okay."

"When it comes to meaning, one may typically find that through hobbies, career, family, community. Those are just a few, but if you were to pick which one of those that resonates with you the most, which would it be?"

I think about my hobbies, which pretty much solely consist of drinking, online impulse shopping, and most recently, stalking hot yet oddly sensitive Italian men then abruptly kicking them out of my house. So, yeah, let's not go with that one. Career, um let's see. I failed at being a concert pianist, I failed at being a teacher, and now I babysit life-sized American girl dolls while they pound the keys of a grand piano worth more than three years of their private school tuition. Looks like career is off the table too. Family? Family... You know what, I'm not even going there.

"Community," I blurt out.

"Community, okay, great. Let's explore that. What does community look like to you?"

"Having friends, I guess."

"Alright, interpersonal relationships, people who you connect with. Tell me, what are your current friendships like?" Dr. Veizer looks me up and down. I can tell she's lining up her pieces, waiting for the exact right moment to push them over.

"Um, I don't really have any." Saying that out loud, I feel... I don't know, like the biggest loser on the planet.

"Mhmm."

"I mean, I guess I sort of do. I'm on the fundraising committee at the country club in my town. I see those women at least once a week."

"That's great. Are there any women on the committee that you feel a connection with?"

Charlotte Vanderheiden's cherry red hair and her evil green eyes flash through my mind. Daisy or Dixie's fake smile accompanies her. Anastasia's Russian accent and fake Chanel bag follow behind like a puppy looking for its owner.

I shake my head. "No, not really. They're kind of all, um..."

"Bitchy?"

I giggle like a schoolgirl. "Exactly."

"I know the type," Dr. Veizer sighs, "It's like high school never ends for some people."

"Yes! That's exactly how it is with those women. How do you know?"

"I lived it. I know that you don't like to talk about your past, but I know a kindred spirit when I see one. But anyway, back to you. There's no one on the committee that you feel like you could form a real connection with?"

"Well," I trail off, "maybe one of them. Sebastian, he's the only man on the committee. I always thought he was amusing but we had never actually had a conversation until the other day. We talked for a while."

"And?"

"And… he's cool, I think. Talking to him doesn't feel like how it does with the other women on the committee."

"How does talking to him make you feel?"

"It makes me feel… I don't know."

Dr. Veizer points to the feelings chart on the couch cushion to my right. I roll my eyes a bit, not at her, at myself. I pick up the paper and search the little faces for a viable answer.

"Understood, I guess."

"Understood," she reflects my words.

"Yeah, like he wasn't judging me. I felt like I could be honest with him. It felt…" I search my brain. "It felt… really fucking nice. The last time I was that honest with someone was…"

No.

"Never mind. Anyway, I think Sebastian is the most tolerable of the group. But, even if I did find a way to get closer to him, how do I know that he'll be a good friend? How do I know I'm not just going to get screwed over yet again? My God, I feel like I'm in middle school. Making friends as an adult is so hard."

"It is, Delilah, it really is. It's much easier to make friends as a kid, before you know how cruel the world can be. But I commend you for being open to people again… Ever since what happened."

I peer back out towards the rain, trying telepathically to let Dr. Veizer know not to go there right now. I told her months ago that I'm done talking about that in this room, she's not going to trick me into it. She's not winning the game this time.

"Tell me something, do you believe Sebastian is a safe person?"

"A safe person?"

"Yes, a safe person."

"How am I supposed to know?"

"Well, does he feel safe? Do you feel safe when you're around him?"

I look away again, glaring at the window. I'm beginning to despise this window. I don't know what she wants from me, I can't remember the last time I felt safe. Everyone I have ever trusted made me want to be anybody but myself. They wanted a specific part of me, and the rest of me that I hid in the shadows was punished and shunned if it ever dared to peek through. I had to agree with things that I knew were wrong to not be hurt or isolated. I had to compete with everyone and everything around me to get affection, and I somehow always lost. Life has and always will be a competition that I am losing. Everyone is an opponent, including the wise woman with the notepad sitting across from me.

"I don't know if he feels safe. I know you hate it when I say, 'I don't know' but I truly don't." I inhale loudly.

"That's okay. Thank you for your honesty. You know, I believe that one way we can tell if people are safe or not is if their values align with ours. Do you know what Sebastian's values are?"

"Um, no. I mean, he likes a stiff martini, does that count?"

Dr. Veizer laughs. "Not exactly. Do *you* know what your core values are?"

"Core values?"

"The things that are the most important to you, that matter the most to you. *Meaning*."

This meaning shit again. What's the most important thing to me? The most important thing is gone. And now, nothing else matters.

"I know you hate this, but I really don't know." I bury my face in my hands out of exhaustion. My head is starting to pound, I need another drink, now. I pick my head up and glance at the clock.

"That's okay!" Dr. Veizer exclaims, "most people that I ask that question to don't know the answer because they've never thought about it before. I do have an intervention for values exploration. Are you open to trying it?"

"What's an intervention?"

"It's just an activity."

"Sure."

"Alright then." She gets up from her chair and heads to her desk before returning with a clipboard, pen, and paper.

"What's this for?"

"You'll see."

Ugh.

"I want you to write down about five people who you truly admire. People who have qualities that you love. People that stand for something. These can be friends, teachers, family members, celebrities, politicians, made up characters. Anybody."

"I don't—" Fuck it. I put the pen to the paper and write down the numbers one through five. I scribble and scribble until I hear the sound of an alarm.

"Okay, time's up. What do you have for me?"

"I'm not sure if I did it right."

"Well, there's no wrong way to do this which pretty much guarantees you did it right."

"Okay then. The first person I thought of was Otis Redding."

"Oh, I love him. That's a great one. Who else?"

"I wrote my brother, Liam. He's had a rough go of it the past few years, but he still has the biggest heart."

Dr. Veizer smiles sincerely and nods her head.

"Okay, and then I have, um…" my face blooms to a familiar shade of red, "sorry if this is weird, but I wrote down Dr. Veizer, you."

Dr. Veizer smiles bashfully, and she looks surprised.

"Sorry if that's weird."

"No, no, not at all. I'm just flattered. Sometimes it's hard for me to take a compliment, even at this age. But thank you, that means a lot." Dr. Veizer brings her nail to the corner of her eye. Is she wiping a tear? I can't tell if this is another one of her strategies to win this game of dominos or if she's being genuine.

"Anyway," she continues, "what are the last two names you have for me?"

I glance down at my paper without moving my head. The black letters practically jump off of the white page. I draw a thick line through the fourth name.

"Sorry, I could only think of three."

"That's okay, we can work with three. Next question, these people you chose, what are at least two qualities they have in common?"

I rack my brain. "I guess you and my brother, neither of you have ever judged me. I don't know about Otis Redding though. I love his music, but I don't know him personally, obviously."

"Okay, so nonjudgmental. Do me a favor and write that down."

I oblige her.

"And Otis, he's an incredible musician, there's no denying that, but how do you feel when you listen to his lyrics?"

I'm yanked back into Lilah Land by a familiar warm breeze and the smell of seawater.

I see myself laying down on the old wood, listening to 'Dock of the Bay' on my iPod, drenched in Abercrombie or Hollister or whatever was the must-have brand back then. Little me looks peaceful, enjoying the calm outside before getting washed away by the storm that lives inside. To this day, I don't know if I've ever found a place happier than that dock. Of course, it wasn't just the sunset and sea breeze that made it so.

"Delilah? Did I lose you?"

I grab my adult self and yank her back down onto the therapy couch. "No, yes, I mean, I'm here."

"Where did you go just now?"

"Uh, nowhere. Sorry, what was the question?"

"I was wondering how Otis Redding's lyrics make you feel."

"Like, he gets me, I guess. Almost like I could have written some of the songs myself. Not that I write songs, well, not anymore."

"You wrote songs?"

"No..."

Dr. Veizer is silent. I look around the room, neglecting to acknowledge the awkwardness between us. I wonder if Dr. Veizer can tell when I'm lying to her. I wonder if she can read me like that. What am I even saying, she's a therapist not a psychic.

"It sounds like Otis Redding's lyrics make you feel understood."

"Yeah, I suppose they do."

"So, you can go ahead and write understanding down. It sounds like I apppreciate people who are nonjudgmental and understanding. I'm going to go ahead and assume that the person you crossed off of the list earlier shares those qualities as well."

Shit, maybe she is a psychic.

"Now, last thing. I want you to look at those qualities."

I listen to her and look down at the list.

"Those are your core values. Those are the things that mean the most to you. These are qualities that you, yourself, have whether you can see that or not. These are your values, Delilah. Cherish that piece of paper with those words written on it because this is who you are."

I look down at the list again. I take the piece of paper from the clipboard and clench it in my hands.

"Finding people who align with those values is how you will find safe people. Because there are safe people in the world, Delilah."

"There are?" My eyes well with tears.

"There are." Dr Veizer pushes her domino, toppling me over along with all the rest in a line. She won.

I bring my hands to my face and cover it. My chest jerks forward as my heaves catch the sobs my mouth won't let out. I hold my breath, keeping my face covered. I catch my breath and try to tuck my tears back into my eyes. Once I'm calm and straighten out my dress, I notice that Dr. Veizer hasn't said anything in minutes. How does she do that? Is silence not violent to her too? I reconnect my eyes with hers and stare at her for what feels like a long time. Uh, is she going to say anything, or...

"Delilah, I know you don't like to talk about your past, but I'm going to take a shot in the dark here. I'm going to hazard a guess that you haven't had a lot of safe people in your life, especially when you were young."

"No."

"And I'm going to guess that the people whose sole job it was to protect you ended up hurting you the most."

I nod, the tears fighting to make a vicious return.

"They should have protected you, Delilah. You deserved that. You deserved to be protected. You deserved to feel safe."

I cover my face again in anticipation of the rainfall, but to my surprise, my eyes are dry. Maybe I've cried all of the tears I could possibly cry for one lifetime.

"You didn't deserve to be hurt the way you were. You did not deserve it." Dr. Veizer's eyes become glassy, and I notice a tear of my own fall onto my cheek. I guess I haven't cried all the tears yet.

"How do you know?"

"Because I know, Delilah. Trust me, I know."

"You've seen the rain too?"

"I guess I have. I like that saying."

I look back to the window, the sky has stopped crying, but the drops are still there. The corners of my mouth flare up.

"Sebastian, the guy from the committee' he said something like that. He said that when he saw me, he knew I had seen the rain, like the bad stuff, the dark stuff. The things I wish I would have never known."

"I see. You know, this Sebastian, I think he may just be a safe person for you in this world. Next time you are with him, keep your core values in mind and see if what he says and does aligns with those values. Because like I said Delilah, there are safe people in this world. And you deserve to know them."

I inhale hard and nod.

"And I want you to think back to when you were young, if there was anybody that made you feel safe. And I want you to identify what it was about them that was safe."

My mind jumps back in time to two of the most breathtaking eyes I have ever seen and the most captivating voice I have ever heard. I stay in 2009, gazing at how striking and perfect the boy in front of me is. I can't stay here long, but maybe, I can stay for a little while. Just a little while longer.

Dr. Veizer's phone buzzes. "Well, that's our time for today. I appreciate how honest and vulnerable you were today. Before you go, I want to give you a little homework assignment."

"What is this? High school?"

she laughs, "bear with me. Since we talked about how it's difficult for you to identify your feelings, I want you to practice. You can take the feelings chart with you. At least three times a day, no matter what you're doing, I want you to look at that chart and identify your emotion. Then, I want you to give yourself an affirmation. I want you to say out loud 'today, I am feeling, insert your emotion, and that's okay."

"Are you serious right now?"

"I know it may seem silly, but I'm telling you, this is how we learn to identify and accept our feelings. Let's do a practice round, I'll go first. Today, I'm feeling overwhelmed, and that's okay."

My eyebrow shoots up. Is she really feeling overwhelmed? I hope I didn't cause that.

"Your turn.".

"Fine. Today I'm feeling… fucking ridiculous."

"And?"

"And that's okay." I say it like an apathetic child responding to her teacher.

"Three times a day, deal?"

"Deal," I nod and grab the paper off the couch.

As I'm driving away from Dr. Veizer's office, on my way to a date with Belvedere and Pornhub, my mind wanders to 2009. I can't help but think about those eyes staring not at me but into me. Those eyes. I would give anything to see them again. Too bad that will never happen. God, I need a fucking drink.

Chapter 21
2009- Richmond Hill, Georgia

The keys vibrate below my fingertips. I straighten out my posture and close my eyes, allowing my ears to take over and my hands to travel where they want. My fingers graze the piano with a legato ease. The chords float above me like clouds while the melody transports me to heaven. The bass strings and treble strings dance with each other like two teenagers in love. My body sways with a harmonious tranquility. The rest of the world disappears for a glorious moment as I fly my ship away beyond the sky. I'm halfway to space when my ship plummets back down to earth and burns my five minutes of peace to a crisp. My Otis Redding cover is cut short by loud footsteps behind me. My heart skips at least three beats.

"Don't let Dad hear you playing that. Only classical compositions for the prodigy, Delilah Monroe."

My hand flies to my chest in total relief when I hear Liam's voice instead of my dad's.

"Jesus, fuck. I thought you were him."

"Calm down, squirrelly. William's out with colleagues at the club and Katherine is... I don't know, doing whatever it is

Katherine does. Bible thumping, or shopping, or kicking stray puppies in the street for fun."

"She's not *that* bad."

"She's not?"

"Okay," I sigh, "she's pretty bad, but she's nothing compared to William. Dad's been a complete asshole lately."

"Did something happen?"

"He… he just… never mind. Nothing significant, just the usual William Monroe fuckery."

"Ah, I know it well," Liam says as he takes a seat next to me on the piano bench. I'm relieved he's not asking more questions. There's nothing I want to do less than revisit that night and how disgustingly Dad treated Mom. The smell of bourbon still stings my nose like my nasal passages have their own set of memories.

Suddenly, another smell from that night wafts over me like a black tarp of doom and confusion. I shake my head, trying to break my mind free from the memories that chain me.

"Did I lose you to Lilah Land already? That was fast. Didn't think I was *that* boring," Liam teases.

"No, I'm good. It's all good."

"I liked your playing. You were really feeling it. You always look way happier when you play that kind of music."

"Yeah, too bad that's not the path for me."

"It could be."

I let out a big exhale. "No, it couldn't be. Because William Monroe is the only being on planet earth who gets to decide what path one will follow."

"True that. That's why I'm a finance major."

"Speaking of, what are you doing here? Shouldn't you be at school, partying for a living?" I focus my eyes on Liam's aqua irises. I scan his face up and down and can't help but notice the white tint in his skin. Sweat gathers on his forehead, making him glisten like a porcelain doll. That's strange, the air conditioning is blasting in here, making the house like the arctic, just how Dad likes it.

"Liam," I say looking down at his shaking hands. I grab one of his clammy palms. "Are you okay? You don't look so good. What are you doing here?"

Liam runs a shaky hand through his dirty blonde hair. "Yeah, well… Exams are coming up, so you know I gotta take Adderall to study, obviously."

Obviously?

"But then sometimes I get too wired, and I need something to calm me down so I can sleep. And I need something to help me sleep, obviously."

Obviously?

Liam trips over his words. "So," he continues, "I was getting Xannies, ya know, Xanax. I was buying from my hookup on campus, but then some narc tipped the cops off and his place got raided. Now, no one on campus wants to sell because they're afraid of getting caught. So, I came back here to get some stuff from my old high school dealer to get me through exam week. But he's not answering his phone. Think maybe he changed his number."

"So…"

"So, I'm fucked!" Liam shouts, his voice bounces off the walls and it reminds me of William's roar.

"Jesus, Liam, chill out. I'm sure you'll function through exam week just fine without pills."

"No," Liam sighs, "I won't." He turns from me and stares down at the floor. He looks defeated and desperate. He shivers yet sweat is still forming on his neck and chest. He really doesn't look good. I feel so… I don't know, worried. What has he gotten himself into? I'm about to get up and offer him a glass of water when he shoots his head up.

"What about Philly? Or one of the football guys? I'm sure they have some stuff. I'll take whatever they got. Anything, I'll take it," he pleads with eagerness.

"Is it that bad?"

"Can you just text Philly?"

I shake my head.

"Please, Lilah," he begs as tears well in his light eyes. "Please."

I sigh. "Ugh, hold on, I think I have something that can help."

I rise from the piano bench and quickly walk upstairs to my mom's room. She has commandeered the master bedroom, banishing my Dad from the entire top floor. I believe he's sleeping in the basement, but he hasn't been home much, so it's hard to say where he's laying his head, or who he's laying it next to. Once I swing open the door to the master bathroom, I rifle through Katherine's drawers until I find the little orange bottle that I'm looking for. I shut all the drawers and head back down the stairs and into the piano room.

"Here. I'm not sure if this is exactly what you're looking for but it's what Mom has been taking. It seems to mellow her out."

"What is it?"

I try to pronounce the word on the label slowly. "Al-praz-o-lam."

"Alprazolam! Fuck yeah! That's the scientific word for Xanax." He jumps up with glee and snatches the pill bottle out of my hand. He pops three in his mouth and swallows them dry.

"Are you sure that's not too much?"

"Very fucking sure. This will help with the chills, but it'll barely make a dent." He fishes three more pills out of the bottle. "This is all I can take for now without Mom noticing. Don't want to experience that woman's wrath ever again." He points to the spot on his head where he had stitches after Mom cracked it open when he was trying to protect her from William. "I'll need some more in a few hours. Can you text Philly to see if he has anything or has a hookup in town?"

The smell of urine wafts over me again as a pang in my stomach pounds like a bass drum. "Oh, uh, I don't know."

"Trouble in paradise?"

"Kind of. I don't really know, to be honest. I never know where I stand with him. It's complicated."

"Well, y'all have been an item practically since you could walk. Dad and Sheriff St. James are butt buddies at the county club. Philly's like part of the family. What's complicated about that?"

"It's…" I hesitate. "Nothing. Never mind."

"D, tell me. What's going on?"

I sit back down on the piano bench and Liam joins me. "How do you know if someone is a good person or not?"

"Are you wondering whether or not Philly is a good person?"

"I guess so, yeah."

"Well, the world is not that black and white. It's gray as fuck."

"Um, in English, please."

"There are no good people or bad people. We're all just people who do both good things and bad things."

"Some more than others." I roll my eyes towards the wall of family photos to our left. It's filled with framed photos of Liam and I when we were little in matching white outfits at Forsyth Park and old photos from my parents' wedding in the 80s.

"That's for sure. But you really can't label anyone as good or bad because there's no criteria. There's no number of how many bad things someone has to do to be considered a bad person."

"But, what about the people who go to hell? You may not think there's an exact number, but I bet the devil is counting."

"I thought you didn't believe in God and all that."

"I don't but… I don't know. How can you know anything if you believe in nothing?"

"Very astute," Liam laughs, "deep. You come up with that just now?"

"No, uh, it's something that I heard someone say before."

"Who?"

"Just a friend." My eyes linger around as we sit in silence. They land back on the wall of photos, fixated on a photo of my dad on a riverboat holding a big fish that he probably paid someone else to catch.

"Do you think that Dad is a bad person?"

Liam snorts. "He's definitely done a lot of bad things, but he's done some good too. The question is if the good outweighs the bad."

"What good has he done?

"Look around," Liam puts his hands in the air. "He's provided us with a more than comfortable life."

"I'm not sure that constant screaming and drinking and hitting is comfortable."

"That's fair. He is a piece of shit. But we could just as easily have been raised by a poor piece of shit in a tiny shack in the mountains, no pot to piss in. At least with William, we have pots."

"That's true. Imagine William Monroe if he was poor."

"Ah," Liam shivers, "the only thing scarier than a wealthy and powerful William Monroe would be a poor and starving William Monroe."

"True."

"Anyway, back to Philly. I'm sure he's not always a saint, none of us are, but do you think his good outweighs his bad? Or do you think he's like Dad?"

I shake my head. "Of course not. Philly is nothing like Dad. If Philly ever treated me the way that Dad treats Mom, I would send him to jail and never talk to him again."

"Glad to hear it. You got a good head on your shoulders, kid." Liam pats my arm.

"I guess so," I say with my eyes glued to piano petals under my shoes.

"So, the pills. Can you text Philly to see if he has a connect?"

I think for a moment then stand up. "You know what, I was thinking of going over there, actually. I haven't been to his house or seen his mom in a while. Can you drive me?"

"Of course," Liam says, excitedly, "and you're going to—"

"Yes, yes. I will ask about the damn pills. But you have to swear that after exam week, you ditch them for good. You're a scary sight today. I don't want you getting addicted or anything."

"I swear. Monroe's don't do addiction. We're too strong for that."

"Yeah, yeah. That's what Mom says after her 12th martini of the afternoon."

We both laugh and head out towards Liam's Mercedes.

Philly's house has not changed a bit since the first time I came here in kindergarten. It's a big, classic southern house with white columns, black shutters, and a wrap-around porch with two rocking chairs in the front. They have these gorgeous floor-to-ceiling windows in the kitchen that look out onto the pool and the most beautiful magnolia trees I've ever seen. I've always loved this house and the energy inside of it. Philly's Dad inherited the house from his Dad who inherited it from his Dad. And, one day, it will be Philly's. He's an only child, so there's not much competition.

I press my finger to the doorbell as I hear Liam drive away.

"Oh, good evening, Delilah. How lovely to see you. Is Philly expecting you?" Nancy asks in her sweet, Tennessean accent.

"Oh, no. He's not. I just wanted to stop by to ask him something. Sorry if it's a bad time. Um, is he here?"

"Nonsense, you're always welcome here. Philly is out back. Why don't you come inside? I'm sure Mrs. St. James would love to see a familiar face."

"Okay." My feet almost trip over each other as I hesitantly follow Nancy into the house. We don't have to travel far before we're in the downstairs guest room where Philly's mom lays, comatose, in her hospital bed.

"Mrs. St. James, look who's here. It's Delilah!" Nancy, Mrs. St. James's nurse, sings to her in a soft voice, but there's no response. "We haven't gotten many visitors lately. I know her wishes were to keep her condition private, but I was hoping that some of her family and friends would stop by before…" Nancy trails off. "Anyway, we're happy to see you. I'll go get Philly from the backyard and tell him you're here."

"Thank you," I say, aching for her not to go. I'm scared of being alone with Philly's mom when she's like this, and I immediately hate myself for it.

"H— hi Mrs. St. James," I stutter. I sit down on a small space on the bed next to her. I can hear her breathing over the monitor, but her eyes are closed and she's completely limp.

She has countless wires hooked up to her, I almost can't bear to look. Her once beautiful, long black hair is gone, and her face is paler than a corpse. She looks like she's dead already. Oh my god, did I really just think that? What the hell is wrong with me? I look around the all-white room, it smells of sickness. My heart shatters at how much the energy in this house has changed. Breast cancer stole it, it stole everything. My eyes travel back to Mrs. St. James. I can't help but miss her rosy cheeks, her beautiful dark eyes, her kind nature, and above all, her famous mouth-watering pecan pie. I put my hand on hers, and it's ice cold to the touch.

"I'm very glad to see you, Mrs. St. James. I know it's been a while. You look great." I have no fucking clue what else to say. Shocker. Can she hear me?

"She can't hear you." I hear a voice read my mind from behind me. I whip my head around to see Philly standing in the doorway, his black eyes glistening with sadness. Nancy comes up behind him with freshly pressed blankets.

"I got that Nancy," he insists, taking the blankets from her. "Why don't you go relax or get something to eat. You've done enough for tonight."

Nancy puts her hand to Philly's cheek. "You are such a good boy. Such a good son."

Philly smiles politely with an air of melancholy in his black eyes which are accompanied by dark circles. Perhaps he hasn't been sleeping much either. Nancy makes her way through the doorway and disappears down the hallway. Philly walks towards me with the blankets, and I hop up off of the bed. I inch out of his way as he lays the blankets over his mother.

"I, um—" *Say something, you idiot.* "I didn't know it was this bad."

"No one does. She took a turn for the worst a few weeks ago. At this point, we're just making her comfortable. Won't be long now. Cancer fucking won."

"Philly, I'm so sorry." I walk around the bed and put my hand on his arm, but he shrugs me off of him. I shouldn't have done that. "Sorry," I repeat in a lulled whisper.

"It's fine."

"It's not."

Philly pulls the blanket up to her neck and tucks it under her shoulders. He stares at his mom. "No. No, it's not," he sighs.

I watch as his already sparkling eyes begin to sparkle more with tears. I haven't seen tears in Philly's eyes since his dog died in eighth grade. He cared for that dog with so much love until her final breath just like he's caring for his mom now. Some things never change.

Philly turns away from me and wipes his face. He walks towards the window. I follow behind, keeping a wide berth to give him space.

"Where's your dad?"

"He's on duty all night at the station. As he has been every single night for the past six months."

It's strange that Sheriff St. James would be that busy in a town with a basically negative crime rate. You'd think they would allow him to be with his wife on her final days.

"He's avoiding her," Philly looks back towards me, "And me. And everything. He can't bear to watch her die. He says he loves her too much."

I inch closer, hesitantly.

"Fucking prick. Like I want to watch her die? Nobody fucking does. But I'm not going to leave her here to die alone." Philly's voice rises slightly. He takes a deep breath and turns back towards the window. I move closer until I'm next to him and join him in staring out the window. Philly's parents have always shown an insane amount of love and affection for each other, always touching and kissing each other. They're nothing like my parents. I know that the Sheriff adores his wife, everyone in this town with eyes can see that. But, like my dad, Sheriff St. James is a tough man, a guy's guy. He's the town hero, he can't afford to be emotional. I could see him avoiding this type of pain at all costs.

"So, you've been dealing with this all alone?"

"Yep."

"I'm sorry."

"You said that already."

"Oh right... sorry. I mean— I just want to make you feel better."

Philly sighs, "I know you do, but you don't. You don't understand. You don't understand *anything*, Delilah."

"I'm sorry."

Philly wipes a palm over his defined cheekbone. "God, stop fucking saying that. Just shut up."

I bow my head down. He's right, I don't understand. I should stop pretending to. "Does anybody else know? Any of our friends?"

"No. My dad doesn't want anyone to know." Philly turns around and walks back towards his mom. He picks up her limp hand and holds it in both of his.

"Nancy is right, you know. You truly are a great son."

Philly sighs, "right." He drops his mom's hand and heads for the door. "I need a beer." He walks out of the doorway.

I'm frozen in place.

Suddenly, his head pops back in through the frame. "You coming?"

I scurry out of the room and follow him to the kitchen.

214

I'm perched up at the granite kitchen counter, already halfway through my beer when Philly asks, "so, what are you doing here?"

"I, um… I don't know."

"You don't know why you trekked all the way across town and showed up at my house unannounced?"

"No, I— I mean…"

Philly stares at me, expectantly. He's obviously irritated. "Say something, Delilah."

The words continue to escape me until I remember who drove me here. "Liam!" I blurt.

"Liam? Your brother?"

"Yeah, he's home from school. He was wondering if you had anything…"

"Anything like?"

"Xanax, I think. Maybe Adderall."

"Ah. Link's got some stuff, we bought a bunch last weekend. He's got Xannies for sure, I don't know about Adderall, but I think he has Ritalin. I doubt Liam cares, it's all the same shit. Does he have Link's number?"

"I'll give it to him. Thanks."

"All good. Is that all you came here for? You could have texted or Facebooked me." Philly gets another Corona from the refrigerator and cracks it open.

"Yeah, well…"

"Well, what?"

"I kind of wanted to talk about the other night."

"What about the other night?" Philly chugs his beer.

I study his black eyes; they seem to be filled with apathy.

"You know, when you— when we…" I can't bring myself to utter the words. "When you like, did that thing?"

"The sex thing?"

"No, the other thing." Red blotches spread from my chest to my face, staining my cheeks.

Philly sips his beer without a care in the world. Frustration swims through my boiling blood.

"The pee thing," I finally yell. "You peed on me, Philly!"

His eyes widen with shock. He looks around the kitchen, probably making sure Nancy, the sweet southern nurse, didn't hear me. The surprise is short lived once he takes another sip, his muscles relax.

He rolls his eyes. "So? Who cares?"

Shivers cool the red blotches on my skin. I wrap my arms around myself. Philly sets his beer on the counter and sighs. "Look, it's not a big deal. I saw it in an old porn DVD. My dad has a big collection. I was just trying something new. You don't have to be so sensitive all the time."

Tears form at the corners of muddy eyes. I have no idea how to tell him what I felt in that moment when he was over me, pushing me down, looking at me like I was a piece of trash on the street, like I was fucking nothing. It made me feel... I don't know, like I didn't matter. Like I don't matter, to Philly, to anyone. My hand flies up to my eyes, desperate to catch the tears before he sees them fall.

"Hey, hey," Philly rounds the kitchen island and puts an awkward hand on my shoulder. "You don't need to cry about it. I was trying something new. I've banged plenty of girls but never done that with a girl. You were my first. I thought you would like that you were my first."

"Well, I didn't," I whisper, physically unable to speak at a normal volume.

Philly rubs my back. "Okay then, we don't have to do it again."

I cover my face so he can't see me sob. I try to will the tears away, but my body is betraying me.

"Look, there's no need to be this goddamn dramatic. If you can't tell, I've got a lot on my fucking plate here."

Guilt rises up my throat like acid rain. He's right, he does have a lot on his plate, more than I can imagine dealing with. I shouldn't have come here. I shouldn't have put this on him. "Sorry, I'll go." I slowly rise from the highchair.

Philly puts both hands on my shoulders and gently pushes me back down. "Delilah, look at me." Philly takes his hand off of my shoulders and stares down at me. He picks up my hand and moves it away from my face. "We don't have to do that again. Hell, we don't have to have sex ever again. I don't care that much. I just want to be with you."

"You— you do?" Shock fills me, widening my eyes and sewing my lips shut.

"Yeah, I do. I wanna be *with you* with you. Like, for real."

And then, there he is. The boy who chased butterflies with me, the boy who was too afraid to go to the pool party because he was self-conscious about his stomach. The boy I've always loved. Philly puts his hand on my thigh and bites his bottom lip. His eyes spear through mine, my leg tingles at his touch with desire.

"Like… as my boyfriend, kind of?"

Philly laughs. "If that's what you wanna call it, whatever."

Excitement floods me as images of our future flash through my mind. Images of us holding hands in the hallway, us getting married, us having kids, us growing old in this very house. Images of us, finally, us.

"Could we even, like, change our Facebook statuses to in a relationship?"

Philly rolls his gorgeous eyes. Shit. Was that too much? Did I just ruin this before it started?

"Sure," he smirks, "whatever you want."

I jump out of my chair with glee and wrap my arms around his neck. I cannot believe this is happening. Philly just asked me to officially be his girlfriend. Well, kind of. He even said he'd give up sex for me. A teenage boy giving up sex is like Beethoven giving up music. I can't believe he's willing to do that just for me. Maybe he really does love me as much as I love him. Should I tell him I love him? Is now the time?

Philly shakes me off of him and grabs his beer from the other side of the counter. No, now's not the time. I'll know the right moment when it comes. My smile stretches across my face like a clown, and I can't seem to wipe it off as I gawk at his lips wrapped around his beer bottle, his chiseled face looking sharper and sexier as he puckers.

"Philly?"

The cloud I'm floating on disintegrates when Nancy walks into the kitchen.

"Sorry to interrupt, I wanted to make some food and feed your mom before I go."

"I'll help you with that. She loves my potato leek soup," Philly tells her.

He is such a good son, such a good person. Liam was right, we're all capable of doing bad things, but the important thing is that our good outweighs the bad.

My phone buzzes, and I remember that Liam told me he was picking me up in half an hour.

"I better be going," I tell Philly and Nancy.

"I'll walk you out."

Philly leads me to the front door. I stop in the foyer.

"Sorry for being so dramatic."

Philly shrugs. "You always are, I'm used to it."

"It must be my time of the month."

"Gross."

"Oh yeah, gross. Sorry."

I try to salvage the moment by pulling Philly in for a kiss. I grab his hair from the back of his head and he slides his tongue between my lips. I feel his edged cheek bone graze my face. Our tongues dance together in perfect rhythm the way they always have. Philly pulls me into him, pushing our pelvises together. He grinds on me slightly as a quiet groan escapes his mouth that's entangled with mine. He slowly brings his hand from the small of my back up to my head. He grabs a handful of my copper hair and clenches it tightly in his grasp. He then smashes my face deeper into his, his sharp features nearly cut me like a knife. It's like he can't possibly get closer to me. That's sweet… right? All of the sudden, I feel an intense pressure searing on my bottom lip. I try to pull away, but my lip is trapped between Philly's teeth. I stand like a statue for a moment, but the shrill pain becomes excruciating when he bites down harder. I remove my hands from Philly's hair and push them off his chest.

"Ow." I step backward, bringing my fingers to my mouth. I wipe my lip and bring my hand into my focus to see scarlet blood tinting the snow-white skin. I look back towards Philly, who's smile has grown across his face, exposing the W-shaped white stain on his front tooth. I can't help but mirror his smile, it's been too long since it's made an appearance. I swipe the rest of the blood from my lip and wipe it on my dress. I laugh bashfully, embarrassed that I've never done anything like that before. I'm sure it's normal. Love is pain.

I hear the honk of Liam's horn from the driveway and straighten myself out.

"See ya tomorrow, boyfriend!" I turn on my heels and open the front door.

Philly laughs. "Oh God, what have I gotten myself into?"

Chapter 22
2009- Richmond Hill, Georgia

"I can't believe Mr. Stoff got fired."

"He did?" I ask, setting my salad and sweet tea down on the lunch table.

Mia puts her pizza down and takes the seat next to me. She flips her long hair, laces her glittery nailed fingers together, and patiently awaits the latest gossip. I look at her side profile, which is perfectly made up for tonight's football game, her cat eyes could claw a heart out. She's incredibly precise with her liquid eyeliner, but my hands aren't as steady with an eye pencil as they are on a piano.

"Well?" Mia glares at Chloe, who, judging by her empty tray, has decided to forego her lunch today. Perhaps Mia's little comment about overeating got to her. Or maybe she's trying to stay thin to impress Philly.

I've been floating on a cloud ever since he and I made our relationship official, but that doesn't mean I've forgotten about how strong Chloe has been coming onto him. I know that she knows that we're official. We're Facebook official, which means literally everything ever. We're as good as married. But I'm still watching her. Now that I have Philly for real, I am not losing him, to anything or anyone. Especially not Chloe Black.

"Mr. Stoff," Mary Lu chimes in, her mouth full of pizza, her hazel eyes full of amusement. "Our English teacher. He got fired, like yesterday. You haven't heard?"

"Guess not," Mia says, reaching over to steal a sip of my sweet tea.

I glance around the table. The girls are in their black and white cheer uniforms as usual. I look around the rest of the cafeteria, searching for Philly. My eyes trail up and down the lunch tables and lunch line, and I can't help but notice people huddled together, whispering, laughing. Looks of shock and jaws dropping to the floor fill the cafeteria.

"What the hell is going on?" I ask.

"Sup hoes." Link's shrill voice and his almond eyes come into my view. I glance past him to see if his best friend is behind him, but still no sign of Philly. Where is he? I haven't seen him all day.

"Hey."

My lips form a child-like grin at the sound of his voice.

"Here," Mia says, getting up from her chair, "you can take my seat. Can't separate the love birds."

Philly rolls his eyes and sits next to me. Mia walks around to the other side of the table. Mary Lu, who's sitting on the other side of me, immediately gets up and lets Mia have her seat.

"Wow, Mary Lu. Could you be further up Mia's ass?" Chloe chirps.

Mia glares at her, then grabs her plate from across the table. "Lord knows I'm not sitting next to Link. I don't want to catch Gonorrhea… Or rabies."

"You wish, you fucking slut!" Link hisses.

Mia rolls her neck. "I sure hope the girls you've gotten with had all their shots. If you *have* gotten with any girls, that is."

"Fuck you, Mia."

"Clever." She adjusts her uniform and continues eating.

It's silent for a moment. I look over at Link who seems deep in thought... well... deep in thought for him. Who knows how many brain cells that kid has left. He keeps his head down until he finally snaps it up with enthusiasm. "Hey, hey Mia!"

Mia flutters her freshly mascaraed eyelashes up at him.

"This isn't the wax museum!" Link bursts out into laughter at his own joke, then repeats it again under his breath.

I peek around the table to gauge everyone else's reactions, but they seem as confused as I am. Okay good, I thought I missed something. Mia looks ready and amused.

"Huh?" Mary Lu grunts.

"Like the wax museum? You know, like she's wax because she wears a lot of makeup. You know, like the figures at the wax museum!" Link hits Philly's chest with the back of his hand, looking for backup.

"The wax museum?" Philly asks, annoyed.

"Yeah, the wax museum, like Madam Tussauds."

"Bro, who the fuck is Madam Tussauds, my guy?" Philly breaks out into high pitched laughter which is contagious to the rest of the table. Philly has that effect on people, he can always make us smile or laugh, even with all that he's going through with his mom at home.

"Yo, you gotta chill on those Xannies, bro. You're losing it. Madam Tussauds. Sounds like a lady that would be on a syrup bottle, or a weird ass porno."

The table continues laughing at Philly's jokes. I stare at his smile in awe, watching his lips part and his teeth show. I see his perfect tooth, the one he hates but I adore. I continue to gawk at his smile until I feel eyes burning with adoration in the same direction as mine. I whip my head and glare at Chloe, who's eyes stay fixed on Philly's smile. Anger runs through my bones, causing me to want to break all of hers. I take a deep breath and put my hand on Philly's arm. This is probably a bad idea. I'm being ridiculous, like a dog marking its territory. Philly will hate it. I close my eyes and brace myself for the public embarrassment. But, then, a few seconds pass, and he doesn't. He doesn't move, he just continues talking and laughing. Okay, maybe this is good, maybe it's okay to do this kind of thing now that we're official. I can see our entire future together. We'll go to colleges up north then move to New York City so that I can pursue my dreams of playing piano in the New York Philharmonic. Philly will love New York, he can be anything he wants to be. Maybe a Wall-Streeter, an artist, maybe a cop like his Dad. The sky is the limit in the big apple, unlike Georgia, where the meaning of fine dining is a pig roast.

My mind wanders out of Lilah land to see Philly's perfectly imperfect smile fixated on me. I swoon as I feel my cheeks blush with passion. Our eyes twirl in bliss together for six heavenly seconds… until a third pair of eyes cut in.

The reflection of the cafeteria lights illuminates the gray behind his eyelashes. It stuns me. The silver specs in his eyes slice my perfect moment in half like a knife to a wedding cake. I'm shell shocked as Sam stops in his tracks. His tall, tanned body towers over the lunch table. His backpack drapes over his shoulders and his black hoodie hugs his chest. It's too small for him, like most of his clothes. I want to tell him that he's outgrown it, and that Liam has hundreds of hoodies leftover in his closet. Most of them are too big for him now, he's lost a little weight since being at college. They'd fit Sam perfectly though. But I know that my offering would make him feel like a charity case.

"Hey," Sam says, with the confidence of a hundred knights.

Every head at the table turns toward him. My 'friends' look shocked, like they're flabbergasted that Sam knows how to speak.

"Uh, hey," I stutter, realizing that the 'uh' probably makes it seem like I don't want to talk to him, like I'm embarrassed to be talking to him, which I'm not. I'm really not... right?

"What's up!" I shout, too animated, overcompensating.

"Nothin'." The corner of his mouth flares up in that side smile that he does. I can't help but smile a little when I see it, picturing the last time that I did. Only that time, the moon kissed his bare chest like it was his lover. His big arms parted the cold bay water with ease. I bobbed up and down in silence, treading the thick water, trying not to be swallowed whole with the way Sam said my name. I watched as he dunked his head under, just long enough for my heart to race faster than it was already. When he emerged from the water, he flicked his head, and drops from his black hair splashed on my face. Salt water shouldn't taste good, but it did. I licked it off my lips and continued to stare. My eyelashes fluttered as he swam closer to me.

"What?" He asked.

"Nothin'." I smirked and turned away from him, swimming in the other direction. I could feel his eyes on me, trying not to notice the way my legs parted when I swam away.

"You coming?" I called out.

Sam followed behind me, his breaths were even as mine became heavier and heavier. When I had no choice but to slow down, I began to tread. I spun in the water to face Sam. His gaze took in my bare chest, as mine did to his. The water from the bay froze every inch of my skin, but I didn't care, nor did he. He treaded in that very spot, almost out of eyesight of the dock. We stared at each other's bodies, taking in every goosebump, every scar, every freckle. I wanted to stay there forever.

"Can we help you, bro?" Philly's voice crashes into me as he puts his arm around my shoulder, something he has never done while sober. "Whatever the fuck your name is."

Philly and Link start laughing. Mia and Mary Lu exchange awkward looks with each other. Chloe… well who cares what Chloe is doing. I shoot my head down, terrified.

"See ya around," Sam gestures to me, half smile still intact, not the least bit deflated. He walks away from the table and out the back door.

Why was Philly so rude to Sam? His sister just died, and his family lost their home, can't anyone just give him a goddamn break? I take my hand off of Philly and subtly inch away. He doesn't look at me. Fuck. Did he pick up on something? Was that why he was rude? It can't be because there is nothing to pick up on. What happened with Sam was a mere fluke, a weak moment because I was angry with Philly, and anger will make you do crazy things. But I finally have everything I've ever wanted here, with Philly. That's what matters, that's what is real. I grab my sweet tea back from Mia.

"Fucking skeleton twin," Link mumbles under his breath.

"Forget him," Mary Lu interrupts, "back to the drama with Mr. Stoff."

"He got fired, right? For what?"

"I heard that he was looking at porno films on a school computer! Can you believe that? Porn!" Mary Lu shouts.

"Oh please, like you're so pure. You're no nun. I bet you watch porn on the reg," Chloe spits.

"I do not!"

"Nothing wrong with a little porn. Ya'll ever seen Two Girls One Cup?" Link asks.

"Ewwwwww," the whole table groans in unison.

"Hey, don't knock it till you try it."

"I heard," Philly's low voice chimes in, commanding the table, "Mr. Stoff got fired because he had an affair with a student."

Everybody gasps.

"What? Where did you hear that?" I ask, turning towards Philly.

"My aunt told me. She and him run in the same circles. Apparently, he frequents bars in the south historic district in Savannah. I'm pretty sure he went out with one of my aunt's friends. But yeah, she said that he was hooking up with a student, that's why they fired him."

"I bet it was Mia," Link barks. "No dudes left in the grade she hasn't boned so she had to move on to teachers."

"Ew, fuck off, Link. I might date guys a few years older, but I draw the line at gray hair. Mr. Stoff could, like, be my grandpa."

"Now that would be a great porn."

"Once again, Link, fuck off. Go suck your two-inch dick."

"Whore," Link whispers.

"My bets are on Chloe." Mia's eyes flash over towards Chloe who finally looks up from the floor.

"Clearly, she's desperate. And now that Philly is officially off the market…"

Chloe's small body shoots up from her seat. She pushes her empty lunch tray towards the middle of the table, tightens her blonde ponytail, and walks away. It seems like she's had enough for one day. I'm sure I contributed to that, marking my territory with Philly. I kind of feel… I don't know, bad. I'm a bitch.

"What's up her ass?" Philly asks.

"Not you, that's why she's so pissed." Mia laughs, the others join in.

"Hey, what if Mr. Stoff banged the other skeleton twin?"

"Bailey?" I ask, my voice accidentally booming.

"Whatever, who cares what her name was. But maybe she fucked him then got scared people would find out so she…" Link makes a hanging gesture with his hand as he tilts his neck.

"My God, Link," Mia hisses, "you're seriously messed up."

"Whatever, that's my theory."

"That's not what happened. She was raped," I snap..

"How would you know?" Philly asks.

"I— I just— that's what I heard."

"Yeah, I heard the same thing," Mia says.

"Me too," Mary Lu agrees.

"Well, Mr. Stoff banged someone at this school," Philly reminds everyone.

"And detective Link and St. James are on the case!" Link puts an arm around Philly that looks more like a headlock than a friendly gesture. The two of them laugh.

"Well, with Sherlock Homo and Nancy Dickbreath on the case, it's sure to be cracked," Mia jokes. I laugh so hard, I choke on my sweet tea.

I'm about to throw out my untouched salad when I hear my ringtone blare through my bag. I riffle through and flip open my Razor phone.

"Who's texted?" Mia asks.

"No one!" I yell, slamming my phone shut. "It's just… um, my mom…" I lie through my teeth.

"Drunk again?"

"Ha, yeah. Of course, you know Lady Katherine." I laugh awkwardly. "See you at the game!" I emergency exit out of the cafeteria, nearly knocking over multiple freshmen. I pray no one saw the name on my screen.

Chapter 23
Present Day

"Ma'am, do you need any help in there?"

"No, that's alright. Thank you!" I shout the words through the dressing room door, my head stuck in the neck hole of this black dress. I yank the hem down past my waist until my head finally pops through the hole. I pull it over my hips, zip the side of it, and flatten out the creases. I'm surprised by how easily it zipped right up. I turn to the side, to the back, to the other side, attempting to see the dress from all angles, how everyone at that reunion could possibly see me. I've always hated that I can't see myself through the eyes of others, but hell if I'm not going to try. It was after my last therapy session that I made a decision. Well, *decisions*. I decided that I will no longer drink a sip of alcohol before 5pm, with the exception of committee meetings at the country club. I decided that I'm going eat at least two meals a day, and I'm going to start frequenting the gym. I decided that I will no longer partake in self-sabotaging pastimes, like cheating on my husband with the neighbor's gardener. Last night's escapades, aside.

Salvatore clenched my neck as he railed into me, pool water splashing and creating the perfect friction. I tightened my legs around his torso as I bounced up and down on his cock. My hands played through his hair, tugging the strands as I threw my head back, a loud whimper escaping me. I clasped my hand over mouth, quieting the roars as he slid in and out, each thrust feeling deeper and deeper. Our naked bodies feverishly entagled, our wet stomachs collided as I arched my back. The pool water submerged my hair and I whipped my head back to Salvatore's mouth, catching his lips between my teeth. He squeezed my butt as he yanked me forward and back, crashing into him with fluidity. I slid my hand over his pecks and felt each one of his defined abs as my finger tips explored his smooth olive skin. He thrust into me with circular motions, his hips making ovals in the water. Gliding our interwoven bodies through the small waves, he pushed me up against the edge of the pool. The warm autumn night wrapped us in a delicate embrace as Salvatore floated his tongue over my breasts, licking the salt water off.

"Salvatore!" I squealed.

A smile flickered across his face as he quickened his thrusts.

"Oh my God, Oh my God!"

My back smashed into the edge of the pool behind me as Salavatore grabbed my neck. He rammed his manhood into me, each time with more force. His fingers dug into my skin as I bit down on his shoulder. Whirlpools of sensations swirled through my body as my heart beat out of my chest. My insides vibrated and pulsation touched each corner of me. Electricity shocked every nerve, palpitations rocking me as the orgasm captured and held me hostage.

"Still doing okay in there, ma'am?"

"Yes, I'm fine!" I shout. I squeeze my legs together, hoping my thighs are strong enough to crush the memory into a million pieces. It's fine, everything is fine. It was a minor indiscretion, a slip up, if you will. It will never happen again. Anyway, back to the new me. I decided I'm going to look for a part-time job that gets me out of the house more. And most importantly, I decided to block that unknown number that's been harassing me, well, block it again. Then I'm going to snap out of my paranoia and walk into my 15th year high school reunion with my head held high and my Louboutin's higher. That's why I've been raiding all of the local boutiques in Savannah today. I am committed to finding the classiest yet sexiest dress this city has in its inventory so I can turn the heads of everyone who's ever doubted me. I haven't received any cryptic texts since that last one. And it truly feels like the end of it. Besides, he can't *that* many phones. I probably read too much into it anyway. Maybe it was a mistake or a prank. There are infinite possibilities, but I know that him being at the reunion is not one of them. It can't be. He would never show his face at that school again, not after what he did.

I stare at my golden locks spilled over the long, velvet sleeves of the dress. Today is the first day I'm not hungover in I don't know how long. Last night, I only had three drinks. They were double shot vodka and sodas, but still, only three.

I flash my veneers with a seductive smile in the mirror, and I can't help but notice how still my body stands. No shakes, no chills. Today, I'm feeling… relieved, and that's okay. Look at me, I'm even using Dr. Veizer's therapy things. This must be it. This is what healing looks like. This is the part where I put my past to bed once and for all, and the weight of it never drags me down to the abyss again. This is the part where I get off the ground.

I slip out of the dress I'm wearing and take the other one off the hanger. I pull it over my head and stuff my arms into the sleeves. I yank the hem down, but I can't pull the dress down past my waist. I pull and pull until my fingers feel like they're going to fall off. I glance up at myself in the mirror. The bottom of my stomach is sticking out, leaving my scar in full view. I had almost forgotten. *Look at you, you're disgusting, Delilah.*

It's fine, it's fine, it's fine. I'll just take this dress off and put on the other one. I don't know why it's so small, it's my size. Perhaps it's sized wrong. Yes, that must be it. I lift the bottom of the dress up and attempt to squeeze my breasts through. Get this fucking thing off of me. It's halfway up my chest when I hear a rip. I drop my hands. My stomach turns at the thought of having to explain this to the sales associate. I stare at my disheveled hair that drapes over the dress that looks like the casing of a sausage. I poke the layer of fat that rests under my scar. Today, I'm feeling... disgusting, and that's okay. Is it okay?

My phone buzzes in my purse. It's probably Sebastian wondering where I am, reminding me that Charlotte will chew my head off for being late to a committee meeting again. I leave the dress that's clearly designed for toddlers clenched around my rib cage. Reaching into my purse, I grab my phone, and unlock it.

Unknown number: You think you can block me and I'll go away forever? You can't get rid of me that easily. Not this time.

My heart sinks back into the abyss. I knew it was too good to be true. Every time things are going well, the other shoe drops from a skyscraper. I should have learned my lesson by now. *You're so fucking naive, Delilah.*

I throw my phone on the ground as if it just burned the skin off my hand.

"Is everything okay in there, ma'am?"

"Yes, uh, yes, it's fine!"

"Are you sure? I can get you another—"

"I said I'm fine!"

I pull my white caftan over my head and pick my phone up off the ground. The new crack in my screen matches the old cracks in my splintered heart. I rip my bag off the hook and sprint out of the dressing room.

"Ma'am? You have to pay for that!"

I hear the sales associate faintly as I launch myself out the door. It's fine, they have my credit card on file. I stumble down the street aimlessly until I'm on River Street. I throw my head over the ledge in front of me, jerking my face towards the river. I heave and gag into the water as tour boats pass by. Eventually, when no vomit comes out, my body settles a bit. I stand up straight and catch my breath. I stare out straight onto the river. Where am I?

I search around the area. I see boats and birds and shopping stands. I peer back towards the water, and I notice that the sun is shining directly onto the ripples in the river, making the teal waves glow a shade of orange, my favorite.

No.

My phone buzzes. My shaky hand barely has the strength to bring my cracked phone up to my face.

Unknown number: I am right here.

My head shoots up as my chest heaves in and out. He's watching me. He's here. I spin around to look behind me, then spin around again, and again, again. I don't see him. I don't see... anything. Everything goes dark, too dark to see.

Chapter 24
2009- Richmond Hill, Georgia

I duck my head and squat as I tiptoe my way under the bleachers. The sounds of students squealing over a gym class soccer game torture my musical ears. I creep along the edge of the bleachers, trying to stay out of sight. When I move closer to the center, I see a familiar cloud of cigarette smoke.

"Sam?"

Sam spins on his heels, the smoke from his lit cigarette following him, gliding through the air. "Delilah, hey!"

I press my lips into a flat smile, my eyes twitching between Sam and the boy to his right.

"Oh. Delilah, this is Ronny. He's a buddy." Sam smiles warmly at his friend.

"Delilah Monroe, come here often? Doesn't look like a place girls like you would be caught dead in." Ronny puffs out a breath of smoke and a little cough. The area under the bleachers fills with the smell of skunk.

"Yeah… well…" My cheeks stain pink as I rub the pale skin on my arm raw.

"Ronny was just leaving, right Ron?"

A confused look douses Ronny's small features. "Oh, right, yes. That, uh, report. It's not gonna write itself."

"What's your report on?"

Caught off guard, Ronny stumbles. "Oh, you know… Christmas… I mean… Whales… in… Paris… Whales in Paris on Christmas."

"There are whales in Paris on Christmas?" I ask, giggling.

"No, uh, no, turns out, there are not. That's my stance on the report, that contrary to popular belief, there are no whales in Paris on Christmas…" Ronny's eyes flicker over mine and Sam's. "Okay, bye." Ronny saunters away with speed.

"He's funny."

"Yeah, not like your usual crew, I'm sure." Sam chokes out smoke as he approaches me.

233

"Book and cover, Sam. Or did you forget?"

"No," he says inching closer, "I didn't forget. I'd never forget anything you say. You look great, by the way, you always do. I like your shirt."

I insecurely tug on my over-sized T-shirt from piano camp. He can't be serious.

"Okay…" I say, turning away from him. I lean my back on the edge of a bleacher. "So, what was so pressing that I had to ditch sixth period to come here?"

"I'm impressed that message sent. I sent it over AIM. I used a computer in the library. You were right, fascinating things in there," he jokes.

"Yeah, well, with how much you like philosophy and the Bible, I'm surprised you're not a regular."

"Wouldn't really fit with my whole ne'er-do-well image."

"I thought you didn't wear a mask?"

"Touché."

I peek through the bleachers to see if anyone is within earshot.

"What's wrong? You embarrassed to be seen with me?"

"No, it's just… What is it you needed to talk to me about?"

Sam throws his cigarette on the ground and comes in close to me. I can taste his whisper, the smell of cigarette smoke slowly becoming my favorite aroma.

"I thought we should talk about the other night, don't you?"

"What is there to talk about?"

Sam's features pinch together in conflict. "What is there to talk about? I don't know, about what happened."

"Nothing happened." I jerk my head down, shunning his eye contact.

Against my wishes, my mind roams back to the night in question, the night that I stripped off my shirt and convinced Sam to dive into the water because I was afraid to confront my feelings about him. After Sam followed my many strokes, we stopped to devote our stares to every inch of each other's bodies. My arms started to faulter from treading.

"You okay?" Sam asked, but I couldn't answer, my words were clenched in my throat. My upper body was betraying me with fatigue as much as my lower body was betraying me with thirst. I was starving for him, it nearly knocked the wind out of me.

"Here..." Sam swam closer and grabbed my arms gently, wrapping them around his neck, "hold onto me." I squeezed his traps with the crevasses of my arms, digging my nails into the back of his neck until I caught my breath. I interlocked my head with his, taking in the smell of his sweat. Sweat isn't supposed to smell good, but it did. Sam rubbed my shoulder and collarbone with tenderness, ignoring that my bra strap had fallen down completely. I looked up to the stars and let out a hungry breath. I prayed for him to move his hand from my collarbone to my breast, but he didn't, he just stroked my cold skin, warming me up. Without thinking, I kicked both of my legs up and wrapped them around his waist, squeezing his torso with my inner thighs. Sam's hands gripped my back. They lingered up there until they finally surrendered down towards my butt, holding me up while he treaded in the cold, dark river water. I pulled my face away, unlocking our necks, and I peered into his eyes. His silver, deep, wolf-like eyes. The dichotomy of his dark skin and hair with his eyes, it's like nothing I've ever seen. My wine-stained lips grazed his cheek, his stubble tickling my chin. I pressed my legs deeper into his waist, savoring the feeling in my jeans, until I felt something bulging, hard, on my inner thigh. *What the hell am I doing?* I thought. I unhooked my legs from him and breast stroked as fast as I could back to shore without explanation. I gathered my shirt and wine glass, feigning exhaustion before running back towards the house before Sam could say another word.

"I wouldn't call that nothing." Sam's low voice tugs me back into the present under the bleachers.

"What would you call it then?" I bite.

"Uh, I don't know, like skinny dipping?"

"Please. It's hardly skinny dipping if my jeans were on."

Sam's eyes widen and his brow furrows. "I was worried when you bolted off so quickly after, you know. I'm sorry if I did anything to make you uncomfortable, I didn't mean to."

I squeeze my eyes and open them. "No, no, Sam, you didn't. It wasn't like that. If anything, I was the one who was... you know."

"So, what happened then?"

"I have a boyfriend, Sam," I blurt out.

"You do? Since when?"

"Since... recently. Philly. We finally made it official."

"Philly? The quarterback? Delilah, that guy is a dick. He always has been, and you know it."

"You don't know him. You don't know him like I do, no one does."

"And does he know *you*? The real you, the Delilah without a mask?"

"Of course... yeah..." I stutter, "of course he does. He's known me since kindergarten. He and I have history."

"And what do *we* have?"

"We... We have nothing, Sam. We are nothing. We're just neighbors for the time being, that's it. Once your Dad is back on his feet and ya'll move out, everything will go back to normal, just the way it was before."

"What if I don't want it to go back to normal?"

"Well..." I sigh, "you can't always get what you want."

"The Rolling Stones... really? I thought you were exclusive with Otis Redding." The corner of Sam's mouth flares up, his smile traveling to the left side of his face.

I sigh, trying not to smile at his effortless charisma. "Look Sam, I think you're really cool. And obviously there was… something between us at some point. But it's over now. It has to be over. I have a boyfriend. So, no more sunset chats or midnight swims, okay? From now on, we're just neighbors, nothing more."

Sam leans in close enough until his forehead touches mine. His warmth on my skin makes me feel… I don't know, tranquil, like the whole world is obsolete except for this present moment. A swarm of guilt flies through me.

"We're not just neighbors, Delilah. We'll never be just neighbors. What happened the other night, you don't do that with just a neighbor."

I yank my head away from him, stumbling back on my feet. "So, what? I'm a whore then for having a fleeting moment with someone? Is that it?"

"What? No, of course not."

"Am I just the biggest fucking slut in Richmond Hill now because I went swimming with you?"

"Delilah, no, oh my gosh. That's not what I meant at all. I don't think that. I would never think that. I'm sorry if it sounded like that. I promise you, that is not what I meant. I was trying to say that what we have is special." Sam reaches for my hand, but I rip it away before he can grip it.

"It's fine, whatever. I gotta get to class. See you around." I turn on my heels and speed-walk out of the dark bleachers and into the light.

"Delilah, I'm sorry! Can we talk about this?" Sam yells after me as I make a mad dash onto the freshly mowed field.

The boys are still hooting and hollering at the top of their lungs when we make it back to Mia's after the football game. The Richmond Hill Jaguars defeated the Bluffton Bulldogs in the final quarter. It's a big deal, seeing as they're our rival team, at least, that's what I'm told. I find sports challenging to keep up with. Philly has explained the rules of football to me many times, but it never sticks. He says it must be because I'm bad at math, a class that I'm pretty sure he's failing. I told him that I'll learn how to play football if he learns how to play piano. But he said that will never work because I'm not a guy and he's not a loser. So, I guess that's that.

"Deeeeeee!" Link smashes his body into mine, "let's see those skills!" He hands me a plastic bottle of who the hell knows. "Hey! Put on that shot song!"

Mary Lu walks over to the guy whose iPod is hooked up to the auxiliary cord. Within a minute, "Shots" by LMFAO blares on the speakers. I oblige Link's request by chugging from the bottle. The acid stings my throat like a swarm of bees.

"Ugh, what is that? It tastes like lighter fluid."

"Ha, don't know!" Link skips away, much more energetic than usual, most likely thanks to the pharmacy he's currently running out of his bedroom. I hope he didn't give Liam whatever he's on. I should call Liam, check-in, make sure he keeps his word about quitting the pills after exams.

"Wooooo!" Mia hip bumps me and she puts an arm around me, "'we won!" She grabs both of my arms.

"Well, you won. I didn't do anything."

"No, listen to me. You listen to me, you beautiful creature. You play piano like… like…"

I stand still in her drunken grasp as she attempts to think of famous piano players.

"Like Jesus! Like Jesus. You play piano like Jesus. Wait… did Jesus play piano?" Mia's words are blurred together like a Monet painting.

This is the worst part about having such a high tolerance to alcohol, nobody else does. It makes parties like these feel... I don't know, lonely. There's no one I can actually have a conversation with, except...

"Hey, Baby." Philly's warm hand clasps mine. Butterflies flutter all throughout my stomach, and they're faster than the one we chased when we first met in kindergarten.

"Hey!" I blink my eyelashes at him as he strokes his angular jaw. I inhale his cologne scent and swoon at the aroma. It's like I just walked into an Abercrombie & Fitch at the mall. He smells clean and sexy and familiar. This is how guys are supposed to smell, not like cigarette smoke.

I pick up a solo cup and gulp the stale beer, willing the image of Sam out of my head. I look back at Philly, his sharp features and glittering eyes nearly blow me away. This is what I've always wanted, for Philly to think that I'm good enough for him, and finally, he does.

"Wanna shot?" Chloe saunters over, bouncing her stupid blonde hair.

"We're good."

"Sure!" Philly shouts. He's quite energetic as well, something tells me he partook in whatever Link did. I imagine it involved dollar bills and smooth surfaces.

Philly, Mia, and I watch as Chloe bends down to pour a shot of tequila. Her skirt is hiked up so high, I can see her entire thong as she points her round butt up to the air.

"Jesus, Chloe. Pull your damn skirt down. You have a team to represent," Mia yells.

"You're one to talk," Chloe gloats, handing Philly a shot. She touches hers to his then takes her double shot without making a sour face.

"Nice," Philly remarks.

"That's not all I can swallow."

"Holy hell, Chloe, take a damn hint. I can practically smell the desperation on you. Philly is Delilah's boyfriend. He chose her. And you could never hold a candle to her, everybody knows that. Get a life and get lost."

Everybody? Chloe looks like she's going to cry as she flips her hair and speed walks away. That was kind of harsh...

"Don't worry about her, she's just jealous." Mia's train of thought is interrupted when one of those wrestling dudes yells her name. "I'll leave you two love birds alone."

The Pussy Cat Dolls blast on the stereo, filling every corner of the basement. My ears are used to hearing constant music, but not from speakers this loud or this cheap. I feel a vibration in my ear drum and touch my palm to it.

"You wanna go somewhere quieter?" Philly suggests.

"Yes, please."

We walk into Mia's sister's bedroom a few minutes later. I reach my hand up to turn on the lights, but Philly grabs my wrist. "I thought you liked the lights off."

"Well, yeah... but that was when—"

"Shhhhh." Philly grabs both of my hands and leads me to the bed. He sits on the edge of the mattress atop the black and white duvet.

"What are we doing in here?"

"What do you think?" He grabs my hips with both hands and pushes me down to my knees.

I shoot back up to standing. "What are you doing?"

"C'mon. I played my ass off tonight. We won. Don't I get a little reward from my *girlfriend?*" He grabs my hips again and pushes me back down.

"I— I'm really proud of you, but..."

Philly leans back and unbuttons his pants. "But what?"

"You said." I rise to my feet.

"What?" He whines. "You don't like touching me?" He takes my dainty hand and puts it on his chest. I feel his heart beat, it's slower and steadier than mine.

"I do, I really do," I sink my height down.

"Do you like kissing me?" He pulls me between his legs until my knees touch the edge of the bed. He slowly peppers my face with kisses across my forehead, my cheeks, and finally my lips. I melt into myself.

"I do, of course I do."

"Then what's the problem?"

"I like all that stuff. I *love* all that stuff. It's the other stuff. I just don't think I'm ready right now."

Philly scoffs, "you're really going to do this to me? Seriously? Do you know how bad blue balls hurt? I can't believe you could do this to me. I thought you cared about me."

"I do care about you, I more than care about you, I—"

Wait, what the hell are blue balls?

Philly grabs my hand and places it on the bulge in his pants. I try to yank it away, but it's locked in his grasp.

"You said that we don't have to have sex again. You said you just wanted to be with me."

"I do want to be with you. I want to be with your mouth on my dick." He pulls his pants down as I back away, but he leans over the edge of the bed and pushes me back to my knees.

"But..." I hesitate. *Should I just do it? I don't even know how to.* "You said you don't care about doing it anymore."

"Ugh," Philly sits up, "you didn't actually believe that, did you? I said that to chill you out, you were being crazy. I didn't mean it. What guy would ever agree to have a girlfriend that doesn't suck him off? You are nowhere near hot enough for that. You're so fucking naive, Delilah."

I push myself up to my feet. Tears rim my eyes as the stabbing feeling in my stomach jabs harder and harder.

"Ugh, fine. You don't have to suck it, just lay down."

"What?"

"Well, if you're not gonna give me head, you gotta do *something*. You can't leave me with blue balls."

I want to give Philly what he wants, but when I look down at this bed, I can't help but see myself there on my back, covered in urine, sobbing in the fetal position.

"I— I can't."

"Yes, you can." Philly grabs my hand and pulls me towards the bed. I rip my hand out of his grasp and glare at him with anger.

"You came in here with me."

"Because you said you wanted to talk."

Philly looks my body up and down with disgust. "Fine. Have it your way, fucking slut."

"Excuse me?"

"You heard me."

"Was anything you said the other day in your kitchen true? Any of it?" I plead, begging for any type of humanity in him. Begging for the boy I use to chase butterflies with to come home to me.

"Couldn't tell you. I took way too many Percocet. I don't remember anything after breakfast that day," Philly laughs. And, for the first time, his laugh is not contagious. I bring my hands to my eyelids.

"I— I thought you loved me." I cry.

I feel... I don't know, stupid. And used. And worthless.

"Me?" Philly scoffs, "me love you? I'm a St. James. My family has been here for centuries. My parents are actually respected in this town. Unlike your morally corrupt father and gold digging whore mother."

"Go to hell!" I scream, tears falling onto my shirt. I turn around and head towards the door.

"Alright, guess you don't care if your little secret gets out," Philly sings, diabolically.

I turn around. "What?"

"Oh, you know, you and Mr. Stoff."

My eyebrows raise in confusion. I walk back towards him. "Our English teacher that got fired? what about him?"

"Well, word on the street is that Mr. Stoff banged a student. And I just so happened to hear that that student was you."

"You know that's not true." I roll my eyes, tired of his sick game.

"Oh, but it is. See, my aunt knows him and all his friends. They could have easily shared this bit of information with me. It would make sense. Mr. Stoff always did pay you extra special attention, the other kids in class could attest to that. And given your family's reputation in this town. Your dad and his many mistresses, the rumors about your mom and her minister, your drug addict brother…"

"Fuck you!"

"Just think, if that's already your family's reputation, what's gonna happen to it when everyone finds out that Delilah Monroe threw herself at a teacher and seduced him into getting fired?"

"No one would believe you. Everyone knows that's not me."

"Do they though? Wanna bet?"

I gaze into Philly's black eyes. They usually sparkle in the moonlight, but right now, they don't sparkle, or gleam, or shine. They're just black. Completely and utterly black.

"You're a monster," I whisper.

I spin to turn around and start towards the door. Then, I feel a hand on the back of my shoulder, yanking me from behind. Philly pulls me backward and throws my entire body down on the bed. The whiplash steals my vision for a second. Philly has his full body weight on top of me. He grabs one of my wrists and pins it down. I try to punch him with my other hand, but he grabs it. Before he can pin it down, I slash the side of his neck with my nails. He shoots up, stunned. I try to get up until I notice one of my wrists is still pinned down. Hiking up my skirt, he rips my underwear off. The fabric cuts into my raw skin. He yanks his pants down his thighs. I throw my head to the side, unable to look at it. I press my free hand into the mattress and spring off my back, flipping my body over to my stomach. I inch my knees up until they're under me. While Philly is fiddling with my skirt, I see a quick opportunity and throw my head back, smashing his nose. I can tell by the sound it makes that I hit the back of my head hard, but I don't feel anything. Philly brings his hands up to his nose and falls backwards onto the bed. I don't know if he's bleeding or not. I don't fucking care. I leap off of the bed and run towards the door.

"You're gonna pay for this, you fucking whore!"

I hear him screaming words like 'whore' and 'slut' and 'bitch' as I run down the hallway. I grab my coat and my bag then sprint out of Mia's Basement. I walk 7 miles home in the rain. Of course, it's fucking raining. But I don't feel the sting of the wind or the drench of the rain at all. All I feel is... I don't know. I feel nothing. I am nothing.

Chapter 25
Present Day

I ball my hands into fists then extend my fingers out over and over again underneath the table. The tingling was a nice little bonus that was added onto the chills that started washing over me on the drive here. Luckily, the dizziness wore off before I got back in my car. Being awakened face down on the pavement by the manager of Joe's Crab Shack was not on the to-do list I wrote out this morning. I laid there on the pavement near the river, limp, for what felt like a lifetime as I tried to make out the sights around me. *Get off the fucking ground, Delilah.* Once I could see again, I sprung up to my feet, shrugging the stranger's helping hand off of me. I declined the nice man's offer to call the ambulance or to come inside for water. Instead, I broke out of his gentle grasp and sprinted up the hill.

I take a sip of the dry martini in front of me to settle my stomach. It was truly idiotic of me to believe that I was magically healed. I should have known better. Some flesh can never be sewn together. Some sheets can never be washed. And some people can never be healed.

I gobble half of my martini down my throat and set it on the table. I pull at the tight ripped dress that still suffocates my rib cage under my caftan. Whoever invented caftans is an angel from heaven. Charlotte's shrill voice can be heard throughout the whole country club, just as she intends it to be. I couldn't tell you a single thing she's said the past hour. I glance around the table at a mix of both intensely focused and dreadfully bored faces. Blanche, our resident widow, swirls her red wine around in her glass. She touches it to her paper thin face. It's clear that she doesn't get Botox or filler like the rest of the women at this table, myself included. Perhaps she stopped when her husband died, maybe she didn't see the point anymore. Her grief radiates around her like an aura, you can practically smell it on her. She puts her glass down and continues to swirl it around in silence. That's what I think of when I think of Blanche, silence. Painfully lonely silence. Though I bet the sounds in her head are far shriller than Charlotte's high pitched demands. I would know, the louder the mind, the quieter the mouth. Blanche glances my way. *Shit.* She probably felt my eyes on her. I whip my head down and keep it fixed on the table. Out of the corner of my eye, I see Blanche straighten up and look towards Charlotte, pretending to listen to whatever tirade she's on. I clearly rattled her. She's probably not used to people staring at her. She's probably not used to being noticed at all. Something I learned long ago, you're invisible when you're sad. And feared when you're angry. And judged when you're scared. And abandoned when you're ill. Maybe Dr. Veizer was right about never being safe to feel my feelings. But is anybody really?

I keep my eyes glued to the table and take a sip of vodka, thrilled that these ridiculous meetings and dial tone women give me an excuse to break my new no alcohol before 5pm rule. I take my Chanel off the back of the chair and dig for my phone. I press the home button. No new messages. Is he really following me? What does he want? I can't play this cryptic game anymore. I throw my phone back into my purse and drain the rest of my glass. Today, I'm feeling... ugh. I. Don't. Fucking. Know. And that's the truth.

"You okay, Sugar?"

I'm dragged out of Lilah Land by my hair when I hear Sebastian's charming drawl and feel his hand on my knee, stabilizing it in place.

246

"You're shakin' like a leaf."

I blink at him blankly, my body stiffer than the martini in front of me. *Say something, Delilah.*

"Sorry. I'm fine. I just didn't eat today, I forgot."

"Oh honey, you're preaching to the choir. I 'forget' to eat just about every damn day. But look who fit into his favorite Armani suit this morning. Usually, these pants are so tight, you can see my religion. But look at me now." Sebastian arches his shoulders back and simulates flipping his hair.

I pretend to laugh. Sebastian looks at me with sympathetic eyes and grabs a bowl of cheese straws from the center of the table. "Here you go, Sugar."

I stare down at the bowl of grease. I want to reach my hand into it and stuff every single straw in my face. But something inside of me won't let me.

"Don't worry," Sebastian whispers. "The kitchen air fries these things nowadays. Better than passing out on the floor of the Richmond Hill Country Club."

Damn, how did he know? He reaches into the white bowl and pops a cheese straw in his mouth. I smile, sheepishly, and do the same. My jaw clicks as I slowly chew the cheese straw. Anastasia's head jerks towards my direction. I avoid her eyes and look around the room as if I heard the same noise and am trying to figure out where it's coming from. Once Anastasia loses interest, I relax my shoulders and look back towards Sebastian. I'm starting to get the sense that maybe Sebastian wants to be my friend, like actually my friend. The realization gives me a mental high.

"Hey," I lean over and whisper in his ear, "would you want to stay after the meeting and get a drink at the east wing bar?"

Hives creep up my neck and I feel my face begin to burn hotter than the equator. I shouldn't have done that. Of course he doesn't want to stay after the committee meeting. These things are painful enough, why on earth would he want to subject himself to more torture? I am such a fucking loser. Making friends as an adult is an actual Greek tragedy. I wish things were still as simple as a cute boy in my kindergarten class chasing a butterfly with me, or the cool girl in school liking my piano riffs.

"Oh, Sugar…"

The rejection. Here it comes. Dear Lord. I want to scoop my eyes out with a spoon.

"I thought you'd never ask!" Sebastian picks up his glass and touches it to my empty one for a cheers.

I feel my hives begin to fade and my smile begin to grow.

"Um, are we interrupting?"

Mine and Sebastian's heads whip over to Charlotte's sharp voice. She sounds like a cheap piano, out of tune. Sebastian and I both blush then open the folders Charlotte spent a ridiculous amount of time creating. We pretend to pay attention for the rest of the meeting, but I can't stop thinking about the fact that for the first time in 15 years, I may have a real friend. I haven't been this happy about something in a long time. Nothing can ruin this moment, this day. Nothing.

My phone buzzes and I reach for it in my purse. I open it up to my messages app.

Unknown number: I see you.

Chapter 26
2009- Richmond Hill, Georgia

By Monday morning, the rumor mill began running over-time. The entire school, students of all ages, teachers, staff, every single person at Richmond Hill High had heard that I had an affair with Mr. Stoff and that's why he got fired. Kids from other schools, parents, older siblings, little siblings, first cousins, seconds cousins, fucking fifth cousins. It seemed as though, by fourth period, every single person in the world had heard this rumor. Girls were whispering about it every time I entered the bathroom. People screamed 'Mr. Stoff!' when they passed me in the hallways. Someone wrote 'slut' on my locker… in Sharpie, a nice touch. Someone even threw a condom at me on my way out of the cafeteria. Every 'friend' of mine acted sympathetic when talking to me alone, then distant once there were other eyes on us. It was as if they were afraid my bad reputation was a contagious, infectious disease. I overheard freshmen talking about the rumor. I overheard seniors. I even overheard teachers talking about it. They were saying that 'they always knew I was bad news, like mother like daughter'. I heard a history teacher say to our janitor that 'it's such a shame Mr. Stoff had to be fired because of that girl's choices.' Mr. Stoff has been labeled a 'fine man' who was taken advantage of by a stupid little girl with a big crush. While I have been labeled, so far in the past 9 hours, as a slut, a whore, a tramp, a hooker, a floozy, a tart, or as Mrs. Johnson put it 'a wicked little harlot'. Even Mia asked me if the rumor was true. I was shocked that she had to ask. I vehemently denied it, and she said that she believed me, but I'm not completely sure that she does. The thing is, I don't know if Mr. Stoff is a fine man who didn't deserve to be fired. Because I don't fucking know him. I have had no interaction with him other than in class. I never once thought of him as attractive. He was never flirty, or inappropriate, or weird to me, and nor was I to him. We have never even had a conversation one-on-one. But, as it looks to everyone from the outside, I am a worthless, desperate slut who seduced a respected gentleman into my chambers. I snatched him up and spun him in my web, only to defile him in my boudoir. And now, I must pay the price. I must have a scarlet letter pasted on my chest, or I must be burned at the stake like a witch in the town square. This might be the worst, most rapidly wide-spread rumor Richmond Hill High has ever seen. *Philly*. Fucking Philly. Fucking me. I should have known he wasn't bluffing about spreading this rumor. Philly doesn't bluff. I should have shut my mouth and done what he wanted. If I hadn't fought him off, if I had just stayed still, none of this would be happening. I hope and pray my parents don't find out about the rumors. Lady Katherine would be horribly humiliated. She would say that I tarnished the family name once and for all. Luckily, it seems like my parents' newest battle will keep them both busy for the time being.

The Spanish moss dances in the cool fall breeze, using the sky as its dance floor. I keep my head tilted up towards the clouds as I walk across the backyard. The fresh-cut grass tickles my feet as my steps get wider and faster. My yearn to get as far away from the screaming fuels my pace. This week's latest crisis entails Lady Katherine's Porsche breaking down. And, since she's not allowed to drive any of William's vintage, mint condition collector's cars in the garage, she has no way to get to church and ministry outings this week. Although he can more than afford it, Dad is giving her a hard time about getting her car fixed because he says my mother is no longer worth a dime of his hard-earned money. And, that was probably the tamest thing I overheard him say while he was on the phone with his lawyer in the basement. Because of this little snafu, insults have been flying back and forth through the house like crows in the sky. I don't know much about cars or car repairs, but I'm sure screaming about it will fix the Porsche. Makes total sense.

I roll my eyes and I continue through the yard, past the pool and the magnolias. I walk faster and faster until I find what I'm looking for. I see a small cloud of cigarette smoke floating in the air above the dock. I tip toe quietly towards it. Sam is laying down flat, looking up at the sky. He has his too-tight white shirt on again. I can already see little brown stains forming from laying on this old wood. His hand is still in the air, holding his cigarette when I creep over towards him and sit down next to him, dangling my bare feet over the ledge. I look back at him. He spears me with a devilish look as the corner of his mouth tips up.

"Hey you."

"Hey." I glance down at the wood beneath me and he follows my stare. We're silent for a beat. And then another beat. And then another.

"I'm sorry!" We both exclaim at the same time. Both our lips press into smiles as I giggle.

"Jinx, you owe me a soda."

"What are you, five?" I chuckle.

"Potentially." Sam dabs his cigarette out on the dock then lifts up until we're at eye-level.

I try to ignore the way his gray eyes match the gray sky.

"For real though, Delilah. I'm sorry. So so fucking sorry. I didn't mean to make you feel like I was calling you… you know. I would never call you that or think that. I'm sorry that it came off that way and I'm sorry about everything else I said that day. I didn't mean to make what happened a bigger deal than it was. You were right."

"No, I wasn't. You were right, I shouldn't have—"

Sam cuts back in, "it was nothing. Just two crazy kids out for a swim, it meant nothing."

My heart sinks a little remembering the way Sam looked at me that night, like he saw deep through my mask. And the way that he looked at my body, like it was something to be treasured instead of trashed.

"Right, yeah. It was nothing." I glance around the dock and stare out onto the bay, looking for something, anything else to make conversation about. "You just out here for a smoke?" *Really. That's the best I can do?*

"Well, that, and this." Sam sits up and grabs something to his left. He sets Bailey's little black notebook down on my lap.

"The investigation continues. How's it coming?"

"No leads."

Sam whips out his lighter. I stare at the cigarette at the corner of his mouth, caught between his big lips. I envy that cigarette. I envy anything that feels the pleasure of Sam's warm touch. My gaze strokes Sam up and down. I revel at the way his shiny black hair falls over his forehead. His deep eyes light up when they catch mine. His smile grows radiant, exposing each one of his white teeth.

"What?"

"Nothin'." I smirk.

"Hey, that's my line."

I shrug as the smirk lingers on my pouted lips. I open Bailey's journal to the cover page, re-reading her handwriting. *Property of Mileena Gale.*

"You know, I had an alter ego once."

"Yeah?"

"Gazana."

"Gaz-what-a?"

I laugh, "Gazana. Just a random name I came up with. It was supposed to be the part of me that was outgoing and friendly. Anytime I had to be in a social situation, I would pretend I wasn't Delilah anymore, but Gazana, a free-spirited, confident girl who didn't care what anyone thought. I thought it would make it easier to talk to people if I wasn't me."

"Did it work?"

"Yeah, actually. It worked so well that I came up with names and characters for each part of my personality. It was fun, playing pretend. But then, I walked into the living room while my mom was watching Oprah. And, she was interviewing a woman with multiple personalities, it's like a real psychological thing. Everything that woman said about her personalities was basically the same as me and mine, so I forced myself to forget about Gazana and the rest of the herd."

"Aw, that's kind of sad. Cool, though. I love the way your mind works, it's creative, like Bailey's. I bet if you two had gotten to know each other, you would have been friends."

I push down the nauseous thought that I wouldn't have been able to be friends with Bailey Garcia and keep my social standing at Richmond Hill High. The fact that I care about things like that, well, *cared*, makes me want to jump off of this dock and drown alone in my vapidity.

"I'm glad we're friends though." Sam takes a drag and looks out onto the clouds over the river.

I pivot my eyes away from his face. "Right… friends." I stare at the gray sky in defeat, like it's not entirely my fault for ruining whatever this was.

"I need you."

My head jerks back to the side of Sam's face. "You do?"

"Yeah." Sam ruffles his hand in his black hair nervously. "Well, you know, you were so helpful at cracking Bailey's code and solving her riddles last time, I thought maybe you could help translate some of her journal entries again. You seem to be the only one that understands her thought process."

"Oh... right. Of course." I sigh internally and flip the notebook open to a random page. "Look at this!" I hand the notebook back and point to the page. The first words on the page are 'Dear Sam'. "This is addressed to you, maybe it's a letter." I focus my eyes to read the sentence that follows, but it looks like it's in a different language. "Can you read that?"

Sam is silent as he scans the page. "Obrigado por ser sempre o meu Afro-íris depois da tempestade."

I stare at Sam, dumb founded. My uncultured ignorance is dripping from my pores.

Sam smiles widely. "It means thank you for always being my rainbow after a storm. It's a Portuguese saying. My mom used to say it to us when we were little. I can't believe Bailey remembered it."

"It's a very beautiful saying."

"Yeah, it is." Sam's half smile stays active on his lips, which are very full, like his arms, like his pecks. I can't stop staring, it's like my eyes are magnets and his body is a refrigerator door.

"Whatcha looking at?" Sam asks without turning his head. Panic surges in my veins. I play it cool and shrug my shoulders, attempting to emulate his confident half smirk. However, I don't think my pale, less-than-full lips do it justice.

Sam flips a couple of pages forward in the little black book. "Hey, look at this."

"Looks like a poem." I take the book and read Bailey's words aloud. "I knew there were no butterflies in the basement. But that didn't stop me from following him down. No one told me his wings were laced with poison. And now I'm trapped down here for eternity. Someone upstairs might hear me if I scream. But I stay down here counting the bruises like sheep going over the moon. Infected by his laugh, haunted by his grasp. But the world wants to believe that my wings are still fluttering. So, I let them. All because he bought me black roses."

"Wow," Sam sighs.

"There it is again, the black roses." I hand the journal back to Sam. "What do you think she meant when she said she's counting the bruises? Do you think he, the guy who, you know, do you think he hit her? Do you think it was an on-going thing, not just that one night?"

"It's possible." Sam looks up at the sky and shakes his head. I look up with him and notice that the sky is fading to a darker shade than Sam's eyes.

"If it was an ongoing thing, how could she have hid that from us? From me? I'm her twin. How could I possibly miss something like that?"

"Well," I sigh, "you'd be shocked how much people can hide. You can never know who anyone really is. Like you said, we're all wearing masks. That's why you can't trust anyone." I reach down to my side to pick up my drink until I realize that I never poured myself one tonight. There was no point. I knew that the pain from seeing Philly's true colors couldn't possibly be numbed by alcohol.

"Right… about that. I wanted to ask you, but I didn't wanna pry."

"Ugh." I drop my shoulders and sink down onto the dock. "You heard too?"

"I did." Sam turns to me with concern. "Are you okay?"

"Am I okay?" I ask, utterly shocked.

"Yeah. Are you okay?"

"I— I don't know. You're the first person to ask me that."

Sam's sympathetic eyes stare deep into mine. "You don't have to talk about it if you don't want to. And, you don't have to tell me if it's true or not. But, if it is, just know that I'm here for you. I'm here to talk or to listen. I'll even go to the police station with you if you want."

"The police station?"

"Yeah. They've been no help with the investigation for Bailey. But maybe you'll have better luck with them, being a Monroe and all."

"We are talking about the same thing, right? The Mr. Stoff thing."

"Yeah," Sam brings his hand to the back of his neck and rubs it. I trace the defined bulge his bicep makes. He catches my stare, and I yank my head away.

"I don't get it. Why would I go to the police?"

Sam raises an eyebrow. "Because you're a kid, Mr. Stoff is an adult. That's statutory rape."

"Statutory..." my voice lulls to a whisper, "rape?"

Sam dabs his cigarette on the old wood. He takes his free hand away from the back of his neck and puts it on top of mine for a second or two. But he rips it away when he sees the perplexed look on my face.

"Sorry... I just, I hope you know that it's not your fault. That fucker took advantage of you. He deserves way worse than being fired. He was your teacher, he was supposed to protect you, not... you know. Guys like that need to be locked up for good. Dude's a predator."

I shake my head and let out a breath I've been holding in for way too long. "No... he isn't. At least, I don't think so. Not to me. The rumor isn't true. I don't know how it blew up so badly, but Mr. Stoff never touched me, and I never touched him. I barely know him. He was just a mediocre English teacher to me. I'm not sure why he got fired, but it had nothing to do with me," I plead my case, knowing that it's a lost cause. "Whatever. It doesn't matter, I'm sure you don't believe me, nobody does." I peer out onto the bay. Fog is rising above the tide where the sun usually sets. We sit there in silence for a moment.

"I believe you."

"You do?" I swing my head back towards Sam.

"Of course I do. Why wouldn't I?"

"People don't tend to believe girls like me."

"Or Bailey."

"Or Bailey," I agree.

"So, how did this rumor become a thing then? Someone made it up?"

I sigh. "It's a long story."

"That's a fucked up thing to make up about someone. Who the hell would want to do that Delilah Monroe? Everybody loves you."

"No, they don't. They really don't. Especially now. I'm now and will forever be branded as the school slut."

"What? How would being statutory raped by an old creep make you a slut?"

I sigh. "When you're a girl in a town as small as this one, just breathing makes you a slut. Besides, I don't think the rest of the school sees it like you do. They see me as their new punching bag."

"You shouldn't have to feel that way at school. You should tell everyone the truth, shut them up."

"People don't believe girls like me… or Bailey. Remember?"

"Yeah." Sam takes out a pack of cigarettes and lights another. "I'm sorry, Delilah. Fuck this town."

"For real." I laugh a little for the first time in I don't know how long. "*Fuck* this fucking town. I can't wait to leave here and never look back. Maybe I'll change my name and join the circus, like Bailey said she would."

"Well, Bailey wasn't going to join the circus, Mileena Gale was."

"Mileena Gale, right. Being someone else sounds pretty good right about now." I lean back on my elbows and look up at the gloomy sky. Sam leans back and brushes his shoulder on mine. It's warm, despite it being quite chilly by the water. I hesitate to look his way. He holds his cigarette away from me and turns his face to meet mine, our noses are practically touching.

"I'm glad you're not someone else." Sam's silver eyes burn into mine. His face is so close, I can taste his warm, sweet breath. His eyes travel across my face, and I feel... I don't know, seen. The current beneath us quickly picks up as Sam's head jerks away from my face. He takes a drag of his cigarette and keeps his gaze on the bay.

"So, what does your boyfriend make of all this? The rumor and all that."

"He's..." I trip over my words, realizing that I haven't had time or space in my brain to think about what Philly and I are at this point. I don't know what I'm going to do about him, but I do know that the thought of him makes me feel... I don't know, scared and sick. "He's not my boyfriend," I insist, flatly. Once the words come out, I know that they need to be true.

"He's not?"

I shake my head.

"Well, good. Guy's a prick. Always has been."

"Yeah. I used to think he was just misunderstood and hurting."

"And now?" Sam's eyes re-lock with mine.

"I still think he's hurting. He's got a lot going on, family stuff. But I'm starting to understand him completely." My mind wanders back to the look in Philly's dead eyes in that dark bedroom. They were cold and vacant. The more I remember it, the more familiar that look becomes to me. He looked like… William Monroe.

I snap out of it. "Anyway, you're right, Philly's a prick. I'm done with him."

"Glad to hear it. You're too good for him. You're too good for anyone in this town."

"I don't know about all that." I giggle and blush, inching my hand towards his. "But I definitely don't want to be tied down to this place for any reason. I don't want to become like my mom. Like honestly, shoot me if I ever become like any of the women in this town. With no passion, no vision. My sole purpose in life to be a wife and a mom, dying within a mile from the hospital I was born at. It's pathetic."

"Damn," Sam chuckles, "tell me how you really feel."

"Sorry." I hang my head down. "It's been a long day."

"You don't have to be sorry. I get it. Well, as much as a dude who's never been publicly shunned and labeled as a—" Sam catches himself, "you know, can."

I nod and force a flat smile.

"So, if you're not gonna end up like your mom, how do you want to end up?"

"Well, my Dad hasn't decided if I'm going to a top conservatory or an Ivy university yet. But, after I graduate, I know I want to go to New York and play for the New York City Philharmonic. Then, after that, the sky is the limit."

"The philharmonic. I'm not gonna pretend to know what that is, but I'm sure it's awesome. And New York, big city."

"Exactly. That's what I want my life to be like. I want it to be big. I want it to have... I don't know," I trail off.

"Meaning?"

"Yeah, meaning."

The corner of Sam's mouth flares up into the half smile that is becoming my favorite sight. I flutter my eyelashes and twirl my copper hair. When I've properly knotted it up, I panic and begin to smooth down my locks. Sam stays focused on my face as he brings his hands up to my hair, lacing his fingers with mine. He brings our interlocked down to his lap, slowly.

"What?"

"Nothin'."

I smile and roll my eyes, giving a gentle squeeze to his hand that cradle mine. I look out towards the gray sky, wanting to paint it with love letters. Sam may not be able to chase the clouds on the bay away, but he has sure as hell chased away mine. I look back towards him, straightening my arms and sinking into my shoulder like a giddy schoolgirl.

"What?"

"Nothin'," he repeats. "I just like how big you dream. That's all."

"I want to matter, you know?"

"You do matter." Sam squeezes my hand and shakes it lightly.

"You know what I mean. I want to *really* matter." Sam's eyes linger over to his cigarette burning on the wood. He unlaces our fingers and grabs it. I try to hide the disappointment that my hands hold when they're not holding his.

"Anyway, what about you? Any hopes or dreams? Plans after high school?"

"Nah. We don't have money for college, so probably not getting a fancy degree like you."

"But, there's scholarships and loans and stuff. Right?"

"Yeah… they're not exactly lining up to give guys like me scholarships. And, my parents' credit is shot, hence why we can't find a place to live. So, no loans either."

"I'm sure there's something you could do. Maybe I could talk to my dad?" I regret the words as soon as they slither through my teeth. Could I possibly sound more like a spoiled princess? I turn my head away from Sam. He's likely angry at me, disgusted with me. Just like everyone else is. Suddenly, I feel a warm palm on my back, and I want to melt.

"That's nice, Delilah. I appreciate it. You have a great heart, you really do. But your family has done more than enough by letting us crash here. I'll be okay. School isn't my thing anyway."

"But… you're like, so smart. You and all your philosophies. You're the smartest person I know."

He laughs, "which is why I'll be okay."

I study his face and body language. How Sam manages to be this comfortable with himself yet dashingly humble at the same time is beyond me.

"But, getting out of this town no matter what sounds like the best plan on earth."

"Amen. New York is a really cool place to live, you know. Just saying." I nudge him.

"I'll keep that in mind."

"You got a bright future, kid." I joke as I pat Sam's shoulder. Sam's rests his hand on top of mine, clinging it to his shoulder. My eyes flutter up towards his as he slowly guides my hand from his shoulder to his chest. My body arouses as my fingertips graze over his nipple. Sam continues sliding my hand until it's placed directly over his heart, his hand still holding mine in place. I stare down at his chest as his heart beats to the rhythm of my sadness. I swoon as I study his chest, the way his pecks bulge through his white T-shirt, the way little black hairs make their way up his neck, peeking subtly out of his shirt.

"Hey, where's your cross necklace? The silver one you always wear."

"Oh." Sam drops my hand from his heart. "I think I lost it that night when we... went for a swim. It's fine though, no big deal."

"Wait for real? Holy shit. Let's go find it." I shoot up to my feet through the cold, windy air. Sam dabs out his cigarette and rises to his feet. "Don't be silly. It's freezing. Like, actually freezing this time."

"I'm going in." I step towards the edge of the dock.

"No, Delilah. I'm not letting you go in there." Sam points to the cold water that has turned a shade of black thanks to the dark sky. Sam grabs my hand and turns me to face him.

"No, I have to. That's the necklace that you shared with Bailey, it's special. You lost it and it's all my fault. Everything is all my fault. Everything I touch gets ruined!" I scream the words out into the cold air, colder tears rimming my eyes.

"Hey!" Sam yells.

"What?"

Sam grabs my hand and drapes it over his shoulder, it barely reaches with his height. He takes my other hand and cups it, moving his free hand to the small of my back.

"Dance with me."

"What?"

"Dance with me." Sam whispers insistently, his voice low and masculine. He begins to sway both our bodies from side to side. I hesitate at first, then begin to sway to a familiar rhythm. My fingers curl around the nape of his neck. A light mist falls on us, ever so slightly.

"What Otis Redding song is playing in your mind right now?"

My jaw drops. "What? How did you know?"

"I just know. Come on, let's hear it."

My smile grows wide. I begin to hum quietly then sing in a raspy whisper.

It's a rainy night in Georgia,
Such a rainy night in Georgia,
I feel that it's raining all over the world,
I feel like it's raining all over the world...

Sam closes his eyes as his smile stretches. I bury my face in his neck, my mouth grazes the skin of his throat. My hum vibrates off the night sky, when suddenly, I feel a cold drip on my head. Sam takes his hand from the small of my back and holds it to the air. He catches a raindrop in his palm.

"Damn. I didn't know you could control the weather like that."

"I'm a witch, didn't they tell you?" I laugh.

The rain slowly picks up, adding more drops onto the wood. We continue humming and swaying until it begins to pour.

"Come on!" I yell over the sound of the pouring rain. I grab Sam's hand and jump off of the dock, he follows. I lead him underneath the dock and we stand face to face, next to old kayaks. Our feet sink into the wet, muddy sand.

"Are you okay?" Sam grabs both of my hands.

"Yeah. I'm not actually a witch, ya know. I don't melt in the rain."

Sam laughs. He takes his hands away from mine and puts them on both sides of my face. He brushes back the soaking hair that sticks to my forehead. *Shit*. I probably have mascara running down my cheeks and I'm sure I smell like a wet dog. My head falls towards the ground below us, but Sam tilts it back up with a gentle finger on my chin. I stare into his silver eyes. He stares back into my mine, holding my face parallel to his. We study each other, bewitched and enchanted. What is he doing to me? Is he going to kiss me? He is. He'll probably want to go further than that too. He heard all the rumors about what an experienced whore I am and now he wants a taste of what he thinks everyone else has had. I put my hands on top of his and lower them away from my face.

"Hey."

"Hey," I sigh and roll my eyes.

"Hey."

"What?" I yell over the rain splashing on the dock above us. *Just tell me what you want from me and get it over with.*

"I need to tell you something."

"What?"

"Hey!"

"For fuck's sake, what!"

"You matter." Sam grabs my hand. "To me, you matter." Sam brings my hand up to his chest. Tears fill my eyes like the rain drops fill the sky. I lean towards him and collapse into him. He stretches his big arms around me, wrapping me in safety. My head rests against his chest. His heart thumps like it's beating just for me. I don't move a muscle. I keep my body thrown into his, and he lets me. I don't want him to ever let go. I inhale his scent. He smells faintly of smoke and something else that I can't put my finger on. He doesn't smell like cologne or body spray like the other guys at school. I don't know if he's wearing anything at all, but I know that he smells like home.

"Sam? Samson? Are you out here? Va la! You're going to catch a cold."

Sam's arms break away from me at the sound of his mom's voice. I wipe the devastation off my face before I look at him.

"I, uh, I should—"

"Yeah. Me too." I'm about to turn around and make a run for it back to the house until impulse possesses me. "Hey, what are you doing tomorrow after school? My dad will probably be working late then getting trashed at the country club, and my mom has some sort of church fundraiser."

"Yeah, my mom's going to that too. She's been baking cookies all day."

"And your dad?"

"Working. Why?"

"Come over. Well, you live here. But, I mean, come inside. I want to show you something."

"Inside your house? Like just us?"

"Samson! Va la!" Sofia yells into the air.

"Tomorrow, 5pm. You can come in through the back door promise?"

We hear the screen door of the guest house slam.

"Yeah, yeah. 5pm. I promise."

Chapter 27
Present day

I continue to frantically glance over my shoulder as Sebastian switches from dirty martinis to moonshine.

"You can take the boy out of Louisiana, but…" He tosses the whole drink back in one sip. I fane a small laugh, but I'm too distracted to appreciate good old fashioned alcoholism right now. Though, on any other day, I'm its number one fan.

I keep scanning the room around me. The East Wing Bar looks the same as it did 15 years ago when my mom was sitting in this very chair night after night. Oh God, did I take her place? I shiver the thought off of me. I don't have time to worry about that considering that I am now officially being stalked. I could have faked sick and gone home after the committee meeting, but I feared that he would follow me to my house. Does he know where I live? He clearly knows where I am today. But it's safer here, in plain sight with Sebastian right next to me, than anywhere else.

I shoot my head up as someone walks through the doorway. *Thank God.* It's not him. It's not him. I put my hand to my heart.

"You okay, Sugar? You seem a bit… jumpy and such."

"Yeah, I'm fine, I just need another drink."

"Well, I'll drink to that." Sebastian raises his glass. "Bar-keep! You've been about as useful as a steering wheel on a mule. Get that sweet young booty over here."

The bartender scurries over to us. I see the country club is still hiring boys that look like they should be in second period chemistry, not behind a bar. He pours a healthy serving of Belvedere and Vermouth into a cocktail shaker and begins to shake it up and down.

"Dang, that cocktail shaker is one lucky son of a bitch."

I laugh and spit up my martini a little.

"Are you spoken for, Sugar? You got a fella?" He leans over the bar. "I'm not quite as girthy as that there cocktail shaker, but I can assure you what's inside my shaker will taste better than any of your top shelf liquor."

"Jesus Christ!" I slap Sebastian on the arm. "He's like 16. You're gonna get yourself arrested."

"Oh, I'm just kidding 'round with him. You know I'm just kidding 'round with you, right barkeep?"

"Uh... yeah. Ha ha." The bartender pours me another martini and awkwardly inches away from us. I don't blame him.

"I see the loyal devotion and fidelity to your husband is going swimmingly," I joke as I taste my martini. It's perfectly stiff, just as Mother used to like it.

My head jerks towards the door when I see another person walking through it. Again, it's not him. I unclench. Fuck it. If he wants to approach me, if he wants to yell at me or hit me or murder me, he'll have to do it right here in broad daylight in front of every wasp in this room. And he wouldn't dare... would he?

Sebastian takes a big sip of his drink and laughs. I had almost forgotten he was here.

"Oh, don't even remind me. That bastard is in the doghouse, right where he belongs."

I scan Sebastian's skin for new lashes or bruises. "Did he... you know... again?"

"No, Sugar. Much, much worse. Last night, that buffoon dropped a bomb on me. Get this, he said that he wants to adopt a child. A child! He said it would bring his life meaning, or some dunderheaded crap like that. Can you believe that?"

"Well, yeah, kind of. We're not getting any younger."

"Speak for yourself, darlin'." Sebastian pats his face. "You best believe I pitched a hissy fit. I love my husband, but he hasn't got the sense God gave a goose. Why, he's so dumb, he could throw himself on the ground and miss. A child? Who in the hell does he think ought to raise that snot-nosed demon?

Him? With all the hours he works? I can promise you this, it will most certainly not be me. No, ma'am. Not I, rabbi."

"What is your vendetta against children?"

"Childbearing is for people who don't have lives. They have kids because they're bored and they think their babies will be perfect little angels, then those little succubi bleed them dry of any identity and personality they had. They'd never say it, but if I were a betting man, I'd say most parents regret shootin' their buttermilk load into the clam bake."

My palm on my lips hides my giggle. "You're ridiculous. You really think that's true though?

"I know it is."

He may have a point. Both of my parents seemed to regret having me from the moment I arrived.

"So, I take it you're pro-choice then?"

"Oh honey, no!" Sebastian brings his palm to his chest. "I am as pro-life as it gets. I am a good, wholesome Christian woman."

I laugh at his joke. It *was* a joke, right?

"Trust me, Sugar. Baby having is not in the cards for people like you or me. It's for people who aren't doing anything important with their lives."

"And… what are we doing with our lives that is so important, exactly?"

"This!" Sebastian raises his glass of moonshine for a toast.

I cheers him and take a stiff sip. "Well, considering the fact that you're constantly on Grindr trolling for men, and your husband…" I consider my words carefully, "has the temper he does, maybe not bringing humans into the world is for the best."

"Amen, Sugar. What about you? You ever wet your whistle where it don't belong?"

I raise an eyebrow at him.

"You know, step outside your marriage, get a little stank on your hang down?"

"Oh my God!" I spit my drink all over the bar counter in front of me. I quickly grab a napkin and wipe it up. "Sorry," I mouth to the bartender who has practically glued himself to the window as far from us as possible. I turn to Sebastian. "I don't have a hang down, so I'm gonna go with no."

"You never know. We're all creatures of God, and he loves us all just the same."

"No, I haven't stepped out of my marriage." The words mock me as they leave my lips.

"Well, good for you then. You must have a good one."

"I do." *If he ever comes back home. I'm not getting my hopes up though.* I open my mouth wide to take a big sip of my martini. The clicking sound in my jaw can be heard from the golf course.

"What was that?"

"Oh, nothing. My jaw makes that noise sometimes. I broke it when I was younger."

"You broke your jaw? Hot damn. I need to hear that story."

"Another time," I say flatly as my face reddens. "So, anyway, how did Jeremy take it when you told him you don't want to adopt?"

"Not well, honey, not well." Sebastian takes off his Armani suit jacket and pulls down the collar of his dress shirt, revealing huge bruises and deep scratches. How he deals with this regularly yet manages to be so whimsical is beyond me. The only thing that beats *me* every night is my own brain, yet I wear every wound like a Vera Wang wedding dress.

I assess Sebastian's injuries. "Jesus, Sebastian. That's not good."

"Maybe not, but that's my lot in life. I know what I signed up for."

"Did you though?"

Sebastian nods and drains his moonshine. He holds up his glass and the young bartender hurries over from the window to pour him another.

"Well, you know, it's not too late to get out."

"And go where, my love?"

"Anywhere. You could stay with me for a while, as long as you want."

"That's a nice offer, Sugar. I appreciate it, but I'll survive. I'm a survivor."

I continue to stare at him, searching his eyes for some sort of help signal.

"I'm okay where I'm at, Sugar, really." He puts his hand on mine and squeezes it lightly.

"You're okay with getting beaten every time you step out of line?"

This martini is making my lips too loose. I may end up losing Sebastian as a friend before I ever really had him.

He takes a big swig from his glass. "So, you're telling me you've never been knocked around by a man before? Never?"

Acid boils in my throat. My brain conjures the memories I've been trying to forget for over a decade. The countless insults, the bruises, the smell of urine. The no's he ignored, the no's I didn't even bother to say. That's the thing about no's. Once the word has been discarded enough times, you begin to discard it yourself. Eventually, you forget the word entirely.

I lift my martini to my lips and gulp down as much as I can fit in my mouth. I sit and wait for the sun to come out, to forget all the things I don't deserve to know. But the images of him flashing in my brain stay put right where they are. I should have known. My mind hangs onto memories like the Spanish moss clings to the trees. They follow me all day and beat me bloody in my bed when the sun goes down. I wonder if he still thinks of me at night like I think of him. Probably not. He broke me. He broke me like a promise. And I bet he sleeps like a baby, while I'm still afraid to close my eyes. I hang my head in shame, terrified to see the look on Sebastian's face.

"Thought so. I told you; I know when someone has seen the rain. And you, my darlin', have seen the rain." I choke back tears.

Sebastian gently rubs my back. "Don't worry, Sugar. Like I said, it's just our lot in life."

Maybe he has a point. I suppose my lot in life is to never light a fire, yet always get burned.

"So, what's your sob story then? Who's the fella that knocked you around?"

Then all of the sudden, I open my eyes. I'm on the floor, my back is against the wall. There's so much screaming but all I can feel is the throbbing, searing pain in my jaw. I look beneath me and I see a pool of scarlet lurching towards my Manolos. And immediately I know that he's dead. How did this happen?

No.

"Bella?"

I jump at a noise and a warm hand on my right shoulder. I swivel myself around in my chair to get a glimpse of what startled me. My gaze trails the attractive man up and down. His olive skin radiates from the sun shining through the windows. *Salvatore.*

"Oh, um… Hi."

"Buongiorno." Salvatore lowers his head in what looks like a bow.

"Ha, Buongiorno," I mutter.

Sebastian swings himself around, moonshine in hand. "Well who's this little slice of pecan pie?"

Salvatore smiles at Sebastian then reverts his eyes back to me, expectantly.

"Oh, this, this is Salvatore. He's um... he... He, um, trims my neighbor's hedges and helps in her garden. We met the other week while he was doing that."

"I'll trim *his* hedges any day," Sebastian murmurs. He reaches out his hand. "Nice to meet you, Salvatore. Charmed, I'm sure." Sebastian leaves his hand out with his wrist flicked down, waiting for Salvatore to take it. And do what, exactly, I'm not sure. Kiss it? It wouldn't surprise me. It takes Sebastian about 6 drinks until he believes he's Dolly Parton.

"I'm Sebastian," he continues in a comically long, low southern drawl. I roll my eyes and turn my attention back towards Salvatore. The light from the windows is still reflecting on him in the most flattering way, illuminating his soft features. It's then that I notice he's wearing all black, just like the bartender and the rest of the staff here.

"Do you work here?"

"Work here?" he asks, pointing a finger to the ground. "Yes. I work at country club this week. I text you." He holds up his phone and points to the message he sent to my number. *Damn.* It was Salvatore that texted me 'I see you'. I forgot that I gave him my number, I guess I never took down his. That makes perfect sense. Wow, my paranoia really is getting the best of me. *You are delusional, Delilah.*

My relief is short-lived when I notice the silence that flurries in the air between Salvatore and I. He stares at me with sullen eyes. A pang of guilt stabs at my chest. I think I hurt his feelings the other night when I kicked him out right after he made me cum for the third time. I should apologize, but I haven't the slightest clue how to explain my behavior.

"Well, anyway. It was great to see you, Salvatore."

"Nice to see you, Delilah. I call you?"

"Uh… yeah," I hesitate, my eyes flickering between him and Sebastian. "About the hedges."

"The hedges, yes…" Salvatore winks his thick eyelashes at me. I squeeze my thighs and adjust in my seat, attempting to squander how viscerally Salvatore's smooth accent turns me on.

"Nice to meet you, Sugar." Sebastian takes a sip of his drink as Salvatore walks back towards the kitchen, his olive skin still glowing. I watch his toned body as he leaves.

"Well, that boy was cuter than a speckled pup under a wagon with his tongue hangin' out."

I laugh and shake my head.

Sebastian sets his empty glass down on the bar. "How long you been fuckin' him?"

"What?" I ask far too loudly, my head turning so hard, I feel a kink in my neck.

"You know, doing the tango, choking the chicken, twirling his pasta."

"I, um… I—"

"I see the loyal devotion and fidelity to your husband is going swimmingly," he mocks me.

There's no use in denying it at this point. "Oh, hush up," I sigh.

"Relax, Sugar. You know I'm never one to judge."

He's right. In fact, he has never once made me feel judged from the moment I met him.

"Besides, you could do way worse. That body, that accent. Oh!" Sebastian fans himself. "He got me sweatin' like a whore in church. Where's he from anyhow?"

"Ascoli Pecino, it's a little town in Italy."

"Well, I bet you're eatin' good. I loved me some Sunday sauce back in the day if you know what I mean."

"I'm sure I could hazard a guess. Ugh, I don't know how I let this happen."

"We're wasps, Sugar. It's a right of passage. You think our husbands aren't messing around behind our backs? All those long hours at the office, the impromptu business trips. Not to mention all the shit we take from them. You know what they say, when you marry for money, you always end up paying for it. We pay the price; we might as well have some fun with it."

"I didn't marry for money."

"Of course you didn't, Sugar. And this is the nose I was born with." Sebastian winks at me.

"I love my husband. At least, I did." I shrug my shoulders, defeated.

"Me too. There's nothing like the allure of a powerful man. The way they command every room they walk into, especially the bedroom. The way they wine and dine you and look at you like you're the most precious jewel they've been searching for their whole life."

"Yeah," I sigh, "I remember those days. It seems like so long ago now, the way it was before..." I stumble on my words, too sober to be honest but too buzzed to shut up. I take another sip of my drink. "Before everything changed, I mean. When did it all go south with you and Jeremy?" I ask, mostly wanting to steer the conversation away from me and my failures, my losses, my sham of a marriage.

"It was about two years after we got married that I noticed the shift. Don't get me wrong, it was hard, it was. When the magic wore off and real life reared its little turtle head. Jeremy's temper got real bad, and his true colors came through. But it was my fault."

"Your fault?"

"For believin' in fairytales."

"But I thought it *was* a fairytale. You and Jeremy. That's how you made it sound. You said he saved you."

"Oh, Sugar. I make things sound exactly the way I want you to hear them. We're all wearing some sort of mask in this town."

"So, I've heard," I sigh, refusing my brain of memory recall.

"And Jeremy did save me. You should see the shit hole I came from, the one he pulled me out of. It's a waste land full of hicks, homophobes, and men far meaner than Jeremy. He saved me from that, from poverty, from a wasted life. But, no one can save you from the riff raff that goes on in your head. No one is equipped to save you from that. Most people are just as broken as we are. You can't ask a broken man to cradle a shattered heart."

I stare straight ahead of me at the full bar stocked with the most premium liquor. I feel… I don't know, dumbstruck. I can't decide if Sebastian is the most ridiculous or the most authentic person I've come across.

"Hey, I have a question. It's kind of a weird one though."

"Sugar, I'm nuttier than a squirrel turd. Shoot."

"Do you know what your core values are?"

"My core values?"

"Like the things that give you meaning. The things that matter to you the most."

"Do Cuban cigars and top shelf liquor count?"

"Absolutely."

I sigh with a comforting relief. We clink our glasses together and drown out all the other noise. And suddenly, the sun comes out.

Chapter 28
2009- Richmond Hill, Georgia

I twirl and spin in front of the mirror, having too much fun with my solo fashion show. I take a few steps back towards my keyboard then catwalk forward until I'm face to face with myself. I smooth out the white fabric with delicate hands. It's no shock that Lady Katherine demanded I wear white when we went prom dress shopping last month. It's usually a difficult task to get my mom to do anything with me, especially an outing that requires her to be sober enough to drive. But her need to make sure her daughter doesn't look like a 'crack-brained tramp' in front of the whole town persevered, winning the battle against her usual mid-afternoon martini. I flip my copper hair over the short sleeve corset top which is elegantly beaded with pearls. The A-line dress flares at the waist and drapes down well past my feet. I practically trip over the train as I hobble over to the closet. I slide on the white Manolo Blaniks we bought to pair with the dress. They make me almost a whole foot taller. I do a couple more spins in the mirror until I hear a loud noise coming from downstairs. What the hell was that? I open the bedroom door.

"Hello?" I yell out with wide eyes. No one is supposed to be home all night. *Thump, Thump, Thump.* There's a hard knock on the door. I wonder if I should ignore it and lock myself in my bedroom or go investigate. *Thump, Thump, Thump.*

"Who's there?"

"Delilah? It's me."

Oh shit, Sam. I almost forgot. What time is it?

"Be right there!"

I run down the spiral staircase. I open the back door with urgency. I'm halfway stunned when I see his dark skin and gray eyes lit up by the sunset. His half smile flares as he scratches the black scruff on his chin.

"Hey, you look…"

"What?"

"Nothin'."

"What? Oh fuck." I look down at the dress I forgot I was wearing. "This is— it's not—"

"You getting married or something?"

I roll my eyes and gesture for Sam to come inside. He walks through the doorway into the kitchen.

"I was just trying it on. It's for prom, or it was, at least."

"Was?"

"Well yeah, I'm not going anymore. Seeing as I no longer have a boyfriend and everyone thinks I'm a tramp who got their favorite teacher fired."

"Nobody thinks that."

I roll my neck. "Yes, they do. It's okay. It is what it is."

"Well, I don't think that." Sam looks deeply into my eyes, intention rages in his.

"I know."

We continue to stare at each other. The only sound in the room comes from the central air conditioning. I'm almost at eye level with him in these heels. Wait, that's bad, boys hate it when you're as tall as them. Philly always scolded me for it.

"Sorry," I mutter, reaching my hand down to my ankle.

"For what?" Sam's heart shaped mouth purses as his brow furrows.

"The heels, they're… they're too much." I kneel down to unfasten the strap when Sam reaches for my arms, gently pulling me back up.

"They're not too much, they're beautiful. And the dress is beautiful too. Delilah, *you* are beautiful."

I want to believe his words. I want to live inside each one of them. I want to pour them over my head like bay water and let them soak me in safety. But, for some reason, I can't.

I turn my head and Sam loosens his grasp, letting his warm hands fall away.

"Anyway, I wanted to show you something. Come on." I lead Sam out of the kitchen, through the dining room, the living room, past my dad's study, through the foyer and into the piano room.

"Holy shit. This place doesn't end." Sam walks around the piano room marveling at the photos on the wall. He seems bewildered. He picks up a photo and studies it. "Is this you? You were so cute."

I walk towards him. And snatch the picture from him. I look at the photo inside the frame of two children at a pumpkin patch. "That's my brother, Liam."

"Are y'all close?"

"We are. You'd love him, he's the best person I know."

"That's great. Hold him close. You never know how long you have with people." Sam sighs and continues studying our family photos. "Wow, you and your family, you look so…"

"What?"

"Perfect."

"Yeah, well, our family is not as black and white as those photos."

"Are you saying the esteemed Monroe family has… secrets!" Sam teases.

I giggle. "I'm saying, things are rarely as they seem."

"Don't I know it. Everyone's got their mask on."

I look up at the ceiling. "I covered the fire detectors in here earlier this afternoon, so you can smoke if you want."

Sam laughs, "I appreciate that, but I'm good."

"You sure? Because I really don't mind."

"I'm sure. But you do whatever you want, have a drink if you want."

"I think I'm good too."

I walk over to the piano and sit on the bench. I pat the space next to me and Sam comes over to sit. Our shoulders touch, and I feel paralyzed by his warm, comforting skin. I imagine the broadness of his frame makes me appear as a garden gnome in comparison.

"So... are you going to prom?" I ask.

"What do you think?"

"I think prom isn't your scene."

"Rats," he snaps his fingers. "Guess I can't count on your vote for prom king then?"

We both laugh, and I nudge him with my body. I turn my face towards his, and we're barely an inch apart.

"It's a masquerade ball. It'll be fun to see what everyone wears."

"I thought you weren't going."

"Oh... right. I'm not." I shutter at the realization. I've been dreaming of prom night since I was in middle school. But, seeing as my prom date is a blood thirsty monster who destroyed my reputation, amongst other things... I think it's safe to say that dream is dashed.

Sam stretches his arm around me and rubs my shoulder, like any good friend would. Because that's what we are... right?

"You know any Otis Redding, prom queen?"

I roll my eyes and begin to play "Dock of the Bay" on the piano. Sam and I both hum the first verse quietly until he bursts out into a full belt at the chorus. His voice cracks, completely off key. It sends me into full belly laughter until my eyes tear and I can't see the keys anymore. Sam slams his hands on the black keys an octave above, making a hilariously dreadful sound.

"Am I... better than Otis Redding? I think I might be," he jokes.

"I think you may be the one who gets to play for the New York City Philharmonic."

He laughs and puts a hand on his stomach. "Nah, that's all you. You're really freaking good. At piano, I mean."

"Thanks." I smile bashfully. "I don't normally get to play that kind of music."

"How come?"

"I have to play classical. That's what's played in the philharmonic and every other major symphony. Besides, it's the only genre my dad wants me to play."

"And, what do *you* want to play?

"I— well, that's actually what I wanted to show you. I wrote a song."

"You did? That's amazing."

"Oh no, it's nothing, really. There's no words or anything. I was just sitting here the other day, thinking about you and how hard you're fighting to get justice for Bailey. I was thinking about how beautifully she wrote, or how Mileena Gale, her alter ego, wrote. I just felt... I don't know, inspired."

"That's really nice, Delilah." Sam stares into my eyes like he doesn't see the muddy watercolor everybody else does. He darts his silver irises down to the piano. "Well, let's hear it. What's it called?"

"It's called Black Roses."

I straighten my posture and hover my hands above the piano, assuming my regular performance position. The only difference between this performance and all of the others is that I don't choke. I don't feel panicked, or anxious, or like I want to disappear. For the first time while performing in front of someone I feel... I don't know, peace. I stroke the keys in a melodic legato, augmenting and diminishing the chords to sound darker, more ominous. I close my eyes and sway to the sound that I can't believe my own hands are playing. I allow my fingers to flow freely up and down the scales imperfectly, reminding me of why I fell in love with this instrument. I press my Manolo on the pedal, forgetting everything else. I'm unsure of how I want to end the song until I finally press my fingers into a beautiful arpeggio, creating a harmony that fills the entire room. My eyes are still closed when I feel two fingers lightly touch my chin and tilt my head up. I suck in a deep breath. I open my eyes, and I'm face to face with Sam's full, heart-shaped lips formed into that gorgeous half smile. Without thinking, I press my face to his, finding his lips and puckering mine. Sam caresses my cheek and holds the back of my head with gentle hands. I slip my tongue between his lips and stroke his. His soft tongue waltzes with mine as both our breathing picks up. Our pace gets faster, our bodies grinding into each other. Lust consumes me to point where I want to cry. I think I have died and gone to heaven when Sam pulls away from me. Oh no. Maybe I shouldn't have—

"Hey."

"Hey..."

"Go to prom with me."

"What?"

"Go to prom with me," Sam repeats.

"Prom? I thought it wasn't your scene."

Sam grins. "I never said that, you did."

"Are you serious? You really want to go with me?"

"I am. And I do, I really do. But I should let you know now that I *will* be wearing that exact same dress," he points at my outfit, "I hope that won't be a problem."

"Oh God, I forgot I was wearing this fucking thing."

"It's beautiful. You're beautiful, Delilah."

Distrust begins to fill my gut again. I narrow my eyes. "You actually want to go to prom… with me? Why?"

"You really need to ask that?"

"Yes."

"Fine. If you must know, I think you're the most talented, most special person I've ever met. You dream big, and you see the world differently than everyone else. Like it's not black and white, but gray. You've opened my eyes to a whole new perspective. And there's something dark about you…"

Dark? Great.

Sam continues, "and it's the most beautiful quality I have ever seen in a person. The way that you were able to understand Bailey's mind with just a few pages of scribbles, it was amazing. You're truly like no one I've known."

I blush. "Back at you."

"When I'm with you, I just feel…"

"Peace?"

"Yeah, peace. Don't get me wrong. You make me nervous; you make me nervous as hell."

"I do?"

"You do. But it's a good kind of nervous, an excited kind. Like I can't wait just to sit next to you and listen to you breathe or feel the goosebumps on your skin when I pretend to accidentally brush against your hand."

My smile widens as Sam scoots even closer.

He cradles my face in his hands. "Like I can't wait to watch you twirl your hair, or watch your fingers play an invisible piano in the air."

"Shit. You've seen that?"

Sam's grin is plastered to the left side of his irresistible face. "I've never had this with anyone before. But I'm starting to think that it's everything I've ever wanted."

I press my forehead to his, fighting back tears. "Me too."

"So, will you go to prom with me?"

"Yes!" I cry. "Hell yes!" I grab his face and slam it into mine, practically breaking his teeth. But I can't help it. I want to absorb him. Sam pulls me in closer and I fall into him. Our lips dance like they knew each other in a past life. I grab the back of Sam's hair, pulling it as hunger gushes out of me. Sam lets out a quiet moan as his hands lower down to my waist, squeezing it lightly. My pulse quickens and our kiss deepens. I bring my hands to his neck, gliding my fingers over every inch of it. Our chests bump against each other as the ache for more of him takes over. I can feel his chest hair tickling my collarbone as I smash into him with desire. I crave his warm hands and his soft tongue all over every part of me. I'm fucking ravenous. I reach my hand down to one of his and clasp it with mine. I slide it up the front of my body. Over my belly button, my diaphragm, my ribs, until I press it firmly to my breast. Sam pulls his face away from mine.

"Does this make you nervous?" I whisper.

Sam gulps. "Yeah."

"Do you want to stop?"

"No," he whimpers, starving as much as I am. "Do *you* want to stop?"

"No."

"Are you sure?" Sam studies my face like he's looking for any sign of hesitation.

"I'm sure." I press his hand deeper into my breast, and he squeezes his fingers around it. His breathing picks up as he squeezes faster and tighter. The sensation is like nothing I have ever felt before. I arch my spine and lean my head back, breathing heavily as his hands explore my chest. I pull the sleeve of my dress down slightly and pick my head up. His hungry eyes connect with mine.

"Have you ever… you know?" I ask, Sam's big hand still pressed on my chest.

"No. Have you?"

"Yeah. Well, kind of."

Sam removes his hand from chest. "What do you mean?"

"I mean," I stutter, "yes. I have. Is that bad?"

"No, of course not. Why would that be bad?"

"I don't know. I thought it would make you think I was like… disgusting."

"No, oh my gosh, no." Sam grabs my hands, both of ours are sweating. "Why would you think something like that? Who's putting these things in your head, Delilah?"

My head shoots down towards the ground. "No one, nothing. So, are you like celibate or something because you're Christian?"

Sam laughs. "I think we've established I'm not your typical Christian. Nah, it's nothing like that. I just haven't found anyone I liked enough. Well, until I met you."

Panic floods me, my stomach flutters.

"Not that I'm saying we should do it now, or ever."

I unlace my fingers from his and bow my head down.

"Not that I don't want to, or that– shit." Sam lets out an embarrassed laugh and ruffles his black hair with his hand. He then brings his fingers to my chin and tilts it up. "Hey."

"Hey."

"I would be the luckiest dude in the fucking world to get the privilege of sleeping with you. But I want to do it when *you* want to. When you're sure you're ready."

I sigh at his charming words. "What about you? When will you be ready?"

"Honestly?"

"Honestly."

"Uh, the minute I looked into your beautiful hazel eyes. I know I didn't know you well, but it felt like my soul did. That's corny, sorry," Sam laughs.

I grab his face and pierce his eyes. "No, it's not." I pull him towards me and inhale his face, gripping the back of his T-shirt in my hands. Sam wraps his fingers around my neck as it curls through his fingers. Our torsos crash into each other on the piano bench as his hands make their way down to my hips, he grips them firmly then moves them to my butt. There's not much to grab, but he finds it somehow. My nails dig into him as I search for the bottom of his T-shirt. I rip at it until I've lifted it to his pecks. Sam pulls away from my lips and stretches his arms up, allowing me to pull the shirt over his head. Our eyes stay connected, mulling over every color and detail. Sam abandons his shirt on the floor as I slowly lean back on the piano bench, rolling each vertebrae as our eyes stay fixed on each other. Sam follows me down and puts his hand under my head like a pillow. He grins at me like no one ever has. Finally, he leans down towards me, and our lips lock in a way that only a key could break into.

"Eh hem."

And... there's the key. Sam jumps off of me and leaps from the piano bench, fumbling on the floor to find his shirt. I shoot up from my back and onto my feet. I pull up my sleeve and wipe my mouth. I stiffen my back, standing as straight as a soldier in a line-up drill. I stare blankly at the sergeant in front of me. *Katherine*. Fuck. I look to Sam who is frantically putting his shirt back on.

"Hi Mrs. Monroe," he grimaces. "We were, we were just—"

"I saw clear as day what you were doing." Mom's face is expressionless. Her lips are together in a straight line. Her eyes are fierce yet vacant. The veins popping out of her neck and forehead tell me that she's clenching her teeth, holding herself back from making a scene. This is bad. This is so bad.

"I, uh, I thought you were going to be at the church fundraiser all night."

"I was until your brother called and said he was driving home from college tonight."

"He is? Shouldn't he be taking exams this week?"

Mom ignores my question. "Sam, you best be going now. I'm sure your mama would like you home before dark."

Home before dark? Since when is that a concept Lady Katherine cherishes?

"Yes, ma'am."

"I ordered supper from the country club. We will be eating in the dining room when Liam arrives. I reckon you go change, unless you plan on wearing... that."

Damn, I keep forgetting I'm wearing a freaking wedding gown. I look down at the white dress then back up at my mom's face which is now wearing a disgusted look. Sam heads for the door.

"Have a good night, Mrs. Monroe." He lingers a second, awaiting a response but Lady Katherine merely nods without looking at him. He walks out of the door, and my heart gains a new crack with every yard that is put in between us. My mom looks at the door, making sure he left, then her head swivels back to me. This is not going to be good.

"Did he respond yet?" My mom asks eagerly, her French tips taping impatiently on the base of her martini glass. I flip my phone open.

"No, he didn't."

"Ugh, where is that boy? He's slow as molasses."

My mom drains the contents in her martini minus the lemon twist. I get up from my chair and grab the cocktail shaker from the ice bucket in the center of the table. I walk over to the other head of the glass dining table. I keep my footsteps quiet, attempting to shrink my presence down to a peanut. I pour Mom another martini with shaky hands. Putting the shaker down, I walk back to my chair at the opposite side of the table. I stab at cold mac and cheese on the China plate in front of me and shovel it into my mouth, as I have been for the past hour. My logic is that my mom can't ask me any questions and expect me to answer if my mouth is full.

Katherine taps her fingers on the glass table. "This is just ridiculous. He said he would be here over two hours ago. I went through all of this effort to make a nice supper for him, and this is the thanks I get."

I can't blame her for getting antsy. We've been sitting at this table in silence for an hour waiting for Liam. He had called Mom earlier today in a chaotic state. He said he was driving home from college and wanted to have dinner with her and I. But he never showed up, and he's not answering any calls or texts. I even Facebook messaged him. When I called his college roommate a half hour ago, he said that he hasn't seen

Liam in days and that his behavior has been alarming lately. My mom is quite obviously annoyed at Liam's absence, but remembering back to how he was that day in the piano room, how desperate he was for pills, I'm starting to really worry.

"Maybe we should call the police."

"Don't be so childish, Delilah. This is not a police matter. Your brother is just being his bratty self. I swear, that boy, he could make a preacher cuss. He's just like his father, selfish and entitled, no regard for anyone else's time."

"I'm just saying. He could be missing, or he could have gotten into an accident."

"For heaven's sake, Lilah. Do not speak like that."

"Sorry." I shrivel low in my seat. I glance over at the place setting next to me and grab the martini I had poured for Liam. It's no longer cold, as it's been sitting here for a while, but who gives a shit? I press it to my lips and savor the feeling as the vodka burns my throat.

"Besides," Mom continues, "the police in this town are as useless as a screen door on a submarine."

"So I've heard," I sigh, thinking about how badly the police department handled Bailey's situation.

"I reckon Sheriff St. James is getting loaded with your father at the bar as we speak."

Based on what Philly had said about his dad avoiding his mom's final days, I'd bet that Lady Katherine's theory is correct. *Philly.* How am I going to explain to Philly that I'm going to prom with Sam? What will he do? Will he try to fight him? Will he even care? No. Fuck that. I don't care if he cares. Philly and I are through. He's a monster. I need to have more respect for myself. I am not going to grow up to be a woman like... well, like the woman across the table from me. *Katherine.* She's been so focused on her anger towards Liam for being late that she seems to have forgotten about what she saw in the piano room. I'm sure I need to explain myself, but I don't want to. I don't need a drunken lecture about how God punishes sinners. And I don't need to listen to her call me a whore, I've gotten enough of that at school this week. I don't want to hear what she thinks about me or Sam. I don't want to sit through ramblings of offensive comments towards him and his family, saying that they're beneath us and we're nothing but heroes doing a good deed by giving them a place to stay. I don't want to hear her say that Sam's twin sister committed the ultimate sin of suicide, so her brother must be crazy too. I don't want to hear that my feelings for Sam are a silly phase, and that I am meant to marry a man like Philly St. James, a boy that has made me feel worthless for over a decade. It's no wonder I ended up with a guy like Philly, look at the example Katherine set. The finger she wags at me dug my grave. But now, I'm digging myself out. I'm getting out of Philly's haunting grasp and jumping into the arms of something warm, something soothing, something enchanting. I'm done pretending to be who my parents want me to be, who my friends want me to be, who Philly wants me to be. I. Am. Done. I want to be happy; I need to be happy. I don't know how long I can hold on otherwise.

"Mom!" I shoot up from my chair, liquid courage coursing through my veins. "I have to tell you something." I say it sternly, slamming my hands flat on the dining room table. "What you saw in the piano room, Sam and I…"

My mom purses her lips and waits to answer, taking a long sip of her martini.

"I only need to know one thing," she says, looking off into the distance. Her drawl is long and intimidating, her eyelashes flutter with superiority. This is it, this is the part where she screams profanities at me for being a 'tramp' and tarnishing the Monroe name.

She gets up from her chair and walks over to my end of the table. I stand still in place. I stare into her ice blue eyes. Is she going to slap me? I begin to brace myself for the hit when she takes both of my hands. I stare at our interwoven fingers in awe.

"Is he anything like your father?"

"What?" I look up at her with trepidation.

It's then that I notice tears rimming her eyes. She blinks sharply, allowing a drop to fall onto her high cheekbone.

"This boy, Samson. Is he anything like your father?"

"No... no, he's not. He's warm and captivating. He's like... sunset."

"Sunset?"

"Yeah, like when the sunset casts it's shine onto the blue river, making the teal waves glow orange."

"You're favorite." Mom nods.

"You... you knew that?"

"Why of course I do, darlin'. I know my tongue can be sharp, but it doesn't mean I don't love you like biscuits love gravy."

I grin at her words. Mom strokes my arm up and down. "My mama used to say that."

Tears well in my eyes as my voice shakes. "I love you too, Mom."

"Oh, hey, well don't go gettin' all hysterical now. Tell me more about this boy."

"Well, he's... he's... he's the safest person I have ever known."

"Safe?"

"Yeah, safe."

"Well good then." Mom says as she releases my hands. She leans in close to me and whispers in my ear. "Then go ahead and let him love you."

Chapter 29
2009- Richmond Hill, Georgia

"I can't believe you're actually dating him." Mary Lu's voice echoes throughout the black and white cafeteria. She re-applies her Dior lip gloss then hands it to Mia who does the same.

"We're not *dating*. At least, I don't think. I don't really know what we are."

"What *do* you know?" Mia asks excitedly, freshly glossed lips in a pout.

"I know that I like him. I like him a lot."

Word about Sam and I traveled like wildfire throughout the school this morning. I had called Mia late at night after the talk with my mom. I blurted everything out right when Mia picked up the phone, not knowing she was in her basement pulling an all-nighter with Mary Lu and Chloe after cheer practice. Those two chirping birds immediately went on their phones and blasted the information out to everyone they knew. I haven't seen Sam since this morning. We both snuck out at 5am and watched the sun rise on the dock together. It was freezing, but absolutely worth every second. It made me believe in magic again. The feeling I get when I'm huddled in his arms, burrowed in his neck, it feels… I don't know, like everything. However, I didn't expect the rumor mill to have started their engines this early in the school day. By second period, everyone was talking about Sam and me, giving them a nice little break from gossiping about the Mr. Stoff rumor.

Though, I'm sure nobody has forgotten. Reputations have a habit of being permanent and irreparable around here.

"So, you're really going to prom with him?" Chloe squeaks over another empty lunch tray. She's wearing disgust on her face, and it is not her color.

"Yes, why?"

"Why? He's a homeless person living in your shed. Fucking skeleton twin."

Anger intoxicates my blood. "Chloe, go fuck yourself. You don't know the first thing about Sam. He has more kindness and intelligence in his pinky nail than you have in your entire body!" I yell, hands slapped on the table, splashing sweet tea out of my cup.

"Damn," Mia laughs.

"What?"

"I just didn't know you had it in you. Well done. I taught you well." Mia sips her diet coke. "And she's right, Chloe. Skeleton twin? You sound like Link."

"Fuck off."

Mia ignores her. "That reminds me, what does Philly think about your newfound romance? Is he pissed?"

"I don't know."

"Philly doesn't care," Chloe gloats, "he was done with you the minute you whored yourself out to that geriatric English teacher. Besides, he says you're horrible in bed anyway. He told me that all you do is lay there like a dead fish."

Dead fish? What was I supposed to do? I didn't want to have sex in the first place. Perhaps that should have been his first signal, not that he would have cared regardless.

"Chloe, what the fuck?" Mia hisses.

I touch my hand to her arm gently.

"It's fine. I don't give a single fuck how Philly thinks I am in bed or what sea creatures he wants to refer to me as. He is officially irrelevant to me. And for the last time, I did not sleep with Mr. Stoff, or kiss him, or have any interaction with him alone. And if I did, apparently that would be considered rape. Anyone ever thought about that? No one has a problem with that? Of course not. So, thank you, Chloe, thank you so much for your concern. What a kind heart you have," I hiss, sarcastically. I know I should stop there. I should walk away and cool down, but… "You are trash, Chloe, complete and utter trash. No wonder you and your family were denied membership at the church this year," I snap, word vomit. That was of the lowest blow variety. I guess Mia was right, she has taught me well, but I don't think I like the new skill I've acquired. I look around the table. Chloe hangs her head down. Mia and Mary Lu pick their jaws up from the floor and look at me with bewildered expressions.

"Sorry," I whisper. "I'm just tired. I'm tired of all this Richmond Hill bullshit. I can't do it anymore."

The table sits in silence for a moment.

"And, FYI, I don't care what Philly thinks about Sam and me. He lost the right to have an opinion a long time ago."

"Yeah… what ever happened with you and Philly anyway?" Mary Lu asks.

"It's a long story." I stare down at the floor, tears well in my eyes as I try to force my brain out of going back to that night.

Mia catches my demeanor and attempts to distract the group. "Well, the story is that Philly is a dickhead, we all know that. Delilah is too good for him, and she's finally come to her senses. It's about damn time."

Mary Lu nods. "He is a dick. He and Link are practically the same person. Neanderthals."

"Amen sister," Mia adds.

Chloe doesn't agree or disagree, she just sits silently with her head down. I feel… I don't know, horrible. What I said to her, it was uncalled for. I only know that her family's membership at the church was revoked because I overheard my mom gossiping about it on the phone. I suppose the fraud and embezzlement charges against Chloe's dad were too salacious for the church to handle, so they booted the whole family out.

"Chloe, I—"

"There's Sam!" Mary Lu shouts.

"Sam! Hey! Come here, sit with us." Mia invites Sam over to our lunch table, and I begin to feel the chicken I ate make its way back up my windpipe.

"Uh, hey," Sam hesitates as he inches over to us, cautiously yet confidently. I don't know how he does that.

"Pop a squat. This is Mary Lu, Chloe, and obviously you know Delilah. I'm Mia."

"I know who you are." Sam lowers himself onto the open seat next to me. I don't dare hazard a glance towards his magnetic eyes.

"Well yeah, of course. We've been in school together since elementary, but I've never formally introduced myself. I'm sorry about that."

"All good."

"I knew your sister though, Bailey. We did an English project on The Outsiders in seventh grade. She was my partner. We didn't know much of each other before that, but I was so happy I was paired with her. We ended up writing a bunch of poems for our project."

"I didn't know you wrote poetry," I interject, quite shocked.

"I didn't. Bailey introduced me to it. She was good at it. She taught me all about stanzas and similes. She even taught me how to write a haiku," Mia smiles reminiscently. "We got an A on our project. And the stuff we wrote for that wasn't half as good as Bailey's other poetry."

"Bailey showed you her poetry?" Sam asks, his eyebrows pinched together, matching mine.

"Yeah, we did most of the project in her bedroom. My parents were still together then, so my house was a war zone, but Bailey was nice enough to offer hers. She had dozens of journals filled with poems. I liked reading them. A little dark, but beautiful." Mia takes a sip of her soda. "I'm a patron of the arts, D knows." Mia nods to me. "Oh, oh!" Mia continues, "and your mom made us these delicious grape dessert things. What were they called again? Supreeso—"

"Surpressa de Uva. It means grape surprise in Portuguese."

"Yes, that's it. They were amazing. I couldn't get enough of them."

"I— I can't believe that my mom made you Surpressa de Uva, and that Bailey showed you her poetry. I didn't even know that she wrote poetry, until…" Sam trails off. "I just can't believe you were in my house."

"Well, believe it. Most fun I've ever had working on a school assignment. And I really liked Bailey. I'm sorry she's gone."

"Me too," Sam nods at Mia then looks over at me. I can tell he's admitted to himself that he was wrong about Mia. Like I told him, she's a wonderful person.

"So," Mary Lu creeps into the conversation, "I hear y'all are going to prom together. That's a surprise."

"How so?"

"No, nothing, I just didn't think guys like you went to prom."

"Yeah, I've been getting that a lot lately," Sam smirks at me again and winks. I practically melt onto the cafeteria tiles. I grab his hand underneath the table and flash him a bright smile.

"How cute." Mia and Mary Lu gawk, but I can barely hear them over my own swooning. I look deeper into the gray flecks in his eyes. His heart-shaped lips continue to melt me like water to a wicked witch. I squeeze his hand tighter until I hear Mia whispering.

"Oh, no."

I burst out of my bliss bubble. I follow Mia's eyes over to two boys standing a few feet away from our table, lunch trays in hand. Philly's black eyes catch mine like a net and tangle me up. His eyes, those eyes, the ones that went from being the most majestic to the most soulless, now they look… sad. I've never seen them look like that, not when his dog died in eighth grade, not when he talks about his ill mother. His mother, I wonder if Mrs. St. James is okay. Should I ask him how she is doing? Should I ask him how *he* is doing? I can't stand to see him like this. *No.* I can't spin around in his cycle anymore. Even if things with Sam and I don't work out, one thing is for certain; I am no longer going to be fooled by Philly St. James's sparkling eyes. He can go ahead and turn all my friends against me, bar me from every party, tell the world that I slept with every teacher in the state of Georgia. I don't care, I am done with him. I untangle myself from the netting of Philly's gaze and turn back towards Sam who has a concerned look on his face. Fuck. How long was I staring at Philly for? I keep my focus on Sam. I notice Philly and Link walk away out of the corner of my eye. I look back towards the rest of the table. Chloe, who has been silent the past few minutes, stands up and grabs her bag. It's not until I see her dump her tray and trot behind Philly that I realize she's following them to a different table.

"Wow, could she be any more desperate?" Mary Lu laughs.

"Good riddance." Mia flicks her hand and takes a sip of her soda. She pulls out her Blackberry and opens Brick Breaker. "Sam, are you coming to my party tonight?"

"Your party?"

"Well, yeah. Now that you're D's… well… whatever y'all are, we should get to know you more. It's tonight after the game."

The game. How is there always a freaking game at this school?"

"Thanks for the invite, but I promised my mom I'd help her cook for her church bake sale this weekend."

"Ah! Please tell me she is making those grape things!"

Sam laughs. "She is. I'll swipe a few for you, bring them on Monday."

"Oh, thank you! Those things are like crack." Mia nudges me, "D, I think he's a keeper."

"Shame you can't come tonight, but you should at least come to prom with us. Mia's mom got us a limo," Mary Lu exclaims.

"A limo, wow."

"Yeah, well, my mom is dating a guy who owns a limo company. Well, dating is a strong term. But, with the moans that are coming from her room every night, the least that dude can do is make himself useful and spoil my friends and I. This night only comes once in a lifetime, and it'll be the most magical night of our lives."

"What about your wedding day?"

"Oh, I plan on doing that way more than once." Mia laughs. We all join in.

"Your friends are pretty cool," Sam whispers.

I rub his arm with a smile stretched ear to ear.

"So? You'll come?"

"Absolutely," Sam agrees.

I wrap my arms around his broad neck and pull him close.

"Aw, young love." Mia locks arms with Mary Lu as they watch us like a Hallmark movie. How did life get this good? I hope it stays like this forever.

Black Eyed Peas blasts through Mia's basement speakers. I keep my head tilted down towards my phone, avoiding contact with everybody here.

"D, you want some face paint?" Mary Lu asks as she stumbles by the folding chair I'm sitting on.

"Maybe later."

I watch her pour herself another beer from the keg. She holds up her solo cup and nods to me. I lift mine up and pretend to take a sip. Beer has never been my drink of choice, but I decided that I would nurse this one tonight to avoid people handing me bottles to chug out of. I'm not in the mood to get wasted tonight. Hey... I've never said that before. Interesting. I squeeze my red solo cup between my thighs and stare back down at my phone. I've read and re-read the sweet text Sam sent me.

G2g. Mom needs my professional baking skills. Have fun with your friends tonight. Can't wait to kiss your beautiful face tomorrow <3

I nearly collapse thinking of Sam's wet lips on cheek, my neck. But it'll have to wait. I sigh, taking a sip of my piss-water beer. When I look up from my cup, I'm met with a ping pong ball flying through the air, gunning straight for my head. I face the white wall beside me and feel a splash hit my wrist.

"Oh! That's double points! Drink up, D!" Link screeches from across the ping pong table.

I roll my eyes and chug the stale beer. Tilting my head back down, I flip open my phone and read Sam's text for the 15th time.

"Hey."

My head shoots up. Philly hovers above me in a black cotton sweater. It looks soft and cozy. *No.* No, it doesn't. Philly's sweater does not look soft and cozy because there is nothing about Philly that is soft and cozy. I look back towards the white wall and sip from my empty cup. I study the little lumps of paint that bubble over the smooth part of the wall.

"Are you not even going to look at me?"

I r turn my head back towards Philly. It's then that I notice the red circles around his eyes. They're swollen, like two wounds. The skin looks rubbed and raw. Has he been… crying? He blinks slowly, giving me that same look he had in the cafeteria, only worse.

I shoot out of my chair. "What's wrong? Is it your mom? Did she…"

Philly runs his hand through his chocolate hair. His lips part and I catch a glimpse of the W shaped mark on his tooth. It's almost as white as his porcelain complexion.

"No, no. She's fine. Well, she's the same, dying. Cancer, ya know?"

My brow furrows at his awkward attempt to make a joke.

"Sorry. Long day."

"Yeah, you lost."

"I did." Philly bites his bottom lip.

I turn my head away and avoid his smoldering stare. "The game, I mean."

"Oh yeah, that too."

I study Philly's angular face as he rubs his eyes.

"I don't care that we lost the game."

"Okay… what are you upset about then?"

"I lost you." Tears begin to well in his eyes as he turns away.

I sigh. I didn't realize the news about Sam and me would hurt Philly like this. I never want to hurt him. I thought he hated me, that's why he started that Mr. Stoff rumor.

"Since when do you care about me?" I ask, folding my arms.

"Since forever, D. You know that."

"I do?"

"Yes, of course. You are the only person in the world who knows me, whether I like it or not. I know I fucked up. But, you know, everything with my Mom. It's making me lose my goddamn mind. I love her so much. I don't want to lose her."

"I know," I whisper, "I know."

Philly takes my hand and I'm stunned. I look around the room at the drunk cheerleaders dancing on Mia's coffee table, Link cheating at beer pong by leaning over the table. Everyone is too drunk to notice us, it's like the rest of the world has disappeared.

Philly squeezes my hand and leans in close, brushing copper strands away from my face. He brings his lips to my ear and whispers, "I love you, Delilah."

Heat surges through me from my toes to my hair follicles. My skin burns with the passion of the sun. I feel queasy, like I may vomit. He said it. He finally said it. Philly finally admitted that he loves me. This is everything I have ever wanted. But, why now? Why did it take him this long to say it? I have been in Philly's corner for over a decade. For 12 years, all I ever did was love him, and all he ever did was punish me for it.

I'm about to open my mouth when a pair of deep gray eyes and a half smirk flash through my mind. *Sam*. Fuck. *Sam*.

I pull my hand out of Philly's grasp and back away from him. Philly clasps his hands behind his back. "It's okay. You don't have to say it back. I know, I'm too late."

"It's just…"

My thought is interrupted by Link plowing into us. "Sup motherfuckers!" Link puts one arm around Philly and one arm around me. Philly shrugs him off and I do the same. "Oh, am I, like, interrupting?"

"Yes," Philly says sternly through his teeth.

Link puts up his hands. "Alright, alright, sorry man, my bad. But, D, hey, D." Link puts his arm back around my neck and I cringe at the smell of tequila on his breath. "You should not be with that freak of nature skeleton twin. Dude's a loser. He's not good enough to breathe the same air as us. You had your fun but it's time to dump the loser and get back with my boy here. That's where you belong."

I look up at Philly with obvious anger in my jaw.

He puts a hand on Link's shoulder. "Bro, fuck off. Please."

Link's eyes widen. He nods and scurries away.

Philly grabs my hand again. "Can we go talk?"

"I, um…"

"I just wanna talk. Come on, D. You owe me that much."

I ruminate in stillness for a second, utterly torn.

"So, can we?" Philly asks again.

"Okay. But, just to talk. Not in Mia's sisters—"

"No, of course not. Let's go outside."

"Okay."

Philly continues to hold my hand as he leads me up the stairs of the basement and out the front door into the driveway. I don't know if I feel the same way about him as I did before.

Before I saw the devil in his black eyes. Before I saw sunset in Sam's gray ones. I have no idea how I'm going to explain my relationship with Sam to Philly, but I at least owe him a conversation.

The air is brisk outside. I shiver, hugging my arms around myself. Philly scans Mia's driveway for prying eyes. I can still hear the hum of music coming from the basement. My teeth chatter as I see Philly rounding the corner of a black Lexus.

"So, uh, what did you want to talk about?"

"Not here, come with me." He takes my freezing hand and leads me to a small shed in the front yard. He pushes on the door, but it doesn't budge.

"Follow me."

I follow him around to the back of the shed. My hand still cupped in his. I see my breath linger in the cold air. I'm beginning to get annoyed.

"Look Philly, I—"

"Shhhhhhh." Philly presses his index finger to my lips. He grips both of my wrists tightly in his hands.

"But I—"

Philly grabs both sides of my face and pulls it towards him.

"What are you doing?"

"Come on, you know what I'm doing." Philly presses his open, wet mouth onto mine and shivers radiate throughout my body. I put my hands on his chest and push him away.

"Philly, what the hell? You said you just wanted to talk."

"We *are* talking." He grabs my hand and puts it on the bulge of his jeans.

"Philly, it's over. We are done."

I can't believe I fell for his shit again. He just made my decision a whole lot easier. This needs to end. I pull my hand back, but he grabs it again. He begins to rub it up and down on his pants.

"Stop!"

I try to yank my hand away, but he grips my wrist with more force. The zipper on his jeans scratches my skin. He lets my hand go and pushes me down to my knees. I fall backward onto the pavement, my tailbone catching my fall. The whiplash has blurred my vision so much, I barely realize that Philly has unzipped his jeans and pulled down his boxers.

"What the fuck are you doing?"

He kneels down and pushes my shoulders back. The back of my head slams on the pavement.

"Get off of me or I'll—"

He pins me down with a stern hand glued to my chest. "You'll what? What will you do? Tell on me? No one would believe you. It doesn't matter if I rape you. I can do whatever the fuck I want to you."

"Rape me? What?"

"No one would fucking believe you."

He lowers himself on top of me, crushing me with his heavy body. I squirm underneath him.

"Stop, please, stop," I cry in a whisper, my throat unable to get anything else out.

He pushes inside of me with brutal force. I hold my breath. He pins both of my wrists down on the pavement and whispers in my ear.

"No one would believe you. You don't fucking matter, you fucking whore."

At the sound of his words, my body goes still. I'm paralyzed. I float up out of myself and watch from above. Why am I not moving? Why can't I move? I yell at myself from my floating state. Get off the ground. Get off the ground. Get off the ground. Get off the fucking ground. Get off the fucking ground. Get off the fucking ground, Delilah.

I didn't get off the ground that night, and I never would.

Chapter 30
Present Day

My foot taps heavily on the ground as my leg bounces up and down. I adjust the collar of my short sleeve turtleneck and wipe my clammy palms on my black jeans. I fish my phone out of my YSL purse and place the silver chain on the back of my chair. I unlock my phone and open the message I've been staring at all morning.

Unknown number: Please, Delilah. I just want to talk.

Talk... I know what that means. There is no way that I'm going to risk 'talking' to him. I'm not 17 anymore. I know how short life can be, and I know how horribly and vulnerably mortal I am. I am not going to put my life at risk again, not for him.

I stuff my phone back in my purse and stare at the white wall in front of me. Smooth jazz plays softly in the waiting room of Dr. Veizer's private practice. I close my eyes and attempt to focus on the music, hoping it will cool my body down somehow. I listen for each individual instrument, savoring their sounds separately from all of the others. I sway from side to side, squeezing my folded hands in between my thighs to keep me from playing along to the piano riff. I feel a bullet of sweat roll down my back. Ugh, withdrawal sweat. When I made that rule for myself that I can't start drinking until 5pm, I never specified when I needed to *stop* drinking for the night. Usually, my last drink is consumed around 2 or 3am when I fall asleep, but that didn't happen last night because I never fell asleep. I was watching Fried Green Tomatoes with a dirty martini when the anonymous text came in. I blocked the number again then proceeded to run around the house, bolting every door and window. I thought it would make me feel safer, but it didn't. I took shot after shot as the movie played and replayed in the background. You'd think that vomiting up Belvedere and olive juice in the kitchen sink would have stopped me, but it didn't. All it did was give me a clean slate to forget all the things I never deserved to know, again. I began drinking straight from the bottle around 1am, trying to sedate myself. But the monsters under my bed are rarely scared off when I turn on the lights. It was about 7am when I realized that sleep was not in the cards no matter how much I drank. I forced myself to drain the rest of my last bottle in the sink. I had about eight hours to sober up, and now that I am completely sober, I wish that I wasn't. Chills float over my skin as goosebumps form underneath the sweat. I hug my body and rub my arms, hopelessly trying to warm up and cool down at the same time. I take the chain off the chair and open my YSL bag. I curse the empty space where a flask of vodka used to reside. This's what I get for trying to be healthy and committing to therapy. Damn these therapy sessions. Damn this therapy office. And damn that terribly wise and uncomfortably comforting therapist.

"Dr. Veizer!" I shoot up off of the chair, dropping my purse and spilling its contents. I bend down to pick up my phone, wallet, lipstick, and keys.

"Good afternoon, Delilah. Did I startle you?"

"Oh no, no. It's not you. I'm just... you know me!" I laugh and avoid her eye contact for a moment. When I look up, I see that Dr. Veizer isn't laughing, but instead looks concerned as her eyes flicker back and forth. She's probably deciding what game she's going to beat me at today.

The wind swirls around outside, causing the window next to me to hum loudly. Dr. Veizer is still looking for something from the closet behind her desk when I quietly yank my phone out of my bag and check for any new messages.

"Found it!" Dr. Veizer sings from the closet. She walks over to the coffee table in front of me and sets down something that looks like a sandbox for a doll. There's a little rake in it.

"What's this?"

"It's a sand tray."

Okay, so exactly what it looks like.

"It's a therapeutic tool. I thought it might help; I noticed you seem a bit jumpy today."

"Okay... um, what am I supposed to do with it?"

"Whatever you want. Some people like to plant their hands in the sand, some people like to rake it, some people like to use the figures to create a story within the box."

I look to the right of the box and notice a plastic bag full of figurines. I look back up at her, confused and a tad bit offended that this is what seemed appropriate to her based on my mental maturity.

"You don't have to do anything with it if you don't want to. But I find it can be grounding when talking about some of the heavier topics. And I thought it would be a nice way to ease into inner child work." Dr. Veizer sits on her leather chair and flips open her notepad. "Tell me, did you ever play in the sand as a child?"

Scenes flash through my mind as if I'm watching a montage on the Hallmark channel. I see the sand under the dock of my childhood home. I see my seven-year-old-self digging my toes into it, burying my legs. I see Liam and I pulling a heavy kayak through it. I see Mia and I balling up the wet sand and throwing it at each other like summer snowballs. I see it all. The sand, the dock, the bay. Then, I see *him*.

No.

I shake my head and turn it away from the children's toy in front of me. I glance back down at my phone and refresh my messages app.

"Everything okay? Do you need to make a call?"

"No! No, I'm fine." I turn my phone off and stuff it in my purse. Focus, Delilah. I wipe sweat from my neck and clasp my hands together to stop them from shaking.

"So, Delilah, how are you feeling today?"

I sigh as Dr. Veizer points to the feelings chart on the couch cushion next to me.

"Have you been practicing the feelings identification that we talked about last session?"

"Uh, yeah, actually. I did."

"That's great. Let's do some of that now."

"Okay." I scan the chart of faces. "Today, I'm feeling… calm, and that's okay."

"Mhmm. Calm. Tell me more about that."

I stare at her. "What is there to tell? I feel calm, that's it."

"That's it?"

"Um… yes?"

Dr. Veizer seems to be playing Twister today, and suddenly, I feel like the least flexible person in the world.

"I've noticed that you're glistening, yet your skin has goosebumps as if you're chilly. Would you feel comfortable telling me when your last drink was?"

"Um, a few days ago," I lie, quite obviously.

"How many days is a few?"

"I don't know."

"What *do* you know?"

Jesus Christ.

"I really don't remember. A few."

"Okay then," Dr. Veizer states in clear disbelief of my story.

I ball my hands into fists and shake my feet out, trying to ease the pins and needles before the numbness takes over. Dr. Veizer stares at me intently, probably trying to decide which spot she will move to first. I stare back at her, taking a big gulp to clear my throat. I quietly choke on my saliva and cover my mouth.

"Correct me if I'm wrong, but I'm noticing some heightened anxiety today."

"I'm always anxious, hence why I confide in the bottle, hence why I'm here."

"No, it seems like there's something else going on, something you're not telling me. So, I'm going to ask, point blank. Is there something that you're not telling me, Delilah?" Dr. Veizer spins me, hoping she'll land on the right color.

The numbness in my hands and legs travels from the toes up. My lips begin to tingle. I try to bring my hand up to touch them, but it's locked in place. I am locked in place. Dr. Veizer clearly knows that I'm lying. There is something I'm not telling her, there are a plethora of things I'm not telling her. But, it's not like I can tell her that there's a potential monster on the loose, stalking me, watching me, sending me threatening texts. If I told her that, I'd have to tell her everything. And, Lord knows I can never do that.

"I screwed my neighbor's gardener," I blurt, all of the air and energy draining from my body.

"Oh."

I focus my eyes on her. I find it surprising that that's the craziest thing she's heard at this job. Unless, was it? Am I her most bat-shit patient? Embarrassment fills my gut more than the alcohol did last night.

"I know, I know. It's horrible. I cheated on my husband. I'm a cheater. I'm a terrible person." I bury my face in my hands.

Dr. Veizer leans forward and gently reaches her hand out to the coffee table, touching it with her fingertips. "You're not a terrible person."

"Yes, I am. I cheated. Only terrible people cheat."

"Says who?" Dr. Veizer crosses her arms and tilts her head.

"Um, I don't know, everyone. God."

"I thought you didn't believe in God."

I sigh and look out the window. "I don't know what I believe." I take a deep breath and glance at Dr. Veizer whose head is still cocked to the side. "So, you don't think cheating is a terrible thing?"

"I think it's a complicated thing. It's not black and white, nothing ever is. Besides, who am I to dictate what's right and what's wrong?" She adjusts herself on her chair. "So, tell me more about this man. He is a man, yes?"

"Yes," I laugh. *I'd never be interesting enough to hold the attention of a woman.* "His name is Salvatore. He works for my annoying neighbor, Beth. The affair started… well, I don't even know it would be considered an affair."

"Let's call it whatever you would consider it."

"A distraction, I guess."

"A distraction," she repeats after me. "A distraction from what?"

"Me."

"I see." Dr. Veizer scribbles in her notepad. "It sounds like he's serving some sort of purpose, like alcohol does. You typically use alcohol to self-regulate, to feel better."

"I guess so. I guess I used Salvatore too."

"Mhmm. What did you use Salvatore for?"

"I guess to not be bored, to not feel lonely."

"I see." She jots a few notes down then stares down at the page.

"What?"

"Well, it makes sense that you would look for a distraction from boredom and loneliness. I've always found that affairs, whether they're physical or emotional, have less to do with the temptation and more to do with insecurities and unfulfillment. Tell me, when's the last time you saw your husband?"

I sigh, rolling my neck. "I don't want to talk about my husband."

"How come?"

Dr. Veizer spins again, landing on a color she can't quite reach.

"Because you know everything there is to know about him."

"Do I?"

"Yep."

She scribbles a bunch of words down then flips to a new blank page. I'm always shocked by how much she tries to challenge me, how much she cares to. If I were in her shoes, I would just tell all my patients what they want to hear for an hour then cash their checks. I guess it's good that I'm not a therapist. I'm not anything.

"Alright, if you don't want to talk about your husband, fair enough. What do you want to talk about?"

I scour around my brain. "I'm looking for a job."

"That's great. What kind of job?"

"I have no clue, actually. But I thought it would be good to have something to get me out of the house. A distraction to get me out of the house that doesn't come in the shape of a glass bottle or a devastatingly sexy Italian man."

Dr. Veizer laughs, and I'm happy that I was able to make her do so.

"I think it's an amazing idea. But I like to think of a job as less of a distraction and more of a social role."

"A social role?"

"Something that allows us to contribute to society in one way or another. It helps us feel useful, purposeful. Which gives us a sense of… fill in the blank, Delilah."

"Meaning?"

"Ding ding ding!" Dr. Veizer holds her thin arms up as though she's a game show host, and the levity of it soothes my nerves.

"Yeah, some meaning would be nice," I smile at her.

"So, have you begun the job search yet?"

"Not yet. I find the whole thing feels a little… overwhelming."

"Good identification of your feelings. It's almost as if that silly assignment I gave you actually did some good," Dr. Veizer jokes. "But yes, job hunting can be overwhelming. So, why don't we start at square one and take it slow. What field are you looking to get into? Teaching again?"

And, just like that, the levity is smashed on the ground like a piano in an old cartoon. I hang my head in shame and exhale a breath of melancholy.

"You know I can't. My license was revoked. Hence why I now babysit the spoiled offspring of wealthy stage moms twice a week while my eardrums bleed."

"I wasn't sure if there was a statute of limitations on that in Georgia."

The light mood continues to be covered by a dark, wicked cloak.

Dr. Veizer looks at me with sad eyes and closes her notebook. "How long has it been since you lost the baby?"

I inhale sharply, resenting the oxygen for being too clean to kill me.

"Three years," I inhale again, "two months," I inhale again, "and six days." I hold my breath, wondering how long I can hold it until my heart gives out and my brain shuts down. "I was fired and had my teaching license revoked a year later."

I silently curse that damn sophomore choir girl that ratted me out after she took my water bottle from a music stand when I was in the bathroom. She spit it out with a squeal before running to the front office to report me. When they searched my music room, they found dozens of water bottles filled with vodka in my desk.

"It's been two years since I taught at Richmond Hill High. That's around when I started coming here. My husband threatened to divorce me if I didn't clean up my act."

"I remember," Dr. Veizer nods her head.

"Having to unlock my desk drawers for the police, knowing what they'd find, being escorted out of the building in front of everyone… It was humiliating. I thought that once the dust settled, the embarrassment would fade."

"But it never did?"

"No. I'm still repulsed with myself. Not a day goes by that I don't think about it."

"You're repulsed with yourself?"

I glance my head towards the window and let my gaze turn into a stare. My mind wanders to a place far away.

"Yes… What I did, what I let happen."

Then all of the sudden, I open my eyes. I'm on the floor, my back is against the wall. There's so much screaming but all I can feel is the throbbing, searing pain in my jaw. I look beneath me and I see a pool of scarlet lurching towards my Manolos. And, immediately I know that he's dead. How did this happen?

"I am completely fucking repulsive." My eyes stay fixed on the window, but I can no longer see anything clearly, and I don't want to.

"Delilah?"

I jerk my head away from the window and back towards Dr. Veizer. She broke my stare; I hate it when people do that.

"What happened just now? Where did you go?"

"Nowhere. What were we talking about?"

I'm completely disoriented at this point. I think I'm having hangover hallucinations.

"You were saying that you felt repulsed by yourself, you called yourself repulsive."

"I am," I doze off again to my left.

"Because you got fired?"

"What?" I look back towards her, groggy.

"You said you felt repulsive because you got fired. Unless… there's another reason that you're not telling me."

"Oh, yeah. I mean, no, no. That's it."

She laces her thin fingers together and folds her hands in her lap. "You know, Delilah, plenty of people lose their jobs, and I'm not sure that you would label all of them repulsive. Why are the rules any different for you?"

"Did they all lose their jobs because they were slurring through an AP music theory lesson, drunker than a sailor?"

"Maybe some of them. My point is that you're being brutal on yourself for something you were doing to ease the pain of the miscarriage. It was a huge loss. The pain and grief you were going through is unimaginable. It makes sense that you did what you did to survive the hardest part."

"But I never stopped."

"Right, the avoidance of pain and feelings with the numbing of alcohol continued, which is one of the reasons you're here."

"I should feel bad though, about what I did. Shouldn't I?"

"I don't think 'shoulds' are helpful. There is no right way to feel. Sometimes, it's helpful to look at unhealthy behaviors that lead to consequences, like getting fired, and label them as bad so that we don't repeat the behavior. That's why guilt can be helpful to us, it gives us a moral compass that will keep us from repeating mistakes. But the thing is, I don't think that you feel guilty about drinking on the job and getting fired. I think you feel ashamed, and there's a big difference between guilt and shame."

"There is?"

"Yes. Guilt is a realization that your behavior may have hurt you or others, it recognizes that behavior as a mistake."

"Um, okay…"

"Shame focuses on the self, recognizing *you* as bad, or *you* as the mistake. And you're not a mistake, Delilah."

"I'm sure my parents would beg to differ."

Dr. Veizer's lips press into a frown. I know my legs are not strong enough to hold me in this spot on the twister mat, but I also know that I'm going to stay in place, muscles shaking, for as long as I can.

"Do you see what I'm saying, do you see the difference?"

"I guess so."

"Guilt may have been healthy. Guilt may have prompted you to stop drinking. But, you didn't because shame took over, making you hate yourself, stealing all hope you had for the future. And, why would someone who hates themselves and who thinks they have no future stop drinking?'

"Welp, guess that's why I never did." I bring my hand to my temple as it throbs. I glance at the clock and wince that we're less than a half hour in. I cannot sit here for an entire hour today, I just can't.

"What I'm saying is that your shame is unmerited. We are the stories that we tell ourselves about ourselves. And, in your story, you're alway the villain. It's not like you killed anyone, Delilah."

My head shoots up. "Who says I didn't?"

Dr. Veizer's chin sinks into her neck as her whole body moves backward on her chair. She turns her head and studies me, trying to decide which color she'll move to next. I stare at her, stoically.

"Are you…" She hesitates. Her voice is soft. "You don't— You don't believe that you killed your baby, do you?"

My eyes travel left to right in confusion, my gaze above her head towards the paintings on the wall behind her.

"Delilah, you miscarried in the first trimester due to natural causes. It happens all of the time. You weren't drinking or being reckless. You didn't do anything wrong, it's just an unfortunate reality of early pregnancy. You did not *kill* anybody."

"Oh, right. Yes, that. Sure."

"Unless… you're not referring to the miscarriage. Unless you're referring to something else, someone else."

I feel a vibration from inside of my purse. My body shivers at the feeling and the sound. It's him, I know it. I need to get the fuck out of here.

"Delilah, did you…"

I shoot up to my feet.

"Dr. Veizer, I'm sorry but I have a horrible migraine, it just came on, and I didn't bring any Excedrin with me. Would you mind terribly if we reschedule to sometime next week?"

She stands and stretches her small body. "Oh, are you sure?"

"Yes, yes. I'm sorry, it's a really bad one."

"Of course, I understand. When you're feeling better, you can call my secretary to reschedule."

"Thanks, will do."

I turn on my heels towards the door. "But before you go!"

Ugh.

"I have another assignment I want you to do before our next session. It's an easy one, I promise. In preparation for inner child work, I want you to go through some old photo albums and find one of yourself at the age that resonates with you the most. Then, I want you to study that photo. Look at what you were wearing, what your hair looked like, what environment you were in. Notice your expression and try to tap into what you were feeling and thinking at that moment in time. Can you do that for me?"

"Yes, I can do that. Sounds good. See you next week!" I yell and rush out the door before she can say anything else. I know it's rude to bail on Dr. Veizer like this, but I can't do this. I can't. Dr. Veizer will have to just deal with the fact that she didn't win the game for once. Though, I'm not so sure I won either.

Chapter 31
2009- Richmond Hill, Georgia

The DJ blasts Akon through the gym of Richmond Hill High.

Nobody wanna see us together,
But it don't matter,
No cuz I got you..

The song couldn't be more fitting. I can't help but laugh a little when I look into Sam's wool-gray eyes. He grins a half smile as I rest my head against his broad chest. It's warm, just like him. He lays his head on mine, and I feel… I don't know, in love, maybe? I've been so elated; I barely noticed the boys who screamed 'Mr. Stoff!' at me in the hallway when I exited the bathroom. *Good one*, I thought. Clever, creative. It didn't matter, nothing could tug me down from the cloud I was floating on. Everything about tonight has been absolutely perfect, magical even. When I descended the staircase into the foyer of my house, Sam was waiting at the bottom of the steps with a corsage. It was a black rose. I still have no idea where or how he found a black rose, but it was the most beautiful flower I had ever seen. Sam's mom and Lady Katherine gushed as they took photos of us in the backyard. I was surprised that Sofia was supportive of Sam and I, but I guess my mom had a heart-to-heart with her. Lady Katherine's support of this union has been the most shocking twist of these insane past few weeks. When my mom lured Sofia into the house and all but forced her to drink a martini, I took the opportunity and pulled Sam away from the house and under the large magnolia tree towards the end of the backyard. Birds chirped in faultless harmony as I made Sam close his eyes. I grazed his thick neck with my fingers as I clasped the silver cross necklace around him, replacing the one that now shines from the bottom of the bay.

"I know it's not the exact same one that you had with Bailey, but…"

"It's perfect." Sam fiddled with the silver cross hanging between his pecks. "Pretty interesting gift to get from someone who doesn't believe in God. Unless my master plan worked and I turned you into a bible thumper like our mothers," Sam joked.

I shook my head. "I don't know what I believe, but I know I believe in you. Besides, how can you know anything if you believe in nothing?"

"Who said that? He must be pretty wise and devastatingly handsome."

"He has his moments," I laughed.

Sam smirked as he tilted my chin up with two fingers and pressed his lips to mine. *Sunset*. We tied our masquerade masks to our faces.

"Ready, Sam?"

"Ready, Delilah."

We emerged from under the magnolia tree and headed towards our future.

The limo ride over here was something out of a movie scene. Mary Lu scream-sang Beyoncé at the top of her lungs as Mia danced with her head out of the sunroof. Sam thought that they were both hilarious and sang along to songs I never thought he'd know the words to. We were having so much fun, we didn't even feel the need to pop the bottle of Veuve Clicquot I swiped from my dad's collection. We were all high on life. Chloe declined to join us. Instead, she rode on a party bus with most of the football team including Philly, of course. *Philly*. Fucking Philly. I didn't tell Sam about what happened that night in Mia's front yard. I didn't tell anyone. Because Philly was probably right. No one would believe me. No one cares, no one ever has. I am not going to talk about it. I don't even want to think about it. I just want what happened to go away. And maybe if I don't talk or think about it, it will. Maybe if I focus on the sun, there will be no more night. Philly has been radio silent since that night. He hasn't given me or Sam any trouble. He hasn't even given us a lingering look. I want to keep it that way.

I pull my head away from Sam's chest, hoping I didn't get makeup on his suit. I mull over the details of Sam's black and white mask. His mom painted both of ours with perfect precision. The contrast with his silver eyes is spellbinding. I run my fingers over the mask's fabric.

"I thought you didn't wear a mask," I tease.

"For you, I'd wear a thousand."

My glossed lips stretch with glee as I hold his tall body tighter, pushing it into me.

"Hold on, I'm gonna go see if I can request a song," Sam says with excitement.

I smile at him as he makes his way over to the DJ booth. His confident walk thrills parts of me I didn't know I had.

"D!"

I jump two inches off of the ground and shuffle backwards as I swing my body around. I trip over my own feet.

"Jeez, are you okay?"

I loosen my muscles and sigh in relief at the sight of Mia's face, made up to perfection, of course. Her sparkly silver mask, tight black dress, and cherry red lips light up the gymnasium.

"Yeah, I'm fine."

She tilts her head. "You sure, D? You're jumpy."

319

"Yes." I snap, smoothing out my copper hair.

"Well, okay then," she conceits. "You look gorgeous, D."

"Thanks." I tilt my head to the floor and smile bashfully. "So do you, your makeup looks perfect."

"Well, of course. Always. Wax museum my ass." She flips her long hair. "Anyway, I wanted to make sure that you and Sam are coming to the after prom party at my house. My mom is gone for the night, and my sister scored us some nice liquor. Like real liquor, top shelf stuff."

"Oh, um, I don't think so."

"D, did you not hear me? Top shelf liquor. What more incentive do you need?"

"It's not the liquor. It's just… Philly. I don't want to see him."

"Well good because he won't be there."

"He won't? Really?"

"I didn't invite him or Link. I'm over Philly's cocky attitude, and Link like vandalizes at least one piece of furniture in my basement every time he comes. I tolerated them because you loved Philly. But now that you're over him, good riddance."

"Wow, I, uh… I didn't realize you would be so…"

"So, what?" Mia crosses her arms and raises an eyebrow.

"So… I don't know, understanding."

Mia lifts an arm and puts it around me. "Of course, D. I've always understood you, and I always will. You're my best friend."

"And you're mine."

My heart warms as I pull Mia in for a long hug. Once the length of our embrace approaches that of the sapphic variety, I notice Sam out of the corner of my eye.

"Hey!"

"I didn't mean to interrupt."

"Don't be silly," Mia flicks her wrist. "I was just making sure y'all are coming to my after prom party. Don't worry, no douchebags allowed." Mia motions over towards the punch bowl. I follow her hand and see Philly and Link sulking in front of it. They no doubt spiked it. Philly's eyes lift from his cup and beat into mine. I try to look away, but for some reason, I can't. My skin crawls and I hug my chest, shivering.

"You okay?" Sam asks.

"Yeah." I sever eye contact with Philly.

"So, you'll come?"

Sam looks to me, and I look back towards Philly who is now stroking Chloe's arm.

"Yeah, of course we'll come."

Mia claps her hands and brings Sam and I in for a quick hug before running away to find one of her wrestlers.

Sam puts his hand on the small of my back and takes my hand in the other. It feels so dainty in his, but so right. He stares at me with a devilish smile on his face.

"What?"

"Nothin'." He points towards the DJ who changes the song as per Sam's request.

But I just want to tell them they don't know
For as long as you're in love with me
Our love will grow wider
Deeper than any sea

I wrap my arms tighter around Sam, almost suffocating him. I bury my face in his chest as we slowly sway to the music. He pets my hair and tilts my head up to meet his gray eyes.

"Hey."

"Hey."

"Remember when I said that heaven was on your dock, on the water?"

"Yeah."

"Well, I was wrong. That's not heaven, this is. You are my heaven, Delilah Monroe."

I swoon as my smile grows so wide, it might jump off of my face. I lay my head back down on his chest and soak up every second of this perfect night.

"And you are my sunset."

The limo ride back to Mia's was even more magical than it was on the way there. Sam and I got custody of the sunroof and Sam smoked a cigarette out of it. The cool breeze brushed us both like leaves in the wind. I felt so... I don't know, free. I still feel that way, even standing here in Mia's basement, with its beer stained carpet, where everything bad has happened. Where solo cups of shame have been poured over my head, when all I've ever wanted was to be soaked in safety. I stare at the corner that I glued myself to the last time I was here. I can still see Philly's face that night. The night he—

"You are so gorgeous, Delilah."

I fly out of Lilah land and straight into Sam's kind eyes.

"I am?"

"You are the most gorgeous woman I've ever known." Sam touches his lips to my ear, the vibration of his whisper tickles my cheek. "I want to kiss every inch of you."

I tilt my head down and blush, knowing the redness of my cheeks will be traveling throughout the rest of my body shortly. But, for once, I don't care. Sam is the sweetest human being on this earth. And he's wildly romantic. I used to consider myself lucky if Philly texted me back or gave me a drunken butt grab. *Philly*. Why the hell am I still thinking about Philly?

I look into Sam's dark ocean eyes and try not to drown in the beauty. I can't do this to him. As much as I want to stop the world and melt with him, I still have this sick tie to Philly. Because I am an absolutely fucked-up, sad excuse for a girl. Sam deserves more than me.

"You okay?" Sam furrows his brow. "You're not. You can talk to me, you know, about anything. Or… anyone. I'm here for you," he says, earnestly. And it turns my stomach as much as it breaks my heart.

"I have to pee!" I yell, eyes wide as a barren meadow.

"Oh, okay then. You want me to walk you upstairs?"

"No, I got it!" I yell over my shoulder, already 12 feet away from Sam.

Sam.

My fairytale night comes to an end when I lift my white dress over my hips and sit on the cold toilet seat in Mia's bathroom. I take my phone out of my purse and flip it open. I hadn't realized that my period is an entire week late until now. Fuck. I flush and pull my underwear back on. I smooth out my white dress and begin to wash my hands. I stare at my reflection in the mirror, trying not to cry. It's not possible… is it? Philly wasn't wearing a condom that night. Did he… finish? Would I know if he did? *Him. Philly*. Fucking Philly.

"Philly?"

I look up from the sink and see Philly's reflection behind me in the doorway. I spin around as fast as I can and sure enough, there he is, still in his tuxedo and masquerade mask from prom. His mask covers half of his face like a phantom, highlighting his sharp angles. The masks were fun under the lights on the dance floor, but here, in Mia's moldy basement bathroom, Philly looks frightening, like a monster. He quickly shuts the door and locks it.

"What the fuck! Get out!"

"Relax, D. I just want to talk."

"What are you doing here? Mia didn't invite you."

"Luckily, Link knows her garage code. And, that slut is nowhere to be found. Probably getting railed by the whole wrestling team in her mother's bed."

He walks towards me. He's smiling. His voice sounds malevolent, demonic even. He inches closer and I back away, holding myself against the sink. He glares at my prom dress, scanning me up and down like a hunter stalking its prey. He no longer looks like the boy who chased a butterfly with me. Or the boy who wouldn't go to the pool party because he was self-conscious about his stomach. Or the boy who smiles with his mouth shut because of the W on his tooth. Or the boy who cried in my arms for hours when his beloved dog died. He is not the boy I remember; he is now someone else. Someone sinister. Someone dangerous.

"Just please get out," I plead.

"Not until we talk."

"You never want to just talk, Philly. I learned my lesson. You are a bad fucking person. I'm done with you."

"So what? You're gonna be with him? That fucking loser? The fucking skeleton twin?"

"I don't know!" I yell. "All I know is that I want nothing to do with you. Get out of my way." I push the side of his arm with all of my might, but he doesn't budge. He grabs my neck with his hand and lifts me off the ground.

"I don't give a flying fuck what you want, you fucking whore! You're nothing! Do you hear me? You're fucking nothing!"

He clasps my neck with the other hand and squeezes so tightly until I can't breathe. I gasp for air as my vision starts to impair. Philly rips me off of the sink by my copper hair and drags me though the air. He slams my head into the toilet seat, smashing my face. I wait for everything to go dark, but it doesn't. I feel the crack in my jaw as it shifts to the left side of my face. I feel the stabbing sensation that starts at my neck and travels all the way to the top of my head. I feel my arms and legs crumbling underneath me, unable to help me in any way. I feel the pain. I feel it all. Philly lets go of my hair and pushes me onto the cold tile. I'm on my back, looking up at the blurry ceiling. I hear the door swing open but I still can't see or move. I'm paralyzed.

"Delilah!"

I feel warm hands on my cold body, they're trying to lift me up.

"What did you do to her? You fucking monster!"

I hear his voice, *him*. Suddenly, the warm hands are no longer beneath me. I hear a loud crash, then a bang.

"What did you do!"

I hear Sam screaming and grunting and punching. I hear smashes against the floor, the wall, the door. And I hear… laughing? Is that laughing?

The black and white tile ceiling becomes clearer, and I can make out the shapes and colors. I lift my arms and put them beneath me. *I can move, I can move. Thank God.* I struggle to lift myself up to a seated position. I tuck my feet under me and grab the toilet, trying to stand. I get halfway up until a horrific pain surges through my body, pushing me back down to the ground. I bring my hand to my face and feel my jaw in a place that it's not supposed to be. My chin throbs. I push the bottom of my jaw over and shriek at the pain. It doesn't move. I keep a hand over my jaw and open my eyes. In front of me, Sam and Philly are wrestling on the ground. Sam is on top of Philly, holding him down with his knee. And Philly is… laughing. He's fucking laughing. The door slams into the wall as another figure runs into the bathroom.

"Get off him you freak!" Link's shrill squawk is unmistakable. He lunges towards the ground and rips Sam up by the neck of his suit shirt and throws him into the sink. Philly hurries up to his feet and pushes Link out of the way. He grabs both sides of Sam's shirt collar and rams him into the wall. Sam tries to squirm out of his grasp, but Link pins him to the wall by his chest. I see Philly's face moving closer towards Sam's until his mouth is up to his ear. I can hear him whispering something in between ungodly laughs. I squint my eyes and attempt to make out what he's saying, but it's still unclear. Philly let's go of Sam's collar and Link takes his hand away from Sam's chest. Philly is still laughing. Sam's face is blank, and he doesn't move. He looks at Philly, then at me. His eyes are wider than I've ever seen. Shock consumes him. His eyes travel back towards Philly and suddenly, they change. His face fumes with anger as his entire body becomes red with rage. Every vein on his body pops out when he lunges towards Philly and throws him down to the ground with one hand. He begins punching Philly's masked face over and over, beating him to the ground. Link jumps on Sam's back and he elbows him in the stomach.

"Sam! Stop!" I yell as I grab the toilet seat with both hands and hoist myself to my feet. I hobble over to Sam to pull him off of Philly, but before I know it, Philly is on top of him drilling his face from side to side. Link is kicking Sam in the ribs, and I hear him yell out in pain.

"Stop! Get off of him!" I stumble more and pull at the back of Philly's shirt. Link steps on Sam's chest, crushing his lungs. Philly turns around and shoves me into the wall behind me. My head hits the back of the drywall so hard; my vision goes blurry again. I sink down to the tile floor, my legs betraying me again. My head hangs down, and I try to keep my eyes open. But, everything goes dark, too dark to see.

Then all of the sudden, I open my eyes. I'm on the floor, my back is against the wall. There's so much screaming but all I can feel is the throbbing, searing pain in my jaw. I look beneath me and I see a pool of scarlet lurching towards my Manolos. And immediately I know that he's dead. How did this happen?

Chapter 32
Present Day

I swirl my martini around in the glass I have clutched in my hand. I lower my head to the rim and breathe in the sharp but sweet aroma. It's flowery today, rose petals being my garnish of choice. My jaw clicks as I take a long sip. I shiver in my white slip dress; I wasn't able to find my silk robe this morning. I waltz over towards the central air controller and turn up the heat. I look down at the goosebumps forming on my shins and stare at the dark bruises on my thighs. I've been bruising like a peach lately on account of not being able to keep food down, hence the rose petals taking the place of where olives usually live in my crystal glass. I head over towards the piano and relish in its beauty. I tend to admire it a whole lot more on the days in which I know I don't have to entertain children butchering 'Ode to Joy'. I inch closer towards the piano bench, wondering if today is the day I will play again. I haven't done so since I had the miscarriage. Since then, everything that once brought me joy now brings me nausea. It's been years since I lost myself in the keys. I walk closer and sit down on the small bench. I keep the top over the keys as I debate what I might play. 'Clair de Lune' maybe? No. 'La Campanella'? No, it's been too long to jump right into Liszt. Maybe some Chopin, he was my dad's favorite. Eventually, a simple melody creeps into my head, violating my vodka haze, the forcefield that keeps me safe from feeling. I let a few notes play until I admit what song it is, who it's by, who it reminds me of. I close my eyes.

I've got dreams,
Dreams to remember,
Listen honey, I've got dreams,
Rough dreams, dreams to remember...

I open my eyes and loosen the grip I have on the martini stem, trying not to break another glass. I look down at the pool of vodka with the white rose petals floating inside of it. I stare deeply, the song still playing on the Victrola in my mind. Slowly, the color begins to change, tainting the petals until they become black. *All because he bought me black roses.*
No.
I leap off of the piano bench and throw my drink out of the glass. Vodka and rose petals land on the piano, splattering with a vengeance. Hyperventilating, I bring my hand to my chest and use box breathing until I feel the wings of my heart begin to flutter at a normal pace again. I look down at the piano, it's soaked in vodka like my brain is. The rose petals are scattered across the top of it. They are white, not black. They are not black roses, they never were. *Jesus Christ.* When will these wild hallucinations end? Maybe I should try to eat something..

I head to the kitchen for paper towels and a snack. I open the refrigerator door and scan the contents inside. Cocktail olives, string cheese, and Belvedere. My stomach turns at the thought of dairy or salt right now. Fuck it. I grab the Belvedere off of the shelf, untwist the cap and take a sip directly from the bottle. It goes down smoother than any food has within the past few weeks. I shut the refrigerator door and am startled, yet again, to see his young, unwrinkled face on our high school reunion invitation. I lock eyes with the boy in the photo. Not a day goes by that I'm not haunted by his ghost. I study the shape of his cheekbones. The photo is a bit grainy. The 2000s camera could not do him justice. Oh, photos! I almost forgot, Dr. Veizer's assignment this week was to look at a photo of myself as a child.

I quickly clean the vodka and rose petals off the piano and rip through old photo albums. I bring one over to the kitchen table and start flipping. This one documents the years 2006-2009. My mom must have put this together for me on one of her Christian healing retreats. She went on a lot of those after Dad passed away from a heart attack. With him gone and her all alone in that big house, she set out on a mission to find herself. And she did find herself, she found herself in Texas with a whole new husband and a whole new small town of sinners to save. She seems good though. Ever since Dad passed, she's seemed lighter. She found a nice man who sells insurance and makes corny Dad jokes. Katherine now lives a much more modest lifestyle than she used to, but she radiates much more joy than she used to. She stopped getting Botox, she stopped killing her lungs with the many designer perfumes, and she even stopped drinking. Well... she stopped drinking hard liquor, at least. She switched to Pinot Grigio, which is pretty much sobriety for that woman.

I flip quickly past the photos of my dad, though there aren't many. I keep flipping. There are photos of Mia and me, her cheering me on at my piano recitals, me cheering her on at football games. I flip more and see photos from eighth grade graduation, Philly and I's families posing together. I flip the page and see Liam and I smiling and laughing at some Ivy League school during his college visits. Wow. His face was so full, his aqua eyes so clear. He hasn't looked like that in a long time. The drugs came for him. Addiction crashed over him like a wave and washed him away. He's been lost at sea ever since. He dropped out of college after his sophomore year, or maybe he was kicked out, it's hard to remember. My dad shunned him and disowned him in the last few years of his life. I wonder, if William knew how limited his time on earth would be, would he have spent it differently? Would he still have spent it chasing the dollar, ignoring me, abusing his wife, abandoning his son, and drinking his meaning away? I glance at the bottle of vodka in my hand and set it down on the far end of the table. Not me. I'm not going to let it get me like it did my dad, like it did Liam. I tried to keep in touch with Liam throughout the years. Katherine did too, after Dad passed. She sent him to rehab a couple of times to help him get clean, but nothing stuck. Now, we have no idea where he is. It's been years since we've heard from him. A tear escapes from the duct in the corner of my eye. I wipe it away and continue to do Dr. Veizer's assignment. I keep flipping through the photo album, waiting for a picture to jump out at me. I'm about to flip past when I do a double take of a girl in a white gown with a black rose on her wrist. She's standing under a magnolia tree next to a boy with a black suit, dark skin, a silver cross necklace, and the warmest gray eyes I've ever called home. My hands shake as I grasp the page.

Then all of the sudden, I open my eyes. I'm on the floor, my back is against the wall. There's so much screaming but all I can feel is the throbbing, searing pain in my jaw. I look beneath me and I see a pool of scarlet lurching towards my Manolos. And, immediately I know that he's dead. How did this happen?

No.

I shake my head and slam the album shut, sliding it down the kitchen counter all of the way until it falls off the edge, landing in the trash can. I grab the bottle of vodka and saunter over to the floor to ceiling window that displays a full view of the backyard. I try to stand out of sight as I watch Salvatore plant peony seeds in the ground for Beth. She's sitting on a towel in the grass. She's wearing a tankini and has what looks like a Pina Colada in her hand. Where does she think she is, St. Barts? I watch as she strokes her straw and licks the rum off her lips. Her oversized shades are very Lolita-esque, which is ironic considering she's the one robbing the cradle in this version. I watch as sweat drips from Salvatore's olive skin. His swollen muscles are flexed as he holds himself up in the dirt. Salvatore is unnervingly sexy, but there is also something extremely pure about him. Something I cling to, and maybe people like Beth cling to it as well. Perhaps he hasn't seen the rain quite yet. I hope he hasn't. I should apologize to him for how rude and careless I've been acting. Maybe I'll write him a letter, in Italian. Something thoughtful and heartfelt, and completely generated by Google translate.

I continue to watch Salvatore, and to watch Beth watch Salvatore until my phone buzzes. I jump at the horrific sound. I slowly walk backwards towards the kitchen counter. I set the bottle down and hover my hand over my phone, but it's shaking too much to pick it up. I finally slam it down and yank the phone from the counter. I type in my passcode at least seven times before it unlocks. I hesitate, then press the messages app.

International number: Sorry I've been off the grid, my VPN wasn't working so I got another phone to use internationally. It's hectic over here. I'll do my best to make it to the reunion, but no promises. Sending kisses from Denmark. Love you, honey.

It's just my husband, thank God. That explains why he hasn't been answering any of my texts and calls. That's a relief. I thought he was ignoring me because he was busy writing up divorce papers. But perhaps this marriage stands a chance after all. He even said he'd try to make it to my high school reunion. I hope he does. I need him there on my arm, especially if I'm forced to see *him*.

I drop my phone back on the counter. I look at the bottle of vodka, debating another sip. The smell of the clear liquid sings to me like a siren. I want another sip, I want ten more sips. But, instead, I twist the cap on and stash the bottle back in the liquor cabinet, carefully avoiding the photo on the refrigerator. I wrap my arms around my shivering body and head back over to the window. Beth is now standing and so is Salvatore. Her fake lips form a smile as she pets his arm muscle like it's a dog. Her boobs are pushed up so high, they could touch her chin. They honestly look like they could pop any minute. Salvatore smiles bashfully at her as he backs away slowly. She has a sour look on her face as he lowers himself back down to the garden, rejecting whatever advance she was making. Beth stomps away like a child throwing a temper tantrum. I continue to watch Salvatore plant peonies. He's gentle and fluid with his movements, as if he treats every seed he plants like a precious work of art. I watch as he picks up his gardening shovel and digs more holes.

Suddenly, I hear a loud bang. I jump and gasp for air then crouch down behind the window curtain.

Thump thump thump.

Fuck, someone's at the door. It's probably something from Amazon I drunkenly purchased. Or it's Mrs. Chamberlain and her American Girl Doll looking daughter, Ashley. It wouldn't be the first time that she's mixed up the lesson days then asked me to watch her child anyway while she plays pickleball with other Prada princesses. Pickleball is a made up sport, by the way, and it's fucking stupid.

I drag my feet over to the foyer and open the front door.

"Sam?"

"Hey."

Chapter 33
Present Day

I stand, paralyzed, face to face with the most beautiful, magnetic eyes. They're warm, still. As warm as they ever were. I shut my eyelids and open them again. This isn't real, it can't be. It's another hallucination. I drank too much, or not enough, or… I inhale sharply as I study him up and down. His tall frame is broader than it used to be. It's real, it's *him*.

Sam's eyes circle my face. "You haven't aged a day, Delilah. You look… Wow."

"What are you—"

"I got out a few weeks ago, and you were the first person I wanted to see. I texted you, but you didn't answer. I thought maybe you changed your number or something. Or that these pre-historic phones are useless."

Sam reaches into his pocket, and I flinch. He pulls out a flip phone that looks like it was bought at a gas station.

"These things only have like 100 minutes on them, and I use most of them when my mom calls, so I have to get three of them at a time."

That explains the different numbers texting me.

"Can I come in?" Sam asks as his familiar half smile grows at the corner of his mouth.

I don't want to let him in. I shouldn't. Everything in me tells me that I shouldn't, but for some reason unknown to me, I step aside and he passes by me, entering my home. I shut the door. I'm careful not to lock it in case I need to make a quick getaway.

"Wow, nice place."

"What are you doing here, Sam? What do you want?"

Sam puts his hands up. "Whoa, no nice to see you, Sam? How were your last 15 years rotting away in prison, Sam?"

I close my eyes and clench my teeth. I feel my hands and feet begin to tingle.

"I'm sorry, bad joke. I've been isolated from regular society for quite some time. I'm a little rusty on the social graces."

"What are you doing here, Sam?"

"I wanted to talk to you."

Sam's eyes look earnest as he inches towards me. I immediately back away and wrap my arms around myself. It's then that I realize I'm wearing only a white slip dress and no bra. I take a few more steps back.

"What's wrong?" Sam cocks his head to the side. His eyebrows pinch together, creating a wrinkle he didn't used to have. Sam continues, "are you... afraid of me?"

I don't respond as a shiver travels up my spine.

"I'm not dangerous, Delilah. I would never hurt you."

"You killed someone," I whisper.

"Not exactly." Sam hangs his head.

"I'm sure it was accident. I'm sure you didn't mean to kill him, but you did, Sam. You killed Link."

"I'm not completely blameless. I should have never gone after Philly the way I did that night. I should have gotten you to safety and called the police, but I didn't and I will regret it for the rest of my life. But I did not kill Link."

"Wh— what?"

"I blacked out on the floor. I didn't even realize that Link cracked his head on the corner of the sink until it was too late. When I came to, he had already bled out. He was already gone."

The memory of blood rushing towards my feet impales me. I cover my mouth to keep from vomiting.

"Then who killed him?"

"Philly did. The last thing I remember is Link trying to pull him off of me. He was yelling 'that's enough, he's had enough'. Philly pushed him into the sink, then I fell unconscious. Philly, that fuck, got off scott free with his dad being the sheriff and all. They pinned the whole thing on me, Delilah. Philly told everyone that I broke your jaw and pushed Link into the sink. He said he found you both unconscious in the bathroom with me standing over you, so he knocked me out. By the time I was conscious and realized what happened, I was handcuffed to a hospital bed. Nobody believed my story and my parents couldn't afford a good lawyer, so I went to prison for manslaughter while that fucker probably went on to live a happy life. I took the fall, I did the time, and I carry Link's death around with me every waking minute. He shouldn't have died; he didn't deserve to. I would do anything to change that night, Delilah, anything. I would never intentionally hurt anyone. I thought you would know that. I thought you knew me better than that."

I let out a huge breath and uncrossed my arms. I study Sam's face. Could he be telling the truth? Could it really have been Philly who killed Link and not Sam? I shoved that night so far down in my brain that I barely remember what happened. I merely believed what I was told. Like everyone else, I labeled Sam as a killer and dropped the memory of him off the edge of the world.

"I'm sorry. I should have visited or called or something. It was all just so…"

"I know," Sam nods his head, "I know."

I'm still not totally sure that I believe him. Philly is a lot of things, but he's not a murderer. He would never want to hurt Link, he loved him. He couldn't have done it, could he? I need more information.

"Here, come into the living room. I think it's time we have a real talk."

Sam nods. I begin to walk when he gently grabs my arm.

"You really do look great, Delilah. Beautiful."

I twirl my honey-colored hair with my finger. "Yeah, I finally got the blonde thing down. No more copper hair, no more looking like a penny," I laugh, nervously.

"I always liked it."

I give him a polite smile and continue walking; he follows me into the living room and takes a seat on the white couch.

"I'll get us something to drink."

I head over to the cupboard and fill two glasses with water. "You still haven't told me exactly what you're doing here. Why would you come back to Richmond Hill after, well, everything?"

"I'm going to the reunion."

I turn off the sink faucet. "You are?"

"Yeah, to explain myself. I want to tell everyone what really happened. That I wasn't the one who pushed Link. I want them to know why I went after Philly that night, what he did to you. How he hit you and broke your jaw. I want to tell them everything. And I was hoping that you would do it with me. We can finally tell the real story, the truth. Then they'll put that prick in prison where he belongs."

I walk back over to the living room, silently, and set the two glasses down on coasters.

"So, will you?"

"Will I what?"

"Will you stand by me? Tell everyone the truth with me?"

"I…" My heart falls down into my stomach. "I can't."

"Why?"

"I just can't," I snap.

"15 years, Delilah. 15 years. That's how long I've paid for this crime. I've had so much time to think about what I would say to everyone in this town if I ever got a chance. That's what kept me going when I was getting the shit kicked out of me for refusing to join a gang. When I was standing under freezing shower water with 10 dudes waiting in line behind me. When I watched my mother sob into the phone each time she came to visit. When I was staring up at the ceiling every night, thinking about Link, thinking about Bailey, thinking about you. There were times that I wanted to die. I finally understood how Bailey was able to take her life, how she got to that dark of a place. I knew what it felt like for your humanity to be stripped, for life to be completely meaningless. But I stayed. I held on for the chance to one day get out and tell the world what really happened. And now, with the reunion, I have the opportunity. Philly is dangerous and should not be walking around. You know that. Why wouldn't you want everyone to know the truth?"

I turn my head away from him and close my eyes. I hear him sigh as he gets up from the couch. He walks over towards the flat-screen television, and he begins to admire the wall of photos.

"Wow. I can't believe it's been 15 years since I last saw you. You have any kids?"

I shake my head, keeping my eyes shut.

"Lots of swanky vacations you've taken, I see."

I suck in a deep gasp of air. I hear Sam take a photo off of the wall.

"Wait…"

I hold my breath.

"Wait…"

I swallow hard.

"Is this… Philly? That's Philly. That's fucking Philly. This is a wedding photo. He's your husband. You married him. You married Philly? You fucking married him? You married that fucking monster!"

Tears stream from my squeezed eyelids. I knew this was coming.

"How could you?" Sam drops the wedding photo onto the floor and it shatters with his heart. He brings his hands up to his mouth and covers it in shock. "How? Why? Why, Delilah?"

I begin to sob as I cover my face. "You… you don't know him like I do. I love him!" I cry.

"He hit you, Delilah. He broke your jaw over a toilet seat. He's a monster. How could you love him?"

"He's changed," I plead. "He hasn't laid a hand on me our entire marriage. You have no idea what it was like when you got sent away. I was so depressed and felt so guilty. It's my fault that Link died. If I hadn't gotten involved with you, if I just left you alone instead of sucking you into my dark, fucked up world, none of it would have happened."

Sam sighs and takes a seat on a chair opposite the couch. "It's not your fault, Delilah."

"It is. Everything I touch burns to the ground, including you." My sobs ease up and I wipe the tears from my face. "After you went away, life was meaningless. I couldn't see a point to anything. I didn't send in college applications, so I never went away for school and never made it to New York. I barely graduated high school. I would sit day after day staring at the basement wall, unable to do anything. I had nobody to talk to. Mia fucked right off to Paris after graduation and found bigger and better people to hang out with. Last I heard, she's a big shot marketing executive in LA." I don't look up at Sam as I continue. "I was completely and utterly fucking alone. Just me, my thoughts, and a bottle of vodka. Eventually, my mom forced me to enroll in community college here. My dad cut Liam and I off financially as a punishment for embarrassing his family name. I was working at the dollar store when Philly graduated from Miami University and moved home to bury his dad and take over the family estate." I try to catch my breath as the words continue to tumble out of my mouth. "He reached out to me. Both of our fathers died that year. He needed a friend and so did I. I had no one else, no one. But Philly was there. And, eventually, the relationship evolved. He inherited this house, got a high paying job with good benefits. He wanted to provide me with a good life, and I accepted."

Sam looks around. "I thought I recognized this house. This is the old St. James house." Sam gets up from the couch and walks around, studying the interior design. Before he gets to the floor to ceiling windows that overlook the magnolias in the backyard, he spins around and faces me. "So that's it then? You married an abusive fucking monster because you were lonely? You and that asshole, that murderer, are gonna live happily ever after?"

I stand and cross my arms. "Like I said, he hasn't done anything since we've been married."

"And before that?"

I look away from him, not wanting to get sucked into his silver eyes that wrinkle at the corners now, and God knows I would.

"I took him off the market, didn't I? He didn't get the opportunity to hurt anyone else. Doesn't that count for something?"

Sam mirrors my body language and crosses his arms. "So, what does that make you, some sort of martyr? Con-grat-u-fucking-lations, Delilah. You hate yourself just enough to save all womankind from the wrath of Philly St. James. You deserve a metal, really."

I march over towards Sam in a haze of frustration. I try not to be stunned by his good looks when I come face to face with him. He's scruffier, his black hair is longer, and his skin is lighter than I remember, but he still looks like my teenage dream.

"I think you should go, Sam. I'm glad that you got out of prison and can start a new life, but like I said, I can't help you. And, if you know what's good for you, you'll skip the reunion. Better yet, skip town, and don't come back."

"That a threat?" Sam cocks his head to the side, partially smiling. Why the fuck is he smiling? And why the fuck does he look so good doing it?

I will the temptation away. "It's not a threat."

"You know, you're not the only woman that Philly hurt, Delilah."

"What? How would you know?"

"He raped her. Bailey, my sister. He raped her the weekend that she killed herself. He was the one she reported to the cops. He told me himself. He whispered it in my ear the night that Link died, that's why I went after him the way I did."

My mind turns over and over until it lands on the memory of that night. Of me, on the floor, hanging onto the toilet, watching Philly whisper in Sam's ear while laughing.

"It was him, Delilah, it was *him*. When Bailey went to the police, Sheriff St. James must have covered it up or threatened her or something to protect his rapist son. That's why she killed herself. Philly is the reason why. He's the person she was talking about in all those poems. Philly is the one who bought her black roses."

I drop to my knees as the air escapes the room. Sam squats down and puts a hand on my back.

"Whoa, you okay?"

I try to breathe, I try the box breathing thing, but my lungs refuse to inhale. There's no air coming in or out. Suddenly, every lie I've ever told or believed to protect and love Philly regurgitate from my stomach, through my esophagus and out of my mouth onto the white carpet. Pressure pushes on every inch of my chest, neck, and face as the vomit keeps coming. I gasp for oxygen in between heaves, but it won't stop. Sam holds my hair back with one hand and rubs my back lightly with the other.

"It's okay, it's okay. You are safe. You are safe," he whispers.

Eventually, the vomit lets up. I try to stand with one leg but it collapses under me.

Sam catches me. "Hey, hey. Just take it easy, okay? Let's sit for a minute."

Sam sits across from me cross legged. I wipe my wet face with my slip dress and grab his hand. It's warm, of course it's warm.

"I'm sorry. I'm sorry. I'm sorry!" I wale.

"Hey, hey. It's okay. You didn't know. He brainwashed you, that's what abusers do to their victims."

I look up at him in confusion.

"I, uh, read a lot of psychology books in the pen. Not much else to do." He shrugs his shoulders.

My head hangs back down and I continue to sob. Sam puts his hands on my arm and pulls me in for a hug. I cannot believe I'm in his arms again, his huge arms.

"It's okay," he whispers, "we can't stay here long, but maybe, we can stay here for just a little while. Just for a little while longer." Sam rubs my back as I cry into his chest. He begins to hum a melody I'm sure we've both tried to forget.

I've been loving you,
Too long,
To stop now,
Oh, I've been loving you,
Too long,
I don't wanna stop now...

Chapter 34
Present Day

My hands slip off of the railings as the sweat from my palms leaves a slug trail in my wake. I trip up one of the stairs, nearly rolling my ankle. I leap up three steps at a time, clearing the rest of the staircase. When I finally reach the top, I swing open the door and push my way into the lobby. I'm panting as I look around at the empty chairs and white walls with minimalistic artwork hanging on them. Dr. Veizer's waiting room looks as it always does, but something's wrong. Her secretary isn't at her desk, there are no other patients waiting, and there's no music playing. Maybe she left for the day. It is 7pm, after all. But the door to the waiting room was unlocked and the lights are on, surely she's got to be here. I charge over to the door of her office, still out of breath. I'm about to knock when the knob turns and the door swings open. "Same time next week?" I hear Dr. Veizer say as she escorts her patient through the doorway.

"Charlotte?"

Shock puddles under me when I see that familiar, fiery red hair and her lime green eyes staring at me like a deer in headlights. *Charlotte.* What is she doing here? I scan her up and down with the backdrop of the therapy office behind her. Wait… is she a patient here? Is Charlotte Vanderheiden in… therapy? Charlotte pushes past me without a word, without looking my way. I watch her red locks bounce as she walks out the door with her head held high. Charlotte Vanderheiden, the empress of Richmond Hill. The queen of the country club goes to therapy. I want to pull out my phone and text Sebastian this hard-hitting gossip until it hits me. If Charlotte is coming here every week, doing therapy with Dr. Veizer, there must be a good reason for it. Maybe she's hurting too. Maybe she's just as fucked up as the rest of us. Maybe there's a price that she's paying. Maybe there's a hell of a lot that I don't know about Charlotte Vanderheiden. I book and covered her. I should have known, everyone has an abyss they can't swim up from, that's why we go to people like Dr. Veizer, so they can teach us how to swim.

"Delilah?" Dr. Veizer checks her watch in confusion. "I don't remember having an appointment scheduled today."

"Yeah... I..." I wipe my sweaty palms on my white jeans. "I... just..."

"Is everything okay?"

I try to come up with words to say but nothing comes out. Instead, I shake my head.

She checks her watch again. "I have some time now, why don't you come in?" She lightly touches my elbow and guides me into her office.

I watch the sun setting from the window as Dr. Veizer begins with her usual line of questioning, but I can only hear her voice in my peripheral. I can't make out what she's saying. It's like I'm watching myself from above. I spread my fingers and look down at my hands, but I barely recognize them.

"Delilah? Delilah?"

"Yes." The present moment slaps me in the face like I'm playing chicken with a Mack truck. "Yes, that's me."

The blur in front of Dr. Veizer's face evaporates and I can see her clearly. She's wearing a nice blouse over black pants that flare at the ends. I look down at my hands again and recognize them as mine, French tips, oval diamond wedding ring and all.

"Sorry." I blush. " I zone out a lot. Sometimes I forget where or who I am. My mom used to call it going to Lilah Land."

"Lilah Land?"

"Yeah, but it's nothing. I'm just not great at focusing."

"It sounds like more than that. I noticed you looking at your hands before, it was as if you didn't know who they belonged to. Am I correct?"

I shrug.

"It sounds like dissociation. It's a brain's response to heightened emotions such as anxiety, depression, or trauma. It shuts down as a way of protecting you from the pain of feeling when it overloads you. It's often a result of deep rooted trauma, typically childhood trauma."

I'm already regretting coming here. Maybe I should leave, it's late, and I'm sure Dr. Veizer has a million and one better things she could be doing right now. I can't remember when I made the decision to hop in my Range Rover and speed over here. I barely remember the drive.

Dr. Veizer looks at me expectantly. I wonder what game she's playing today. Whatever it is, maybe I can cheat my way to the finish line. I have nothing left to lose anymore.

"So, are you going to tell me what brought you to my door tonight?"

"I— I don't remember."

"You don't remember?" She studies me. "That could be a form of dissociation as well. Sometimes we lose time, block out memories that are too painful, get confused about who and where we are. Squeezing ice in your hand can help bring you back into the present. You can try smelling something strong like incense or a candle. I've also found it helpful to look at your surroundings and describe what you see or write down the facts about yourself that you know to be true, like your name, your address."

"I doubt I'd ever forget my name." I roll my eyes and laugh a little, even though I know it's not funny.

"You'd be surprised. The mind will go to extreme lengths to prevent you from feeling your feelings."

"But, if the feelings are so bad, why would I want to feel them?"

"Because you gotta feel in order to heal."

I look down at my hands again and ponder her words.

"So, did you get a chance to do that inner child assignment we discussed?"

"What?" I ask in confusion until the fog in my brain dissipates. "Oh, oh, the picture thing. Yeah, I pulled out an old photo album and went through it."

"Great. Did any of the photos speak to you?"

"All of them did, I guess."

"And how did they make you feel?"

"I don't kno— No, no, I do know. I do know!"

Dr. Veizer smiles at me. "I taught you well."

I return her smile and try to remember the different emotions on that feelings chart she gave me. "The pictures, they made me feel… sad. A lot of the memories were good memories, but they make me feel sad when I think of them now."

"Mhm, tell me more."

"Things have changed so much since then. Even though I'm in the same town I grew up in, going to the same country club, everything is different."

"What is different?"

"The people around me, I guess. My family, friends. My best friend, her name was Mia. I thought we'd be friends forever, but we slowly lost touch after she moved away for school. She immediately thrived after leaving this town. She continued to grow and level up in the world, while I stayed stagnant. We would try to catch up from time to time, but at some point, we had nothing in common anymore. It was like she outgrew me. I unfollowed her on social media a few years ago because I couldn't take seeing all of the career moves, private planes, and fine dining. It made me feel… hold on, wait, I got this…"

She smiles again.

"It made me feel like a failure. Like she won the game of life, and I lost it."

"And is that how you view life? Like a competition?"

"Honestly? Yeah, I do. I think of everything as a game. Every interaction, every conversation."

"Do you view these sessions as a game?"

I put my head down and stay silent.

"There's no wrong answer here."

I stretch my head back up. "I guess I do. I'm sorry, I know that's bad."

"Who says it's bad? If that's how you view it, that's how you view it. Let's go with this."

"Um, okay."

"So tonight, this session, what game are we playing tonight?"

"Uh, I don't know."

"Well, let's pick one. What was your favorite game as a kid?"

I laugh. "My family wasn't exactly the board game and bond type. We were the drink heavily and avoid each other type."

"I see. So, you never played any games as a kid? None?"

"Well, I guess Liam and I played Monopoly a few times when we were little."

"Monopoly, perfect. Let's go with that. Tonight, we are playing Monopoly."

"Okay. Monopoly."

"So, tell me more about the photo assignment."

"Well, seeing pictures of my brother, Liam, it made me feel… It made me feel kind of hopeless."

"Hopeless," Dr. Veizer mirrors my words.

"Yeah, hopeless. In the photos, he was young and handsome. His eyes were bright, his face had color. But he got into drugs in college, and it was all over from there. He was a full blown junkie by the time he was 21. I'm not totally sure if he's even… Never mind. I'm not going to even think like that."

Dr. Veizer nods with sympathy.

"Seeing pictures of my mom was weird."

"How so?"

"In the old photos, she looked younger and thinner, and her skin was tighter, but she also looked… miserable. She looked angry to be alive."

"And now?"

"Now, she's lighter, more relaxed. She's almost, like, pleasant to be around. I actually get excited when she calls."

"I see. She aged well."

"She did."

"So…" Dr. Veizer adjusts herself in her seat. "If you were to speculate, what do you believe made your mom miserable back then at the time the photos were taken?"

"My dad, definitely my dad."

"Your dad," she nods slowly.

"Yeah." I look off towards the window. The sun has set, and it's dark out. It's kind of strange being in this office at night. I look back to Dr. Veizer. "I didn't feel anything when I looked at photos of him. He passed away suddenly a while ago, and I remember it being a dark time back then. But now when I think of him or see photos of him, I feel nothing. I don't miss him. Is that bad? That's so bad."

I bring my hand up to my mouth, punishing myself for my harsh words.

"I don't think it's bad at all. Dying does not magically make one a saint. Those who were assholes in life will remain assholes in our psyches for eternity."

"Damn, Dr. Veizer." I can't help but giggle.

"Well, it's true," she giggles with me.

"I don't disagree."

If we're playing monopoly, then Dr. Veizer just moved five spaces.

"So, tell me what else came up for you when you looked at the photo album." She rolls her dice again.

I swallow hard and glance at the clock. I cross one leg over the other and take a deep breath. I need to tell her. I need to tell her everything. I need to tell her so she can help me figure out what to do about the reunion. What to do about Sam. What to do about Philly. *Philly.* Fucking Philly.

"I saw my prom photo."

"Wow, okay. And, what emotion came up for you there?"

I don't hesitate, I don't over think it, I don't say 'I don't know'. Instead, I'm honest, for the first time in a long time.

"Love."

"Love?"

"Love," I repeat.

"I assume you're referring to your prom date."

"Yeah."

"Tell me about him." Dr. Veizer moves forward a space, takes her Monopoly money, and hands the dice to me.

I think of *him*. I think of Sam. I think of his warm gray eyes and smooth dark skin. I think of his black hair flowing in the wind by the water, his scruff framing his face perfectly. I think of his low raspy voice, his infectious half smile. I think of his outgrown shirts that showed off his chest, the cloud of cigarette smoke that circled around him. I think of his James Dean-like charisma, his effortless confidence. I think of how philosophical he was, how perceptive he was. How he chose to believe in heaven while he was in his own hell. I think of his quest for life's meaning, his undying loyalty to seek justice for his sister. I think of the way he loved his mother, the way he loved me. I think of the way my lips felt when they grazed over the skin of his neck, how my legs felt when they were wrapped around his rock-hard torso. I can still feel every peach fuzz stand up with goosebumps when his hand touched my breast. I can still see the way he stared into my eyes the whole time, like he was the luckiest boy on earth to be touching my body, like he cherished it. I can see us, hear us, feel us, taste us. Singing and swaying to Otis Redding on the piano bench, reading poetry on the dock, skinny-dipping in the cold bay, watching the sun set and the stars shine. I can't help but think of *him*, all of the long nights, all of the secrets shared, all of the black roses. He once told me I was his version of heaven, but honestly, he was lucky if I could make it through the night.

No.

My mind falters. Dropping from the light of the sun into the darkness of the cold, cold night.

Then all of the sudden, I open my eyes. I'm on the floor, my back is against the wall. There's so much screaming but all I can feel is the throbbing, searing pain in my jaw. I look beneath me and I see a pool of scarlet lurching towards my Manolos. And immediately I know that he's dead. How did this happen?

I shake my head and grunt at the same time. I squeeze my eyelids together and slap myself in the head. "Why won't the memories go away? Why won't he stop fucking haunting me!" I scream.

Dr. Veizer springs up from her chair and sits next to me on the couch. "What memories? Who's haunting you?"

I shake my head and cry.

"Who's haunting you, Delilah?"

"I can't."

"Yes, you can."

"I can't! I can't! I can't!"

"Okay, okay. That's okay." She pats the top of my hand and returns to her chair across from me. "I know this is difficult for you to talk about. I didn't mean to push you, but I do believe that there is something, some trauma that may be the root of all this pain. I'd like to explore it further, but first I want to do some de-escalation exercises. Are you open to that?"

I nod.

Dr. Veizer takes me through box breathing, the 54321 grounding technique, music therapy. It's all stuff that we've done before. This isn't the first time I've freaked out like this when talking about my past, and something tells me that it won't be the last. My breathing and heart rate are back to normal by the time Dr. Veizer returns to the office with two plastic cups of water. I put down the stress ball I'm squeezing, pick up a cup, and take a sip.

"I wish this was vodka."

She laughs and takes a big gulp of her water.

"So, what now?" I ask.

"I want to take you through a guided inner child meditation. I'm hoping that it can open a pathway into any trauma that may have been repressed over time."

I shiver at the thought of that night, prom night. Everything that happened in that bathroom, everything that happened after. Link's funeral, Sam's sentencing, years and years of sleepless nights and drunken cries. I don't want to remember exactly what happened that night on the bathroom floor, but I know that I have to. I have to do this in order to decide if I'm going to help Sam at the reunion or I don't know… maybe fake my own death at this point.

"Delilah?" Dr. Veizer comes back into view. "Are you ready to start?"

"Yes. Yes, I'm ready."

"Okay, you can go ahead and get into a comfortable position then close your eyes."

I lay my head back on the couch cushion. Dr. Veizer plays calming music from her stereo. I try not to focus on the chord progressions of the song and instead fixate on her voice, her words.

"Imagine yourself as a teenager, go back into that time period. What do you look like? What is your hairstyle? What are you wearing? What does your voice sound like? What do you smell like? Feel the clothes on your body, run your hands through your hair, listen to your younger voice, smell the perfume from your wrist."

My mind takes me to the backyard at my parents' house. I run my fingers through my copper hair and touch the stitching on my jean skirt. I smell the Pink Sugar perfume mixed with the scent of crisp ocean air. I take in the sights around me. The magnolia trees stand tall and regal, their leaves blow in the wind. The Spanish moss hangs above me as it dances from side to side. The grass is itchy on my feet, so I walk towards the dock. I see the sun setting over the bay, making the teal ripples glow a shade of orange, my favorite. I inhale the salty air as the wind tickles my face.

I can hear Dr. Veizer's calming voice guide me.

"Now, I want you to take a hard look at your surroundings. Take it all in. Appreciate everything that you see and hear and smell and feel. Then wave goodbye, and head over to another place, a new setting. Go wherever your mind takes you without judgment."

I walk away from the sunset and out of my yard. Suddenly, I'm transported to another realm. I can feel the cold ground beneath me, but I can't make out where I am. Everything is dark. Oh God, this must be it. Prom night.

Tears stream from my eyes and down the sides of my face, landing on the couch. I keep them shut and brace myself.

"Are you there yet?"

"Yes," I whisper.

"Okay, now feel the ground beneath you. Inhale the air around you, let it consume you. Open your ear drums and listen to the sounds. What do you hear? Who do you hear?"

Screaming.

"Slowly open your eyes in this new realm. What do you see?"

I tap on the cold ground beneath me and open my eyes. Wait, this is not the bathroom in Mia's basement. But I do recognize it. I look to my left and see concrete under me, a car parked, a shed. This is Mia's front yard. Why would I be here? Then I look up, and I see his face. Philly is on top of me. His weight holding me down. I hear him panting and grunting, he sounds like a monster. I stare into the eyes above me with confusion. They're black and barren. His jabbing motions cut me to my core, and I let out a yelp. I try to move my hand but my wrist in pinned down. I try to squirm and scream and kick, but he's stronger than me. Philly puts a hand over my mouth, leans down and whispers in my ear.

"No one would believe you. You don't fucking matter, you fucking whore."

At the sound of his words my body goes still. I'm paralyzed. I float up out of myself and watch from above. Why am I not moving? Why can't I move? I yell at myself from my floating state. Get off the ground. Get off the ground. Get off the ground. Get off the fucking ground. Get off the fucking ground. Get off the fucking ground, Delilah.

Suddenly, my body shoots up off the therapy couch without warning. My eyes are still shut as I launch up and land on my knees on the rug beneath me.

"Get off the ground! Get off the ground! Get off the ground! Get off the fucking ground. Get off the fucking ground. Get off the fucking ground, Delilah!" I scream and scream until my voice box shatters and I'm gasping for air. I'm hunched over as Dr. Veizer runs towards me and kneels on the carpet next to me.

"It's okay, Delilah. It's okay. You're safe. I'm right here. It's okay. You are safe here." Dr. Veizer puts a hand on my back and rubs gently. "You are safe."

I cover my face with my hands and begin to sob.

"I remember! I remember it all. He's a monster. I married a monster! What he did to me—" I gasp for air, "he did it to Bailey too! It was him. It was him all along. He bought her black roses. He was the one who bought her black roses. I have to tell you. I have to tell you everything."

"Okay, okay." Dr. Veizer puts both hands on my shoulders. "Then you'll tell me everything. I will stay here with you all night, Delilah. I'm here for you, and I'm not going anywhere."

I continue to hyperventilate as she keeps her hand on my shoulder, steadying me in place.

"Dr. Veizer?"

"Yes?"

"Why did he want to hurt me so badly? And why did I let him? Why didn't I get off the ground?"

Chapter 35
Present Day

I yawn as I check the time on my phone for the third time. Where is Sam? He said to meet here under the bleachers at 6:15pm on the dot, and it is now 6:18pm. I press the lock button on my phone and tap my foot on the gravel. The space underneath the bleachers looks just as it did when we were in high school. I can still see the wounded look on Sam's face, and the scorned one on mine as I professed my devotion for Philly and accused Sam of calling me a whore because I couldn't handle how turned on his deep thoughts, his built body, and his heart-shaped mouth made me feel.

My skin crawls at the erotic sensation that tantalized every part of me when I saw Sam towering over me in my doorway. Looking like a harder, more masculine version of the boy I used to call sunset.

I do progressive muscle relaxation with my hands and attempt to deep breath. My third inhale becomes another yawn, and I bring my palm up to cover my mouth. Damn, I'm tired. I was at Dr. Veizer's office until midnight going over every detail of my childhood. I told her everything. The way my parents used to fight, the way they hit us and each other. I told her about my mom's alcoholism and the beauty queen standards she set for me. I told her about my dad's temper, his sharp tongue, and the way he demeaned my mom every day. I told her about Liam, and how his once gold heart and charm turned into heroin shakes, angry outbursts, lying, cheating, and stealing. I told her about Chloe and Mary Lu, and how all of the kids at school tormented me as much as they idolized me. I told her about Mia and how I sought safety in her as a friend. I told her about Link and his immature, vicious ways. Most importantly,

I told her about Philly. I told her about how we chased butterflies together, and how I was the only one he let see him cry when his dog died. I told her about how he would put me down, how he would be extremely sweet one minute then shit all over me the next. I told her about how cruel he became when his mom got sick. I told her about how he peed on me, how he ruined my reputation because I fought him off when he tried to attack me. I told her how he… how he raped me. How he raped Bailey. How he made us feel like we didn't matter. I told her about prom night, about how Philly broke my jaw, and how he ruined three separate lives on that bathroom floor. I told Dr. Veizer everything. And, she sat with me and listened, with absolutely no judgment. We talked about high school, and everything that happened after. We talked about how Philly and I came together again, how he won my affection back. We talked about the good times, the courting stage, the honeymoon stage. Then we talked about what happened when the veil was lifted, yet again. We talked about the constant insults, the ignored texts. We talked about the affair he had when I was pregnant. We talked about the fact that it was with none other than the famous Chloe Black when she was in town visiting her parents three Christmases ago. We talked about how when I found out and told him I wanted a divorce, he threatened to punch me in the stomach, kill our unborn child then leave me on the street to die. We talked about how the stress may have caused the miscarriage. We talked about my drinking and losing my teaching license. We talked about my failed dreams of being a concert pianist in New York. Dr. Veizer told me that Philly is a narcissist who has been using something called intermittent reinforcement since the day he met me. She says intermittent reinforcement is when someone love bombs you one minute then takes away their love the next, creating a pattern that forms an addiction.

Apparently, I mistook chaos and toxicity for passion and excitement. But, Dr. Veizer says that healthy relationships don't look like that. She said that healthy relationships should be peaceful and feel like home. She said that the way my parents fought and the way my dad abused my mom normalized abuse in my brain, not allowing me to recognize situations as abusive in the future. She also said that the emotional abuse I endured from my parents and Philly caused internalized beliefs that have caused me to abuse myself for the past 15 years. Dr. Veizer said that Philly brainwashed me just like Sam said he did. She said that he set his sights on me at a young age and chose me as a sponge to soak up all of his insecurity. She said that we have to re-wire my brain to challenge those internalized beliefs to be able to see myself and the world around me clearly.

Philly. Fucking Philly. I prayed to God that he wouldn't show up at the reunion tonight. Like, I literally got down on my knees and prayed to God. I haven't done that since… ever. But I needed a higher power or something in this damn universe to protect me, for once. After hours and hours of going over every moment I've ever spent with Philly St. James, I was reminded of just how much evil he's capable of, and it's an evil that I never want to see again. I just want to go into this God forsaken high school, stand by Sam and truth, then let the police take it from there.

Speaking of Sam, where the hell is he?

"Hey."

I hear a voice from behind me and spin around on my heels to see those silver eyes that have been haunting my dreams for 15 years. I evaluate every centimeter of his face as if he's a poltergeist that may evaporate into the air any minute. There are crow's feet at the corners of his deep eyes, like he's seen more life than he should have. There's a little wrinkle on top of the corner of his side smirk, like he hasn't stopped smiling in spite of everything. He's older, more worn down, yet somehow, more attractive. His arms are bigger than they were, and he almost seems taller. My eyes slide down Sam's large body, and I curse the inappropriate, naughty signals my mind sends me. Being face to face with Sam after all these years feels… wait I've got this; I know how I feel. Seeing him feels surreal, like it's not happening. For 15 years, he's only existed in my memories, but all that time there was a real, flesh and bone Samson Garcia walking the same earth I walked, suffering even more than I was.

"Hey," I respond.

Sam stares at me, my little black dress, and my strappy Louboutins up and down.

"What?"

"Nothin'." He smirks, and I melt like lava. "You look great."

I cross my ankles and squeeze my thighs together, blushing. I look Sam over again. He's wearing a black shirt, black jeans, and a black leather jacket. He clearly abandoned the cocktail attire dress code. That's Sam for you, never conforming, never following the crowd. Not a sheep nor a shepherd, but a lone wolf watching the masses from afar. No primal need to prove to anyone that he matters.

"We're matching." I smile at him, predicting the half smile that grows on his big lips, and it does.

"Sorry I'm late. I was on the phone with my mom. I love her but that woman could talk to a brick wall for hours."

"Your Mom? Is she still in Richmond Hill?"

"Nah, my parents moved back to Brazil about 5 years after I got locked up. Wasn't much for them here anymore, and they couldn't exactly afford it."

I bow my head down and nod.

"But she's doing great, Dad too. They were able to retire in a small beach town down there. My mom tans and listens to true crime podcasts all day, so they're pretty much living the life."

"That's great to hear. I'm glad they're doing well. I'm sure they went through hell when you went away."

"Yeah, you have no idea." Sam rubs the back of his black hair, just like he used to.

A lightning bolt of guilt strikes me.

"What happened to the cloud of smoke that used to follow you?"

"Ah, I gave it up when I went inside."

"Oh, right."

I'm a fucking idiot. I keep forgetting that this man has been in prison for the last 15 years, partially because Delilah Monroe did what she does best, stayed quiet.

"Sorry, I forgot."

"Nah, it's all good.

"I guess they don't have cigarettes in…" I search my brain for a more casual word than prison, but I don't think one exists. "In there."

"You'd be surprised," Sam laughs, "you can get just about anything in prison if you're motivated enough."

"Oh, good to know."

"Not that it was a luxury cruise by any means."

"Right, of course." I shake my head as I feel hives begin to form on my bare arms. Shit. Spaghetti straps were probably a mistake. I wish I could reach inside of my black Prada and whip out my flask, but alas, I left it at home, on purpose. Dr. Veizer and I discussed that while tonight will be brutal no matter what, I need to feel it. I need to feel it all in order to one day heal it all. I rub my arm up and down and replace the strap that fell back on my shoulder. When I look up, Sam's wolf-like eyes are on my collarbones. He keeps them fixed on that spot, and I casually push the strap back down, away from my shoulder, and let him look. I like that he's not pretending not to stare.

"What?"

"Nothin," he smirks, "you just look…"

"What?" I lean in closer, blinking my long fake eyelashes at him.

"You look…" Sam leans in closer, I can almost taste his sweet breath again when he suddenly takes a step back and fanes a nervous cough. "Uh, cold. You look cold. Here, take my jacket." Sam tears his leather jacket off and hangs it around my shoulders.

"Oh, right. Thanks." I step back and try to mask my humiliation.

"So, you ready to do this? I'd understand if you wanted to back out."

"No, no. I'm ready."

"Okay, good. Do you remember the plan?"

I twirl my honey hair. "Remind me one more time."

"Once we go in there, we'll go our separate ways. There's supposed to be a half hour for mingling, then a distinguished guest alumni is speaking on stage, then more music and a cocktail hour, then the memorial. Ronny, a kid I used to smoke under the bleachers with is working the sound system. I think you met him once, here actually. We kept in touch over the years, he was one of the few who believed I was innocent. He agreed to help us out tonight. Once the guest speaker is done and the music starts, wait for the cue."

"Right, yes. And, what's the cue again?" My brain is absolute mush after last night's five-hour therapy session and the gallons of tears I cried.

"It's the third verse of Dock of the Bay by Otis Redding. Once you hear him go into the verse, sneak backstage and meet me there."

"Okay, got it."

"Alright, let's do this."

Sam turns to walk out of the bleachers, but I grab his big hand and pull him back.

"Sam, wait."

He turns back. "What's wrong?"

"I just… I— I wanted to say… sorry. I'm sorry. I am so fucking sorry. About everything." A tear escapes from my eye.

Sam cups his hands on both sides of my face. "Delilah, I don't blame you for what happened. It wasn't your fault. He hurt you, for years. He abused you, just like he did Bailey. He's the only monster here. And we're going to finally expose him for what he is."

"But if I had come to visit. If I had asked more questions, if I had found out what really happened, maybe I could have saved you from years of torture. But I was scared. I was scared to know the truth. It was easier for me to stay silent, so I did." My volume begins to rise as anger fumes in my gut. "If I had just opened my motherfucking mouth. If I had just gotten off the fucking ground."

"Hey, hey. Delilah, look at me." Sam takes two fingers to my chin and gently lifts it. "I'm okay. It was hell, but I'm still here. You're still here. Philly may have gotten Bailey, but he didn't get us. Because we are still here, and we are going to fight."

I keep my eyes glued to the ground. "But you were locked away for over a decade. How can you not be angry? With me, with God even?"

"Well," Sam sighs, "I was angry at first, but I had a lot of time to think in there. And I realized that being abused and degraded by someone like Philly can make one do things that don't make sense. Yes, it would have been nice if you had reached out or told the police about Philly's violent nature after they arrested me. And, it also would have been nice if Bailey didn't kill herself. But someone wise once taught me that the world is not so black and white. She told me that sometimes life is just too painful to live, and sometimes it just hurts too bad to be you."

I smile through my tears. "She doesn't sound so wise to me."

"She was, she is. And, as for God, you remember that bible story I told you about all those years ago after Bailey died, the story of Hannah?"

"Yeah, I remember."

"It's okay to be angry with God. And it's okay to be upset that life isn't fair. It's okay to feel."

"You gotta feel in order to heal."

I look up at Sam's eyes which are just as warm as the hands he has on my arms.

"Exactly. We should sew that on a throw pillow or something," he giggles, I giggle too.

"You know, there wasn't a day that went by that I didn't think about you. I tried my hardest, believe me. Distractions, affairs, pills, and all the vodka Russia has ever produced. But you always popped into my mind, silver eyes, smoke cloud and all. I tried to erase you, but I couldn't. The way you saw me, really saw me, and never judged me. The way you walked with confidence yet no arrogance. The way you loved fiercely and felt deeply. The way you never wore a mask and didn't need anyone's validation. The way you untangled my twisted mind and chose me on the days I wouldn't choose myself. The way you absolutely sucked at singing Otis Redding."

We both laugh, and I should stop at the point of levity, but I don't. Instead, I inch closer to him. "The way your half-smirk made me believe in fairytales. The way you believed in God and justice, even after all life handed to you. The way the moon sparkled on your wet chest." I feel my body heating up as Sam leans closer. "The way the silver in your cross necklace flirted with..." It's then that I notice the tiny silver cross dangling on his black shirt, between his nipples. "The necklace, you kept it? You kept it all this time?"

Sam takes his hand and brushes it over my cheek. I lean my lips towards it and give it a quick peck. His skin tastes like I remember.

"I thought about you too. I thought about you every waking fucking moment," Sam whispers into my lips with desire.

We allow our instincts to overtake us as we smash into each other, colliding like two cars on a stormy night. Our lips fasten together, latching like they never forgot each other. Our tongues swirl and pirouette in a way that is much more adult than they once knew. Sam rips the leather jacket off of my shoulders and squeezes my waist. I grab a handful of his black hair and dig my nails in his back. Sam puts his hands beneath my butt and hoists me up with ease as if I'm light as a feather. I wrap my legs around him and squeeze my inner thighs against his pelvis, savoring the feeling. He keeps his mouth on mine as he carries me over to the edge of the bleachers, pressing my back up against them. Our bodies continue to frolic like we're in a dark, enchanted forest until the buzz in Sam's pocket strikes lightening down at us. Sam slowly lowers me to the gravel as I unwrap my legs from his torso. He presses his forehead to mine as he silences his phone. He plants another sweet kiss on my painted lips before embracing me in his big, safe arms. I inhale the natural scent from his neck. *Sunset.*

"Sorry. I forgot my mom usually calls around this time. Like I said, the woman can talk."

I laugh as I wipe Sam's sweet saliva from my lips. He backs away slowly and grabs the leather jacket off the ground, allowing me to pull up the straps of my dress.

"Here." He hands me the jacket.

"I'm okay, keep it. It completes your look. Gives you a whole rebel without a cause thing."

Sam's big lips flare into a smirk as he pulls his muscles through the jacket. "Sorry about that. I think maybe we got caught up. It's just, you look so... And you make me feel so…"

"I know, I know," I press my hand to his chest and can feel the fine hair under his shirt. "But we shouldn't. I— I clearly have a lot of shit to sort out. And you and I… we can't. Too much has happened, you know? So, as much as I want this, as much as I've always wanted this, we can't," I say, deflated with disappointment.

"I hear you. We're not teenagers anymore. And, there's a lot I gotta sort out too."

"Right. I've caused you enough pain for one lifetime."

I secretly wish Sam would protest, but instead, he nods.

"Friends?" Sam extends his hands.

"Friends, right." I take his hand and give it a soft shake, but when I try to pull it away, his fingers are still clamped around my dainty knuckles. Part of me hopes he'll yank my arm, pulling me back into him. But he doesn't. He releases my hand, and I suck in tears.

"Maybe in another life then," Sam says, gray eyes glassy.

"In another life, we will dance to Otis Redding together at sunset."

"You got yourself a deal, Delilah Monroe." Sam sticks out his arm like he's my escort to Cotillion, like we're not about to burn this whole town to the ground. Sam leads me out of the bleachers.

"You know, when I got out and looked you up, I assumed you'd be in New York playing your heart out, getting standing ovations every night."

I sigh. "Yeah, well, obviously that didn't happen."

"Never too late."

I squeeze his hand and smile. "Alright, let's do this."

We sneak out from under the bleachers, turn the corner of our old high school and approach the wide double doors.

"Ready, Sam?"

"Ready, Delilah."

"Good evening, please grab a name tag and a marker and stick it on."

Sam and I lean over the check-in desk and begin to write our names. Sam writes 'SA' in big letters.

"Wait! Maybe you shouldn't write your name. This is supposed to be a memorial for Link, and everyone believes that Samson Garcia... well... you know."

"Damn, didn't think about that."

"I wish we could wear masks. But this isn't prom, despite being in the same dingy gymnasium."

"Who says we can't?" Sam stares at his name tag and draws an L. "There, Sal. Hi, I'm Sal. Remember me? I was captain

of the lacrosse team and the sole heir to my father's fortune."
Sam mimics a waspy accent.

"Metaphysical masks, I like it. I'll do one too."

I uncap my marker and write a name down on the tag.

"Who are you gonna be? Let me guess, Tiffany Johnson,
captain of the beer pong squad?"

I hold the name tag up to Sam. He smiles with nostalgia.

"Mileena Gale, you remembered."

"How could I forget?"

A glimmer appears in Sam's glassy eyes. He gives a little
embarrassed laugh and chokes it back.

"Alright, remember the plan?"

"Absolutely. Let's do this."

Sam and I reluctantly part ways and head into the gym.

"Champagne for you, ma'am?"

I jump at the waiter's voice from behind me.

"Oh, oh, sure. Thank you." I take a glass of champagne off the
tray and bring it up to my nose. It smells spectacular, but I
made a promise to Dr. Veizer that I wouldn't drink tonight.
And it's a promise that I want to prove to myself I can keep.
But there's no harm in holding the glass, I need something to
do with my hands. I linger behind a table in the corner, hoping
to hide in plain sight. The last thing I want to do is have idle
conversations with a room of people I don't care about and
who don't care about me. The chatter I've overheard so far
features topics such as careers, promotions, weddings,
pregnancy, kids, and investing in crypto. All things that I have
no points to add on.

I move slowly from corner to corner, keeping my back to the
wall. I scan the room for any sign of Philly. All the former
football players are standing in a group, reminiscing about the

glory days. All common cases of high school heroes, life zeros. Not that I'm one to talk. I look at my phone to check for any missed calls or texts from Philly, but there's nothing. I haven't heard from him since that last text in which he said he'd try to make it to the reunion. Lucky for me, he has never kept his word on anything in our entire 10 years of marriage.

I linger over towards the back of the gym and spot Chloe and Mary Lu, attached at the hip, on the other side of the room near the DJ booth. I turn away and walk back towards the bathroom. Chloe, the home wrecker, is the second to last person I want to see. After I learned of the affair and had the miscarriage, Philly swore he would never see Chloe again. I, however, was not so lucky. I saw her out shopping with her mom around the holidays last year. She looked dolled up and gorgeous, and it made me want to die. We avoided each other like the plague, like the two polite southern women that we are. None of that matters anymore. Philly is no longer mine and I am no longer his. And, if I have anything to do with it, no woman will bear the burden of being his ever again. I glance back at Chloe and Mary Lu. They're both dressed like it's New Year's Eve, and they're whispering and laughing as people pass them by. Looks like some things never change. I'm surprised to see Mary Lu here. Last I heard, she moved to Utah, became a Mormon, and popped out like 6 kids.

I turn around and keep walking towards the bathroom. I pass a few cops on my way, some of them I recognize as old classmates and some of them are younger. I suppose they need police here to keep drunken sloppiness to an appropriate amount. However, I'm hoping that they will hear Sam's side of prom night and re-open the case.

I swing the door of the bathroom open and head into a stall. I sit down and ball my hands into fists then stretch my fingers out. I then put a hand over my heart and begin affirmations.

"I am safe, I am safe, I am safe. Everything is going to be okay," I whisper. After a few beats, I stand up and flush. I head out of the stall and put my hands under the faucet. Looking up into the mirror, I examine my face. It looks way older than it once did under this fluorescent lighting. I dry my hands, grab lipstick from my purse, and begin to apply it in the mirror.

"Delilah?"

I glance up and do a double take of the pregnant woman in the mirror behind me.

"Mia!" I spin around. "Oh my gosh!" I hesitantly open my arms to give her a hug. She leans in and kisses me on the cheek. I pull away after the first air kiss, but she pulls me back in for a second, third, and fourth. Okay, I guess we're doing that now.

"It's so good to see you, Delilah. It's been ages. How are you?" Mia asks with high-pitched enthusiasm. Her tight white maxi dress shows off her baby bump elegantly. Her face is perfectly made up with neutral tones and contouring that is noticeable yet subtle. Her hair, now black, is up in a tight bun, highlighting the beauty of her bone structure. She looks glamorous and put together, just as she always has been.

"Oh, I'm, you know. I'm fine. But how are you? Congratulations! When are you due?"

"Oh, not soon enough." Mia puts a hand on her back and slowly walks over to the sink. From the looks of it, she's due pretty soon.

"I didn't know you were coming, I figured you'd be too busy with all the companies you own and stuff."

"Well, I am, but you know. I wanted to be here for the memorial. Link may have been a complete dickface, but he was our dickface."

"Yeah," I sigh.

Mia washes her hands and checks her teeth for lipstick marks.

"So, I didn't know you got married. Is your husband here?" I ask, trying to make conversation.

"I'm not married."

Fuck. "Oh, oh I'm— I'm sorry. I shouldn't have assumed."

Mia laughs, "no worries. I went the sperm donor route. I want my child to have the most high-brow DNA possible. The donor is a six-foot-four Harvard grad with blue eyes, can't get better than that."

"Wow, that's great."

"Yep," she dries her hands with a towel. "Do you have kids yet?"

"No, I don't. I'm not sure that I want to anymore." The words come out before I have time to tailor them. But this is the first time I've been asked if I'm a mom and haven't felt a stabbing sensation in my stomach. It's also the first time I haven't hesitated with the answer. Although, that probably wasn't the most ideal thing to say to an expecting mother.

"Yeah, it's definitely not for everyone. This is my first, so we'll see how it goes." Mia leans back on the sink and turns around to face me. "So, what else is new? What have you been up to? What are you doing for work these days?"

I look quickly back and forth, pondering various lies I could tell, but instead… "Honestly, nothing. I don't have a real job, I don't have a child, I don't have hobbies, I don't do much of anything, really."

Mia's face looks a bit stunned by my bluntness at first but then her perfect features relax. "Well, that sounds pretty nice, honestly. I'd certainly like a break from all the noise. I feel like I'm freaking drowning."

I tilt my head to the side. "Drowning, you? But you seem so put together, like you have it all figured out."

"Oh D, no one has it all figured out. We're all just guessing. Trust me, I'm flailing just as much as everybody else. I have like a million failed relationships because every man I've been with felt emasculated by me and unable to deal with my work schedule. And well, eventually, I got tired of waiting and my eggs were rotting so I bit the bullet and did in vitro with a donor. I figured it was my last shot. I wanted a legacy, you know? Something more than just a career. I thought I'd push out one baby, hire a nanny, go on kicking ass at work but still be there for the fun parts of having a kid. I thought pregnancy was going to be this magical thing, like women say it is, but it has been freaking hell. I've hated every minute of it. My brain is murky, I'm not as sharp at work, I can't fit into any of my shoes, and I feel like crap all the time."

"Oh damn. That sucks, sorry. But you're due soon, right? So, not much longer."

"I'm due in five months."

My brow furrows. "But... you're..."

"Huge? Yeah, I know. Well, get this, I'm having fucking triplets. Triplets!"

"Holy shit," I gasp.

"Damn right, holy shit."

Mia and I both start laughing.

She touches my arm. "No one ever has it together like you think they do, including me. We're all just doing our best."

"I guess you're right. You're always right."

"Well, some things never change."

"Some things do... hopefully."

"Like what?" She asks.

"Mia? Mia White? Are you in there? You're on stage in two." A voice shouts into the bathroom.

"Be right there!" Mia yells back. "Sorry, gotta go."

"You're the guest speaker? The distinguished alumni?"

Dumb question, of course she is.

Mia pulls me in for a hug. "It was wonderful to see you, D. Let's get together next time I'm in town or you're in L.A., sound good?"

Because I'm always flying to L.A. for all of the very distinguished and high-brow things I do.

"Sounds great. Break a leg!"

I follow Mia out of the bathroom and take a seat at a table in the back. I recognize some of the people at the table, but they don't seem to recognize me with lighter hair and my tag that says Mileena Gale. I haven't performed in years, but I'm sure I'd still burn under the spotlight if I did. As for Mia, it's like she was made for it. I ogle at her as she gives her speech. She's articulate, regal, and motivational. There's a fire in her eyes that I wish I had. My flame burned out the night Link died and Sam was taken away in handcuffs.

Mia talks to the crowd about her accomplishments but somehow does it without bragging. She talks about her philosophy toward her career, marketing strategies, and what it's like having a seat at the men's table. I always had a sneaking suspicion that Mia would run shit like this one day, and I'm happy to see that I was right. I'm proud of her.

Mia talks for another few minutes and then ends her speech with a quote by Maya Angelou. She exits off the stage as all of our old classmates applaud and cheer. I search around the room for Sam, but I don't see him. Did he go backstage already? No, not yet. I'm supposed to wait for the song, then we both go back.

I cling to a wall in the back of the gym, avoiding eye contact with everyone. I keep smelling my champagne, illogically hoping the smell will give me a buzz. Enough of a buzz to give me the confidence to go through with this. I hold my champagne up to my nose as I wait for the song, but the DJ continues to play music that was popular when we were in high school: Katy Perry, Usher, The Pussycat Dolls, and so on. I scan the room again and let out a sigh of relief when I don't spot Philly anywhere. We're over a half hour into the reunion, surely if he was coming, he would be here by now. This is good. We'll just go up there, say our piece, clear Sam's name, and hopefully the police will put out a warrant for Philly, and I will never be spun in the web of his black eyes again.

I keep looking around the room when I hear the first chord progression. I place my champagne on a nearby table and slowly inch my way towards the front of the gym. I put my hair over my face and keep my head down so I won't be recognized. I see a few heads turn out of the corner of my eye. I linger by the stage until I hear the third verse.

Sittin' here resting my bones,
And this loneliness won't leave me alone, listen,
Two thousand miles I roam,
Just to make this dock my home...

I b-line for the stairs and clear all three steps up to the stage. I quickly zoom behind the curtain and crash into someone's chest. I take a step back and gasp, my heart falls out of me.

"Relax, it's just me."

"Philly?"

"Hi, honey."

I'm panting.

371

"What are you— what are you—- how are you—"

"I wanted to surprise you. Surprise! You thought I wouldn't show up, didn't you? I'd never miss an opportunity to rub my success in these losers' faces. You know Mike Hobbs, captain of the wrestling team who was always a prick? He's working at The Dollar Tree now. The Dollar Tree! What an embarrassment."

"I used to work at The Dollar Tree," I say flatly.

"Exactly. Then you married me." Philly lightly presses a kiss to my forehead. A shiver crawls up my whole body and the blood drains from my face. "You can thank me later. C'mon, let's go mingle. Rub our badass life in their faces."

Philly grabs my hand, and I look down at it. It's lifeless, I'm lifeless. Time has stopped. I look up slowly from my hand and glance behind me from backstage. I see Sam standing in the center of the stage under the spotlight, alone. He's staring right at me. He looks down at my hand that Philly's holding then back up at me. The look on his face is indescribable. I think I have just been hit by a train. I yank my hand away from Philly's as quickly as I can and glare up at his chiseled face with wide eyes. His eyes are still beautiful, still twinkling in the light like they did that first day of kindergarten. Philly strokes my arm and bites his bottom lip, and then, there he is. The boy who chased butterflies with me. The boy with the W on his tooth. The boy who wouldn't go to the pool party because he wasn't confident in his skin. The boy who cried in my arms the day his dog died. The boy I loved. The boy I married.

"Philly... I—"

Suddenly, the music cuts out. Sam taps his finger on the microphone then lifts it to his mouth. My head shoots in his direction.

"Who the fuck is that?" Philly asks, pointing to Sam.

"Good evening, Richmond Hill High class of 2010. My name is Samson Garcia."

The crowd gasps and whispers begin.

"What the fuck? How is he here? What is he doing? What the fuck is this?" Philly barks.

"I know we are all here to celebrate the good times and commemorate the life of Link, but before we do so, I have some things I need to say. I am Samson Garcia. In 2009, I was sentenced to 15 years in prison for a crime I did not commit, for the manslaughter of Matthew James Link. My heart breaks for Link and his family. He will always be missed. And while I was involved in the altercation the night that Link lost his life, I was not the one who pushed him, a push that resulted in his death. Tonight, I am here to tell my truth and set the record straight about what occurred before, during, and after the altercation that had fatal consequences." Sam addresses the crowd then looks back at me. I glance down then back up at him. His gray eyes castrate my soul. I want to move towards him, but my body stays paralyzed in place. Paralyzed in Philly's grasp. Sam lets out a sigh and gives me a small nod, assuring me that it's okay.

"What the fuck is going on?" I hear Philly say from behind me. I turn around to face him and he grabs my hand. "Let's get out of here." Philly pulls at my hand but my body stays in place, still as stone. My lips part as my wide eyes stay fixed on him.

"Are you fucking deaf, Delilah? I said let's go." Philly yanks at my hand again, harder this time. My body jolts and I take a few steps forward to catch myself. Philly looks back at me with confusion as my wide eyes become sad ones. Liam was right when he said the world is not so black and white, and so was Sebastian, so was Dr. Veizer, so was Sam, and so was I. I clung to the good memories of Philly until my knuckles turned white because I was afraid if I thought about the bad, then *he* would be all bad. But it's not that simple. We had beautiful times, and we had horrific ones. We had millions of different shades. There are no good people or bad people. There are the people who want to hurt you, the people who want to heal you, and the people who do both. Life is not black or white, it's gray. Beautiful, silver, warm, wolf-like gray. I shake my head at Philly as I pull my hand out of his grip and slowly back away from the boy I loved and his many shades of gray.

"It's time for everyone to know the truth. I'm not going to stay quiet anymore." I take one more step backward then spin around and walk onto the stage, joining Sam by his side.

He gives me a look with his silver eyes and that heart-shaped mouth half smile that doesn't capture me, no. It sets me free. I hold my head up and try not to focus on all the eyes on me at once.

"In the early fall of 2009, my twin sister, Bailey Garcia, was attacked and raped. When she reported this crime to the cops, the police department behaved unethically. They refused to launch an investigation and covered up the crime. The devastation from this caused her to take her own life. In November of 2009, Philly St. James confessed to the sexual assault of Bailey Garcia. This was after I witnessed him physically assault Delilah Monroe and break her jaw."

I hear more gasps and chatter from the audience. I try my best to keep my head up and not look down at the crowd, but I catch Mia's eye. She cups her baby bump as her eyes stretch wider than the open ocean.

"In response to what I witnessed and his confession, I went after Philly St. James. And, while I do not condone violence

374

of any form, I thought I was acting in defense of my sister and my girlfriend."

A small tingle surges in my stomach. Girlfriend? Was I Sam's girlfriend? Oh my God, not fucking important right now. Focus.

"Link joined in on the fight, and once it was two against one, I only used self-defense as I tried to get away from them and get Delilah to safety. Philly was on top of me, punching me in the face over and over until I could no longer see. He grabbed me by my hair and began to hit my head against the floor. I witnessed Link attempt to pull Philly off of me, as I heard him say 'that's enough, he's had enough'. I then witnessed Philly St. James push Link off of him. I heard a loud crash and a scream as he hit the sink, then my eyes closed and everything was dark. I was not informed that Link had lost his life until I was arrested at the hospital. The Richmond Hill police never took a statement from me, and I was denied legal counsel until the trial. I deeply regret using violence that fateful night in November of 2009, but I did not kill Matthew James Link. Philly St. James killed Link. He raped my sister, Bailey Garcia and physically assaulted Delilah Monroe. Philly St. James is a dangerous man who needs to pay for his crime and be sent away from society. Delilah and I will be filing a formal report with the police, but it is my hope that the information you heard here today urges you to—"

Sam's speech is cut short when Philly lunges out from behind the curtain. He sprints onto the stage. Though Sam is taller, Philly is able to take him down by tackling him at the knees. Sam is body-slammed onto the ground. His back makes a loud thud on the stage. Sam protects his face with his arms as Philly drives his fists into it.

"Get off the ground, Sam!" I scream. I look out towards the audience and whale, "police, we need police!"

I see people rushing towards the stage as I hurl my entire body at Philly and knock him off of Sam and onto the stage floor. He hurries to his feet, takes one step towards me, and grabs the back of my neck. I feel an intense smash and hear a crippling crack. Then, everything goes dark, too dark to see.

Chapter 36
One year later

I slip through the turn style and climb my way up the steep stairs. I exit the subway terminal and turn left onto Canal street. I keep my Air Pods in as I walk 5 blocks, drowning out the street vendors selling fake Prada. Though I will say, some of their counterfeit stuff looks pretty legit. I bob my head to the smooth jazz on Spotify. I allow my fingers to play along to the melody in the air in front of me, not giving a flying fuck who sees. I cup my hands over my mouth as a colossal chill of wind rushes towards me. It's freezing in New York this time of year, but that doesn't stop me from roaming the streets every day, admiring the holiday decorations or sipping hot coffee in Central Park.

I hike up my last block and open the door to the bar.

"Hey there, you're here early."

"Hey! Yeah, I wanted to iron out a few new riffs before my shift." I peel my pink parka off and hang it on the coat rack along with my purple knit scarf.

"Of course you did. Always working harder than the rest of us. We're lucky to have you, you know."

"I know." I wink at Simon, our bartender, and head over to the piano.

"Shall I get you your usual?" He asks.

"Yes, please. Thanks!" I yell over my shoulder. I put my bag down and take a seat on the piano bench. I pull out my phone and see a text.

Dr. Veizer: Does 2PM work for Monday's telehealth appointment? I am looking forward to trying some Gestalt activities.

I text her back then pull up the notes app on my phone and re-read the chord progressions I wrote down on the subway. I straighten my posture and begin to play.

It's been over a year since the night of the reunion. I was told that after I passed out, some of the former wrestling guys were able to pull Philly off Sam and hold him down until the police made their way to the stage. Philly was arrested for assault and taken to the station. Sam and I made a formal report with the Richmond Hill police department the next day. Sam told the real story about prom night, and I told them... well, everything. I told them how Philly raped me, how he coerced me, how he degraded me, how he threatened me with violence during our marriage, and how he abused me pretty much from that day in kindergarten on. The case was re-opened and the cops who launched the new investigation took it very seriously. I suppose the Richmond Hill police department vastly improved once Sheriff St. James was no longer in charge. I stayed with Sebastian in a little Airbnb he was renting after leaving his husband and filing for divorce. He had finally reached his limit; he was finally done putting up with his shades of gray. Sebastian was very helpful and supportive throughout everything. He uniquely understood me and my situation, having seen the rain himself and all. Mia helped me find and fund the best criminal attorney money could buy as well as a divorce attorney. Unfortunately, with little physical evidence other than Bailey's old diary of poems, it was our word against Philly's. And even though everyone involved voiced that they believed Philly was guilty, they didn't have enough evidence to convict him. I filed for divorce from Philly and got a restraining order, but eventually he tracked me down and broke into the Airbnb Sebastian and I were staying at. Luckily, Sebastian fought him off with a bat he had handy in case his own abusive husband came looking for him.

It was my mom's idea to change my name and leave the state. She was horrified when I told her the real story of Philly and me. She blamed herself for modeling a toxic relationship with my dad. Since then, we've done a lot of family therapy sessions with Dr. Veizer and we ended up in a better place than I could have ever imagined. Mom is visiting later this month and we're going to see The Rockettes in the Radio City Music Hall Christmas Spectacular. She's excited, she's been looking forward to it for months.

I haven't seen Sam since I moved out of Georgia. The domestic violence protection program I'm in encourages no contact with anyone from your former life except for immediate family. Sam was devastated to see me go, as was I. But he understood that safety needed to be the number one priority. He planned to move back to Brazil and get a place near his parents anyway. I miss him fiercely, but it's okay. I'll see him in another life.

I haven't been contacted by Philly since I left, but he could very well still be searching for me. I constantly find myself looking over my shoulder, wondering if today is the day he'll find me. I brace myself every time I see a customer walk in the bar. I jump every time I hear the buzzer to my apartment, and I carry mace with me every time I walk out the door. I think there's a part of me that will always be scared of Philly St. James, and there will always be a part of me that cries for the sweet young boy I once knew who loved his dog and his mother. The boy with the sparkling black eyes that lit up every room he walked into. But Philly is also the boy, no, the *man* that killed Link, stole Sam's freedom, and drove Bailey to suicide. He is the man who demeaned me, degraded me, and dehumanized me just because he knew that he could. I'm still haunted by the bad times- prom night, that night in Mia's sister's room. The night when I was pinned down to a concrete driveway, when my innocence was yanked out of me and floated up to the sky. Sometimes the vision of me frozen, unable to get off the ground flashes in front of me like a teleprompter with no warning. I think there will always be a small part of me that is frozen on that ground, but I'm learning that that's okay. Dr. Veizer helped me realize that healing isn't linear, or fun, or pretty, or final. There may not be a specific point that you reach where you feel healed from every cut that's ever grazed your skin. But the wounds do close, and scars form in their place. That's what Philly St. James is to me now, he's my biggest scar. But I got out. I broke the cycle. It wasn't easy to say goodbye to the only life I've ever known, unlearn everything I've ever been taught, and start over with a new identity. I'm still getting use to not being called Delilah, D, or Lilah anymore. But I think I picked a good name for my new identity. I chose it very carefully. It's one that has no ties to Delilah Monroe, one that would make it nearly impossible for anyone to find me. Well... all accept one person.

"Here's your club soda and lime, Mileena."

"Thank you, Simon." I grab the drink from him and set it down on the top of the piano.

"I'm hitting a meeting in Bushwick after my shift. You wanna come?"

"Sure, sounds good. I'll catch up with you after last call."

"Awesome, see ya later."

Simon walks back towards the bar. I flip my dark hair back behind my shoulder. I changed it back to my natural color after I left Georgia. I've been sober for about eight months. I get a new chip in a few days. Those first two months of sobriety were brutal. I was an emotional wreck, and I truly did not think I was going to make it. But two months soon turned into three, then four. Staying sober got easier over time, and I eventually stopped craving alcohol. Being able to play piano for a living, especially music that I enjoy and some original songs is what fills me up nowadays. As well as long walks in the park, the camaraderie I have with my friends from AA, my cat, underground coffee shops, vintage bookstores, and new art galleries. I've come alive in this city. It's like I've finally found my meaning. At first, I thought playing at a jazz bar would be difficult to do while trying to stay sober, but it's oddly not. Being around alcohol and drunk people and consciously choosing to not drink feels empowering. Not worrying about where my next drink will come from, or how much I can drink and still drive, or how I can hide my drinking from those around me, plus hangovers, plus withdrawals, plus drunken injuries, plus drunken fights, plus drunken cries, plus one night stands, plus liver pain, plus everything else alcohol has given me… Not having to worry about any of those things anymore, it makes me feel… free. I feel free.

I close my eyes in a moment of gratitude then straighten my back, stretch my fingers, and begin to play. I hear patrons trickling in, seeking solace from the cold. I hear talking, laughing, singing, and my mending heart feels full. I flow through a few jazz riffs I composed myself and sway along to my own music.

Suddenly, I feel a hard tap on my shoulder as my whole body jumps in the air.

"Mileena Gale, is it?"

My body freezes in place as my previously full heart sinks into my stomach. My voice is stuck in my throat as heat rises through me and pulses all throughout my body. I slowly take my hands off the keys and turn around.

"I'd like to make a song request. You happen to know any Otis Redding?"

Tears come to my eyes as my smile stretches wider across my face than it ever has. Sam's mouth flares up at the corner into a half smile as his warm gray eyes cover me like a blanket. And, suddenly, the sun comes out.

Sittin' in the mornin' sun,
I'll be sittin' when the evening comes,
Watching the ships roll in,
Then I watch 'em roll away again,
I'm sittin' on the dock of the bay,
Watchin' the tide roll away,
I'm just sittin' on the dock of the bay,
Wastin' time...

Black Roses Playlist

1. "Dock of the Bay" by Otis Redding
2. "Cherry" by Lana Del Rey
3. "Would've, Could've, Should've" by Taylor Swift
4. "Runnin'" by The Luttrells
5. "2009" by Mac Miller
6. "Have You Ever Seen the Rain" by Creedence Clearwater Revival
7. "Adam's Song" by Blink 182
8. "I've Been Loving You Too Long" by Otis Redding
9. "Medicine" by The Pretty Reckless
10. "The End of the World" by Skeeter Davis
11. "Through the Rain" by Mariah Carey
12. "Georgia on My Mind" by Ray Charles
13. "Car Radio" by Twenty-One Pilots
14. "I Believe You" by Fletcher
15. "Poltergeist" by The Luttrells
16. "Remembering Sunday" by All Time Low
17. "Nobody Gets Me" by SZA
18. "Hangover Cure" by Machine Gun Kelly
19. "Hope is a Dangerous Thing for a Woman Like Me" by Lana Del Rey
20. "Anyone" by Demi Lovato
21. "Reasons I Drink" by Alanis Morrissette
22. "Hometown Glory" by Adele
23. "I've Got Dreams to Remember" by Otis Redding
24. "Six Thirty" by Ariana Grande
25. "Good News" by Mac Miller
26. "Ain't No Way" by Aretha Franklin
27. "Hide and Seek" by Imogen Heap

28. "Play This When I'm Gone" by Machine Gun Kelly
29. "Breathe Me" by Sia
30. "You're On Your Own, Kid" by Taylor Swift
31. "Salvatore" by Lana Del Rey
32. "Rhythm of the Rain" by The Cascades
33. "A Thousand Years" by Christina Perri
34. "The Great Pretender" by The Platters
35. "Crowded Places" by Banks
36. "Make You Feel My Love" by Adele
37. "Nothing Can Change This Love" by Sam Cooke
38. "Clair de lune" by Claude Debussy

About the Author

Deanna Dellia is a full-time clinical psychotherapist in Nashville, Tennessee. She currently specializes in suicide prevention. She uses her knowledge of psychology as well as her personal journey with trauma to help a wide range of people through her clinical work and her social media platforms. Deanna is one half of the R&B musical duo, The Luttrells. She and her husband write, record, and perform music around the country. Deanna is an avid chef, cat Mom, and Bravo superfan. In her free time, you can catch her doing tarot in her witch library with a glass of wine in hand, traveling to foreign lands, planting flowers in her fairy garden, or picnicking in the park. Deanna's goal as a writer is to give a voice to those who suffer from the traumas no one talks about. She hopes that her words make her readers feel seen, heard, and understood. She wants nothing more but to have a long career of writing stories that make you swoon, get you wet, make you cry, and heal your fractured heart. This is Deanna's debut novel. Her second book, Confessions of a Sugar Baby, is coming this spring.

IG: @deannadellia @therapyforartistss @deannadelliapoetry

TikTok: @therapyforartists @darkromancedeannadellia

@blackrosesbook

Turn the page for a bonus chapter from

Confessions of a Sugar Baby

Chapter 12

Under the blanket of a starry sky, the ocean whispers in the background, gently lapping against the shore. The soft glow of the moon reflects off the water, casting a silvery sheen on the sand. Serena presses the glass to her cold lips and tilts the bottle up towards the night sky as she pirouettes in the sea breeze. Her bare feet dance in the sand. She spins and spins, chugging the homemade wine she swiped from my mother's cupboard. It tastes putrid and rotten, but after she coughed up her fourth sip, she found it became more delicious by the minute.

Serena spins her body until the rest of the world begins to swirl with her. The dizziness makes her knees give out and she crashes onto the sand. She buries the wine bottle an inch down next to her to keep it from spilling then she lays her head back down on the ground. The stars in sky flurry around each other rapidly, and she can't tell if they're dancing or fighting with each other. Once the twinkling lights still in the sky, she lifts up to a sitting position. The autumn air is crisp. Pulling her knees to her chest, she tucks them into her over-sized sweatshirt. Her naked body shivers underneath the cotton. The blue Logo reads Shore Regional High School Varsity Soccer Team. It was once Domani's, of course. He was in the habit of giving Serena his sweatshirts. He always said she looked cold, but she knew he just wanted her to cover up so the double takes from the entirety of the male student body would diminish.

She runs her finger along the school letters, cursing every minute she had to spend in those hallowed halls. You'd think all the name calling she endured back then would have prepared her for media frenzy that her life has become now, but it's different when a twenty-to-life is sentence is on the line. She didn't feel the need to defend herself from her bad reputation in high school. She figured she would just become a rich and famous model then prove them all wrong. A sarcastic laugh falls out of her mouth at the thought. She picks up the bottle and takes a swig of the red liquid, it burns as it travels down her esophagus. She slams it back down into the sand and peers out towards the open ocean. The waves crash violently, creating rip tides when they smash into the wet sand. The ripples rage through the black turbulent sea.

"Angry, are we?" Serena asks to the open ocean. "Me too, buddy." She lifts the bottle from the sand. "Me too." She takes three large sips and winces, choking down the stale wine. "So, what's got your panties in a twist?" She holds the bottle out towards the churning water. "Cat got your tongue? So be it. I'll go first." She takes another sip. "Me, I'm currently being investigated for murder. Murder. Yeah, like the shit you'd see on dateline or CSI. And let me tell you, it is nowhere near as glamourous or well-lit in real life like it is on those shows. Turns out, in real life, murder investigations are not so cute. Who would have thought?" She laughs at herself before reality sets in, sobering her slightly. Her face falls and she puts the bottle down. "They want me to burn." Serena lifts herself out of the sand, grabbing the bottle next to her. She steps forward firmly, her feet sinking as she does. She barely realizes she has come face to face with the ocean until she feels a cold wave wash over her ankles. She sways with the strong pull of the current at her feet as she closes her eyes. "They want me to burn," she whispers. She takes a step forward, pushing her deeper into the water. "But they can't burn me if I've already drowned." She takes another step deeper and feels slimy seaweed wrapping around her calves. A tall wave approaches, threatening her stance. *She can practically taste the salty water as the wave crushes her, foam pummeling into her face. The polluted water fills her lungs and pushes into each one of her ribs. She sinks down into the abyss like a rock. Her vision goes blurry and her body goes limp, allowing the current to pull her through the rip tide. Her body tumbles and dances against her will, but her face... Her face looks... free. She stops gasping for air as pain surges through every muscle, bone, vein, and ligament of her body. Until finally, her heart stops. She floats to the surface, allowing the sea to carry her away like a piece of driftwood. Driftwood. Unimportant and forgettable, driftwood.*

"No!" Serena screams at the colossal wave approaching. "This is not my fucking ship. I am not going to down with it." She launches the half empty wine bottle straight into the growing wave and backs away. Spinning on her heels, she walks back towards the shore. She's almost made it up to the boardwalk before she turns back to the ocean for one more look. She holds up her middle finger. "I'm no ship captain. I'm somebody's fucking queen."

Serena stumbles into the confessional booth, her bare sandy feet scraping against the floor. Water drips from her legs. She nearly slipped twice on the way to the church. She shivers as she lowers herself to her knees and imitates the sign of the cross. She's still for a beat as she listens to the angry winds thump on the bones of the old church. She squeezes her eyes shut and allows herself the fall backwards, the bench catching her by the small of her back. She situates herself on the floor as she brings her knees up to her chest and huddles for warmth. Her teeth chatter.

"Innocent," she whispers. "*Innocent*." She wipes her runny nose. "Innocent, that's why he likes her because she's innocent. Like it's a motherfucking choice." She kicks the wall in front of her, shaking the partition. "Sorry. I'm working on that." Serena sits up straight. "It's just… innocence isn't a choice for all of us. Sometimes it's taken…" She wraps her arms around herself. "Stolen." Serena's mind wanders through time to green grass itching beneath her feet, Italian opera singing to her tiny ears, the smell of fresh baked pastries floating through the air. Her braids tight, her teddy bear in her hand, and her school uniform freshly pressed. *His* huge arms wrapped around her waist.

"Ugh!" Serena throws the back of her head into the bench behind her, making a loud thud and shaking the whole booth. Her hand flies up to her skull, the pain wiping away her memories.

"I'm sorry." She combs a hand through her long salty hair and re-positions herself on the floor. "Karoline with a K? Karoline with a fucking K? What is she, a fucking Kardashian?" Serena pleads, out of breath before tilting her head down. "I'm sorry. Oh wait, did I say that already? I'm a lil drunk-y." She giggles, pulling the hood of her sweatshirt over her head. "That's better. Anyway, where were we Padre? Oh, yes, now I remember. You're gonna love this." She smacks her big lips together. "So, after that day at the park with Charlie, everything became crystal clear. This man, richer than God, gave me the code to his psyche. He wanted to own me. And I figured, if he wanted to own me, control me, make me his property, I was going to let him. Or at least, I would pretend to. It's never been hard for a woman to manipulate a man into thinking he holds all the power when really, the pussy pulls the strings. I knew I could embody this man's fantasy of owning me while secretly maintaining all the control. Making *him* feel uncontrollable desire for my touch. Making *him* beg me for more. Making *him* fall head-over-heels in love with me. Making *him* shower me with opulent gifts. Making *him* give me enough money to start a new life. Looking back on it, the whole ownership thing shouldn't have come as such a shock. I mean, the man was famous for literally owning Manhattan. So much so that they made a documentary about him. He wanted it all. The man had a fetish, ya know? Just like Pearson Alcott, just like Avery Davenport. Although, Charlie Bane's fetish was far less depraved, hardly even a category on PornHub. Or so I thought…

One year ago
Serena flips through the pages of a Crockpot recipe book. She memorizes all of the ingredients that she can, creating a mental image of the pictures shown for each dish. She's nearly memorized at least ten recipes when her eyebrow flares up. Tilting her book down, she peeks across the table. Charlie, in his usual leather jacket uniform, leans back in his chair with effortless ease. So comfortable, so self-assured, you'd think this library was his home. You'd think he owned it. Charlie shoots a look across the table when he feels Serena's light eyes on him. He gives her a smirk, charm oozing from his pours while he winks his thick eyelashes. Serena pops her cookbook back up, covering her face. He lets out a quiet chuckle and focuses back down on his investment book. Serena, frowning,

stares at the picture of pot roast in front of her. Her mouth begins to water when she comes to the disappointing revelation that she will never be able to make this pot roast, or any other recipe in the book because she doesn't own a crockpot, or an air fryer, or any other fancy cookware. The oven in her studio apartment doesn't even work. When she tried to complain to her landlord, he kindly reminded her that she is subletting the place and they have no formal lease, so he's allowed to kick her out on her "bodacious ass" at any time. Considering that Serena has no credit and no other options, she's not in a place to make demands. Serena sighs down at the delicious picture. Potatoes, carrots and celery accompanied by meat she knows would just melt in her mouth. She dreams of a world in which she could make this for someone other than just herself. A world with fancy cooking devices, a world with a working kitchen, a world in which she has free will, a world where she has a purpose, a world where she finally has an opportunity to do something good. She sighs, feeling the distance of that world. She looks up from her book to find Charlie staring at her. His copper eyes are fixed on her neck. She sweeps her raven hair from her collar bone. He bites his bottom lip, tinting it a succulent shade of scarlet. Serena watches as he gathers himself. He lifts his arms over his head and up to the ceiling, flexing his biceps as he stretches. He lets out a small grunt that sounds sexual by nature. Serena's mouth salivates, and this time it's not from the pot roast. Charlie runs a hand through his light brown hair and rustles it around. He groans quietly, throwing his head back. Serena wonders if he sounds anything like this when he's getting off. She imagines sliding out of her seat and slithering under the table. She imagines the look on his face when hers appears between his legs as she climbs out from under the library desk. She imagines the shock that fills his eyes when she unbuttons his black jeans and yanks down his zipper. She imagines the shiver that slides up his thighs as she gingerly pulls his pants down to his ankles. She imagines the quiet groans that slip through his lips when she drags her tongue along his thigh, tickling him. She can hear the breath that escapes him when her kisses make it up his thigh and to the base of his cock. She can see the veins throb as his rock-hard dick finds its way between her lips, and she can feel the blood rush to the top of his manhood as she flicks her wet tongue over the tip of him, teasing him. She can hear his loud moan echo through the New York Public Library when she finally grips his balls and shoves his big cock deep down her throat. Never budging, never gagging.

"Serena?"

"What?" She snaps, quickly squeezing her legs together. The slickness between her thighs gathers like a river.

"You okay?" He lifts a thick eyebrow.

"Yeah. Obviously. Why wouldn't I be?"

Charlie shrugs. "If you say so." He gives her another body melting wink and stares back down at his book.

Serena does the same, staring at the pot roast photo again. She knows she's nowhere near close to being able to spend frivolously on any fancy cooking gadgets. And she knows she's nowhere near close to being able to live in the world she dreams of.

"Ugh." She shoots up from her chair and stomps away from the table, losing herself in an aisle of books she doesn't recognize. She keeps walking, weaving through different rows, trying to untangle her twisted mind.

"Serena!"

She hears Charlie whisper call after her. *Good*, she thinks. *He's chasing me, it's working already. Own me, my ass. This millionaire is in the palm of my hand.* A Machiavellian smile plays on her lips.

"Serena!"

She keeps weaving in and out of different aisles as Charlie follows behind.

"Serena, stop."

"Shhhhh!" A librarian spits from afar, ironically much louder than anything else going on in the library.

"Sorry," Charlie whispers.

Serena keeps moving until eventually she doesn't hear Charlie's voice or footsteps behind her. *Shit*, she thinks, stopping in her tracks. She turns to look behind her, then the other way, then—

"Ah!" Her face smashes into Charlie's chest, the hair peaking over his t-shirt tickling her cheek. He smells of oak and leather.

"Where do you think you're going, Sophia Loren?"

"I got bored." Serena steps back and crosses her arms. Her mouth twists into a grimace. "Why did you insist on taking me to the library? This isn't exactly the most romantic date."

"You said this is your favorite place in the city."

Her olive skin flushes and a smile tugs at her lips. "Well, it is, but..."

"But what." Charlie says it as more of a statement than a question as he leans towards her. His broad shoulders surround her as his face comes closer to hers. His breath tickles her throat when he wraps his neck around to the back of hers. His arm reaches out, and the tingle between Serena's thighs returns. He lifts his arm over her, and she reaches hers out as well, ready to accept his embrace.

"Here it is." Charlie's hand snatches a thin book from the shelf behind her and pulls it back. Embarrassment stains her cheeks as he takes a step backward and hands the book to her. She reluctantly takes it, practically snarling, and she reads the front cover.

"The History of Ocean Grove... Sick, dude," she mocks as her face falls flat.

"They say that place is haunted, you know? Crazy history of shipwrecks, unexplained fires destroying the whole town."

"I'm well aware. It's my hometown, numb nuts."

He laughs. "I thought you'd be into all that spooky shit."

"And why is that?" Serena leans her weight to one side and pops her hip out.

"Because you look like you've seen the devil, Serena Snow."

Her breath captures in her chest. She can hear the faint cadence of Italian opera as she inhales a waft of cinnamon levitating in the air.

She shakes the memory off of her. "Whatever," she says, rocking back on her heels.

Charlie smirks with amusement. "Open it."

"What?"

"The book, open it."

She rolls her eyes and opens the hardcover to the first page. She gapes over the cursive letters written in Sharpie. "To my Sophia Loren," she reads. "Wait... did you? How did you—You wrote this?"

Charlie shrugs with a coy grin.

"But how did you—how did you know I would wonder into this section?"

"Perhaps I know you better than you think."

"I highly doubt that."

"Oh yeah? Wanna bet?"

Serena laughs and shakes her head, closing the book.

"Maybe I do. I'm beginning to think you're all talk, Charlie Bane."

He leans in closer, backing her into the book shelf. "I know."

"You know?"

"I know."

"And how do you know, exactly?" She raises a flirtatious eyebrow.

Charlie's hand flies up over Serena's shoulder and lands on the bookshelf behind her. Her eyes widen as he leans his weight against it and hovers over her.

"Because you only think what I want you to think."

Her face flushes as she drops the book to the ground. The stern look on Charlie's face remains as her grabs a fist full of her hair. Serena stands still as a board. Shock fills her when Charlie pulls his face away and circles around her. In one sweep, he pushes all of the books off one of the history shelves.

"Charlie... what are you—"

"Hop up."

"What?"

Serena gasps when Charlie's hands grip her waist. "I said hop up." His fingers dig into her skin as he lifts her up onto the shelf, grabbing a handful of her plush ass.

Serena stills on the shelf, feeling his warm body against her knees. She looks around the aisle for prying eyes.

"Now, are you going to be a good girl and listen to me?"

Serena nods, fear in her honey eyes.

"I can't hear you."

"Yes," she whispers.

"Good. Now open your legs."

"What?"

Charlie's voice is firm. "I said open your legs. Wide."

Serena does as she's told, and she immediately feels the cold library air push through her lace thong. Charlie slowly lifts one of her legs, caressing her calf and sliding his hand up her thigh. He lifts her thin, tight dress over her hips. Chills form all around Serena's body as she peeks around his head, looking for avid history nerds wandering the section. Charlie fingers glide along her thigh and up to her left hip, forming goosebumps with his light touch. His hand travels over her stomach and down her abdomen. He grips the top of her lace thong and tugs at the material.

"Did you wear these just for me?"

"Yes," she whimpers, unable to breathe.

"Good girl."

Charlie's hand slides along the lace, tracing her bikini line and her inner thighs. She lets out a small peep when his hand makes it back to the top of her underwear then slowly creeps down. He rubs the fabric of the thong lightly, and Serena is gripped by the sensation. Her head falls back, hitting a book on the shelf above her. Charlie's rhythm quickens as he presses his hand against her.

"Do you like that?"

"Yes," she whispers, her face coming back to meet his.

He looks deep into her honey eyes with starvation and grabs Serena's ass tighter. "Then spread wider for me."

Serena parts her legs further with trepidation.

"There you go, that's a good girl." He holds Serena's thighs open with one hand as his other slips into her panties. He glides his fingers over her slick folds. "Are you wet for me? Are you fucking wet for me, Serena Snow?"

"Yes," she says, her words needy.

Charlie moves his hand up and down until he finds her clit. He teases two fingers over it, hovering and barely making contact. A rush of lust consumes her.

"Does that feel good?"

"Yes."

"Yeah?" He asks, his voice airy. "Do you want me to press harder?"

Serena nods.

"I can't hear you."

"Yes!" She wails, forgetting where she is.

He adds a third finger and presses harder, making circles on her clit with his hand. Serena moans, pleasure filling her to her core at the unfamiliar sensation.

"Fuck," she moans.

Charlie grunts, keeping his eyes fixed on hers. Serena lifts her hips and his pace quickens, the circles getting smaller. Her head draws back.

"Look at me."

Serena does as she's commanded and presses her face to his. His expression stays stern and savage as their foreheads embrace.

"You're so fucking wet, baby."

Serena moans as he rounds her clit, pressing harder and harder with each circle he draws.

"Oh my God." Her breathing speeds and her toes curl. "Oh my God." She throws her head back.

Right then, Charlie rips his hand out of her underwear. She pants, choking on her own breath.

"Not so fast," he looks at her with a diabolical smile. "You'll cum when I say you can cum. Got it?"

Serena nods.

"Good," he smiles and pushes her thong to the side, spreading her lips wide open. "Are you going to behave?"
"Yes."
He rubs his hand between her thighs, drenching it in the process. He runs three fingers over her clit while gently moving his other hand down. Serena gasps as one of his fingers makes it inside her, gliding up with ease. His one hand rubs side to side over her clit as his finger inside her presses against her, finding a g-spot she didn't know she had. Serena lets out a guttural moan.
"Do you like that?"
"Yes."
"Do you like it when I play with your perfect little pussy?"
"Fuck yes."
"Oh yeah? Do you like being my naughty little librarian?"
"Yes. Oh my fucking God, yes."
"Do you want me to make you cum, Serena Snow?"
"Yes! Please!"
Charlie rubs her clit faster and presses harder against her g-spot. "Please what?"
"Please make me cum!"
Charlie rubs side to side as quickly as he can, flicking his wrist with each motion. He slides his finger deeper into her and she yelps with ecstasy. He slaps a hand over Serena's mouth, muffling her squeals.
"Cum for me," he whispers.
Serena grips the bookshelf, accidently knocking several books down in the process. She ignores it and presses her lips into Charlie's hand, trying with all her might not to scream. She bites down on his palm, hard, and he doesn't flinch. An orgasm rips through her from her toes and travels all the way up over her head. Her legs shake and quiver as she convulses forward, her forehead smashing into Charlie's. A rainbow of color strikes her eyelids.
"Cum for me. There you go. That's a good girl."
Serena continues to convulse as her ecstasy bursts, pulsation and electricity roaring through her. A wave of pure bliss floods the darkest corners of her mind and tickles

nerve endings like she's never felt before. Her muffled moans turn into breathless hums inside of Charlie's palm until he slowly takes his hand off her mouth.

She sits, stunned and lifeless on the bookshelf, unable to process her thoughts. Her breathing is shallower than the dirty New York puddles outside. She feels the slickness between her thighs when Charlie removes his hand from her underwear. Serena tries to catch her breath when he pulls her dress back over her hips and down her legs. She steadies herself, trying not to fall off the shelf. Charlie brings his forehead back to hers and presses against her. He grabs the back of her neck with a tight grip.

"You know what you are now?"

"What?" She asks breathlessly.

"Mine."

www.ingramcontent.com/pod-product-compliance
Lightning Source LLC
Chambersburg PA
CBHW060812030726
47503CB00002B/454